ISBN 9798851449987

Games We Play Series

Series Summary

Elevator pitch

The heirs of two rival mafia families unwillingly fall in love as they navigate the cruel reality of their destinies.

A slow-burn coming of age mafia dark romance series, in which the heirs of two rival mafia families unwillingly fall in love as they come to terms with their cruel fates.

Genre

Romance, Crime, Dark, Contemporary, Contemporary Romance, Adult, New Adult, Fiction

Tags

mafia, morally grey characters, strangers to friends to 'we shouldn't be doing this' friendship, organised crime group activities, slow burn, friends to lovers to enemies to lovers, mafia heirs, billionaires, mafia rivals, coming of age

Warnings

graphic drug use, murder, sexual scenes, criminal activities, violence, psychological abuse, PTSD, gore

Round 1 - Never Have I Ever

Everybody knows Matteo Giudice is the first son of a billionaire who is probably, but not surely, the head of the Sicilian mafia. Everything he does seems to be for his own pleasure, there's a certain darkness to him that seems to follow him everywhere he goes. Burnt-out from a young age due to his generational wealth, being bored is his biggest problem in life.

Valentina is the daughter of a successful Russian businessman and has always flown under the radar at school but now seems to be everywhere and nowhere at the same time. There's something about her, as if she has something nobody else possesses, that stirs up Matteo's interest in the first place.

When Matteo met Valentina during a summer in Italy back in 2019, neither of them knew their destinies had been intertwined for decades. When buried secrets start coming out, their lives turn into a deadly game of power, in which love and war have no choice but to co-exist.

Rule nr. 1: The game of power is won by those brave enough to play it

--

A slow-burn coming of age mafia romance novel, in which the only thing the protagonists know for sure is that fate doesn't care if you're ready for your soulmate.

Games We Play

Round 1: Never Have I Ever

The game of power is won by those brave enough to play it

Family trees at the beginning of Round 1

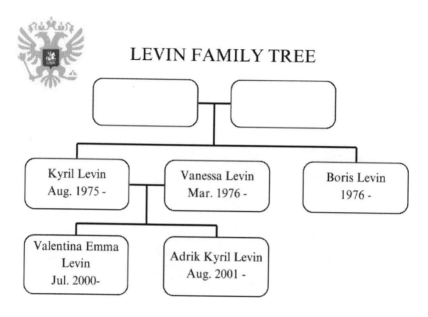

LEVIN FAMILY TREE

Kyril Levin
Aug. 1975 -

Vanessa Levin
Mar. 1976 -

Boris Levin
1976 -

Valentina Emma
Levin
Jul. 2000-

Adrik Kyril Levin
Aug. 2001 -

VOLKOV FAMILY TREE

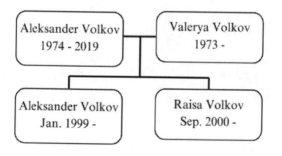

Aleksander Volkov
1974 - 2019

Valerya Volkov
1973 -

Aleksander Volkov
Jan. 1999 -

Raisa Volkov
Sep. 2000 -

GIUDICE FAMILY TREE

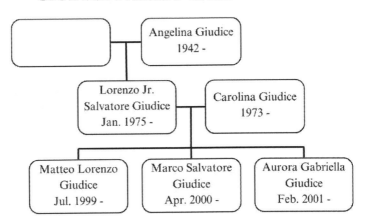

| | Angelina Giudice 1942 - |

| Lorenzo Jr. Salvatore Giudice Jan. 1975 - | Carolina Giudice 1973 - |

| Matteo Lorenzo Giudice Jul. 1999 - | Marco Salvatore Giudice Apr. 2000 - | Aurora Gabriella Giudice Feb. 2001 - |

BARONE FAMILY TREE

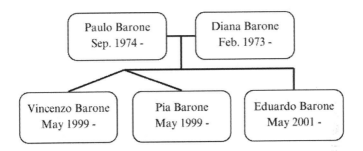

| Paulo Barone Sep. 1974 - | Diana Barone Feb. 1973 - |

| Vincenzo Barone May 1999 - | Pia Barone May 1999 - | Eduardo Barone May 2001 - |

Matteo Giudice

Birthday: 7.07.1999

Eye color: brown | **Hair color**: dark brown

Height: 184cm (6ft)

Tattoos: yes

City of birth: Palermo, Sicily (IT)

School experience:

2006 – 2014: public school in Palermo

2014 – 2018: private international boarding school in New York

2018- : Bachelor in Economics at Hamilton University in New York

Good habits: ? | **Bad habits:** smoking, weed, drugs, sex because he's bored

Life goals: living life on his own terms, become independent and never having to answer to anyone

Fears: becoming his father, having to follow his father's footsteps, disappointing his father

Turn ons: fun, beauty, intelligence, banter, not giving a fuck attitude

Turn offs: obviously desperate people, fake people

Valentina Emma Levin

Name: Valentina Emma Levin

Birthday: 22.07.2000

Eye color: light brown | **Hair color:** dark brown

Height: 168cm (5'6)

Tattoos: yes

City of birth: Moscow (RU)

School experience:

2007 – 2015: public school in Moscow

2015 – 2019: private international boarding school in New York

2019- : Bachelor in Business Psychology at Hamilton University in New York

Good habits: positive thinking, reading, taking baths??, organized

Bad habits: smoking in general

Life goals: Finding something exciting to do every day, not burning out too soon

Fears: being bored, never amounting to anything, living off my parents

Turn ons: someone who's fun, intelligence, banter, humor, confidence

Turn offs: lies, dishonesty

Prologue

The party is starting to get out of hand.

As expected.

It's only been two hours since guests first started to arrive, and yet people are already talking loudly and gesturing far too much. No one's violent yet, there are no guns in sight, and I can see familiar faces, which is usually a good enough sign for me to believe the party will be safe.

And I know he's here. He must be.

Does he think I'm here?

Why do I even care?

I grab a glass of champagne from a tray held out by a waiter as I enter the foyer. The giant room overlooks the Mediterranean Sea, giving everyone a view of the cliffs and its waters below. It's already dark, but the full moon stands high above the water shining on the sea and the city on the western side of the cliffs.

As I browse the room a second time, I realize that there's not even one person in here that I would enjoy making small talk with, let alone spend another hour and a half with them until I'm supposed to meet the guy.

"Oh, Valentina!" Someone behind me exclaims.

The sight of Isabella walking towards me with a glass in hand instantly makes me more comfortable. She's smiling at me in that warm way she always does whenever she sees me.

Coming here alone was a bold move and if anyone but my father had asked, I wouldn't have done it. I didn't know she would be here because she told me she had to pick between two different New Year's parties.

"I wasn't sure you would come!" She cries, hugging me. She takes a step back and knocks our glasses together. "Here's to a peaceful 2022." She says, winking.

"Who else is here?" I ask.

"Pia's here, the entire Giudice family, and the Barone boys."

I nod. The feeling I've had on my way here intensifies in the pit of my stomach. "And uh…where do I leave my jacket?"

"I'm staying in a room on the second floor, you can sleep there too if you want."

I follow her towards the staircase by the entrance. "We both know I probably won't go to sleep before 8am."

She just shakes her head and smiles.

The guest room she's staying in is one I'd never been in, with an en-suite bathroom attached right by the door.

"Where's your brother?" Isabella asks.

"He's in Moscow. Is uh…Ariana here?"

It's the first time I dare to open the subject of what happened with Isabella.

"No." Isabella tells me and sits down on the bed. "Are you okay?"

"Yes, I'm healing," I say and take a seat by the table that has been converted into a makeup table.

"They're not even together anymore! I'm pretty sure it officially lasted two or three days." Isabella adds, even though I didn't ask. It's good to know though.

But that's not why I'm here.

When my father sat me down in his office after Christmas Eve dinner last week, I knew it was serious. He's aware that I know what's going on, what he does for a living, and that I've always kept my mouth shut.

"I need you to go to Sicily for New Year's Eve."

"What for?"

"Talk to the Italians and ask them to consider peace. It can't go on like this, people are dead."

I wanted to tell him that it was partially his fault, but I didn't.

I knew. He knew. "I don't want to go there and try to convince-"

"It's already been arranged. Their second in command is going to be at an event in Sicily and wants to meet there."

"What if I get killed?"

"You won't."

"How can you know?!" I exclaimed. The last two years had contained more death than I'd ever known. Romeo being killed is what reignited this war, and I didn't want my own to also be a part of the story.

"They want peace. They just want to discuss the terms."

"And why me?"

Then I remembered that Romeo being killed is what reignited this war.

"Because Lorenzo Giudice has met you before and knows I put you in charge back in New York."

I rolled my eyes. "What a pleasure that has been."

"Don't be a smartass." He said.

"You can stay the first night at our house in Sicily, and on New Year's Eve I will send a helicopter to take you to the Sulla Scogliera. There's going to be a party there, so dress accordingly."

This brings me back here to this guest bedroom in Sicily in the villa they call *"La casa sulla scogliera"[1]* with Isabella watching me closely, brows furrowed with suspicious worry like they sometimes do.

How am I supposed to tell her that I feel sick? And that beneath my red gown with a left leg slit, there's a small revolver concealed in a thigh holster on my right leg and a micro earpiece in my ear.

This is one of the most dangerous situations I've ever been in, but my father asked me, and he didn't ask unless it was absolutely necessary - not directly, anyway. But it meant that I was his last resort.

---

[1] which means house on a cliff in Italian

"I'm a little nervous. But I'm glad you're here." I sincerely answer as I take a seat on the bed next to her. The gun feels like it's burning holes into my thigh, and even though I know the chances of it happening are close to 0, I keep panicking that it will randomly go off and kill someone.

Maybe me.

Honestly, if it does kill someone, I *do* hope it's me.

"I thought you had a party in Moscow tonight?" she asks.

I hate lying to Isabella. The first and only time I've ever lied to her it turned out that she'd known all along.

"Yes, but it got cancelled last minute. And I didn't want to have to spend the first day of the year with Raisa and her boyfriend."

She smirks. "Alright. Come on, there's nothing better than the first cold Gin and Tonic."

We down our champagne glasses on our way back downstairs and instead of joining the rest of the people in the main room, we detour through a door in the hallway into the kitchen.

"Lime and ice?" Isabella asks, making herself busy with finding us glasses.

"Sure."

I check the clock on my phone – 11pm.

I'm supposed to talk to the guy at 11:30pm.

"I'm going to make a call," I tell Isabella and look around for a way that leads outside. I beeline for a door in the corner of the kitchen which leads to a balcony facing west and I tell her I'll be back in two minutes.

Once I'm sure I'm out of earshot, I dial my father's number and put the phone away in my bag. It's warmer in Italy than it is in Moscow, but the spaghetti-straps of my dress did little to ward of the nightly chill.

"Have you talked to him?"

My dad sighs on the other end. *"No. He said he'd be in touch."*

"If I die, just know it's your fault," I say jokingly, trying to lighten the mood.

He doesn't laugh.

"Valentina."

Shit, he's scared too.

"I will call when I hear from him. He'll give me the exact location a few minutes before you two must meet. Don't be scared."

Thanks for the advice.

"You're there to make peace and reason with them. You're a smart girl, and I know you want this to end too."

I look towards the sea. The moon isn't visible tonight so all I can see is darkness, and if I force my mind to be quiet, I can hear the waves, which usually calms me down. But there is a party going on inside with the music pounding through the windows and my mind is very focused on the gun touching my leg.

"I have a *fucking* gun taped to my leg." I scream-whisper.

I'm spiralling.

"Valentina." He says, raising his voice.

I go silent.

"The gun is there to make you feel safer. You won't have to use it, believe me. Innocent people are dying, and the Italians also want peace. This…this useless power struggle war must stop. You're there to convince them that we want peace as much as they do. They suggested the meeting. They won't hurt you. They'll listen, then we'll talk, and then you'll be back home. I'm sorry it has come to this."

I sigh. I know he's right. Plus, it's not like I protested when he made me his consiglieri.

"Okay. Call me with the location. I'm going to go get a drink."

He hangs up and I take another look at the dark sea before I step back inside.

Isabella extends one of the glasses she's holding. I take it and hold it up, trying to think of a good toast. "To a better 2022." I decide and she smiles, knocking our glasses together in cheers.

The drink is cold and there's definitely more Gin than Tonic. "Ooh, strong." I give her feedback as we make our way toward the living room.

I *really* don't want to dance. I don't want to see people. I just want to go home. The idea that someone might graze against me and feel the gun is making me sick.

***

Dancing with a gun brushing against my upper thigh [2] in the open space living room is overwhelming.

Finally, at 11:27pm, my father calls.

"I need to get this. I'll go up to the room." I tell Isabella, who is busy filling up shot glasses in the kitchen.

"Okay, I'll be here!"

I quickly make my way out of the kitchen and up the stairs while sliding my finger across the screen to answer the call.

"Yes?"

"First floor, second door down the hall. In three minutes."

I nearly trip on my dress as I rush to get to the first floor. Wearing heels was a bad idea; *what if I need to run away? I might as well be dead.*

"Okay."

I hang up and place the phone in my bra as I compose myself. I look down the hall at the door my father had mentioned and stand still for a second, listening for movement. Seeing as I haven't seen some people that I know for a *fact* should be here, they must be upstairs. But there's no sound, no movement, nothing

2 while also keeping an eye out on every single person

There's no carpet on the floor which makes my clicking heels echo through the empty hallway. The bass from downstairs is thumping through the ground but my shoes are still unnecessarily loud compared to the silence on this floor.

Another reason why wearing heels wasn't a good idea.

I go through the first door only to enter another hallway that looks the same except for the two wooden double doors at the end. I take my hand down to my leg and feel out the gun as I walk. All I have to do is slide my hand through the slit on the side of the dress, grab the gun, cock the safety and pull the trigger. After all those complaints about having to go to 'self-defence classes' [3].

I stop in front of the double doors and place my hand on the handle. I have no idea who's on the other side, or what to expect. I've always wondered who the underboss of the Giudice family was. I know who the boss is, but everything else is unknown to me, and apparently to my dad as well.

The door opens with a loud creak, into a dimly lit room. There's a lamp on the desk which provides enough light for me to see a silhouette behind the desk, leaning against the wall by the balcony doors.

The person is wearing dress pants and a white shirt.

I step inside the room and close the door behind me. I don't turn my back to them, not even for a second.

I smell him – tobacco mixed with spice and something sweet - before I even see his face.

Hate that I'm still incredibly attracted to him.

"Of course, it's you." He says.

I feel all the blood in my body rushing to my stomach.

It's him.

Of course it's him.

---

[3] that's what my father likes to call them – he still hasn't come around to admitting that I'm being trained to kill someone if need be

NEVER HAVE I EVER
met someone like you

Chapter 1

Matteo

Palermo, Sicily, Italy – August 8th, 2019

The phone on the wall in Matteo's room rings at around 11am, waking him up from a dreamless sleep.

It was his father.

No one else ever calls the landline – no one would ever bother to learn the extension to each room. He's also the only person on the planet who still uses landlines.

"Come see me in my office please," Is all he says before hanging up.

He sounded serious, like he needs to talk *business*. Not business in a figurative sense, as in, talk about some shit Matteo pulled. Business in the literal sense –*business*.

Matteo started suspecting that his father's job wasn't really as a restaurant "owner" when he was around eight years old. One night after having stayed up past bedtime downstairs in his father's restaurant, a man came in with a gun in his hand. He pointed it at one of his father's friends who was stood behind the counter, then angrily said something in a foreign language before he shot the guy point blank.

He understood, even at that early age, that it had been done on purpose.

The man didn't even clock Matteo hiding under a table in the corner; he just turned around and left after the shooting. When his father found him bawling his eyes out, he told him to stop crying.

"We don't cry when this happens. We take care of it, and we move on."

Matteo didn't know what 'take care of it' meant, but the next morning there was no blood on the walls and no dead body on the floor when he went downstairs for breakfast.

He doesn't think about it as often as one might think. There were no nightmares, no fear of getting shot himself, nor ever talking about it again.

It was the first time Matteo had ever experienced a crime. And the adults around him weren't alarmed.

"The guy who died did bad things. These things happen," his mother said to him that night. Matteo remembers it because it was one of the few times in her life that she actually cared about his wellbeing.

Nobody called the police. And even though Matteo was forced to go to his room, he saw from his window how two men carried the body of the man across the street.

Life went on as if nothing happened.

That same day during dinner, his father announced that they would be moving to the outskirts of Palermo. 'To the countryside' because he was 'tired of living in the city.' They moved out of their townhouse in the city to a big villa with a garden pool and a sea view.

That's when Matteo started seeing less of his father. He would only come home during the weekends, where he would spend time in his office with all types of people who would come in to 'visit'.

His mother became even more distant than she usually was. Now that they were living in a house with ten bedrooms, she would rarely show her face. She started growing vegetables in the garden and made herself busy with the greenhouses on the property. Since their father was away during the week, Matteo and his two siblings grew up surrounded by their maids, nannies, and cooks. The nannies never lasted long. Not because the children were too much to handle – it was always because of 'irreconcilable differences'.

They learned to take care of themselves. Looking back at it now, Matteo thinks that the way they grew up made them bond in a ride-or-die, family-comes-first, loyalty-is-key type of way.

During one summer in 2014 his brother Marco had asked him whether he'd ever seen his mother coming inside with vegetables from that greenhouse she was always tending to. Matteo couldn't answer him.

That night, the two of them managed to sneak into one of the houses said vegetables supposedly grew. The insides were filled with stacks upon stacks of packages; wrapped and sealed with duct tape.

Their father called them into his office the very next day [4]. He'd seen them on the cameras outside and had decided it was time to explain their family history. That's the first time Matteo heard the words *'cosa nostra'* coming from his father's mouth.

Matteo and his brother have always grown up surrounded by mafia action movies, violent video games, and board games such as Monopoly or Poker. They had heard stories about the Sicilian mafia [5], but they never knew that their family played a part in it.

---

[4] Matteo vividly remembers it was a Tuesday

[5] people at school would also sometimes talk about it

The first job he ever did for his father was picking up a shipment on his way home from school. Matteo didn't ask what was in the box. He didn't want to know. He just wanted to get paid.

And it's been working like that ever since then.

That's how Matteo has been able to always live his life the way he wants to. His absent father and busy-with-self mother weren't there to nag him or watch everything he was doing. For one, their nannies never really cared enough to pay attention. Being sent off to boarding school after 8th grade weakened physical parental supervision ever more.

His love for cocaine started developing around eighteen, right after he moved to New York for university where he occasionally filled in as a "manager" for his father at one of their clubs in Manhattan.

One night, a security guard caught someone trying to sell drugs in the club and hauled him into Matteo's office, ordering him to put everything he had on the table.

They watched the man empty his pockets, laying out dozens of small baggies filled with cocaine.

"Where is it from?" Matteo asked.

"Why does it matter?" retorted the guy, eastern European accent heavy on his tongue.

"Is it good?"

"You tell me." the guy said and pulled out his necklace, only to reveal a small spoon attached to it.

The guy and the guards watched Matteo as he dug the spoon into the powder. He sniffed it in one swift motion before passing it down to his security guards.

"What's your name?" Matteo asked him as he gave half of the baggies back to the guy.

The guy wasn't a complete stranger to him; Matteo knew they were in the same year at school. He also knew that he was Russian and that he was good at science.

"Aleksi. Volkov."

Oh, and he had a hot sister that Matteo has always wanted to fuck [6].

Matteo shook Aleksi's hand and pointed to the door. *"From now on, if you want to sell in my club, you come to see me first. And then we can work out a mutually beneficial deal."*

Since January last year, Aleksi Volkov has been sort of a friend to Matteo[7].

His dark brown hair coils around his tired eyes as Matteo groans and rolls out of bed.

He glances at himself in the mirror for a second. His face is always puffy after doing drugs the night prior, hiding his usual pronounced cheekbones and jawline. It makes him look like he's fourteen again.

He remembers reading somewhere [8] that the brain eventually starts to get used to the dopamine and doesn't respond to the same quantities after some time.

Rehab never even came into question; he knows he can give it up if he wants to. There's just nothing else that's as exciting for him as going out and doing drugs.

---

[6] he did a few months ago, it was okay

[7] as well as his dealer

[8] or maybe saw on TikTok

When he was fourteen and moved to the private boarding school his father had arranged, he met an American hotel chain heiress called Allison. She quickly became his girlfriend. They used to do everything together, but he would sometimes go clubbing without her because she was younger. That would always cause arguments that lasted for days.

In 2018, three years after getting together, they finally decided to break up. It worked out perfectly because Matteo started working at the club full-time as soon as he got out of school.

That's when he started noticing how women really acted around him. It was well known that their family was one of the wealthier ones at The Master's International Academy, and Matteo had a reputation. Girls from his school, as well as other schools in New York City, had started noticing him and his brother long before he ever noticed them. It wasn't a challenge to get anyone into bed, especially when he picked up the tab and supplied the party drugs.

He liked his lifestyle, and he knew some girls had crushes on him that he could never reciprocate, but he never gave them false hopes or lied to get them into bed. Being his confident self was enough, and when you add money to the equation, then you don't even have to lift a finger.

He arrives in front of the wooden double doors and doesn't bother to knock as he enters.

"What?" Matteo asks his father as soon as he sets foot in the office and closes the door.

"I need you to do me a favour."

"What kind of favour?"

He's spent the last week just chilling outside with his brother or playing video games in his room, bored out of his mind. He hopes it'll be something interesting.

"Sit down."

Matteo looks at his father. He's 44 but he's always looked younger. They have the same nose and bone structure, but his father's eyes are dark blue [9] and his hair is starting to turn grey.

He's unsuccessful in reading his father's face [10] before he sits down in the chair in front of his desk.

"There's this guy, Enrique, who owes me a favour. He's bringing a shipment over tonight, but he docks in Taormina. I need you to go get it."

Matteo sighs, throwing his head back. "*Taormina*? Can't you ask Marco to do it?"

His father frowns. "Take him with you, I don't care."

Matteo gets an idea. "Are Paulo and Diana still at our vacation home?"

If Vinnie's parents aren't there it would be the perfect opportunity to throw a party. It's been over a month since the last time the entire group got together and it won't be long until university starts up again.

"No."

He stares at the ceiling for a moment before he looks back at his father, crossing his arms. "Can we spend the night there?" If he's going to make the trip, he should at least make it worth it.

"As long as the shipment is in this room by this time tomorrow, do what you want."

Matteo smirks and stands up. "Is that all?"

"Make sure it's ten kilograms. This guy has tried ripping us off before. Take a scale with you. Tonight, 6:30pm."

---

[9] Matteo is the only brown-eyed one in the family "you take after your grandfather" is what people would always say to him

[10] as always

Matteo nods and takes his phone out of his pocket before he's even out the door. He opens the group chat he has with his brother and the Barone brothers.

Matteo's boredom has finally come to an end. He'll tell the guy they'll be picking him up from the docks. Then they'll bring him back to the house where they'll weigh the shipment before sending him on his way.

Their seventeen-year-old little sister Aurora also insisted on coming to the party, saying she's been holed up in her room ever since summer started.

The three of them use their father's helicopter pilot to get to Taormina. It takes an hour by helicopter instead of three hours by car, so they arrive at their home on the cliff around 3pm.

While Aurora calls around to hire someone who can put a party together on short notice, Marco and Matteo call their driver from the city into work so they can arrange the meetup.

If there's one thing all the Giudice men in the family understand, is that Aurora needs to be kept as far away from the back side of the business as possible. Last week, when their father said that they had to go to the cemetery, Aurora was told that they had to go pick up some tools for the backyard. She doesn't even listen to them talking half of the time, but they still do it to protect her. Her father wants her to live a life as normal as possible.

They went to a cemetery an hour away from Palermo with two other men, his father's lifelong friends Paulo Barone and Franco Altieri [11], only to watch a random funeral taking place a few hundred meters away.

"Who is that?" Marco asked, squinting.

"A dear friend of ours sadly had to pass away last month."

Had to??

"Why aren't you at the funeral then?" Marco pushed, and Matteo looked at his father to see whether the questions had any effect on him. He didn't like to explain himself to anyone.

"We wouldn't be welcome." Is all his father said, and Marco knew better than to continue asking questions.

"He's a skinny guy, he probably won't try to pull anything." Marco observes, looking out the window and onto the pier where a lanky man awkwardly stood there with two trash bags.

"Are you Elliott?" Matteo asks, rolling down the window, saying the wrong name on purpose.

---

[11] Matteo is 99% sure they're his consiglieri and second in command

"No, I'm Enrique." The guy answers.

Matteo nods. "Put the bags in the trunk and climb in."

Enrique climbs in the backseat next to Marco before the driver speeds off. His brother makes idle conversation with Enrique when Matteo reminds himself of something else he has to take care of.

He pulls out his phone and searches his conversation with Aleksi.

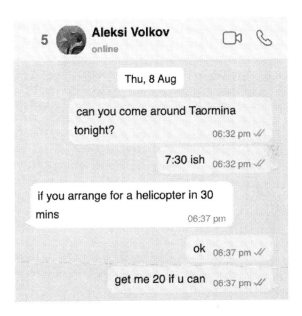

He smiles and turns around to look at his brother. There's excitement in his eyes and a feeling in his stomach that he can't quite place. It just feels like tonight is going to be outstandingly amazing.

Marco smiles back at him, not having to ask in order to know what his brother just took care of.

Chapter 2

Matteo

Palermo, Sicily, Italy – August 8th, 2019

The total comes out to 10.02kg, which is good enough for Matteo.

The extra twenty grams are always a good sign – it either means the seller is happy with the deal or afraid to deliver less than agreed upon.

They make Enrique leave through the back as cars begin to pull up in the front of the house.

He can see familiar faces from the window overlooking the driveway, and the feeling in his stomach grows.

He spots Vinnie climbing out of a black van with Eddie, followed by their sister Pia and two other girls he doesn't recognize right away. The one in the red catches his attention first. His eyes trail over to her friend, and he realizes it's Aleksi's sister Raisa. She was a year below him in school and she has never been shy about having a thing for Matteo [12].

They had sex at the end of the school year, right before Matteo flew to Palermo for the summer and they haven't spoken since. Not that they used to speak a lot before - Matteo doesn't really text any of the girls he fucks because most of the time it feels like a waste of time. Only when he doesn't have anything to entertain himself with is when he opens messages.

---

[12] most of the girls in school did

Aleksi is not with them though, which means that Matteo will just have to wait a little bit longer. A text comes through from their pilot, saying that they've just departed from Capo d'Orlando. He descends the stairs, stopping to grab a drink from the kitchen on the way to go and greet his oldest friends.

The pool area is packed already, and he goes straight to the bar by the pool where he knows he'll find Vinnie.

Sure enough, Vinnie's there, toasting with Raisa and the girl in the red dress.

"We didn't bring our bathing suits." The girl says and takes a sip of her drink.

"It's not the end of the world." Matteo interjects just because he can before he greets his friend. "Vincenzo, how are things? I haven't seen you in weeks, you sonofabitch!"

They do talk in Italian when they're alone (most of the time) but being around so many people from so many different countries for the past four years has altered their conversations into 'Italianglish' [13].

He's missed Vinnie. They're used to being around each other all the time, ever since childhood, so being away from him because he goes to Capo d'Orlando for the summer always reminds him that there's no other person in the world he trusts more than Vinnie. Especially since he's also aware of what their fathers do.

The two girls don't slip his mind though, so Matteo turns to look at them. He studies Raisa's face for a second. She doesn't look like she's carrying any resentment towards him. If anything, she's looking at him like she'd very much enjoy hooking up again.

Then he looks at the other girl.

---

[13] as Isabella calls it when they speak two languages in one sentence

She has deep brown eyes and her hair falls over her bare shoulders in a way that makes her look very sensual. She's already looking at Matteo, but in a different type of way. Her brows are furrowed, and she looks confused, like she doesn't know who he is or that they're at his place right now.

And even though Matteo knows for a fact that they both went to the same school before he graduated [14] he has no idea what her name is or any other information except for the fact that she likes to party. He has seen her around at parties before, that's for sure, but he can't put his finger on when.

"Cheers." He says and toasts with the girls, just as his phone starts ringing. It's Aleksi. Without saying anything else, he winks at Vinnie and then walks away, answering. "Where are you?"

"Just landed, I'm in the car now."

"Come through the back." Matteo tells him. Marco and Vinnie spawn right next to him. He smirks because they can always tell when he's up to no good.

"Aleksi is coming in fifteen, one of you has to get him inside through the back."

One of the things their father taught them early on is that shipments don't go inside the house. If they must, they go through the back. 'The back' being a door in the garage that no one should ever notice except for the people who use it for this exact purpose.

Matteo and Vinnie go upstairs to his bedroom to wait for Marco.

"How's it going with Sofia?"

He knows Vinnie and Sofia have always had an on-again-off-again relationship, so the answer to this question is always like a kinder egg surprise. The only sure thing about it is that it will end with Matteo rolling his eyes and telling him to cut her loose.

---

[14] she looks awfully familiar

"We decided to take a break over the summer. She's in Spain with her parents."

"And you haven't seen her since the semester ended?"

Vinnie shakes his head. "She's just...exhausting, man. She thinks I cheated on her because I went out with you that night and didn't invite her."

Matteo snorts, crossing his arms. So...the usual. "And you're okay with that?"

Vinnie shrugs. "I don't know. I'm definitely happier and have more energy when she's not around, that's for sure."

"I think you need to hook up with someone new." Matteo places a hand on Vinnie's shoulder. He's been trying to hook him up with literally anyone who isn't Sofia Romano. They both look towards the door to his suite – Vinnie because he wants to deflect and Matteo because he's expecting Aleksi.

Finally, the door opens and in comes Aleksi, followed by Marco and Eddie. He has a backpack that contains ten baggies of two grams each. Matteo doesn't care where he gets it from on such short notice – as long as he delivers and it's good.

Aleksi's a nice guy - doesn't mind when people call him "Alex".

Matteo hands him 2000 euros cash in 500-euro bills. They have this thing where Aleksi names the price he buys it for plus the dealer's 25% cut, and Matteo just rounds up the number. Aleksi usually comes to him, not the other way around [15] so the service should be rewarded.

"How was the flight?" Matteo asks him as they warm up a plate with a lighter before spreading two whole baggies onto it.

"Short." Aleksi laughs, looking around. "Can I use a bathroom? I need to make a phone call."

---

[15] from other cities even

"I have one in my room, it's the door right by the door, but you can also use the other bathroom right across the hall."

Aleksi nods and leaves.

"Ariana is coming up with Isabella and a friend." Vinnie says, looking up from his phone.

"Ariana Milanesi?" Matteo asks, surprised.

"Yeah. She texted me at the beginning of summer because she heard I was single again."

"Have you had sex?" Eddie chimes in, surprised.

"Not yet."

The 'not yet' instead of 'no' gives Matteo hope that his best friend might not be a lost cause after all.

"We're going to go into the bathroom then, give you some space with the girls." Marco says, grabbing another plate.

The two of them leave, so it's just Vinnie and Matteo now.

They grew up across the street from each other in Palermo. Vinnie's parents, Paulo and Diana Barone, are also his godparents. They would come into the Giudice restaurant almost every day for dinner, so Vinnie and Matteo inevitably started playing while their parents had 'adult' talks. Back then it never occurred to them that their fathers were almost always absent from the dinner table, or that their mothers talked to each other in hushed tones so their children wouldn't hear.

Matteo had always thought his classmates in Italy had very strict parents because they couldn't hang out after school; their parents made them do their homework or go to extracurricular activities. Matteo's life was different: wake up, go to school and then to the restaurant, where he could do whatever he pleased and eat whatever he wanted. If he wasn't feeling like hanging out there with his brother and the Barone kids, he would go out by himself or with a girl. He's always done whatever he wanted, and his mind still can't comprehend the idea of living his life by following anybody else's orders.

If he's asked to do something he wouldn't mind doing then it's not an order – it's a suggestion.

Sometimes he would do his homework when it was asked of him because Mathematics and Economics came easy to him. He started to get in trouble at school for not doing the mandatory assignments, then his parents would get called in and his father would have a private talk with the principal before it all went away. At some point he stopped getting in trouble for his actions. First in Italy, and later in New York.

And it wasn't even like he was doing anything wrong; he was just using his privilege to do whatever he felt like doing in the moment, never once having to deny himself anything.

"Only you can say 'no' to yourself. Everybody else has a price." his father used to tell him. [16]

Matteo walks over to sit on the bed and pulls out a bill from the pocket of his shorts.

---

[16] He had come home one day upset that his Spanish teacher wouldn't let him go on the class trip to Barcelona because of his behaviour at school – he usually sat in the last row and cracked way too many jokes. He did end up going to Barcelona, and he knew his father had something to do with it. He never asked though.

Ariana Milanesi and his best girl friend since childhood enter his room. Matteo smiles. Every time he gets to spend some time with Isabella he feels better afterward. He used to have a small crush on her when they were younger [17] but that went away with time and they ended up bonding like they were siblings.

"We're here."

She sits down next to him and places a kiss on his cheek.

The girl in red behind her catches his attention again. She looks directly at the coke, like she's trying to figure out whether it's the good kind or not just by staring at it.

Matteo points the rolled bill at her. "You want one?"

"Sure. Can you stand up and hold it, so I don't have to lean down?" she asks, holding her hair back with one hand.

Matteo is taken aback by her question. She wants him to stand up and hold out the plate so she can do lines?

He's never had any girl demand something from him like this.

Before he can even react, she takes the plate from his hand and asks Isabella to help.

"Here you go."

The girl in red looks at Matteo for a second before she bends down and snorts the line.

"Good shit, right?" Ariana asks her and takes the plate.

The girl doesn't look impressed, which sort of impresses Matteo.

"What's your name?" he asks her.

She crosses her arms. "Valentina."

---

[17] maybe five years old

"Valentina." Matteo says, drawing out the "i".

"And you?"

He raises his eyebrows. Everybody always knows who he is. "Matteo."

Valentina nods in acknowledgment and looks around. "Is this where you live?"

Ariana looks at Matteo questioningly, like she wants to see how he'll react.

"Yes," Matteo answers and takes the plate back once it's done the rounds. Just then, Aleksi comes into view. His eyes fall on Valentina and he freezes.

"Alex? I thought you weren't coming tonight." Valentina says, as if they've known each other forever. The way she speaks and accentuates her sentences make her sound like she's from somewhere in Eastern Europe. Probably Russia though, since she knows Aleksi.

Matteo makes eye contact with Aleksi, who looks like his mother has just caught him doing something he shouldn't have.

"I invited him, thought he'd change his mind," Matteo interjects and then stands up to walk over to him. He holds the plate up to Aleksi's chin. "Would you like a line?"

Aleksi looks at Valentina as if to ask for permission, which annoys Matteo even more.

When Valentina shrugs and smiles, Aleksi takes out his little spoon.

Matteo's phone starts buzzing in his pocket again, but the vibrations are different. It means it's his father calling.

He hands the plate back over to Vinnie and tells the group that he'll be right back.

He walks through the door at the end of the hallway, which opens into his parents' side of the villa, and then straight ahead into his father's office. *"When you talk business on the phone, always do it in the office, and always through our private line."* His father told him when he overheard Matteo talking to someone about a shipment in the kitchen.

Matteo figured that the offices on every one of his father's properties were the only rooms where no one could plant bugs in.

"Yes?" he answers once he's inside the office, not bothering to close the door.

"Is it done?" his father asks.

"Yes. Everything went smoothly."

"Are you having a party?"

"Yes."

"Romeo is on the staff floor if you need anything."

"Yeah, thanks."

Romeo has always been their housekeeper. 'Housekeeper' in the sense that he's sort of like a guard dog, who also takes care of the personnel in their Italy homes and keeps the houses in check. So yes, he's a 'housekeeper'. At least that's what their balance sheets say.

As he closes the door to the office on his way out, he sees Valentina at the other end of the hallway.

"What are you looking for?" he asks in an accusatory tone.

She raises a brow at his tone. "The bathroom? The one in your room is occupied."

He believes her. She looks more bothered by his tone rather than caught being somewhere she shouldn't have.

"It's the door across the hall from my room," he points behind her.

Valentina nods before she turns around and walks away. Matteo watches her back for a second, eyes wandering down just for the fun of it and notices a small tattoo peeking out from under her dress.

When he gets back to his room, Marco and Eddie are out of the bathroom, sipping their drinks in the corner and talking about something in hushed tones.

"Let's go do some shots by the pool!" Ariana suggests and stands from the bed. She straightens out her dress as she says something to Vinnie.

The energy suddenly shifts, and Marco and Eddie both stop talking when Valentina enters the room.

"Anybody up for shots?" she asks nobody in particular.

"Sure," Marco responds, and Matteo watches his brother throw a smile in her direction while Eddie looks at her with respect.

Everyone in the room is acting like they already know who she is, like she's always been part of their lives, and yet Matteo feels like she never really existed up until today.

Matteo grabs Isabella's arm on the way to the pool bar.

He recognizes a few people by face – some used to be his classmates back in middle school, others are friends of friends from boarding school.

The pool is packed, mostly with girls waiting their turn to get a picture by the edge of it that faces the sun setting above the sea.

Isabella looks at his hand circling her upper arm, then up at him.

She's the only one who never liked Allison. Kept telling him that she was way too toxic because of how jealous she was of their close friendship. When they broke up, Allison ended up telling Matteo that one of the reasons she acted crazy was because she believed something was going on between him and Isabella. They still laugh about it today and Isabella will never let go of the fact that she was right.

Having a girl best friend has turned out to be a blessing for Matteo because he understands women better and can get input from someone who has his best interest in mind. And even though at the beginning of her 'spirituality, everything is energy' phase Matteo had insisted she was high, her whole belief system about how the laws of the universe work started rubbing off on him too [18].

"What?" she asks, looking towards the group that just left them behind.

"Who's that girl, Valentina?"

"She used to be my roommate in school," she explains. "And we're going to be staying the same dorm at university. I like her, we get along."

"Yeah, but like who *is* she? Have I seen her around before? She looks like she knows everyone here."

Isabella looks at him confused, then shakes her head and smiles. "Ask her yourself, I don't know her life story."

Matteo squints at her, picking up on how she raises brows. It's always been her tell when she's lying. "Oh, but you look like you do."

"It's not my place to tell other people's stories."

"If she used to be your roommate how come I've never met her?"

"You probably have, and you were most probably drunk. Oh, and you were so far up Allison's ass-"

He raises a hand. "Let's not."

"And why do you care anyway?"

"I feel like I don't trust her. She's got one of those resting bitch faces."

Isabella looks annoyed with him. "*I* trust her. And not everything in the world revolves around *you*, you know."

---

[18] he will never admit it to anyone though

He lets go of her arm and she pats him on the head before she turns around and hurries towards the bar.

Judging by the Italian rap blasting from the speakers next to the bar, Marco must be the one connected to them.

Vinnie is taking out glasses from the bar when Matteo sits on the last empty chair next to Isabella. Ariana is sitting between her and Valentina, who's sitting next to Marco.

Aleksi's chatting to Eddie behind the bar when his sister comes up to them and stops right behind Valentina, placing her hands on her shoulders.

"Where have you been? I've been looking all over for you." Raisa smiles. Valentina smiles back and scoots a bit further on the chair to make room for her.

"Aleksi? What are you doing here?"

"I decided to come after all." He answers, making eye contact with Matteo for a moment. Something's weird about the whole interaction, but Matteo can't quite place what or why.

Actually...it's definitely the drug thing.

"What did you come with?" Raisa pushes.

"Where were *you*?" Valentina jokes and gently places her arm around Raisa's shoulders.

Someone behind them screams and jumps into the pool.

"I met one of my friends from school, James," Raisa explains and Valentina looks at her unimpressed.

"You didn't."

"I didn't, I promise!" Raisa laughs and throws up her hands in defence.

"Who wants Tequila, who wants something else?" Vinnie asks.

Valentina, Ariana, and Matteo choose to drink Tequila while the rest of the group chooses Vodka.

"You're Russian and you don't drink Vodka?" Raisa jokes, looking at Valentina.

Raisa Volkov, who Matteo sort of had a thing with at the end of the school year, who is also Aleksi's sister, also knows Valentina. Matteo can't wrap his head around why it feels strange to be the only one who doesn't know her.

The thing that really bothers him though, is that he's never noticed her before even though he *knows* she looks familiar, and suddenly it seems like she's everywhere.

Chapter 3

Valentina

Capo d'Orlando, Sicily, Italy – August 8th, 2019

The sun is starting to burn me alive, and I've only been exposed to it for less than an hour. I stretch my arms out in front of me to inspect whether I've reached the amount of tan that I've been trying to achieve for the past six weeks since we came to Italy.

"Put your hat on." My mother motions from her lounge chair, too engrossed in her book to even look up at me.

I look down at the bucket hat in my lap. "It makes my head too warm."

She puts the book down and throws me an annoyed look. I envy her for how relaxed she looks in her bikini. She looks kind of poetic, sitting alone on our private beach sipping a Martini - only having to worry about how the book is going to end.

She tilts her head and looks at me over the top of her sunglasses. "Then go hang out with your friends. Where are they? Where's your brother?"

I squint my eyes at her. "Nice, mom. Trying to get rid of me like I'm a toddler."

She softens and closes her book. "Honey, you've been complaining for the past five days about being bored. It has nothing to do with me trying to get rid of you. Just go to the beach with your brother next time or go and see what Raisa or Alex are up to."

I sigh. She's right. I haven't seen Raisa in a few days. All we do is go out clubbing or sit by the pool on our phones without anything new to add to the conversation.

First of all, doing some self-care from time to time [19] is way more appealing to me at the moment.

Second, I *just* got my sleeping schedule back under control and managed to sleep eight hours a night for the past seven days. When summer ends, I'll have to return to university and force myself to pass my exams. If I just keep partying and going out I will get myself kicked out.

But in the end, what's worse? Being bored to death or listening to the longest speech about responsibilities from two parents who grew up poor and got rich by working hard?

"I'm just going to eat something," I say.

"Okay."

I start to gather my things; the book I brought along for the summer, my towel, the bucket hat, and the beach bag.

How can I entertain myself tonight?

I could try and find my brother Adrik, see what he's up to. I could open the notifications that have been rotting on my screen since I woke up this morning. I could try doing something with Raisa and her brother. I could also check if any of the Barone boys are around tonight.

I walk up the path leading from the beach up to our garden, pressing on a random notification.

It's a text from Raisa.

---

[19] i.e. smoking a joint in secret when no one's home, making lists of what I want to do with my life and then forgetting about them, sitting in the sun or taking hour-long baths

Our vacation home in Sicily is in Capo d'Orlando, and we've been coming here every single summer since 2008. My brother and I have never actually gone out and explored Sicily because we had everything we needed at our home. Our family friends the Volkov's have always come with us and stayed in a house just a few streets away.

At the beginning of this year, the father unexpectedly passed away in a car crash, so we started the summer with a funeral in Sicily. It was Aleksander Volkov's favourite place on earth, and I always saw him at his best when we were here. It was like he belonged here rather than Russia.

His children are okay though, and from what my mom told me, their mother has also had time to grieve for the past six months and now they're moving on. I think the whole thing affected my father the most, even though he'd never let it show.

I check where Taormina is on Google Maps before I give her an answer.

"Put your hat on." My mother's voice startles me. I completely zoned out and forgot that I came to a halt in the middle of the pathway leading up to the house. My mother is still on the lounge chair, but she's facing me now.

"Where's *papa*?"

She makes a face. It's the nickname I had for him when I was younger. My mom knows I only call him that when I need to soften him up. Usually, I either ask for money or something else that might need some convincing.

"He has some business to take care of."

"Will he be back tonight?"

She shrugs and gets back to her book. "Who knows with your father."

"Didn't he say where he was going?" I ask, trying to estimate when he'd be home judging by where he's at.

"Meeting some business partners, I don't know honey. Do you need help with something?"

I don't like asking her for money. I really don't. I know she grew up poor in a small village in Spain and worked her way up to become a very well-paid ambassador. She has the 'quality over quantity' mindset, so asking her for money to go to a party on another part of the island would be much more exhausting than asking my father [20].

"Mmmm-not yet," I say, knowing she knows what I want anyway.

I quickly walk towards the house, away from her passive-aggressive stare. I walk past the pond, trying to resist the urge to throw myself into it to cool myself off. Our dog, Byk, raises his head from where he's chilling under a tree, hiding from the sun and follows me inside the house, all the way into our kitchen.

After pouring myself a glass of lemonade from the fridge, I click on the message from Vinnie.

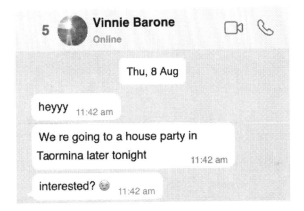

He sent it about two hours ago.

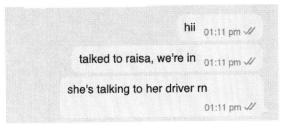

---

[20] he usually just sighs, tells me to be more mindful about it, then gives it to me

I busy myself with getting Byk some food from the pantry as I wait for a reply. My phone vibrates, and suddenly, life feels exciting again.

The little part of my brain that loves seducing men and having fun is slowly defrosting. It usually dies when summer starts and I go away with my family to take a break from the chaotic lifestyle back at school in New York.

I had a long-term boyfriend (Jamie) when I first started boarding school, but after four toxic years we broke it off.

I decided to start fresh three months ago [21].

I wait for him to type out his reply.

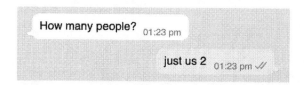

I know for a fact that Raisa's brother won't be coming with us - he never does.

---

[21] for what feels like the third time in five years with all our on-again-off-again fights

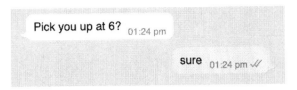

I sigh, looking around for something to do. My eyes fall on my bathroom door. After letting Raisa know about the change of plans, I walk into the bathroom to turn on the water in the bathtub.

Chapter 4

Valentina

Capo d'Orlando, Sicily, Italy – August 8th, 2019

The clock over the mirror shows it's already been three hours since I got into the tub. There's just something about taking a bubble bath while looking out at the sea and reading a book that makes me want to do it forever.

I take the last drag of my cigarette and stub it in the ashtray next to the tub. Then I groan and hoist myself out of the tub.

As I step out of the bathroom in my bathrobe and a towel turban on my head, I hear my father's laughter echoing from downstairs. The other male voice I hear must be the chef, who probably just finished for the day.

I blow dry my hair as fast as I can before I quickly comb through it and rush out of my room towards the stairs. I need to get him in a good mood before my brother comes home and starts cracking bad jokes that my parents take seriously.

My father is sitting at the bar with the chef, laughing and speaking Italian.

"Good evening, welcome home." I smile, placing a hand on his shoulder.

"My daughter is happy to see me home, I wonder why." He says, switching to English and placing a hand around my waist.

"How was your trip?"

He cocks his head and squints at me. "What do you need, Valentina?"

He knows I would never ask about his work [22].

"Raisa and I are going out with the Barone boys in Taormina tonight." I give him my brightest smile. "I need some money."

"When will you be back?"

---

[22] mainly because I don't care

I shrug. "Tomorrow, probably."

He sighs and looks over at the chef, shaking his head. "I'll send some later. When do you leave?"

"Two hours." I press a kiss on his cheek. "Thank you, you're the best!"

In hindsight, thinking that I could get ready in two hours was a mistake.

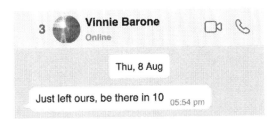

Great.

The Barone family has been vacationing in Capo d'Orlando before we started coming here, and even though they're from Sicily, the kids go to the same boarding school in New York as my brother and me. I don't know what the parents do exactly, but they must be doing something right [23].

They have three children: Vinnie, who's 20, one year older than I am - a very charming guy I've known since I was young when we vacationed to Italy. I was surprised to see him in the year above me when I moved overseas for school.

I've always considered him good-looking because he has a head full of curly hair that he likes pulling up in a man bun sometimes, which always gives off daddy vibes. He also dresses casually, unlike most of the guys I know who are always trying to show off.

---

[23] acutally, I think their mother used to be a model and their father works in construction

Then there's Eddie, a year younger than me, who has also always kind of been around. And finally, there's Pia, Vinnie's twin sister, who I've also known for years but for some reason never really interacted with me. Vinnie always tells me that she just has one of those natural resting bitch faces [24].

I slip into a comfortable floor-length red satin dress from Galvan and begin the staring contest with my mirror.

The more I stare, the prouder I feel about myself. There used to be a time when I was younger when I wouldn't have dared to put on such a dress. The way it clings to my hips and thighs would've sparked a comment from one of my parents for sure – back in the day.

I cannot be bothered with heels and sneakers would be way too warm. I opt for a pair of white ankle-high white and gold Greek sandals to match my white pedicure.

I text Raisa to be at my house in five minutes before my phone ends up in the first white shoulder bag I can find. I throw it in alongside my house keys, credit card, license, perfume, and lip gloss.

My family is gathered in the kitchen when I emerge downstairs, looking sun-kissed and content. And here I am, looking like I want to get over my ex with the first Italian guy I see [25].

"Where are you going?" My mother asks from her seat by the bar, rolling the chair to face me.

My dad looks at me over her shoulder, eyes glazed as he fills up my mother's wine glass. He frowns. "To impress boys, I see."

"I'm just going out with Raisa and the Barone boys to Taormina. I told you already." I say, trying to get out of it as fast as I can so I don't keep the boys waiting.

I walk over to the bar, barely noticing my brother by the kitchen counter texting away on his phone.

---

[24] like I do sometimes - apparently

[25] which isn't that far from the truth anyway

"Oooh, look who's here." I mock as I pass him.

"Where *exactly* are you going?" he snaps back, finally looking up from his phone. "Where is this *party*?"

The truth is, I don't know. All I know is that I need to be entertained. I want to feel like I'm doing something exciting, otherwise I'll rot in my bedroom upstairs. And of course, Adrik knows it too, but he's just trying to be a smartass in front of our parents.

I sit down next to my mother by the bar. "Taormina. I think the party is hosted by a friend of Vinnie and Eddie's." I explain, even though I have no idea whether that's true or not. It probably is.

"And you go dressed like that?" Adrik continues.

"What's your problem with my look?" I ask, slightly getting offended.

"Nothing. You're a walking red flag." He says and I look at my mom hoping she'd say something. She shrugs, not wanting to get involved.

I turn back to my brother. "How so?"

"Everybody knows a white pedicure is a red flag. Plus, you're literally in a red dress."

I look down at myself. I like what I see. It's time to turn the spotlight back onto him.

"Where have you been, hm?" I retort and reach for my mother's glass. She looks at me disapprovingly as I take a sip.

"At the beach."

"You've been going quite often to the beach recently. Even though we have one in the backyard." I point behind me.

"Mooom." He says, not being able to handle it anymore.

"Kyril." My mother turns to my dad.

"Valentina."

I roll my eyes. Of course, *I'm* the problem.

"I need to go," I say, getting up from the chair and looking at my dad. "Can you please send me some money so I can..." *take shots? Order random shit online?* "...have money?"

"Oh, yes, I forgot."

I kiss both my parents on the cheek before I pass by my brother, trying to kiss him on my way out as well. He struggles but I manage to grab his chin and press a kiss to his cheek with a loud noise.

"Buona notte, familia!" I exclaim, grabbing one of my jackets from the downstairs dressing room on my way out. I feel a rush of adrenaline in my body, excited about having something new happen.

There's a black minivan with tinted windows outside our gate, and I run down the driveway as if an extra ten seconds would make a difference. I quickly spray a bit of perfume on myself as I go.

"Sorry for making you wait," I say when the driver opens the door and I climb in.

The two rows of seats are facing each other, so I take my place next to Raisa, right across from Vinnie, who's between his siblings. I haven't seen them in about a month since we went out to Catania.

"It's fine, we didn't wait long," Vinnie says, and I smile.

Vinnie has such a good vibe; I like hanging out with him. He's one of those people you just instantly get along with and could talk about everything forever because he's interesting and smart.

One summer I described him to Raisa, and she asked whether I'm in love with him. I was startled by the question but also confused as to why I had to think about the answer.

"Where are we going exactly?" I ask as soon as the car starts moving and the silence gets a bit too loud.

I usually have no problem talking to the Barone brothers, but having Pia here with them makes me feel uneasy. I feel like she's always judging me and is not very fond of me for some reason.

"A family friend of ours has a vacation home in Taormina. They're out so we're hosting a party with everyone who could attend on short notice." He explains. "A lot of people from school are coming."

"How many people?" Pia asks, not looking up from her phone.

"About sixty."

The car stops. When I look out the window, I realize it's a small airstrip.

"We're taking the small plane, it's only thirty minutes that way."

Going to a party and arriving at...*seven*??? What is this?

We board the plane and greet the staff as we do so.

"I didn't know they had these in this town." I say, looking at the small building by the airstrip.

"My father uses it for business purposes. I can borrow it when I want to." Vinnie smiles. He's got a dimple in his left cheek, which makes him even more...*ugh*.

We each take a shot and keep passing the bottle between us once we're up in the air.

It's already 6:45pm by the time we land.

There's another van there to take us to the location on top of a hill, with a beautiful view of the sea and the beaches below.

There are about a dozen cars already parked in the driveway and I recognize a few of them from our boarding school parking lot. I know I'm about to see some people I know in a place I never expected them to be.

I don't ask who lives here exactly, but it smells like a trust fund party.

A bunch of kids born into old money who live their lives the way they see fit, only to become depressed around 25 if they haven't found a thing to be passionate about. I've seen it, and I'm scared it will happen to me too.

People my age basically have unlimited money to spend but don't realize they're destroying themselves with their chronic coke habits and their need to always be chasing...something. Not being able to see that they've passed a certain invisible line and are losing control of their lives just because they want to feel something, anything, that doesn't feel...*meh*.

The house is beautiful, just like all the other houses I've seen in Italy so far. Compared to America or Russia, Italy is definitely a whole other vibe. It's like every one of these places has a certain feel to them, and I can't tell which one I like more. Or which place feels more like home.

The house overlooks the sea, its floor-to-ceiling windows making it seem even bigger than it is.

We get out of the car and I instantly get the feeling of being watched.

"Where is everyone?" Raisa asks as we follow Vinnie through a hallway just off the main entrance.

"By the pool." He answers before he opens a door that leads us to the garden.

This is a pool party??

"I don't have my bathing suit," Raisa whispers to me as we walk down the steps leading to the pool area.

"Me neither." I whisper back.

The pool has a perfect view of the sea below. If I didn't have a fear of heights, I would try to climb on top of the rock wall, which is the closest point overlooking the cliffs. The view of the sea must be insane from there. It's also the closest you can get to falling off and plunging to your death.

There's a bar by the pool where some people are huddled together taking shots. I recognize some girls in the water, as well as some other people chilling on the canopy beds.

"I smell weed," I say to Raisa as soon as we come to a halt by the pool bar. Pia disappeared a few minutes ago and Eddie wandered off to greet some of his friends leaving just the three of us.

"What do you want to drink?" Vinnie asks me as he goes behind the bar.

"Gin Tonic." Raisa and I both answer at the same time, taking a seat on the highchairs.

Vinnie starts mixing the drinks while Raisa and I take a moment to analyse everyone here. I recognize Marco Giudice, one of the Italian boys in Adrik's year, talking to his sister while smoking a joint. I don't remember her name, not really, but I've seen her at some of their games.

I smile. Of course he's smoking a joint.

Marco Giudice was a year below me in school and I got along with him because he used to play ice hockey with Adrik at some point. He's always been a bit mischievous, and nearly all pranks pulled by the hockey team were his idea. I don't know much about Aurora, except for the fact that she used to come to their games sometimes.

Marco catches my eye while talking to his sister. He smiles as he nods in acknowledgment.

"He's kind of cute," Raisa says, leaning over to me so Vinnie wouldn't hear our conversation.

"Who?"

She nods at Marco. "Him."

It's hard for me to think of him as attractive because I still picture him as one of my brother's friends. Nevertheless, she's got a point.

"Yeah, he is."

Yes, he fucking is. He's wearing a pair of orange swim trunks that go down to his knees, showing off his tattoo of a pair of scales in balance. Not to mention, he has no shirt on, which is just-

"Are they dating?" Raisa proceeds to ask.

"What? Those two? No, they're siblings. That's his younger sister Aurora."

"Oh."

"She's still in high school, I think. She's like...sixteen."

We both look back at them, and before I can even think about how we might look like stalkers, Vinnie tells us our drinks are ready.

"Let's get into the pool. Makes drinking more fun," he says, gesturing with his glass towards the pool.

"We didn't bring our bathing suits." I let him know, crossing my legs on the chair as I lean down to take a sip of my drink.

"It's not the end of the world." Someone interjects, and a guy I've seen around before appears in my line of vision.

I catch him looking at me, but he's already looking away before I can figure him out. He pats Vinnie on the back before shaking his hand and pulling him into a side hug.

"Vincenzo, how are things? I haven't seen you in weeks, you sonofabitch!"

His Italian accent is subtle, almost non-existent as he speaks to Vinnie. He looks *really* familiar, but I can't place him. He looks at Raisa, then at me, before raising his glass to us. "Cheers."

Right. I've seen him at parties around Manhattan before, and I know he's a year above me and good friends with Vinnie. Massimo...or something. Looks like one of those guys who know they're rich and good looking at think they can get anything they want because of it (which is also, unfortunately, true).

Massimo's phone starts ringing so he takes it to his ear. He winks at Vinnie then walks away.

"Who was that?" I ask Raisa, who followed him with her eyes.

She laughs and rolls her eyes. "Like you don't know him."

"He looks familiar. Massimo?"

"That's Matteo." Vinnie smiles, like he knows something I don't. "I'm gonna go see what's up with him. See you girls around."

Raisa and I watch him walk away, and as soon as she makes sure no one can hear us, she leans over to me. "That's Matteo *Giudice*."

I look at her, a little shocked. "Giudice as in, related to Marco and Aurora?"

She nods. "He's the oldest, in Vinnie's year. They're best friends."

"How do you know him?"

She shrugs. "We hooked up before summer started."

My jaw drops. "What? How did I not know this!?"

"You were too busy with Jamie to actually notice that I sometimes had a sneaky link."

I look to where she is looking, over to the stairs leading back to the house. Marco and Vinnie are talking to Matteo.

Now that I think about it, I *kind* of know him. I've seen him at parties, in America and Italy, everywhere, really, but just because it was the place to be for people at our school. The reason I noticed him was that he was always shouting something or pouring people drinks – he was drunk most of the time.

Also, he's got tattoos. There's a small pair of scales in balance on his calf similar to Marco's and something on the side of his neck and arms. I can tell he works out by the way his biceps bulge as he crosses his arms.

"He looks good," I say, deciding to look away.

"He fucks good, too."

I throw her a look. "Good to know."

She smiles and then holds her glass up. "Fuck it, let's have fun."

I nod, knocking my glass against hers. "Agreed."

I spot someone sitting down on a lounge chair, talking to a blonde girl I've also seen around.

"Isabella," I say before I'm out of my chair and already making my way toward my roommate. "I'll be right back," I tell Raisa over my shoulder.

She can take care of herself at a party, that's for sure.

Isabella sees me approaching and gets up from the lounge chair, excitedly opening her arms. I like her. She's one of the few people I decided not to cut off after high school. She's the type of friend who you don't have to talk to every day for the friendship to still be intact when you come see each other again. It's based on mutual love and unspoken loyalty because we've been through a lot together. I know that what we talk about stays between us, and she knows it too. I can tell by her eyes.

You can always tell by the eyes.

"Valentinaa!" she exclaims, hugging me when we're close enough. I hug her back, squeezing her a little to let her know that I've missed her.

The blonde looks up and extends her hand without standing up. "I'm Ariana."

"Valentina."

She smiles at me, but based on the way she gives me a subtle and unimpressed onceover, I'm not sure it's genuine.

"What are you doing here? I thought you were in Spain!" I tell Isabella as she takes a sip from my drink.

"I just came back tonight." She smiles. "What have you been up to these past few weeks?"

I think about how I've literally done nothing but pretend to read, scroll on my phone, and watch the occasional movie on Netflix.

"Some self-care." I sum up, wiggling my eyebrows to laugh it off. "You?"

"Same. I just laid in the sun all day and watched hot surfers showing off."

"Well, you had a better summer than mine then," I tell her, just as Ariana chimes in.

"We should go see the boys." She tells Isabella and tilts her head with a look that lets me know that's code for something. She looks at me, then back at Isabella.

"Do you want to come with us?" Isabella asks, motioning with her head towards the villa.

I think about it for a moment because I have no idea what they're talking about or if I'd like to see these 'boys', but I know it can't be that bad.

"Sure."

Ariana replies to a text on her phone and steps out in front of us to lead the way. I look around for Raisa but can't find her, so I decide to text her that I'm going inside for a bit.

We climb up the same flight of circular stairs we came in on, but we go one level higher. They open on the side of a large balcony overlooking the east side of the cliffs.

Ariana slides the double doors open and we enter a large hallway with doors on each side of it. I follow them to the second one on the left, which opens into a suite.

I stop by the door and watch as Ariana opens yet another door on the left of the hallway, only to reveal a bathroom. There are two people in there, and I recognize both of them. One of them is Marco Giudice holding a plate for Eddie Barone to bend down and snort cocaine off of.

"Where's Matty?" Ariana asks as I make eye contact with Marco. He looks at me weird, like he's ashamed that I just caught him trying to snort coke off a plate in a bathroom.

"Bedroom," Marco answers after looking away from me.

Ariana closes the door and walks further along the hallway before finally reaching the bedroom.

"We're here," Isabella announces and plops herself down on the bed next to the guy from before, *Matteo,* then kisses his cheek. Vinnie is sitting on the couch next to the bed, looking surprised to see me.

I look down at Matteo, who is in the process of separating a small pile of cocaine into not-so-small lines.

I should be alarmed by the amount on the plate, but I don't know why I'm not even slightly surprised by the situation. Private schools, private jets, private villas - everything that's 'private' means people have enough wealth to protect their secrets and hide their vices.

My father does it too, even though I'm pretty sure he thinks no one has picked up on it. Private planes, bigger houses, better cars, more money, and more business trips, which he never talks about. Cameras outside and high stone fences. My mother is either oblivious or acts like she is. The first option scares me more.

"You want one?"

I snap back to reality and look at Matteo. He's holding up the plate with one hand while holding a rolled-up bill in the other.

"Sure," I say and take the bill from his hand.

I push my hair back. "Can you stand up and hold it so I don't have to lean down?"

He looks up at me surprised and doesn't move an inch so I take the plate from his hand and ask Isabella to hold it. She shoots Matteo an annoyed look before she stands up and holds the plate for me.

"Here you go."

I look down at the line, then at Matteo, before I lean my head over the plate and snort the line. My nose burns for a split second as I place the bill on the plate. Then it's over.

"Good shit, right?" Ariana asks me as she takes over the plate.

I shrug. My nose hasn't gone numb yet, so we'll see.

Chapter 5

Matteo

Manhattan, New York, United States – October 24th, 2019

When he got the acceptance letter from Hamilton University in New York, Matteo didn't even react [26]. It was the expected outcome after all.

His father had suggested America when he'd just turned fourteen and was about to start eight grade in Palermo.

"Why America?" Matteo had asked. He liked his life in Italy; he had friends, activities, and nothing ever stressed him out [27].

"It's an international private boarding school. It's better than anything you're going to get here in Italy. You're better than Sicily, Matteo. I think you'd benefit from attending an international school and meeting people outside your hometown. If you don't like the first year, I promise you we'll find something else. But a public high school in Palermo shouldn't be your first option."

Matteo listened. Didn't have much of a choice, really.

He met Allison at school in 2014 and she quickly became his girlfriend. Her main problem was her being jealous of his friendship with Isabella. By the time they'd broken up, Matteo had been emotionally detached for months.

---

[26] he didn't even know he'd applied in the first place

[27] that was before he discovered the drug greenhouses in their backyard and saw his father pointing a gun at someone on Christmas that same year

Long story short, he ended up enjoying his first year of boarding school in America because he had learned a lot: if you're smart, you'll always be one step ahead of people because they're easy to read. If you have money, you can do anything you want. And if you're smart and you have money, you're already winning.

In 2018, his father called him into his office in New York and told him he had a graduation present for him.

"I want you to take over one of my clubs in the city, as a manager."

It didn't even take one second for Matteo to think it through. School was done and the past two weeks after graduation had been boring.

"Which one?"

"Either The Candy Club or Redlight."

"I don't want the strip club. Too much work. I'll take Redlight."

He went to New York for the summer and his father bought him an apartment on the Upper West Side so he could be close to the club. When he found out that he would attend Hamilton University to study Economics, he didn't even question why. Didn't even care, really.

He knew his father had talked to someone without bothering to check with him. It should've bothered him but it didn't because he would've ended up studying Economics anyway - at least this way he was spared the stress of admission.

Since Hamilton University is all the way up in Clinton, his father also got him an apartment there so he could attend classes and split up his time. Nearly all of Matteo's friends from school who chose this university were staying in the dorms on campus. But he didn't mind living off-campus; he liked having more freedom and being able to move from city to city whenever he wanted.

He got through the first year, passed all his exams, while also managing to drive up foot traffic into the club.

It's the last week of October and Matteo is sitting in his chair in the office, trying to roll a joint. Vinnie and Marco are also present, with Marco being a new addition since he started his first year of university.

Their father has just bought them a bigger apartment in Manhattan so Marco could learn the ropes of the business.

"What are we doing for Halloween?" Marco asks, not looking away from the TV screen.

Matteo's confused. "What do you mean?"

"It's Halloween next Thursday."

"And Isabella's birthday is the night after," Vinnie says. "I already talked to her about setting up a Halloween party on the 31st, then a second night for her birthday. We can charge twenty per ticket for Halloween and have a costume contest, and Friday can be a theme night for the club which could easily be ten or fifteen per ticket." Vinnie adds.

Matteo stops rolling. "Was this Isabella's idea?"

"Yeah."

"Tell her the club will pay her a grand a night if she puts on a good Halloween event and a good theme party. If it's her birthday, her table will be on the house." Matteo tells Vinnie, smiling.

Matteo likes partying, but he doesn't like planning any further than setting the date and time. He just likes showing up and having fun. Then, when the night comes to an end, he does the math, splits the money the way he was taught and spends his cut the way he sees fit.

***

Manhattan, New York, United States – October 28th, 2019

Isabella comes over to their apartment the next Monday to discuss event planning. She had texted that morning that Valentina had some appointment in the city so they would drive down to Manhattan in the morning and she would come for lunch.

Matteo was planning on being at the club anyway because Vinnie's the one who usually attends classes so Matteo can look through his notes whenever he has time. His job at the club was just promoted from 'general manager' to 'general manager also in charge of money laundering' and is therefore a priority at the moment.

It's not that hard: the money that comes from the illegal part of their business in cash gets divided throughout all the businesses his father owns. One of those businesses is the Redlight club in Manhattan. Matteo's job is to count the money, take his cut, then split it evenly throughout the entire month when he does the accounting [28].

Most of the money generated by the club went back into his father's legitimate company; the biggest shareholder when it came to the club's business activity.

Matteo realized that the restaurant he used to hang out in every day as a kid was probably the first ever business his father had laundered money through.

"I have a few ideas." Isabella takes a seat across from Matteo in his office and drops a binder on his desk.

"You've got a binder and everything." Matteo teases.

She ignores him and opens it.

---

[28] For example: Vinnie brought in a suitcase that contained 500.000 dollars in cash last week. Matteo's job was to take 10%, his cut, then divide the remaining 450 thousand into four parts. Those parts would then be spread equally throughout the weeks of December and added to the balance sheet.

"On Thursday we can do a Halloween Party and have a costume-only dress code. It would be a good idea to charge twenty for each ticket and say that 10% of earnings from the tickets will be the total prize for the costume contest. And we can do single costumes and couple costumes, split it evenly and that'll be it. Your maximum capacity is four hundred fifty, you do the math. Plus what you'll earn at the bar-"

Matteo smiles. "You don't have to convince me that it'll make money, I already know that." He leans forward on his elbows. "Convince me it'll be fun."

Isabella looks confused for a second before she closes her binder. "Fine. We can decorate the club and the upstairs lounge to give it a Halloween scary vibe. We could also use fog machines – that would be fun. I still need to decide on a theme for my birthday, but I want to give out glowing neon bracelets at the entrance so single people can have green and people in a relationship get red. It'll make things more interesting." Her eyes light up. "And the VIP area can have customized menus and everything!"

"Sounds good. Can you do it?"

"I mean, not alone. But I can find people who can help me, that's not a problem."

Matteo shifts in his seat. "You've talked to Vinnie about the whole payment thing?"

If there's one thing that makes him uncomfortable it's talking about money with friends who aren't part of the business. He would never let them do it for free, but he also won't beg someone to take his money.

"Yes."

"Hold on." He opens one of the desk drawers and takes out a credit card. He holds it out to her. "Take this and try to find decorations and whatever else until tonight."

"What's tonight?"

"I'm going to be at the club. Find someone inside and ask them to bring you to the office. You know, where we go to-"

Isabella rolls her eyes. "I know where your little crack den is located. But I'll come with Valentina because she's driving us home."

Matteo throws her a questioning glance.

"We're in the same building this year."

"Thought you were going to be roommates?"

"Turns out there aren't any two-person dorms on campus. And she's one of the very few real people I know."

"She didn't look like that to me." He snorts.

"Just because she's hot and beautiful doesn't mean she's like all the other girls you go for."

Matteo crosses his arms. "What's that supposed to mean?"

"It means that the only good-looking girls you've ever encountered had sex with you and most of them only wanted your money. And while them wanting your money doesn't necessarily bother you because you have loads of it, them not being smart makes them boring and shallow. But that doesn't mean there are no real women out there who also look good." She takes a breath. "I mean, look at me." She motions to herself.

Isabella's dark blonde hair and green eyes have always made her beautiful, and she has always been the smartest person Matteo knows by default.

"Yes, but you're one in a million." Matteo jokes and watches her put the credit card in her wallet. "Code is 0707."

"You shouldn't use your birthday as a code for everything, you know."

"Thanks for the advice, but I haven't been robbed yet. So…"

"Okay this discussion is becoming counterproductive, so I'm going to head out and go shopping."

"When will you be back?"

"I'll text you."

"Alright."

***

Matteo's phone beeps in his pocket around 9pm. He's just about to start a new game of FIFA alone [29].

He turns off his PlayStation and walks over to the desk. He takes a plate full of powder cocaine out of the drawer and quickly fixes himself a line. Sure enough, Isabella's laugh echoes down the hall and the door opens. She comes in with numerous shopping bags, followed by Valentina, who's also holding a vast number of bags.

"We're baaack!" Isabella sings and drops the load of bags on the floor in the corner by the minibar.

"You didn't hold back huh." Matteo jokes. He watches Valentina look around the room for a second, then turns back to Isabella. "So, what did you buy?"

She takes out her wallet and hands him the receipts. "We got decorations, neon glow sticks which we'll turn into bracelets, then we found these cute halloweeny buckets we can use for VIP bottle service- oh! And these web decorations to make it look like the VIP is filled with spiders, and-"

"Tell him about the big spider." Valentina chimes in and starts rummaging through the bags.

"Oh! And we found a big spider prop which we thought would be fun to place at the entrance."

---

[29] since the boys spend their weekdays on campus

Valentina holds up a giant tarantula plush toy.

"That looks…not scary." Matteo smirks. "I mean, it all sounds and looks good to me. If you need people to set it up, use our security."

"I mean, you could also help," Valentina remarks and crosses her arms over her chest.

"Yes, but I can also pay someone do it for me." Matteo smiles back before standing up and grabbing some of the bags anyway.

Chapter 6

Matteo

Manhattan, New York, United States – October 31st, 2019

When Matteo arrives at Redlight on October 31st dressed as the devil, the inside of the club is almost unrecognizable. There's white fog everywhere, orange and black lights moving around the room in sync with the music, and skeletons, spiders, zombies, and other Halloween props scattered all over the place.

He finds Isabella in the VIP area on the couch, talking to Vinnie. The doors opened five minutes ago, and there's a long queue of people outside.

"This is amazing Izzy, well done," Matteo says, hugging her from the side once he sits down, then looks out past the elevated VIP area over to the dancefloor. The VIP section overlooks the entire club - the elevated DJ booth next to the entrance to the left, the two semi-circle bars (one right next to the DJ and one on the other side of the room next to the bathrooms), and the small room made out of glass walls which is the smoking area (Matteo's addition, even though he can't be bothered and just smokes at the table).

"I mean, Valentina helped a lot and had good ideas, so we both deserve the credit." She says, hugging him back. "She even came up with names for the VIP menus. My favourite one is Jack O'Lantern for whiskey. Wait, no. The Gin Skeletonic."

Matteo grabs a can of Red Bull from the pumpkin-shaped champagne bucket at their table. It's their usual table of ten, always reserved for Matteo and his friends – even when they're not there. That way he can easily step back into the staff hallway in the back of the VIP area while also keeping an eye on the club. That's how he spotted Aleksi dealing drugs in the first place.

"What are you supposed to be?" Isabella asks once she takes in his outfit.

"The Devil, clearly." He smirks.

"You threw on some devil horns and a red T-shirt. You're not the devil."

"I could've come out here in nothing and I'd still be the devil."

"Do you pick up girls with that line?" Isabella retorts. "If you do, no wonder why your standards are so low." Matteo pouts and she shrugs. "Am I wrong?"

"I *do* have standards."

"Prove it."

"I dated Allison, who in case you forgot is the heir-"

"She's really-"

Before Isabella can finish the sentence, Valentina and Raisa climb the four stairs leading to the VIP area.

"Hi, oh my *god* what took so long?" Isabella asks Valentina as she helps them drop their bags on the couch, sliding over to make room. Valentina sits down first next to Matteo, and Raisa next to her.

Valentina leans in closer to Matteo, mirroring Isabella, so they can understand each other over the music. "The queue is long as fuck and then the coatroom took forever." Valentina answers.

Great, now they're yelling at each other with Matteo between them. He leans back into the couch, trying to make more space for them while also making a point of being annoyed by the situation (not really, because Valentina smells good but you know - principles).

"Do you want a drink?"

Valentina takes the menu and holds it up so Raisa can also see it. "I'll take the Vodka Redlight. I need some Red Bull to keep me up."

"And I want the bloody Hallowine." Raisa laughs. "I'm guessing that's red wine?"

Valentina excitedly nods while Isabella starts mixing the drinks. Matteo thinks about escaping this all-girls situation, then he remembers Vinnie's there, on the other side of Isabella.

"Why are you so quiet, Vincenzo?" Matteo asks, patting him on the shoulder behind Isabella's back.

Vinnie looks up from his phone. "Nothing. I thought I'd let you two talk." He smiles disingenuously. "I'm fine."

"Is it Sofia related?"

"Let's talk during one of our meetings."

A staff meeting means doing a line or smoking a joint in Matteo's office.

Isabella sits back down and turns to Matteo. "Allison was great-"

"Oh good, you didn't forget where we left off-" Matteo sarcastically interjects.

"-but right now you could definitely do better. She was mommying you and turned you into a passive person. All you did was spend time with her. Everywhere you went, she went. You were with her out of comfort, not because you liked her."

Matteo feels like he's being told off by one of his parents, but deep down he knows she's right. The fact that everyone present can probably also hear what she's saying doesn't make it better.

"Yeah, you're right." He hates to admit it but can't even object.

"And everyone that followed afterward was the same. That's why you said you don't want to settle down anytime soon, because they weren't up to the standards you didn't know you had. I'm not judging you; I'm just saying you can't prove to me that you have standards."

Matteo rolls his eyes but doesn't miss how Isabella's eyes flicker to Raisa for a second. "How diplomatic of you. You should become a politician."

"I'm trying to. I'm literally studying World Politics."

He turns to look at Valentina and Raisa, who are in a conversation of their own. He bumps Valentina's shoulder with his. "What about you?"

They both look at him.

"What about us?" Valentina asks before taking a sip of her drink.

"What do you study?"

"I study Business Psychology."

Matteo raises his brows and turns his head to Raisa, eyes not leaving Valentina. "And you?"

"Law."

"What about you?" Valentina asks.

"Economics."

"Oh really? Did you have Jameson during the first year in Managerial Accounting?"

"Um…I don't really attend classes."

Valentina tilts her head. "Then how do you pass them?"

He shrugs. "I just read the summary notes and go to exams. Vinnie helps me sometimes. And make sure I meet the 60% attendance demand in some courses."

Valentina looks impressed. "How did you pass Managerial Accounting?"

"It's math. And business. People get too caught up in the theory sometimes and forget to read between the lines. You know the 80/20 rule?"

"The Pareto Principle, yeah."

"80 percent of consequences come from 20 percent of causes. So, 80 percent of what I need to know to pass the exam can be learned by doing 20 percent of the work."

Somebody calls Valentina's name, and a girl Matteo has seen around before appears in front of the VIP area.

"I'll see you guys; I'm going to go dance for a bit," Valentina says, looking at Isabella more than anyone else, then stands up and grabs her drink. "You want to come with?" she asks Raisa.

"I'll finish my drink and then come meet you." Raisa decides and then Valentina's gone.

Isabella talks to Vinnie again, and Matteo wonders why nobody else has shown up to their table. His siblings and Vinnie's are expected to show up, and none of them are here yet.

"What did you do this summer?" Raisa asks, trying to make conversation.

Matteo looks at her. She's wearing a tight green bodysuit that shows off her body in a subtle way.

They met at school, so Matteo recognised her when she came to the club the first time last year with a fake ID. Then sometime during the last days of school, she came to an afterparty at Matteo's apartment, they flirted with each other and ended up sleeping together.

"I chilled in Sicily." He says before returning the question. "What about you?"

"Mine and Valentina's family usually spend our summers in Sicily as well, that's why we came to the party in Taormina."

Matteo flashes back to the party at his Taormina house. For some reason, most of his memories from that day are filled with Valentina in the red dress and her unimpressed expression.

"Matteo."

He looks up to see Vinnie looking back at him with a questioning look on his face. Matteo knows exactly what he's asking without asking.

"I'll be back in fifteen," Matteo tells Raisa. He hasn't had sex in almost a month, and he kind of missed having to work for it. Not that he thinks she'll make him work for it – more like wait for it until it's okay to leave.

Vinnie starts venting as soon as he locks the door.

"Sofia ended up not going to Portugal for her Erasmus semester and is coming back. She texted me this morning asking if we want to meet for coffee tomorrow."

Matteo tries to focus on both his friend's problem while fixing them lines.

P. Mazilu

"Do you want to see her?"

Vinnie shrugs. "I don't know. The last times we saw each other it was very toxic, and she ended up draining the life out of me. But I still care about her."

"I mean…man. Look. She cheated on you and then blamed you for not being affectionate enough."

"We weren't…dating."

"You've been dating for *years* and you have never been with somebody else. I think you've lost your self-respect somewhere along the way." Vinnie doesn't look like he agrees. Matteo goes on anyway. "She knows if she as much as lifts a finger, you're going to crawl back to her, because you've proven it to her over and over again."

Vinnie sighs, defeated. He takes a seat across the desk from Matteo and starts rolling up a bill. "Then tell me what to do."

Matteo smirks. "I think you need a new distraction… A new hobby." He pauses. "Or a new girl."

"A bandage wouldn't help."

"Then a new hobby. Maybe golfing?"

"I'm not going to go golfing."

"Then let's go partying."

"We're doing that right now and it's not helping."

Matteo groans. "Not *here*. You need to leave the environment that makes you to think of her. Let's go to Austria in December. Boy's skiing trip. Then maybe France."

Vinnie smiles and nods, thinking about it already. "Alright."

When they get back to their table Marco and Aurora have shown up, and so have Eddie and Pia.

"Are you supposed to be a devil?" Aurora nods at the devil horns headband, unimpressed.

Matteo makes a face at her. "And you're supposed to be…what?"

"A sexy Catwoman." She says, making a twirl.

"You're seventeen." Matteo points out and she flips him off before going over to Pia. He spots Isabella in the corner of the VIP area talking to Valentina.

"Your outfits match." Isabella notices when Matteo approaches them, motioning between Valentina and him.

Valentina is wearing a white corset tutu dress with rhinestones on it and wings attached to the back and a pair of white heels with what looks like leaves on them.

"I mean, he's only got a dusty devil headband on." Valentina notices, a teasing smile playing on her face. "It's not the type of devil my angel would match." She jokes and Isabella seems to find it extremely funny because she starts laughing.

Matteo ignores them and turns around, meeting Raisa's eyes in the process. They nod at each other.

Six hours later when Matteo goes home from the club, Raisa's with him. They kiss as soon as they get into the taxi, and they don't stop until the sun comes up and Raisa falls asleep.

***

He wakes up around three in the afternoon the next day with a faint memory of doing a line with Raisa and Marco in the office.

He remembers ordering three rounds of shots for their table, which had by then been crowded by people. He remembers going home before the club closed, and then kissing Raisa in the taxi.

But now she's in his bed still sleeping, and Matteo feels a pang of regret in his chest. He doesn't like kicking people out, but he enjoys waking up alone without having to make conversation out of courtesy.

He gets out of bed and slips into his slides before walking into the bathroom to brush his teeth and wash his face.

The kitchen in their penthouse has a nice view of Central Park, so drinking his coffee and smoking a cigarette by himself is even nicer with a view.

The machine beeps to signal that the coffee is ready just as Raisa emerges into the kitchen, fully dressed. He doesn't ask her if she wants any coffee in the hopes that she'd leave sooner.

"I'm going to leave. Valentina is picking me up. See you at Isabella's birthday tonight." She smiles, grabs a small unopened bottle of water from the counter and leaves.

"Bye!" Matteo says and waits to hear the door close before he sits down at the island counter.

Finally. He looks at the clock on his laptop. It's 3:34pm, which means he needs to be at the club and make sure everything is set up around 9 or 10. The place would be filled by 11.

An hour later, he decides to take a nap. It's Friday after all.

***

The queue outside is longer than it was yesterday since it's a Friday night, and Matteo is proud to see that people are willing to wait outside in the rain to get in. He thanks the driver and waits for Marco to get out of the car as well before they head inside.

The two girls at the entrance who are in charge of tickets and checking IDs wrap green neon bracelets around their wrists.

"Nice colour." One of the girls (Ashley?) smirks at Matteo. "Single."

Matteo smiles at her out of politeness, then proceeds to walk further down the hallway until he reaches the double doors leading inside.

The Halloween decorations are gone now, and the club looks almost close to normal. UV lights have been installed and neon champagne buckets sit on each table in the VIP area.

"Did you buy new buckets just for this occasion?" Matteo asks Isabella, who's excitedly talking to Raisa about something. "Happy birthday." He adds, planting a kiss on her cheek.

Isabella smiles at him. "Thank you, and yes, we did. I'm curious to see how both nights turn out, financially speaking."

Matteo raises his eyebrows. "I'll call you in when I do the accounting on Sunday then." Then he looks at Raisa. "Hi."

Isabella purses her lips and turns her back to him to get back to the discussion they were having. But the other girl doesn't seem to be focused on that anymore because she's watching Matteo as he pours himself a Vodka Redbull while talking to Vinnie.

"How was last night?" Vinnie asks, a knowing smirk playing on his face.

Matteo gives him a look. "You were here, weren't you?"

"After, I mean. Did you hook up with Raisa again?" he asks.

Matteo shrugs. "Yeah."

"She's looking at you."

"I know. Cheers." He says and raises his glass, but Vinnie is looking at someone outside the VIP area. Matteo turns to follow him gaze.

Valentina is trying to explain to Billy (one of the security guys) that she knows the birthday girl. The two of them walk over immediately.

"It's fine, she's with us." Vinnie says and takes the rope off.

"Get her a bracelet." Matteo adds, and Valentina gratefully smiles at both of them. She looks better than she did yesterday, going from an entirely white outfit to all-black, with her hair up in a ponytail.

"Next time, just tell the girls at the entrance that you're at table 1," Matteo tells her as she sets her bag down on the couch.

"I told them, but they told me they can't do anything."

"That's weird." Vinnie frowns. "I'll talk to them."

"It's no big deal, I'm here now." She places a hand on Vinnie's arm. "But thank you."

She grabs an energy drink from the bucket before she excuses herself and goes toward Isabella.

They both watch her walking away in silence.

"Have you seen her around before?" Matteo asks, eyes falling on the red neon bracelet tied around her wrist.

"Her family has a vacation home in Capo. We're neighbours. Sort of."

"No, I mean around... *here*. School. Clubs. I don't know. She seems to know everyone?"

Vinnie shrugs. "I don't know. Yeah? She went to our school and attended some of our parties with Raisa. Maybe you just never paid attention to her. Or you didn't notice her?"

"Did she have a glow-up or something?"

Vinnie throws his head back and lets out a laugh.

"I don't think so man. Maybe she looks more...not infantile, I guess? Like, she has cheekbones and...longer hair."

"Infantile? Cheekbones?" Matteo asks, smirking. "Maybe she could be your new distraction."

Vinnie rolls his eyes. "Let's get something to drink. Shots." He decides.

"Shots." Matteo agrees.

They spend the next two hours dancing and drinking next to each other, going to the occasional 'meeting' in the office with either Marco, Isabella, or Eddie.

"Maybe we should ask Aleksi to come by in an hour? Is he here?" Vinnie suggests, talking loudly as they enter the staff hallway through the back door in the VIP area.

"I don't know."

They stop in front of the door and Matteo takes the key out.

"Text him and ask," Vinnie says, annoying Matteo with his energy while he's trying to focus on unlocking the door.

"Just be patient for a second, ey?"

The door to the ladies' bathroom down the hall opens and out comes Valentina, stopping as soon as she sees the two of them hunched over and trying to open the door.

"Everything all right boys?" She asks with a knowing smile.

"You want to come with?" Vinnie asks just as Matteo opens the door.

Valentina looks at Matteo for a second. "Sure."

She slings her small bag over her shoulder and makes her way toward them without breaking eye contact. The boys don't move until she steps into the room and looks around.

"We're having a meeting." Vinnie jokes.

"I had one as well," Valentina admits, absentmindedly tapping her index finger over her right nostril.

The boys exchange a look as Matteo opens the drawer.

Valentina steps closer and places her hands on the desk, watching him at work.

"So where's your boyfriend?" Vinnie asks, motioning to Valentina's red bracelet.

She looks surprised and then proceeds to laugh. "Oh, I'm not dating anyone."

"You know red means taken, right?" Matteo asks and starts to separate the powder into three lines with his credit card.

"Yes? But I also know that red looks better on me than green." Valentina retorts and shoots him an innocent smile.

Matteo has learned from being friends with Isabella, that smart *and* beautiful is a very...*annoying* combination in women. Annoying in the sense that they can just weasel their way into your mind because they're not only nice to look at but also interesting to listen to and pay attention to. What's annoying about it is that sometimes you don't realize that they've outwitted you in every way possible until you're in too deep.

His first instinct when he saw Valentina was that he'd seen her around before but that she's probably the type of girl who likes being in the background. But as soon as she opened her mouth back in Sicily, his instinct told him that she's actually *that* annoying combination of incredibly good looking and frustratingly smart. And the fact that she so obviously knows it makes her even more annoying.

Chapter 7

Valentina

Manhattan, New York, United States – November 1ˢᵗ, 2019

Buying cocaine from Aleksi is not how I planned my first day of November to go. But, in my defence, I nearly fell asleep in the club yesterday after driving Raisa's car four hours down to New York, where I got to The Plaza, got dressed, got ready to drink, did it all night, and then woke up again to do the same thing today.

Yesterday, Raisa had left with Matteo and Aleksi told me that he'd sleep in her bed. Before we went to sleep early in the morning, I asked him if he could get me a gram of coke for tonight. All he did was nod, say goodnight, and close the door to his adjacent room.

We met in the kitchen and he placed a baggie on the kitchen table before I handed him a hundred-dollar bill.

"It's eighty."

"Really? I thought it went for a hundred."

"Yes, but you're my friend." He told me and I nodded.

"Oh. Okay. Thank you."

He left afterwards, and I was alone for a couple of hours. I decided to take a bath with a glass of champagne and a joint.

The door to the suite shuts and I sit still, putting out the joint in the ashtray.

"Raisa?" I yell, gathering some foam to cover up my body.

"YES!?"

There's a loud noise, then silence, then footsteps coming down the hall. Raisa opens the door, smiling. She looks tired, but happy.

"How was it?" I ask, wiggling my eyebrows.

"Ugh, *so* good. Maybe the best sex of my life." She sighs and looks at herself in the mirror. "I look like shit."

"I'll be done in fifteen, you can take a bath if you want," I suggest. I wouldn't mind getting a nap in before going to the club. Plus, with the cocaine already scored, falling asleep wouldn't be a concern at Isabella's birthday.

"I'll actually do that, thanks." She smiles. Then she inhales. "Did you smoke weed in here?"

"Definitely."

***

I choose a black cut-out minidress (mainly because I brought four outfits with me and two of them were halloweeny) for the club, even though I usually avoid wearing tight dresses. And heels.

No one forces me to wear heels, but my mother would shake her head if she saw me going out in a dress with sneakers on. She's always been feminine, and I have always admired for that. I wondered how she could be so effortlessly beautiful. She had me when she was young, at twenty-two, and doesn't look over thirty-five even though she's forty-two now.

When I was younger, I would sit on her bed and just watch her sitting by the vanity table doing her night-time skin care routine. She had loads of creams and perfumes on show, but I rarely ever saw her putting makeup on. I watched her spend twenty minutes every night washing her face in the bathroom, sitting down in front of the mirror, and applying what I would call 'magic potions' when I was seven years old.

Now that I think about it, they were sort of magic potions, because they kept her from aging. She's always looked the same to me. When I asked her about it a couple of years ago, she told me that the secret to looking young is also staying young on the inside.

I match the dress with a pair of black heels and grab one of my favourite leather Chanel handbags that looks like it froze from the outside in.

"How are you doing your makeup?" Raisa asks, coming in with her makeup bag.

"Um…nude, I think."

"I forgot my eyeliner at university." She whines and sits down on my bed. "Do you have one?"

"I don't have eyeliner, but I have a black pencil."

"Oh, that's good too."

We don't talk for a while as we both get dressed, but I can tell that whatever happened between her and Matteo last night is giving her extra energy. I'm happy for her; I feel like it's the first time she's been happy since her father died.

Raisa's done way before me, mainly because I cannot decide on which shoes would go better with the dress, so when she asks if I'd mind her leaving before me, I don't hold it against her. I end up leaving twenty minutes later.

The queue is almost two blocks long. The taxi drops me off at the front of the line, which means that I must walk all the way to the back. And to top it all off, it's raining, which means I have to use Isabella's gift bag as an umbrella.

It takes forty minutes until I finally flash my fake ID to the bouncer and get inside, away from the rain and the loud cars outside. Forty minutes which seemed like an eternity, not because of the rain but because of the drugs burning a hole in my bra.

The same two blonde girls from last night are sitting behind a tall marble table by the entrance.

"That will be fifteen." One of them says, looking at me while chewing her gum, looking unimpressed by life.

"Oh, no. I'm here for a birthday party, at table one." I tell her.

"Name?"

"Valentina."

The other one, who looks younger and livelier, looks me up and down while her colleague stares, still unimpressed. Then she looks down at the paper on the table in front of her.

"I don't see your name."

"Fine, a ticket then," I say, taking the cash out of my wallet and placing it in front of them.

"Wait, you need your stamp!" she tells me when she sees me stepping away.

I smile at her. "No, thank you." Then I see the neon bracelets in their boxes and the banner, promoting green as single and red as taken. I take the red one because it's *red* and struggle to put it on my wrist as I walk towards the large double doors.

As expected, I spot Vinnie the moment the VIP area comes into view, talking to Matteo. The bodyguard stops me when I place a foot on the first step.

"I was here yesterday," I tell him, and I know he knows, but his face remains void of emotions. "I'm here for Isabella's birthday, she's my friend."

"It's fine, she's with us," Vinnie says and takes the red velvet rope off.

"Get her a bracelet," Matteo tells the bodyguard, and I smile, a wave of relief washing over me.

The bodyguard looks at me for a second and takes a shiny bracelet with today's date written on it out of his pocket. There's a glint in his eyes that tells me he's just putting up a tough guy front because he gets paid well and is loyal to his bosses.

"Next time, just tell the girls at the entrance that you're at table one," Matteo tells me as I set my bag down on the couch but making sure to not forget about the gift.

"I told them, but they told me that I'm not on the list."

"That's weird. You should've definitely been on that list." Vinnie ponders. "I'll talk to them."

"It's no big deal, I'm here now, but thank you," I tell him and grab an energy drink from the bucket out of habit before I excuse myself and go off to find Isabella.

"Happy birthday!" I say, hugging her from behind.

She's excited to see me so we step away from the crowd to talk in private. I hand her the gift bag and she happily takes out what I put in there. There are three books, all of them mentioned by her in the past few months, one of them being a book for our joint course, which is hard to find.

"You're the best, oh my *GOD!*" she exclaims, hugging me again. Out of the corner of my eye, I see Matteo looking at me while talking to Vinnie.

I've seen him around campus a couple of times since I started my first year two months ago, and it seems as though everyone around me knows him personally, has some history with him, or at least knows *of* him. I don't know exactly what's weird about it but I'm usually very aware of my surroundings and he's somehow managed to be everywhere and nowhere at the same time.

It's weird.

***

I haven't used the cocaine in my bra yet but after two back-to-back Red Bulls during the first hour, it's time to give my heart a break.

When it gets close to midnight, I start feeling as if the alcohol doesn't taste as good anymore and that it's becoming more of a chore rather than something I want to do, so I decide it's time.

I try to be as quick as possible in the bathroom cubicle. I hear two girls come in and drunkenly talk about some guy at their table. He's apparently making a move on both, so I wait for them to leave before I can do my line in peace.

After I make sure there's no residue on my nose, I grab my clutch from the sink and walk out. As soon as I step back into the hallway, I see Matteo and Vinnie at the end of it, hissing at each other in Italian as they try to get a door open.

To do what I just did, I think, smiling.

"Everything all right boys?"

"You want to come with?" Vinnie asks, switching from distressed Italian to calm English.

I look at Matteo, who's still struggling to get the door open, which I find very amusing. "Sure."

The room looks cleaner than the last time I was here to set up for Halloween with Isabella, and the frame of the picture with the landscape has come off, revealing a vault inside the wall.

"We're having a meeting." Vinnie jokingly says.

"I had one as well," I tell him.

Matteo opens a drawer behind the desk, starting what appears to be a routine. I place my hands on the large desk to shift my weight from my heels to my arms.

"So, where's your boyfriend?" Vinnie asks, stepping closer to me and pointing to the bracelet. It confuses me for a moment but then I get it.

"Oh, I'm not with anyone."

"You know red means taken, right?" Matteo asks.

I look down at my bracelet for a second, then back up at him. "Yes? But I also know that I look better in red than I do in green."

Matteo looks at me, feigning annoyance.

I think about asking Vinnie about his girlfriend, but we've never once talked about her. I do know, however, that she's here, because I think I saw her at the bar at some point.

"Can you text him?" Vinnie asks Matteo, who pulls out his phone, this time looking like he's annoyed for real.

We both watch the whole process of him texting someone, getting a reply within seconds, and then looking back up at us.

"Yes, he's on the way. But we've got enough here as it is."

We do the lines and start talking about one of our joint courses at university – even though they're one year above me, some of our courses overlap.

Someone knocks at the door and Matteo goes to open it.

It's Aleksi.

"Hello again." He says, shooting all of us a shy smile.

The scene is a déjà vu of what happened last summer at that villa in Taormina: Aleksi taking stuff out of his bag, Matteo handing over some cash from the desk, Vinnie smiling as he watches it all go down.

And I just stand there, extremely aware of everything around me. I feel that warm rush through my body that suddenly makes me feel like everything is possible, like I could move mountains if I wanted.

"I'm going to dance," I announce to no one in particular before I shift my weight off the desk.

I turn around and walk up to the door, only to find it locked. Vinnie steps towards me to try and help me but I brush him off, unlocking it myself in one swift motion before I'm out the door.

I find Isabella and Raisa at our table, dancing and yelling at each other over the music, so I pour myself a glass before I have them follow me down to the dancefloor.

We dance for what feels like hours until the boys from our table join us. I even dance with Vinnie and Marco for a bit until Matteo spawns in front of us and nods towards the VIP area.

The three of us nod, following him without even speaking. He opens a door across from his office to reveal a pantry (sort of) where the spare alcohol is kept.

The space is a little cramped, but the light is good and Matteo is already spreading out the cocaine on his phone screen.

"Sofia's here," Vinnie says to no one in particular, eyes on the coke.

Right, his girlfriend.

"So?" Marco asks. Judging by his tone, he's not a fan either.

"She told me she still loves me. We met for coffee." He continues.

Matteo groans, rolling his eyes. "Please, she tells you that every time you're about to get over her. She knows she's not going to find anyone better than you, but she still wants to have fun with other guys while you stay loyal to her. It's toxic and she's a fake bitch."

I don't even know the whole story, but I feel like he might be right.

"Yes, and you didn't even hook up with Ariana even though she was *obviously* flirting with you this summer because you felt bad for Sofia." Marco adds.

"But I can't *not* talk to her, I want her."

The boys groan and Vinnie shoots me a helpless look.

I tell him without thinking, "I mean…I don't know the situation, but I don't think you want her, I think you just want the comfort that comes with having her."

This is a lesson I learned while dating Jamie on and off in boarding school; he was the first guy who ever paid me any attention, the first guy who showed even the slightest interest in me. Plus, he was more experienced than I was when we met so the sex just became better and more comfortable. We knew what each other liked and didn't like. It worked. For a while.

In the end, I ended up realizing that I'd spent the last two years with a guy who I knew wasn't for me just because it was comfortable having him around. I ignored all the red flags because he was all I've ever known in terms of romantic relationships.

Of course he wept and cried and everything in between when I broke it off. Asked me to take him back and promised he'd do better but it was too late. I'd detached from him emotionally two months before I finally found an excuse to break up with him.

"There's no com- I love her. I wish I didn't." Vinnie reasons, bringing me back to reality.

"I get the feeling you like the drama she brings with her because you also like to be toxic," I tell him, crossing my arms and looking at him questioningly.

Matteo points and me and smirks. "I like this girl."

"So what should I do?" Vinnie asks, still not understanding what I'm trying to say.

I shrug and watch Matteo do the first line. Before I can answer, Marco buts in.

"Have sex with someone else. There are tons of girls who have a crush on you, and I think you should have fun for a while. You've been with the same person for years now."

"Plus, Austria in December," Matteo adds and holds out the phone and the rolled-up bill to me. I look down at the phone and he holds it up right under my nose so I don't have to lift a finger.

The right side of my face goes numb a few minutes later and I tap it with my fingers.

"Good shit, right?" Marco asks, nodding, and I get a déjà vu for the second time tonight.

"Yeah." I smile.

Out of the corner of my eye, I see Matteo smirking.

Chapter 8

Valentina

Manhattan, New York, United States – November 2nd, 2019

Somehow around ten people end up going to Matteo and Marco's apartment in the city for the after party, including myself. Isabella, Raisa, and Sofia are the only other girls here and we're currently smoking joints around the kitchen table. We're discussing light-hearted topics like how fun the club was and which boy is the best dancer, while the guys chill in the living room.

"So, which one of you is sleeping with Matteo tonight?" Sofia asks, looking between Raisa and me. Her eyes narrow in on me for some reason and it rubs me the wrong way.

"I guess that would be me?" Raisa says, nervously laughing.

"Fun." Sofia smiles.

She raises her glass to Raisa.

"Speaking of the devil." Sofia drawls when Matteo enters the kitchen and walks up to us. I can start to see now why Matteo called her a fake bitch.

"I came for a puff," Matteo says and comes to a halt next to me.

I look at him and take two small drags before I hand over the joint.

"So, whose are you then?" Sofia asks, pointing her wine glass at me.

She loves starting her sentences with 'so'.

Also, what kind of question is that? What does it even mean? Am I too drunk?

"Excuse me?" is the only thing I can think of answering.

"Whose girl are you?" she clarifies, and now all eyes in the kitchen are on me.

"Mine," I tell her, not really knowing how to react.

Either the alcohol and drugs are finally getting to my head or this girl in front of me is very overwhelming and underwhelming at the same time.

Matteo snorts as he passes the joint to Raisa. "And whose are you?" he nods his chin at her.

She blushes and takes a hit without breaking eye contact.

"Yours." She finally answers and I look away.

She should've told him *yours, maybe.* Just to watch him squirm. I shake my head but catch myself in time before people can notice.

Once Matteo leaves everyone seems to relax and we're back to talking mundane things.

My original assessment of Sofia still stands an hour later when we're in the living room listening to music and smoking with the guys. She keeps going on about how she can't do coke anymore but it's okay because she doesn't need drugs to stay awake or have fun anyway.

I'm sitting by the bar in the corner of the living room next to Isabella, people-watching and idly discussing random shit. For some reason, the exchanges between Matteo and Raisa seem the most interesting to me. The way they interact with each other is way too fascinating; he looks like he's bored because he's done this a thousand times and she looks nervous to be talking to him. That, or maybe because it's all happening in front of a huge painting of the woman with a flower head by Dalí.

A tall, thin brunette exits the balcony and walks past the two of them. Matteo tenses before turning his head to watch her for a moment, and I don't think Raisa notices.

"Who's that?" I ask Isabella.

She snaps out of her thoughts. "Who?"

"The brunette talking to Marco."

She rolls her eyes. "Oh. That's Allison."

"You don't like her?"

Isabella shrugs. "She's Matteo's ex. I have no idea what she's doing here. Who even invited her?"

There's definitely more to the story because I've never seen Isabella so close to being angry at someone, but I don't push it. My feet hurt from wearing heels all night and the coke is starting to wear off. If I'm here by the time it starts to get light outside it'll be game over for me.

I place my glass on the bar and turn in my chair to face Isabella.

"I think I'm going to go home."

"You sure?"

I see someone familiar out of the corner of my eye, also talking to Marco.

"Is that my *brother*?" I say in disbelief and take a hold of my glass again before I stand up.

I don't hear what Isabella tells me next as I walk over to him. It's not unusual to see him at the same party - it's weird seeing him at *this* kind of after party.

"Hello, what are you doing here?" I ask, switching to Russian, not giving a fuck whether it comes off as rude to Marco and the girl.

"Marco invited me, I was at another party in the city and decided to swing by. You okay?" he asks, switching the attention on me.

"I'm fine. But I'm coming home with you." I tell him.

Then, smiling, I raise my glass to him and knock it against his. "Cheers," I say English.

It had never really occurred to me before tonight that I could stay at Adrik's when I'm in the city instead of always booking a hotel. Now that he's out of the dorms and in a two-bedroom apartment on the Lower East Side, I could, in theory, sleep at his.

"Cheers."

Isabella looks very amused once I sit back down next to her at the bar.

"Do you think he could tell I've done coke?" I ask.

"I don't know. He might be higher than you are."

I look back at Adrik, who's looking back and forth between Marco and the brunette as they're talking. His eyes are red and smaller than usual, and he seems like he's trying to keep up with their conversation. He *is* high.

"He's adorable." Isabella laughs and shakes her head before taking a sip from her glass. Then she nods toward Sofia and Vinnie, who are talking in hushed tones in the left corner of the room. "She, on the other hand, is annoying." She nods towards Allison. "And her too."

Judging by the way she slurs her words I can tell she's had one too many and is starting to become unhinged. Also, I'm not sure why she doesn't like Matteo's ex since Marco seems to be getting along just fine with her.

"Come to the bathroom?" She whispers to me as she tries to get off the highchair. She wobbles on her heels so I stabilize her by grabbing her arm.

"Yeah, where's the bathroom in this place?"

I let her guide us to the bathroom in the hallway and she shushes me as soon as we get inside and I lock the door. Then she falls to her knees in front of the toilet and dry heaves into it.

"You need to throw up?" I ask, even though it's obvious.

"Uhuh." She says and then proceeds to throw up twice.

I get her some water and try to pat her forehead with a cold towel when someone knocks on the door.

"Isabella? Matteo sent me to check on you." Someone says from behind the door.

Isabella lifts her head and looks at the door. "Bitch." She hisses, before she throws up again.

She wipes her mouth with the back of her hand. "I'm fine, Allison. I'm with Valentina."

"You sure?"

"Yes!" we say at the same time.

We wait for a moment before Isabella finally gets up and dusts off her knees.

"Matteo sent me," she says in a high-pitched voice, mimicking an American accent.

"Was that his ex?" I ask as I help her wash her face.

She nods. "I thought Matteo was done with the bullshit."

"What bullshit?"

"Allison bullshit." She says, as if it's supposed to give me any information.

"Do you want to go home? We can sleep at Adrik's place."

"Why not your hotel?" Isabella asks.

"I think Raisa's brother is there."

Isabella nods. "Call an Uber. I'll wait here."

I go on a mission to find our coats, call an Uber, and also inform Adrik that we'll be leaving. I find him on the balcony, smoking a cigarette with Matteo, Marco, and Allison.

"I'm leaving. Give me your key."

He makes a face but starts looking through his pockets anyway.

"You going alone?" he asks, switching to Russian.

"No, with Isabella. I'll leave the door unlocked."

"I'll sleep here." he says and I shoot him an incredulous look.

"Since when?"

Adrik shrugs. "Since now?"

"Fine."

I hold out my hand to him and he places his keys in it.

"The address is on the family group chat." He adds in English.

"Yeah, thanks."

I wait by the bar for a couple of minutes until a driver accepts my ride, then go to find Isabella when he's five minutes away.

"Do you have your phone?" I check with Isabella while we wait for the elevator.

She's leaning against the wall, looking dangerously close to throwing up again.

"Yes." She smiles, not opening her eyes.

The apartment is on the fourteenth floor, so it'll take us about five minutes to get outside anyway.

When we get inside the elevator, she leans against the mirror, exhaling.

"In case you're wondering what my problem with Allison is." She starts, still keeping her eyes closed. "She made anything she wanted out of Matteo's life for *years*. She was jealous of our friendship and filled his head with lies. She's not a nice person and I thought Matteo was over it - I mean, it's been over a fucking year. But here she is, and if they start again I'm going to lose my shit. He deserves better."

I smile. "You love him."

"Of course, I do. That's why I want what's best for him."

I nod, just as the elevator comes to a halt and the double doors open to reveal an empty lobby, save for the night-shift receptionist.

The car is already outside by the time we stumble out into the cold and I help Isabella climb inside before I lean her against the other window.

"I'm not going to sit by and watch him be a doormat anymore." She drunkenly says, then dozes off against the window for the rest of the twenty-five-minute car ride.

***

I wake up around two in the afternoon the next day, well-rested but with a puffy face and a weird taste in my mouth. Isabella is still sleeping next to me in the guest bedroom, so I grab my phone from the nightstand and quietly walk out of the room.

I open one of the kitchen windows and light a cigarette as I press on my conversation with Adrik.

I press on the cappuccino button of the coffee machine and look at the photos taped to the fridge while I wait for him to answer.

There's a photo of our family this year in August for Adrik's eighteenth birthday, smiling from ear to ear because we went to Sardinia for the occasion. There's another one of him and his teammates at an ice hockey championship they won last year and several more of him and his friends from school, at parties, and in aesthetic places.

I've never even seen these photos because he only posts on Instagram like three times a year and doesn't really share his life with me or our parents. At least not as much as I do, anyway.

My eyes fall on a photo buried under three others in the downright corner of the fridge. I crouch down to take it.

It's of Adrik on the beach, kissing a girl's temple. She has blonde hair curled at the ends and is turned with her back to the camera, hugging his waist.

There's another photo of him holding the same girl as she jumps in his arms, with her face covered by her hair. But I recognize the beach, even though the sky is cloudy in the photo. It's in Capo d'Orlando, where we'd sometimes go at night to eat dinner by the sea.

My phone buzzes on the counter so I put the photo back and go to check my messages.

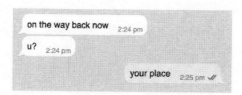

I lean against the open window with my coffee and light another cigarette.

Who's that girl in the photo?

The intercom rings fifteen minutes later and I buzz my brother into the building.

"You look well." I sarcastically say when I see his dishevelled hair and the dark circles under his eyes.

"Spare me," he replies, groaning as he drops down on a chair in the kitchen.

"Do you want some coffee?" I ask, even though the actual thing I want to talk about is that girl in the photo. But talking to him about his personal life is like walking in a field full of landmines.

"Yes, please."

We're silent as the coffee machine gets to work.

"Are you hanging out with Marco Giudice now?" I ask.

"Yes."

"Since when?"

He rolls his eyes at me. "Since last year. You know, we used to be on the same team before he quit."

I knew that, but I didn't know they were close enough to hang outside of practice.

"Do you have any girlfriends?" I continue, realizing that I sound exactly like mom.

"You sound like mom," Adrik confirms my thoughts and runs a hand through his hair.

"I saw a photo on your fridge with a girl," I cut straight to the point. He raises his eyebrows and leans back in the chair.

"And?"

"Who's that?"

"I can't tell you."

"Oh, come on."

He shakes his head. "She asked me not to tell. Plus, it's over now anyway."

I purse my lips, not satisfied with the answer.

"Do I know her?"

"Valentina." He sternly says and crosses his arms over his chest.

"I do, hn." I smirk, then put the coffee in front of him.

"Don't start snooping." He points a finger at me. "I mean it. Just find something else to do with your life, or I swear."

"Ouch."

"I'm serious, Valentina. I promised her nobody would find out."

I laugh. "Seriously?"

"Yes. We ended it when school started."

"Fine." I know it's all I'm going to get out of him right now, so I don't push it.

I watch him drink his coffee. "Are you okay though? With the, um, breakup."

He nods, looking genuine.

I sigh. "Fine. Then I'll stay out of it."

Adrik squints at me. "I don't believe you. You can't just let stuff go."

I feel offended for a moment and sit down at the table across from him so he can look me in the eye.

"I *can* let stuff go, and I already have." I lie. "I won't bother you about it. I just want to know your life. We haven't talked in months." I add, truthfully this time.

He shrugs. "I've been busy with my last year of school and you're in university now. I'm *fine*, I just don't like sharing that much."

I sigh. I've been feeling like we're not as close as we used to be when we were younger and still living in Moscow.

Then I get an idea.

"Oh no, no," Adrik shakes his head.

"What?"

"You've got that look on your face when you're about to suggest we play one of your games."

"What games?" I innocently ask, even though he's right on point.

"One of those games where if I lose, I have to do something or share something with you."

I pout. "I wasn't about to do that." Lie again.

He looks me straight in the eyes. "Valentina. I used to play along when we were younger, but right now things are more...serious. And we're not children anymore; we both have responsibilities. Playing games is just...you know. Childish."

"Right." I snort, remembering how my senior year of high school was mostly about me trying *not* to have any responsibilities. And so far, my first year of university is looking pretty much the same.

Adrik stands from the table. "I'm going to go take a shower."

"What if we played on your Xbox?" I try, following him into the living room.

"Haha, you wouldn't last a second."

I raise my eyebrows at him. "Try me."

"Fine. But we're playing FIFA, and you're not allowed to change my controls."

"Fine, then we raise the stakes."

He groans and I smile because that's his tell when he gives into what I want.

"If I win, I get to ask you three questions about yourself and you have to answer truthfully."

He makes a face. "No fucking way."

"Are you afraid you'll lose?" I mock him in that baby voice I know he absolutely despises.

"I can just lie to you if I lose."

I squint at him. "I know you." Then I smirk. "But it's good to know you think I could beat you."

He leans forward, elbows on his knees. "If I win, you give me your first car for an entire year."

My mouth falls open, appalled at his unparalleled audacity. "Three months."

"Six."

We shake on it, and five minutes later I've already picked my Spanish team. He's chosen with his favourite team, as always.

I score the first goal because he keeps answering texts instead actually playing. This makes him lock his phone and focus on playing for real.

"You know that if I lose, I can just lie to you, right?" he asks, eyes not leaving the screen.

"You could, but I'll know."

The game is boring after that and by halftime it's already 5-0 for him but I've missed hanging out with him like this. Before I even get the chance to tell him that, the second half of the game starts, and I end up losing 8-1.

"You did put up a fight at the end, I'll give you that." He says as he watches the highlight reels. "I just can't wait to get your first car."

"Why would you assume that you won't get one first?"

He gives me a look and purses his lips the way Isabella does instead of just saying 'bitch, please'.

"You know dad won't buy me a car until he's sure I'm a responsible driver. He trusts you more than he does me."

I look at his face for a second, and that feeling of love I have for him only makes my heart warm.

"I missed playing with you," I tell him, and his face relaxes into a smile.

"I missed playing with you too." He pulls me into a side hug. "But this need of yours to play games will be the death of me."

I roll my eyes and he stands from the couch with a laugh.

"I'm going to take a shower now."

Chapter 9

Matteo

Palermo, Sicily, Italy – December 24th, 2019

Waking up on Christmas Eve in Palermo always makes Matteo feel nostalgic. He loves the smell of cheesecake mixed with the cigar smoke drifting out of his father's lounge while he has guests over, the sound of his mother cooking downstairs while also trying to teach Aurora something, and the continuous flashing Christmas lights outside his window.

When he was younger, he would go outside and play with Marco until it was time for dinner, then they'd get into bed and fall asleep thinking about the presents they'd unwrap the next day.

The landline in his room starts ringing, which can only mean that it's his father. He groans and gets out of bed to grab the phone off the wall.

"Yes."

"Can you come in the lounge please?"

"Do I really have to?"

The silence on the other line makes him want to groan and swear under his breath, but he just hangs up and walked over to the bathroom.

His father is in the lounge with a man Matteo has never seen before. They're smoking cigars and drinking coffee, which is usually a sign that his father is in a relaxed mood.

"Francesco has a problem with his store." His father goes on, urging Francesco to explain the problem to Matteo.

"Yes, there are two men who have been coming in for weeks now, asking me to give them a spot on the loading docks. When I refused, they threatened to come in today and take it by force."

"Do we know who they are?" Matteo asks.

Francesco shakes his head. "They're not from around here."

"What do you mean?"

Francesco shifts in his seat and throws a look towards Matteo's father.

"They have accents."

"What kind of accents?"

"Eastern European. Polish, maybe?"

Matteo looks at his father, silently asking why he's here in the first place.

"Paulo needs someone to watch over Francesco and drive into town so he can talk to those men." His father clarifies.

Paulo Barone is a tall, muscly guy with tattoos who could intimidate just about anyone who dared to look at him. For the first sixteen years of Matteo's life, Paulo used to be Uncle Paulo - Vinnie's dad. He was also his father's best friend, ever since the two of them were kids growing up in Palermo. Sometimes they would tell stories about how their own fathers (Matteo and Vinnie's grandfathers) also grew up together, and how they managed to turn the family business into the empire it is today.

As Matteo and Vinnie both came to realize, 'the family business' wasn't just waste management, insurance, and real estate - it was also organized crime.

"Why can't Vinnie do it?" Matteo asks even though he knows the answer. Watching the shakedown of some European wannabe-gangsters isn't one of the things he'd like to do on Christmas Eve.

He knows that once he starts getting involved in this type of shit it will all go downhill. He likes taking care of the club and taking his cut without having to get his hands dirty. It's easy like that.

"He's in Taormina." His father answers, calm and collected as always. "Put some proper pants on and then go start the car. I have someone else waiting outside."

Matteo looks down at his sweatpants.

"Thank you, Don Lorenzo." Francesco says, standing up and shaking his hand. Matteo refrains himself from rolling his eyes. "Thank you."

His father waves him off as if it's no big deal, shoots Matteo a look that says '*behave*', then walks through the double doors into the main hallway.

Matteo doesn't change his pants and goes to wait in the car for five minutes until Paulo and Francesco finally get into the car. Paulo gives him the address then lights a cigarette.

"I'm not a taxi driver." Matteo says as he takes out his phone to type in the address on Waze. "Twenty-five minutes." He reads and then puts the car into drive. "Let's see if we can make it twenty."

***

Francesco's bait shop, which also doubles as one of their loading docks for stuff that comes in from the North, is a small, one-story shop located right by the pier. Matteo parks the car a couple of meters away and watches the two men enter the shop.

Matteo rolls his eyes and looks back towards the store. There's literally no one here.

Matteo taps his phone against his chin, eyes wandering to the pier. He can see past the loading docks, further away into the shoreline where people have parked their boats and yachts.

He calls Isabella on video, and her face appears on the screen two seconds later.

"Yes." She answers, obviously annoyed that he woke her up.

"What are you doing?"

She looks at the screen, unimpressed. *"Clearly sleeping, ugh. You?"*

"I'm helping my father out with something. You coming tomorrow?"

Matteo knows that Isabella's parents have been having problems lately, so asking whether they'll attend the annual Christmas dinner is a sensitive subject.

"Yeah."

She doesn't elaborate, nor does she ask why he's asking.

"What are we doing for New Year's?" Isabella continues, turning on the other side of her bed.

Matteo shrugs. "I don't know. Probably a house party here or in Taormina."

"I'm going to invite Valentina."

"Isn't she in Moscow?"

"Yeah, but it's worth a try. I don't want to be the only girl there."

"You know you won't-" Matteo starts.

She rolls her eyes. *"Besides Allison or Sofia or any other girls that are there because of you."*

The mention of Allison's name makes Matteo tense up. It's a sensitive subject for the two of them, mainly because Allison nearly drove a wedge between them in the past.

"She's matured, you know."

"That seems irrelevant to me."

Matteo sighs. "I saw her a couple of times over the past few weeks and she's chill. I think she has worked on some stuff."

"You sound exactly like Vinnie."

Matteo opens his mouth, then closes it. She's not wrong.

"I trust and respect your instincts, but I also trust mine. And mine say not to trust her."

"But you'll be there, right? Even if Valentina doesn't come."

Isabella flips him off. *"Of course I will."*

Matteo looks back up towards the store, just in time to see two men walk inside. He tries to listen closely, as if he could hear through the walls.

"Are you even listening to me?"

Before Matteo can reply, a couple of loud gunshots ring out from inside the store.

"I've got to go. Talk to you later."

He hangs up on her without offering an explanation before he gets out of the car and runs towards the building.

"What happened?" Matteo asks, eyes falling on one of the two men he saw coming in. The man is on the floor with a bullet hole in his head, blood oozing out of it.

Matteo turns to Vinnie's father. "Did you kill him?"

Paulo looks at Francesco, who's hiding in a corner looking absolutely mortified.

"He shot at us first." Francesco tells Matteo as Paulo lifts the other unconscious guy from the floor.

"We need a cleaning crew." Paulo says.

It takes Matteo less than a second to understand.

Everything suddenly starts to make even more sense; How his father would sometimes pick up the phone during dinners and then excuse himself because the waste management business had encountered a problem. Matteo doesn't remember exactly what little white lie his father would give them ('a pipe burst in the city', 'there's a problem with the trash pickup', 'a house needs new recycling bins'), but he would sometimes mention the waste industry.

Cleaning up messes meant getting rid of bodies.

Matteo's hands feel numb as he searches for his father's number in his phone. He was eight the last time he saw a man shot in the head, and it's all coming back to him now.

He watches Paulo and Francesco stuff the guy who's still alive in the trunk of the car.

"Matteo? Is everything alright?"

"We have uh…" He doesn't even know what to say because he's never had to deal with the *illegal* side of his father's business before.

Not the 'illegal' that meant drugs and other shit that people who wrote the law also indulged in. The 'illegal' that meant getting rid of dead bodies.

"Garbage truck needs to come to Francesco's shop."

Silence.

"Okay." The line goes dead.

Apparently, it's all too familiar for his father. And judging by the way Paulo is handling it, it's not the first time he's done this either.

"I will stay here and wait for the crew. You go drive Francesco home."

Matteo looks at him bewildered. "What about that man in the trunk?!"

Paulo waves it off. "Drive straight to your house and put the car in the garage. We'll take care of the rest."

Of course.

Even though he drives Francesco to his house on the outskirts of Palermo before going back to his own house, all Matteo can think about is the unconscious man in the trunk.

There's a thousand ways it could go wrong, and most of them start with the police.

There's a police car on the side of the road, right before the turn leading onto his street.

Every single amount of stress he's ever carried in his body is now pulsing through him, sending hot shivers up to his ears.

The policeman leaning against the car waves at him to pull over.

Matteo debates stepping on the gas and just fucking off, but the rational part of his brain reminds him that they can't search his car unless they have a warrant.

He pulls over behind the police car and waits for the guy to walk over before he rolls the window down.

"License and registration?"

"Is there a problem?" Matteo asks as he looks through the glovebox on the passenger's side for the documents.

"Is this your car?" the policeman asks.

Matteo hands over his license and the papers. "It's my father's."

The officer reads the top of the paper then double checks the license.

"You were speeding up the hill." The policeman says before handing the papers back to him. "Have a good day."

And just like that, Matteo watches the guy get into his car and drive off. It takes him a couple of minutes to come back down from the adrenaline, then then drives the past few hundred meters into his driveway.

The door of the garage is already open and his father is waiting inside, pressing the button to close it as soon as Matteo's inside.

"What happened?" His father asks, stepping aside and revealing Romeo behind him.

"His partner started shooting so Paulo killed him." Matteo says. It comes out cold, like he's telling his father about what he did at school today, not how his "uncle" just shot a guy dead and then beat another one unconscious.

"Did anyone see you?"

Matteo shakes his head. "But a policeman stopped me on the way here."

"That's Russo. He's keeping an eye out on the street for us."

"But he's police." Matteo says, confused.

"He's a *friend* who's in the police." His father corrects him, before pointing to the trunk and looking at Romeo. "Let's take care of this."

While Romeo struggles to get the guy out of the trunk and carry him out of the garage, Matteo's father places a hand on his shoulder.

"Make sure any evidence that you were there is gone."

It's too much for Matteo to handle at once. "What evidence?"

"Anything that could link you to that location at that time."

"Okay."

His father looks at him for a second then, really looks at him. Like he might even be a little worried about how Matteo is handling this. He doesn't remember his father being like this when he first saw that guy murdered in their restaurant.

"Are you paying that policeman?"

"Yes."

"Do you pay the entire police?"

"Not everyone."

There's so many questions Matteo wants to ask but doesn't want the answers to, so he decides to just go along with what his father says for now.

***

Palermo, Sicily, Italy – December 25th, 2019

His father doesn't come home the next day, not even by the time Matteo, Marco, and Aurora are getting ready to leave for lunch at the restaurant. Their mother already left an hour ago to go help setting up, and the Barone family is already there, judging by Vinnie's 'where are you?' texts and Isabella's Instagram stories.

"Aurora, what's taking you so long?" Matteo yells up the stairs.

"In a minute!!" She screams back.

"Every fucking time." He scoffs and looks at his brother through the mirror.

They both look like they put some effort in looking presentable. They're wearing their special occasion tailor-made suits that they get done once a year every January, and black Italian dress shoes. Their hair is gelled back, like their father taught them at a young age.

"We look like jerks." Marco jokes as he checks himself out in the mirror.

If Isabella were here, she wouldn't waste a second to say 'because you are', like she always does.

111

They would never dress like this anywhere outside the family though, but tradition and customs are very important to their parents, so they go along with it on special occasions. He's never been to an extended family event before where someone didn't wear a suit.

"We look like dad." Matteo says. The suit and gelled back hair with a strand poking out are his father's signature look. Throw in a hat if it gets cold and you've nailed it.

"And I look like nonna Angie." Aurora whines, making them turn their heads towards the stairs. She's wearing a green long-sleeved dress that goes down over the knees, similar to the dresses their grandma Angelina likes to wear all the time.

They used to see her nearly every day when they were kids living in their townhouse above the restaurant. Now they only get to see her occasionally or when they're in town.

She's been going to church every Sunday all her life and she's always very well dressed. She's the type of grandma who complains about never visiting but always slips you money after filling you up with a four-course meal.

Her fur coats and shimmering eyeshadow make her look ten years younger than her actual seventy-seven years [30].

Matteo hasn't seen her in a year and sort of feels bad for missing her birthday, Easter, and Liberation Day, because he was too caught up with his life back in New York.

"You look fine." Marco tells Aurora before he takes one more look at himself in the mirror.

Aurora is still on her phone by the time they get into the car. It's a small van with tainted bulletproof glass with six seats facing each other.

"Who are you talking to?" Marco teases, trying to get a look at her screen.

She pulls her phone away towards her chest. "None of your business."

---

[30] She gave birth to their father when she was thirty-three; her one and only child.

"Are you hiding something?" Marco continues, reaching for her hand.

Matteo watches the two of them struggling for the phone.

"I don't check who *you're* texting, leave me alone." Aurora pouts and Marco pulls back, handing her phone back.

Their whole extended family is already there by the time the three of them greet the security guards outside. Matteo recognizes Andrea Calo because he's one of the guys also sometimes working security at the club. The older one also looks familiar, but Matteo doesn't know his name. All he knows is that he's seen him around his father numerous times before.

Grandma Angie is sitting at one end of the table, right across from their father, chatting to one of his mother's sisters. Her expression makes it obvious that she's gossiping.

The Altieri family is also present, with Isabella's dad on his father's right, sitting right across from Paulo Barone and his wife. Matteo looks towards his table (as their grandma likes to call it), happy to see Isabella and Vinnie sitting there.

He walks over to his grandmother first, kisses her on both cheeks before letting her know she looks like she just stepped off a runway in Milan.

"You all love to kiss my ass during Christmas, don't you?" She laughs and smacks Matteo over his arm. "You didn't come see me for my birthday, Matteo." Her voice isn't severe, but Matteo still feels bad.

"Sorry nonna, I'll come to your next one. What are you turning, fifty?" he asks, smirking at the obvious flattery, which makes her exclaim and smack him in a loving way once again.

"Go away before I stand up!" She threatens, eyes glimmering as she waves him off. "Now go, say hello to everyone."

Part of the reason Matteo has so much love and respect for her is because she's the only person in the world with the ability to control his father.

He finally sits down next to Vinnie ten minutes later, grabbing a glass and the bottle of red wine from the table as he does so. It's the usual table at family functions which Matteo and his siblings share with the Barone kids and Isabella. It's been like this ever since they were born; Only back then it used to be called the 'children's table', which has now been filled with a bunch of second- and third-degree cousins Matteo is always obliged to talk to even though he only sees them a few days a year.

"What happened today?" Vinnie asks, lowering his voice.

Matteo knows Isabella is listening and checks to see if their younger siblings are too. Once he makes sure they aren't, he turns to his best friend and lowers his head.

"Had some waste management business to do for my dad." He explains.

"Bullshit." Isabella hisses and leans over the table so she can whisper without being heard. "I heard those shots on Facetime."

Matteo looks at Vinnie, then back at her. "That was a car backfiring."

She rolls her eyes. "I'm not stupid, you know. I'm aware of what's going on in our house." She speaks out the last words, *casa nostra,* in a way that makes the first 'a' sound like an 'o'.

Matteo chooses to change the subject, pretending that he didn't even understand her innuendo. She always thinks she's so clever, and even though she's right, Matteo can't bring himself to discuss the subject right now.

"Let's talk about New Year's plans, shall we?" Matteo smiles, clapping his hands together.

The annual Christmas dinner always starts when Lorenzo stands from the long twenty-person table filled with members of the family he considers close. He faces the rest of the packed restaurant and raises his glass of cognac before giving his recap-of-the-year speech. Matteo never listens because it's always mostly the same and it's not directed at him anyway.

It's directed at the other part of the restaurant, filled with people who work for him and who have been here since before Matteo even became aware of his existence. They make up the extended family of his father, which he treats (almost) equally to his blood relatives.

"Who came from Waste Management?" Vinnie asks, leaning back in his chair when people start applauding.

So, he knows.

"Paulo."

Vinnie nods.

"Did you know about it before?" Vinnie asks.

"Know what?"

Vinnie tilts his head towards him with a 'bitch please' look.

"Let's go for a cigarette." Matteo suggests, standing up and grabbing his wine glass.

There's a special smoking room inside the restaurant but there's always someone there so they go outside, away from the security guys until they're out of earshot. Neither of them says word until they've both lit their cigarettes.

"Did you know about it before?" Vinnie asks again.

"Know about *what*? Explain."

"That they kill people and then make the bodies disappear." He bluntly says, as if he were talking about something trivial.

Matteo shakes his head. "No."

"Have you ever wondered what's in those shipments we've done recently?"

Of course he has.

"It's either drugs or something valuable but illegal, right? Otherwise they wouldn't pay us so much to do it."

'They' is the entire organization, and even though Matteo's father is the boss, there are thousands of people who willingly choose to get involved.

"Is this bad, you think?" Vinnie continues, anxiously puffing on his cigarette.

Matteo sighs. "I don't know. I mean, I don't think this is the first time this happened, and it definitely won't be the last. The only thing that's changed is that now we're consciously aware of it. If you're talking about the guy who died, then yes, it's bad." He tries to joke about it, as he always does when a discussion gets so serious that it makes him uncomfortable.

"Do you feel guilty?"

"Me?" Vinnie asks, surprised. "No."

"In a weird way, neither do I."

Vinnie looks at a couple walking past them, too engrossed in each other to even notice the two of them.

"The only thing- nevermind."

Vinnie makes a face. "Tell me."

"The only thing that bothers me is that it *doesn't* bother me. A man died, Vinnie. He was fuckin' killed, and now he's probably on a way to a crematorium. And I can't bring myself to care about it."

In hindsight, seeing someone shot in the head when he was only eight years old might've desensitised him.

"Yes, but didn't they also have guns on them? Weren't they the ones who pulled the gun on Francesco? My dad showed me the footage."

Vinnie *does* know everything, and Matteo could just as well go and talk to his father about what happened. The only problem is that sometimes (ever since he turned sixteen and was introduced to *cosa nostra*) the line between father and boss becomes very thin, so Matteo prefers to let his father come to him rather than have it the other way around.

"You're right."

Maybe I don't feel guilty because I always knew this was my reality.

They put their cigarettes out on a trashcan nearby, then throw them in.

"Hey." Vinnie says and points at him, making sure Matteo is listening. "No matter what, we always have each other's back, okay?"

Matteo holds out his hand without hesitating.

Vinnie shakes it, eyes going up to Matteo's gelled back hair that's styled exactly like his own.

"We look like assholes." He concludes the conversation.

They look at each other for a moment before they burst out laughing, and suddenly they're kids again, laughing at something they shouldn't be.

Chapter 10

Matteo

Palermo, Sicily, Italy – December 26th, 2019

The party goes on well after midnight, with people drunkenly dancing and excitedly screaming over the music while smoking and drinking wine.

Matteo gets bored after Isabella left, leaving him alone with a drunk Vinnie at their table.

His father is always the last one to leave this type of events, but it's the first time Matteo has ever stayed long enough for them to go back home together.

Sometime around 3am, his father comes over and tells him they're about to leave. Matteo is relieved. With no cocaine or any other drugs to keep his body awake, the red wine is getting to his head.

The car ride home is silent, and although Matteo wants to talk to his father about what he witnessed yesterday, he doesn't - just in case the driver can hear them.

"What's going to happen to the body?" He asks his father as soon as they set foot inside their house, the double doors closing with a thud behind them.

His father looks taken aback by the question. "What do you mean?"

"The guy Paulo killed. What's going to happen to him?"

"Why do you care?" His father asks as he takes off his dinner jacket by the door and places it on the coat hanger. The question makes Matteo's blood boil.

"What do you mean, why the fuck do I care?" He raises his voice, which furthers seems to baffle his father. "A man was killed, another one's body was stuffed in a trunk, and yo-"

"You didn't answer my question. Why do you care?"

"Because killing a man and getting rid of his body is not what I thought your business was about."

His father looks towards the dark foyer. "Take your shoes off and let's talk in my office."

Matteo huffs but listens anyway. He's tipsy and wants answers, so he follows his father into his office.

He accepts the glass of whiskey poured for him, then proceeds to take a seat on one of the chairs by the desk.

He watches his father circle the desk to sit in his chair.

"What do you think my business is about?"

"Construction? Real estate? I don't know, but *not* killing people."

"You're right."

"So why is that man dead?"

"Because he chose his fate the moment he pointed that gun at Francesco and threatened to kill him if he didn't hand over the store. Paulo reacted correctly when he chose to shoot first."

"What if that man had a family?"

"He was a lowlife gangster-"

"I don't give a *shit* if he was a gangster or whatever. *You're* an Italian gangster and you have a family as well."

His father looks at him and Matteo can't say for sure whether it's with pride or disappointment.

"If someone came into my office one day and threatened to take our house away with a gun to my face, what would you do? Would you shoot him, or would you let him take everything before finally killing us?"

Matteo's silence is everything his father needs to continue. "Those two Russians that have been causing problems in Palermo are part of a very dangerous criminal organisation. They came to take the store owned by one of our subsidiaries by force. They had revolvers so they didn't come to play. If Paulo hadn't reacted when he did, Vinnie wouldn't have a father and our company would be involved in a very long police investigation that would eventually lead nowhere and would only cause unnecessary paperwork."

"So it's not the first time you killed someone." Matteo concludes, purposely trying to ignore the part of himself that understands why that man had to die. He's angry; Not because his father is okay with killing people and then making them disappear, but because he feels blindsided by all of it.

When his father doesn't answer, he goes on. "How do you know they were Russians?"

"We found their IDs."

Matteo shakes his head. "You talk about it like what happened was normal, like murdering people and then getting rid of their bodies was the right thing to do."

"There's no right or wrong in this world, Matteo, just like there's no good or evil. We are the ones who make it so."

"That's bullshit."

His father doesn't seem to be rattled at all. He's actually very calm, which makes Matteo even angrier.

"Matteo. Ninety percent of my business is legal and legitimate, but the past always has a way of catching up to you when you thought you've let it go."

Matteo makes a face. "What does that even mean?"

"It means that ever since you were born, I have tried my best to protect you, but now you're older and you've seen enough to know what's really going on."

"Yes. What's going on is that you're okay with killing people like it's nothing."

Although his father wasn't even there when it happened and it was Paulo who had pulled the trigger, Matteo *knows* that this has happened before. He knows, deep down, that his father has given the order to have someone killed before – he wouldn't be so casual about it otherwise.

"No, what's going on is that we have the right to protect what's ours. Those Russians that came into the store might have had families back home, but they were ill intentioned people who came all this way with guns to take something that wasn't rightfully theirs. We protected our territory when they threatened to take away our lives."

He makes everything sound so simple, and Matteo hates the fact that he understands exactly why it had to happen this way.

"You're angry at yourself because you agree with me." His father adds. "I know, I've been in your shoes when I was your age. I've been doing this for over twenty years."

"Do you have a clear conscience?"

"Yes." His father answers without even thinking about it. "If I explain it to you, you wouldn't understand."

Matteo leans forward in the chair. "Try me."

"Do you feel guilty about what happened-" his father starts, and Matteo nearly interrupts him immediately by saying 'yes' "-or do you feel guilty about not feeling guilty?"

Matteo goes silent.

"The second one." He admits, which makes his father smile. It's the first time Matteo can obviously tell that he's proud of him.

"Then someday you'll understand."

Matteo stands up from the chair. He needs to sleep. "I will never kill anyone for you, just so you know."

"I really hope you'll never have to."

When Matteo gets into bed that night, he tells himself that things are still the same.

His reality hasn't changed, not really. The only thing that changed is him slowly becoming aware of the world he was born into.

***

Palermo, Sicily, Italy – December 31st, 2019

They meet at Vinnie's house on New Year's Eve around 8pm to get the last few details in order before the party starts. Isabella and Vinnie mainly took care of the organising and inviting people, but Matteo promised he would take care of the drugs.

Paulo and his wife Diana chose to go to Capo d'Orlando last minute, so their children stayed in Palermo, using the opportunity to throw a party. About sixty people were invited: people from their school, friends they've made abroad and all over Italy, and some 'plus-one's', as Isabella called Allison and Sofia.

Sometimes Matteo wonders why he even thinks about going back to Allison, or why he had sex with her three times in the past few months instead of just going for someone new. He wonders why he sometimes wants her around even though he's barely attracted to her anymore, but then he sees Vinnie going through the same thing and realizes that it's a comfort thing. It's easier to go back to someone you used to fuck rather than bothering to find someone new.

Although they live nearby, Vinnie's house is closer to the city than Matteo's, situated on a one-acre estate close to the sea.

Matteo arrives after everyone has already arrived, and goes straight to Vinnie's room with the bag, only to find that there are seven other people in there.

Ariana Milanesi is also there, and she's obviously flirting with Vinnie right under Sofia's nose, who watches from across the room and clearly talks shit about her to Allison.

"Good evening, everyone." He waltzes over to the desk by the windows and drops the bag on it. "Drugs are here." Since Aleksi's back in Moscow for the holidays, Matteo contacted another guy he knows who lives in Palermo.

Marco hands him a joint as soon as he sits down on the couch.

He takes a few hits to catch up. "Thanks."

His eyes meet Allison's from across the room. She's looking at him with her bedroom eyes, which Matteo doesn't fall for anymore (even though he fucked her in his car just a few days ago, but oh well).

She says something to Sofia before she comes over to him.

"I thought you quit smoking."

"That was two years ago." He replies in a dry tone, puffing the smoke away from her because he remembers that it used to bother her.

She sits down next to him. "Why are you being weird?"

He raises his eyebrows. "I'm not being weird."

"You're rude."

"I didn't even say anything!"

She throws him a look.

Maybe he's coming off as rude because he can't bring himself to care anymore. He enjoys her company, yes, but only sometimes, if he feels like it ('it' meaning either horny or lonely or both).

"You're treating me with indifference." Allison pouts, and his impulse is to roll his eyes even if it makes him look like an asshole.

"You're not my girl anymore, I don't have to treat you like we're together."

She's taken aback by his bluntness but quickly composes herself. "I know that. And I know you've been sleeping with other girls too, and it's fine."

"Why wouldn't it be? It's been over a year since we broke up."

"I meant you having sex with other girls even though we still do it." She clarifies.

"Oh, well, yeah. You're free to do the same."

"So it wouldn't bother you if I fucked someone else tonight?" She asks, obviously wanting to get a reaction out of him.

Honestly? Her focusing her attention on someone else would probably be for the best.

Matteo shakes his head, still leaned back on the couch, looking as relaxed as ever. "Not at all." And he means it. He'd actually be glad, because then she would get taken away by force and he could move on with his life.

"You know I'm the only one who understands you." She says, and she sounds more like she's pleading rather than threatening him to tell someone what his family really does. "And I'm not talking about *that*. I mean from an emotional perspective." She adds, probably having read his face.

Maybe she's right. Maybe one of the reasons he can't seem to let her go is because he hasn't met anyone else who fulfilled his human need to be understood, cared for, listened to. They've had some conversations about life and the meaning of existence which he hasn't had with anyone else, and the feelings that came with those memories are still fresh inside his mind. But he's getting tired of her right now.

"What do you want to hear from me?" He asks.

She huffs and stands up from the couch. "I know you'll come back to me Matteo. You always do."

He watches her walk away and whisper something to Sofia before they leave the room. He just can't deal with it, it's like he's back in high school. He turns his attention back to the room, and as he watches his friends, he smiles.

***

It happens a little bit after midnight.

Matteo kisses Vinnie on the mouth at midnight to make a joke out of it (like they used to do years ago before they both got girlfriends) and although it might be from the drinks and the drugs, everything feels right again.

Matteo suddenly feels like the whole world is spinning while he stands still, so he decides to go out into the back garden and get some fresh air.

After making sure his cigarettes are in his jacket, he leaves Vinnie with the others to go further out into the back garden area, which is shielded from the house by trees.

He sits down on a stone bench facing the sea, taking conscious breaths to ground himself.

"I wish Valentina was here." Isabella says when she joins him on the bench a few minutes later.

"You not having fun?" Matteo asks, throwing an arm around her shoulders as they watch the fireworks over the water.

"I am. But sometimes I just want a familiar presence." She tilts her head. "At least Ariana's here."

Matteo frowns at her. "I'm here."

"Yeah, but you're not *here* when Allison's here. Just like Vinnie isn't here when Sofia's here. And when you both aren't here, I'm not here. You get it?" she rambles, and he nods, switching the subject.

"I think she wants to get back together."

"Obviously. Do you want to?" She asks as he takes the cigarette from his lips.

"No way. I want to not see her anymore, but in a weird way, I need her."

"Bullshit. You just need something to do."

Matteo smiles. "That's exactly what I tell Vinnie."

"Follow your own advice then. And if not yours, then mine."

They sit in silence for a few minutes, listening to the music blasting through the open doors of the house behind them.

She turns to him after a while. "Did you know Vinnie and Sofia had a big fight earlier?"

Matteo looks at her, shocked. "What?"

"Vinnie was flirting with Ariana and asked if he could kiss her at midnight, but she refused because Sofia overheard and made a scene, telling him that the drugs were getting to his head."

"When did this happen?"

"I don't know, half an hour ago? In Eddie's room. You were probably downstairs."

"Fuck. I mean, Vinnie seemed fine a few minutes ago."

Isabella nods. "Yeah, Vinnie's fine, but Sofia isn't. She left."

"What do you mean she left? I saw her at the countdown."

"I'm telling you, she left and then I came over here because you're obviously overwhelmed."

Matteo kisses her cheek as a way of thanking her for being her.

"I hope she doesn't come back." He says in a serious voice, and she laughs as she stands.

Someone yells out *'polizia'* but Matteo doesn't register it until he sees red and blue lights flashing over in the distance. His body freezes. Someone yells it again and he comes back to reality. The sirens are loud as they get closer, so he tells Isabella to run as he himself takes off towards the house. They both know that they need to hide the drugs, otherwise it's over.

"We have half a kilo of cocaine and weed, for fuck's sake!" Eddie screams when they get to Vinnie's room, trying to hide the drugs in a hurry.

Vinnie smacks him over the back of his head. "Shout it louder, why don't you?!"

Isabella is trying not to panic while Ariana and Allison stand by the door, frozen in place with fear written all over their faces.

"It's going to be fine." Matteo tries to assure them, even though he doesn't believe it either.

People downstairs start screaming over the music and soon enough, the music dies at the same time the door to Vinnie's bedroom is dramatically kicked in for no reason.

It's only when he sees policemen pointing guns at them and yelling at everyone to put their hands up and get on the ground, that Matteo starts to realize there's no going back to how things used to be.

P. Mazilu

NEVER HAVE I EVER
felt infinite

Chapter 11

Valentina

Moscow, Russia – December 24th, 2019

We're having Christmas dinner at one of the hotels my father has recently decided to invest in, in a room filled with relatives and business associates.

I stare at the people on the other side of the room. Most of his associates are men dressed in black suits, accompanied by beautiful women wearing long, elegant dresses, just like my mom (who made me wear an uncomfortable red pleated dress that makes me look fifty and a pair of stilettos from her own closet so I would 'look presentable').

It's weird having Christmas somewhere other than at our own house. We used to go to my grandparents on my father's side until I was six or seven years old – when they both died in a house fire.

Going all the way to Mexico to visit my grandmother on my mother's side would be too much hassle; especially since she never approved of their relationship in the first place. She wanted my mother to marry a guy from her own country, but she was too gone for my dad to care.

Everyone seems to be on edge today - maybe it's because our family can't go anywhere without arguing first. In my defence, it was my brother who started it all because he was texting instead of getting ready.

Adrik taps me on the shoulder and I look up at him, coming back to reality.

"I brought you a drink." Adrik says handing me a glass with blueberries in it. "It's blueberry gin."

I squint my eyes at him after I take it and he sits down next to me. "Why are you being nice?"

"I'm bored." He admits and I nod in agreement. There are no other people our own age in attendance besides Raisa and Aleksi.

"Yeah, me too." I say, looking at my mother who seems to be very interested in what Raisa's mother, Valerya, has to say. "What do you think they're talking about?"

Adrik shrugs as he scrolls on his phone. "Us, probably."

Valerya Volkov has always seemed like a strong woman to me, even though I rarely talk to her. It's her first Christmas without her husband and she seems to be very composed about it, which makes me respect her and her family even more. I don't even know what I would do or how I would react if my father were to…

I consciously decide to move my attention elsewhere, so I turn to Raisa, who is quieter than usual. "Are you okay? Why are you so quiet?"

"Yeah." She sighs, placing her phone upside-down on the table.

Judging by her expression and the way she placed her phone, she's about two seconds away from venting about a guy.

My phone vibrates on the table.

"I mean, I've been talking to Matteo over the holidays, but he sometimes takes way too long to reply. I think he's going to ghost me."

There it is.

"Why would you think that?" I ask her, even though it doesn't surprise me in the slightest.

I don't know him that well (or at all, really) but Matteo seems like the exact type of guy who would sleep with several people and not give a fuck what they felt for him afterwards. Plus, there's also the weird vibe I felt with his ex that made me think it's not really over between them. Not to mention that I think Isabella might be in love with him as well.

Raisa shrugs. "I know he's been hanging out with his ex, Allison. And they've been sleeping together."

I lean back, surprised but not really. "How do you know?"

"I figured it out, long story."

I make a face. "Oh, come on, this piece of information is the most interesting thing that's happened to me all *week*."

Raisa smiles and shuffles closer to me, eyes twinkling. "Okay. So I followed her on Instagram and she posted pictures from a hotel a few weeks ago, in a jacuzzi. And she tagged the hotel, which is owned by Matteo's family."

"Maybe she just likes going there." I argue, trying to be rational.

"Yes, but a few days later she posted another story with a bouquet of roses for her birthday and tagged him in it, even though he didn't repost it."

"I mean…okay, maybe. Or maybe they just have history and they like coming back to each other because they're comfortable." I tell her, speaking from my own experience. "During the last few months that I kept going back to Jamie even though we were broken up, I wasn't going back to him because I wanted him back. I was going back because I was horny and lonely sometimes and he was just *there*."

But I also remember being in Raisa's shoes when we used to date, how I would overthink every time he followed someone new on Instagram or when a girl was a little too friendly.

"I don't know. Either way, I'm done with him." She tells me, even though it seems like she's trying to convince herself more than me.

I raise my glass to her. "I support that decision."

She smiles and knocks her glass against mine.

We look out across the room, where people are talking a bit too loud now that the alcohol has sunken in. A few couples have taken to the dancefloor in the middle of the room, trying to imitate a very poor version of the Russian Waltz.

"Who knows." She trails off, nodding towards a table full of men in suits. "Maybe we'll find hot Russian businessmen here."

"They're my dad's age." I deadpan, then look around the room, looking for my him. I haven't seen him since he made a toast in which he thanked everyone for spending Christmas Eve with us.

After a few minutes of silence and people watching, Raisa asks me what we're doing for New Year's, even though we talked about it a few days ago.

"Isabella invited me to Italy- oh, I need to reply to her. But yeah, we're going to that party in Moscow, right? With our friends from middle school?"

I knew some of the people that would be attending the party, yes, although I'm not sure I would call them friends per se. They're just people I used to spend time with when we were younger, before I went off to boarding school.

Most of them stayed in Moscow for high school and then university, but there was always someone we knew who had something going on while we were back home in Russia.

Raisa nods and I remind myself to answer Isabella's text. Honestly, I would love to go to Italy and escape the Russian winter for a couple of days, but plans were made weeks ago and there's no way I can get to Italy on such short notice. Convincing my parents to let me borrow my dad's company plane would be more trouble than it's worth.

I smile. I miss her.

***

Moscow, Russia – December 25th, 2019

Christmas morning always goes down like usual. My mother is up before I can even think about existing, cooking and drinking a glass of wine as she talks on the phone with some of her friends from Spain. My father is holed up somewhere in his office on the other side of the house, also taking calls from people who are most probably not his friends (his only close friend used to be Aleksander Volkov).

I don't bother dressing up today, so I just throw one of my satin robes over my pyjamas, grab my phone, then head downstairs. The Volkov's are going to join us for lunch as they usually do, but there are a couple of hours left until they're supposed to arrive, which means the dress code is basically non-existent until then.

Adrik isn't in the living room, so I go back upstairs, heading straight to his room just because I feel like pestering him a little.

"Do you ever knock?!" He asks, sitting up straight on his bed. The way he's holding the phone in his hand tells me that he's on the phone with someone.

I step into his room. "Am I interrupting something?"

"I'm on the phone."

"With?"

"None of your business."

I raise my eyebrows and shoot him a taunting grin. "With your girlfrieeend?"

"Fuck off Valentina." He whisper-yells and covers the phone with his hand.

"Why are you so cranky?"

"Get out of my room and close the door!" He warns, standing up. I raise my hands in defence, not even pretending to be intimidated by my little brother.

"Jesus, what got up your-"

I squeal and step out of his room when he marches over, watching as he slams the door shut.

"I know, right?" I hear him say to whoever he's talking to, and I flip off the door.

I decide to waste some time staring at the portraits hanging on the hallway's cream-coloured walls. Anything is better than having my mother micro-manage me into doing something.

The portraits of Erik Levin, the grandfather on my father's side, never cease to creep me out. The first one is dated September 19th, 1966, when he was about twenty years old.

He's sitting behind a large wooden desk, leaning back into a chair that looks more like a throne. He's wearing a white shirt with the sleeves rolled up and the first two buttons undone.

He has the same blonde hair dad and Adrik have, but his eyes are blue like my uncle Boris'. There's a boyish smile tugging at his lips as he stares right into my soul, and he looks excited.

He died when I was five so my memories of him are vague and almost non-existent, but this is by my favourite picture of him.

Unlike the second portrait right next to it, dated over thirty years later on June 6th, 1999. He's standing in front of the same desk, dressed in a dark blue suit and leaning against a cane with a carved lion's head for a handle – the family crest.

What terrifies me about the painting is that he looks like a completely different person. His sunken eyes are void of any life and his face looks stern, serious, unlike the man in the previous portrait. He's still looking at the person who's painting him, but this time it's a blank, disassociated stare.

The hairs on my arms rise the longer I stare at it. There's something dark about the way he's just standing there, his face worn by age and the things he must've seen to look like that.

A man's orotund voice echoes down the hallway, from where my dad's office is located, pulling me out of my dazed state. I take one last look at my late grandfather before I walk towards the voice.

I know better than to enter without knocking, so I press my ear against the door.

"How are we going to handle this?" Someone whose voice I don't recognise asks.

"I don't want anyone to do anything about it until I know all the facts."

"It wasn't a misunderstanding Kyril, and you know it."

"I don't know *anything* yet. Let's wait it out and see. And lower your voice, my family is in the house."

There's a moment of silence and I hold my breath.

"If someone else dies, we're going to have bigger problems than your family overhearing."

"Then let's make sure it doesn't happen again."

My dad is using a tone I've never heard before. It's low and authoritarian and demanding. I step away from the door, confused.

Who died? What?

"What are you doing?"

I spin around to look at my mother standing at the top of the stairs with a plate in hand.

"Uh…" I say, stepping further away from the office so my dad won't hear us. "I was just going to see what dad was doing."

"He's in a meeting."

"On Christmas Morning?"

Mom shakes her head and walks up to me. "He's going to be done soon, but emergencies happen." She places her hand on my cheek and gently strokes it. "Don't worry about it."

"I'm not."

But who died?

She squints at me. "Guests will arrive at three." Gives me a onceover. "Dress nicely."

I roll my eyes and she smiles, then leans in to kiss my temple.

***

The Golden Mile, Moscow, Russia – December 31st, 2019

The New Year's party is at a townhouse in a part of the city most people call 'The Golden Mile.' It's close to the Kremlin and is very well known for housing Moscow's richest and most influential people: billionaires, politicians, businessmen, and celebrities.

When I was younger, I would stare at the buildings as the bus passed them by on my way to school, wishing that one day I'd live in one of those townhouses. The dream faded once we moved out of the city to a gated community in Zhukovsky on the outskirts of Moscow. Although nothing beats waking up on Christmas morning in my own room with a view of our gardens covered in snow, I sometimes miss living in the city.

Back when we were celebrating Christmas in our apartment in those communist type building blocks it was always too noisy and too cold-but I was happy. I was happy even when I would cut out photos of my dream houses and dresses that I wished to wear someday and use them to make collages. I guess I was manifesting my life before I was even aware of what being 'rich' really meant.

A girl I know from middle school greets us after we've rung the bell and places two drinks in our hands as soon as we take off our coats. I'm almost certain her name is Sasha, but then again, I was flying under the radar in middle school due to confidence issues. I only knew the names of the popular kids, which everyone knew and talked about.

"This is Sasha's boyfriends' place. His name's Rick. I think you might also know him from school. He was a year above us." Raisa explains as we walk down the hallway.

I nod as if I have any recollection of all these people Raisa is telling me about, but I am very good with faces and numbers so I can recognise about 90% of the people here, could maybe even tell you some of their birth dates, but their names? I've never been good with names.

The townhouse is three stories high and even though it's minus five degrees outside, some people choose to smoke on the terrace overlooking the city. After a few drinks I also become one of those people, so Raisa follows me outside into a corner so we can smoke our cigarettes in peace.

She shows me an Instagram story. It's a photo of Matteo and Vinnie on a balcony.

"He's so hot, ugh."

"Matteo?" I ask, trying to focus solely on our conversation. "Are you still talking to him then?"

She nods, taking a sip from her drink. "Well, we had sex."

"Since Christmas?"

She rolls her eyes. "No. But it's like, *good* sex."

"The best of your life?"

She thinks about it for a second before she nods. "Yes. He definitely knows what he's doing."

I don't know how to continue the conversation, but it turns out that I don't need to because she keeps on talking. "How many girls do you think he's slept with?"

I shrug, puffing out smoke. "I don't know, twenty, maybe?"

At this she laughs, throwing her head back. A few people turn around to look at us but I ignore them. "What, you think he's slept with more than that?"

"Last time I heard a number it was around fifty."

I frown. "Did he tell you that?"

"No, but people talk."

Out of the corner of my eye, I see a group of three girls talk to each other and looking my way.

I turn my attention back to the conversation with Raisa. "Didn't he have a girlfriend up until recently?"

"It's Matteo *Giudice*." She enunciates it like it's supposed to mean something. "Everybody knows everything about him." She stops to look at me for a second. "You really didn't know who he was until this summer?"

"I've known Isabella since ninth grade, and Vinnie even before that. They might've mentioned Matteo in passing, but no, I've never met him before. I don't know him, who he is, or what people are saying about him."

She leans against the railing and holds up her cigarette.

"Well, everybody suspects that his family is in the mafia. His father's a billionaire and he basically owns half of Sicily and half of New York."

I try my hardest not to make a face. It sounds ridiculous, honestly, because come on. Mafia? Owns half of Sicily *and* half of New York?! Please.

"I find that hard to believe."

Raisa glances at me, unimpressed that I don't buy it. "The billionaire part may be a lie, but trust me, there's something shady going on, and I'm pretty sure the Barone family is also in on it somehow."

I wonder if she has ever suspected that our own families might be involved in illegal businesses, but the way she feels so free to speak about such things proves that the thought has never even crossed her mind.

P. Mazilu

She probably thinks that our parents built a conglomerate that got so successful so fast through legitimate means, (even though our families went from living in a two-bedroom apartment in Moscow to a multi-million-dollar mansion in a gated community in less than three years). The math just isn't adding up for me.

A guy walks past and does a double take when his eyes land on me. I watch him walk over to his friend and nod his head in my direction.

"Why would the Barone family be involved?" I ask, thinking about Vinnie and Eddie and how we grew up spending our summers together. I also know their parents who know my parents, and there was never a moment that I thought the Barone family had something to hide. They've always seemed like nice, normal people.

"Because there are thousands of people in the Sicilian mafia. I think Matteo's father is the leader and then people like Vinnie's dad work right under him."

I can't help but laugh. "It kind of sounds made up, Raisa."

"You'd think so, but I've heard stories from Allison's friends."

I raise my eyebrows. "For example?"

"So, you know how Matteo's family is in the insurance b-"

"I thought it was the nightclub industry."

"I think they have more businesses than your father does, Valentina." She rolls her eyes. "Anyway, this 'insurance' business apparently means going to newly opened businesses to get them to sign up for an insurance plan against any possible disturbances. And if someone doesn't think they need insurance, then they'll give them a reason to get insurance...if you know what I mean." She sees my confused face because she continues explaining. "They blow up their stores or send out people to rob them."

"How do you know they're blowing up stores? I mean, come on." It all sounds way too ridiculous.

"Because one of Allison's friend's dads refused to buy insurance for his restaurant and two days later it burned down. He loaned money from the Giudice's to restore it and ended up signing up for an insurance plan."

This discussion is too much for me. I would have never thought Raisa was the type of girl to spread gossip around so easily (well, maybe I did, but not like *this*), especially when she knew how important privacy is for most families at our school. I nod, then change the subject.

We finish our cigarettes and drinks, so we decide to go inside and pour ourselves another round.

"She's with him." Is all she says as I try to get the Gin and Tonic ratio just right.

"Who? What?"

She shows me something on Instagram. It's a photo of a view of the sea from a dimly lit balcony with the tag 'Palermo' and a thirty-minute countdown. "Allison posted this five minutes ago. She's spending New Year's with Matteo. Look." She points to one of the few guys looking out at the sea, who I didn't even spot the first time I looked at the photo. "That's Matteo and the Barone brothers."

I feel bad for her because I can see my younger self in the way she analyses every single photo of an event he's at, wanting to know exactly what he's doing and prepare for the worst.

"Maybe they're friends." I try.

"No, they always get together when they're at the same location. It's like she can't let go. But I guess I understand why she keeps going back. The sex is incredible."

I stare at the two glasses on the counter, trying to remember the last time I had sex. It was months ago, back in June probably, after I'd gone back to Jamie for the last time and swore to myself that I would never do it again. And for the first time, I really did keep the promise I made to myself.

"It's like he knows exactly what he's doing and how he should be doing it. I didn't even have to tell him what I like." She continues.

I smile and shake my head. "Sounds…fun."

"It is. And he's big too, but not to the point it hurts. Just the right amount."

I make a face. "Not really something I wanted to know, but thank you." I joke.

We choose to stand by the bar in the corner of the living room where people are dancing, just to be near the music but also be able to talk. I can tell that she needs someone to talk to about her feelings for Matteo.

A little part of me wishes I were in her place though because I miss having a crush, or someone I can obsess over.

"He's always going to be like this though, I guess I need to remind myself from time to time."

"Hm?"

"He's never going to be able to settle for just one person. He gets bored easily, he always needs a new distraction. And his dick just goes along with it. Doesn't care who it is as long as someone's there. And Allison's always there."

"Maybe he doesn't want love or romantic relationships right now." Not really sure why I'm playing devil's advocate, but I'm a little bored and also a little bit annoyed at myself for feeling like I have to defend him.

"I don't even think he knows what that means."

"Well, he was with Allison for a few years, right? Maybe he wants a break. To have fun."

"I meant that he doesn't know what love is."

I shrug, looking out at the crowd of people. My eyes fall on a guy I remember seeing around school before. I always thought he was cute, but he was a year above me and didn't even know I existed back then. I'm 95% sure that his name is Isaac, but there's a slight chance that I might be confusing him with someone else.

"Who's that?" I ask Raisa.

She follows my gaze and smiles. "That's Isaac. He's at NYU studying World Economics. He dated half of the girls in our year back when we were in middle school. We used to have the biggest crush on him, remember?" she laughs, and I smile. We used to be so close when we were younger and living in Russia. We grew apart at boarding school though, because she always wanted to hang out with people I didn't necessarily like to be around. Those types of people who undermine others and pretend to be someone else in order to be admired by everyone.

I make eye contact with Isaac, and it's incredibly obvious that we were talking about him.

"Oh shit." I say and we laugh even harder now because we've been caught.

"He's coming over here, I'm *dying*." Raisa says and I shush her as we both watch Isaac making his way over to us.

He stops in front of me, and a dimple appears on his right cheek as he smiles. He's taller than I remember him, and the amber eyes with dark brown hair combo still makes him look gorgeous.

"You look familiar." He tells me and I exchange glances with Raisa before answering.

"We went to the same middle school."

"What's your name again?"

"I never told you my name." I tell him. "Valentina."

"I saw you at the club in Manhattan a few months ago, that's why you seem familiar." He says, snapping his fingers and smiling.

"Maybe." I smile at him. He's still so attractive and he's got that sort of baby face with the jawline that I like when it comes to guys.

"You know Matteo Giudice?"

I shrug.

"I know him." Raisa interjects, leaning forward. "Why?"

Isaac turns to look at her. "He's a friend of mine, I think it was his party."

"How do you know him?"

"We were classmates for two years in school. I moved to New York in eleventh grade."

"How come I never saw you at school?"

"Uh…I didn't really attend school." Isaac says, not taking his eyes off me. I pretend to look down at my drink to let them talk, even though I can feel him watching me.

"And what do you study now?" She asks, even though we both know the answer.

"World Economics at NYU."

The conversation drifts off after that and I pretend not to notice that Isaac is going out of his way to make conversation with me while Raisa obviously wants to know everything about him.

A girl that looks familiar walks over to us, looking determined. She introduces herself as Sasha and asks whether we're having a good time.

I realize that everyone around is now subtly watching our conversation, and I get an uneasy feeling in my stomach.

Raisa, thankfully, carries the conversation for a couple of minutes until Sasha is called somewhere else.

"Is it just me or are people staring?" I ask, with the risk of

"Your family is very interesting to people who stayed in our hometown their whole lives."

"Excuse me?" What does my family have to do with anything? "Why would they even know my parents?"

"We left before we were old enough to notice."

"Notice what?"

"You're what Matteo Giudice was for girls at our school."

Matteo Giudice? Who the fuck is Matteo Giudice supposed to be?

"You're saying it like it's supposed to mean something."

Her eyes move to Isaac, who has been watching our whole conversation unfold. It's a look that says he shouldn't be hearing what she's about to say.

"You haven't really gone out that much in the past few years, and it shows."

Two hours after midnight I get bored and decide it's time to go home. I'm surrounded by people who are familiar and strangers at the same time, and I can't do small talk.

Raise decides to stay and keep partying with Isaac, but my entire body is telling me to just go home and go to sleep, so I listen to it.

***

I arrive home around 3am and the house is dead silent. My parents usually have a few friends over for New Year's, but it looks like that has already ended. I know Adrik is with some friends, so I don't even bother checking if he's awake as I make my way to my room.

"What are you going to do about it?" I hear my mother's voice coming from my father's office. There's light shining from under the door, and I take off my boots so I can walk closer without being heard.

"I don't know. I don't want to repeat history again."

"Was it a misunderstanding?"

"They're saying we instigated it." My father replies.

"Did you?"

"No. We didn't send any men out to Europe during the holidays, and I don't want to go back on the peace agreement."

I step even closer to the door.

"What did you tell their families?"

"We told them that they got lost at sea."

So, someone *did* die.

"Does it have the potential to become dangerous?" My mother asks, and I can tell by her tone she's getting worried.

"I think we'll sort it out soon enough. I'll reason with them."

The conversation drifts away from the subject, so I turn around and tiptoe back into my room. I fall asleep wondering who died and why my parents were talking about it.

Chapter 12

Valentina

Private plane, above Russian airspace – January 4th, 2019

We fly back to New York three days later on Saturday the 4th with the company's plane, which always flies us from the private airport outside Moscow to the landing strip near Albany, where a car would be waiting for us to take us to campus.

Adrik takes the seat in the corner closest to the door and puts his headphones on before we even take off. Raisa chooses to sit across from me in the left corner, Adrik goes right to sleep, and Aleksi takes the space across the aisle from us, busying himself on his laptop.

As soon as the plane is off the ground I busy myself with a new book by Paulo Coehlo, but Raisa gets bored scrolling on her phone soon enough so she starts up a conversation.

"Did you hear about what happened in Sicily?" She asks, crossing her legs and leaning back in her chair, ready to spill it.

I close my book, already knowing that it won't be a short conversation if it involves Matteo. But if it's distracting me from thinking about a hundred different scenarios of my parents being involved in a crime, I don't mind it.

"No, what happened?"

"So apparently someone called the police on the party saying there were drugs involved and everyone got busted. Matteo, Vinnie, Eddie and Marco were taken into custody with like half a kilogram of cocaine and weed."

"Oh shit." I say, genuinely feeling worried for Vinnie especially. "Where are they now? What happened?"

"A friend told me that they took them down to the station and let them go thirty minutes later."

My mouth falls open. "What? What about the drugs?"

Raisa shrugs. "I don't know. I think the police kept them."

"Are they under investigation?"

"Not as far as I know." She turns to look at Aleksi, who also seems interested in the conversation. "What do you know?"

Her brother shrugs. "Just that they're fine. They weren't charged with anything."

Raisa looks at me in a knowing way. "See? I told you they were mafia."

I roll my eyes but then I also see Aleksi nodding. "Wait, you believe that shit too?"

"I do."

I look at him incredulously. He's always been the level-headed one in the Volkov family.

"It sounds made up, but they are in the mafia." Aleksi states. "I've seen their bodyguards and what they do."

"Plus, they own the police and that's why they never get into trouble." Raisa adds.

I'm still reluctant to believe them, but Aleksi looks at me with a serious look. "Valentina, you have no idea how deep and dark these things can get."

"Anyway, I'm pretty sure he hooked up with Allison. She posted a photo the day after that from his house in Palermo, and I could see his cat in the background."

Aleksi loses interest in the conversation, probably because he doesn't want to hear his sister talking about some guy she's having sex with.

"How long have you been sleeping with him?" I ask, ready to give her my final opinion on the matter without hurting her feelings.

"Uh…since Halloween?"

"And how often?"

"Every weekend, almost. Whenever we're in the same place we go to his place afterwards."

I nod. "Well, from what I understand, it seems like he just enjoys sleeping around and having fun. I don't think he's got anything serious going on with Allison. Or anyone, for that matter." I'm slightly hinting at the fact that she's one of those people.

"I know." She exhales with a hint of sadness in her voice. "But there's just something about him that makes me want to go keep going back."

"Do you get along?"

"Yeah. He's funny, and he's smart. And *very* good in bed. I get tingles just thinking about it. He talks me through it and he always knows *exactly* what to do."

"If he gives you tingles down there, then you're definitely fucked." I tell her, not even trying to make a joke.

"I know, right?" She exclaims, excited that I'm sharing this with her. "So when did you last have sex? Have you ever had anyone else except Jamie?"

I shake my head. "It was last year and no...I haven't."

"Jesus, Valentina. I would've bet you have at least five by now!"

I shrug. "I don't know, I just-I don't know. I want it to be...spontaneous, you know? Like I want it to be exciting and I want someone to impress me- I don't know."

"You've never had a one-night stand?"

I shake my head.

"So you've only ever seen one?!"

"No, I've done...*stuff* with other guys, but I haven't had *sex* sex." I explain, looking around to see if Aleksi or Adrik are listening. They're not, thank God.

"If you had to pick one of the guys to be a one-night stand, who would you choose?"

"What? Out of who?"

"All the boys you know." She answers, smirking.

I think about Vinnie first, because I've always thought he's cute and attractive, but I never really considered him as a real option because he also has never seemed interested.

"I don't know, maybe Vinnie?" I say.

"Oh my God! I thought you would've said Marco."

"Adrik's friend?" I ask, unwillingly making a disgusted face. There's nothing wrong with him though, he's genuine and good looking and tall and tan and tattooed – a girl could do a lot worse. But he's my younger brother's friend.

"He's friends with Adrik?" She looks surprised. "But he's Matteo's brother."

"Yeah. I've known him for a long time, they used to play on the same team when I was in school. Why would you think I'd choose Marco?"

I look in Adrik's direction, but he looks like he's still asleep.

"Because he's obviously into you and you two seem cute."

"When did you even see us?"

"This summer in Taormina, or at Matteo's apartment. It's so cute how he gets all fidgety around you."

"I haven't noticed." I say, trying to remember the last time I talked to Marco and whether there were any clues. I don't like Raisa putting things in my head because I know she likes to gossip and may make things up just so she could have something to talk about. "And I'm not interested in anyone anyway right now. I want to focus on myself for a while."

"Valentina, it seems like you've been doing that your whole life."

"That's not fair. I was with Jamie for years."

"Yes, and you spent all of your time with him and began ignoring your friends."

I frown. "Not on purpose though."

"Yes, I know. But I'm just saying, it's okay to have sex with someone else if you feel like it. Jamie isn't the only guy on the planet."

"It's not about that."

"Then what is it about?"

"I know exactly who I could sleep with if I wanted to, but having options sometimes means none of them are special."

Raisa looks at me bewildered. "What?"

"I don't only care about how a guy looks, you know? I want to be impressed, surprised...I want it to be *exciting*." I don't elaborate further because I know it's not the right person nor the right place. I just can't be attracted to someone sexually if they don't excite me in any other way.

"Matteo is pretty exciting." She says, like she's trying to sell me the idea of him.

"In what way?"

"He can do whatever he wants, whenever he wants. He asked me to go to the Bahamas one morning because he saw a video on Instagram and I couldn't say yes because I knew I had a project due. He even offered to pay for everything, like he always does. Never even asks or hints at it."

Money is clearly a factor here, even though her family has loads of it.

"We were out eating one evening and everybody knew him wherever we went. Even at the clubs he doesn't own, people know him. He's just so...charming."

"Maybe you like the idea of him."

"I think I've gotten to know him really well over the past few months."

"Do you text?"

"Yes, sometimes. And sometimes he takes days to reply. He's sort of like you." She jokes, even though it's clear that it bothers her.

I take my phone out and text Isabella.

She sends a voice message.

I put my earphones in and press the voice message.

"We were at Vinnie's house and Sofia got mad at him for flirting with Ariana so she called the police on him saying he had drugs. They arrived like, around midnight- I don't even know, the party was busted after that. But I'm telling you Allison and Sofia planned the whole thing-"

"Stop talking shit!" Matteo's voice is heard in the background.

"Fuck off, I heard them talking. Anyway. We're on our way back to New York, the boys were let go and now everything's normal."

"Who are you even talking to about thi-"

The audio cuts off.

After we usually land, there's a six-person SUV waiting to take us on the one-hour trip to Hamilton University.

"Uhh...I think Isabella lands at the same time as us, and she asked me to go in her car on the way to university because she wants to talk to me about something."

Raisa looks surprised but unimpressed.

"Is it about what happened at New Year's?"

I shrug. "I don't know. I think it might be boy trouble as well." I lie.

"Oh really." Raisa says, leaning forward. "With whom?"

"That's what I mean, she wants to tell me in person." I say, and it is clear now that no matter what uninteresting thing I come up with, she'll want to know.

"Alright then."

After a few moments of silence, she asks me whether Matteo's with her on the plane. "Vinnie posted a story from the plane." She explains.

I look up from my phone, taking out my earphone as a sign that I want to be left alone.

"Maybe, I think so." Then I put my earphone back in, consciously ignoring her for the rest of the flight. There's something about her that I've never realized before: how much energy she drains from me when she starts talking about other people and their problems, without even seeing her own. I've got my own shit to deal with. Well, not really, but some peace and quiet would be nice.

***

We land around 9:30pm local time and get into our car. As we leave the landing strip, there are two SUVs just like ours blocking the exit.

"Who's in the cars?" I hear Raisa ask herself as I open the door.

I say goodbye to my brother and the Volkov's before I look straight at the two cars in front me. Isabella pops her head out through the roof of one of them, happily waving.

"Hiii." I greet her as soon as I'm in the car and the door slides closed behind me. She hugs me and as I sit down, I notice Matteo on the seats across from us, on his phone.

"Hi." I tell him and he looks up, nods, then looks back down at his phone. I try not to think about what Raisa has told me about him. Those were just stories as far as I knew, but the way he nonchalantly lives his life makes me think he really doesn't give a fuck about anything.

"So what happened to you?" Isabella asks, crossing her legs and leaning against the opposite wall of the car on our side.

"I overheard my parents talking about someone dying."

"Like a relative or something?"

"No, someone who worked for them got killed. But the weird part is that I think they're trying to keep it a secret, like they have something to hide."

Out of the corner of my eye I see Matteo looking up at me.

"Do you think they had something to do with it?" Isabella asks, genuinely concerned for me.

"I don't know. They're just being secretive about it."

"What does your father do?" Matteo asks me out of the blue.

I turn to look at him. He looks tired and I can see the circles under his eyes every time the car passes under a streetlight.

"He's a businessman." I answer, because in all honesty, I don't know exactly what my father's job is. I'm sure that all he needs is one conversation with Raisa to find out about our family history. For all I know, he knows already. I can't imagine what the two of them could talk about, but it's fascinating to think about it.

"Were you scared when the police came?" I ask both of them.

"Not really, I mean, it's not the first time police have broken off our parties in Italy." Isabella answers.

"It was the first time they took me to the station after they found drugs in my possession." Matteo idly says, head tilted towards his phone but still looking at me.

"And what did they do to you?"

He shrugs, as if he were talking about a trip to the principal's office. "Nothing."

I look at him, trying to read his face, but it looks like he's trying to do the same thing to me. Either he's waiting for a reaction or wondering what I'm going to say next.

"Hm. It means you're one of the lucky ones then."

Chapter 13

Matteo

Manhattan, New York, United States 2020 – January 4th, 2020

Matteo takes out a small silver box from the pocket by the door, then leans back into the seat. Valentina looks at his fingers, which are now holding a pre-rolled joint.

"Lucky how?" He asks, interested in entertaining the discussion.

He can't figure out whether she's joking or being deadly serious, because she didn't even flinch nor ask questions when he told her the police let him go free for clearly punishable offenses.

Valentina watches him light up the joint. "Getting to go free when you get caught doing illegal stuff." Her phone vibrates and she looks down to check her screen, losing her train of thought.

Matteo cocks his head, watching the hair fall over her eyes. "How would that account to luck though?"

He sees Isabella rolling her eyes because she knows that if Matteo is good at something, then that's carrying an argument and seeing it all the way to the end.

He takes a few drags and then looks at Valentina expectantly. "Hello?"

She looks up from her phone. "Right, sorry. What did you ask?"

"What makes me the lucky one in this whole situation? I'm curious."

"The right… circumstances."

Matteo raises his eyebrows and passes her the joint. She takes it without looking down and continues. "Knowing the right people, at the right time."

"That type of luck is made."

Valentina tilts her head and frowns. "Is it your case though?"

Isabella snorts and Matteo looks at her, annoyed. "Maybe not." He's not going to explicitly tell her about how his father probably has the police on his payroll.

"What are you even talking about?" Isabella chimes in, looking between the two of them. "You're chatting legit nonsense."

Valentina hands her the joint. "Join us then."

Matteo looks down at his phone, zoning out but smiling.

***

Utica, New York, United States 2020 – January 6th, 2020

His father calls him on video a quarter after midnight. He was just about to fall asleep, and it's not nothing if he's getting a call so late.

"Fuck. Fuck." He hisses and stands up properly in his bed.

He switches to the App on his laptop. "Yes, hello?"

His father is sitting in his office chair calling him on a private software their company had installed a few years ago for all its members. He looks tired and half of his shirt is unbuttoned.

"What are you doing?"

"I'm trying to sleep."

He's at their apartment in Utica, which Matteo uses when he attends classes.

"Are you in the city?"

"No, I have classes tomorrow." Matteo sighs, knowing damn well his father sometimes checks up on his attendance. Usually at the beginning and end of each semester.

"I talked to the chief of police today. You're cleared of everything. It never happened."

Matteo remembers how Valentina seemed to understand that some people could actually get away even if they're caught doing illegal shit. "Why didn't we get arrested?"

His father looks down at his glass. *"I know the people leading the police force. They owed me a few favours."*

"Do you pay them?"

"Yes."

Matteo nods. He already knew that, instinctively. He wants to ask if it's a monthly payment, but he knows it is.

"What happened to the... stuff?"

"Don't push it. What were you thinking, having drugs in the house?"

Matteo rolls his eyes. "Us doing drugs can't be news to you."

"Not the using, the holding! You need to be more careful-"

"This never happened before, you know. Someone called the police."

His father nods. *"I know. It was Vincenzo's girlfriend, Sofia."*

Everyone suspected Sofia already, but the fact that his father just confirmed it makes it official.

"Do you know why she called the police?"

"Because she had a fight with Vinnie, apparently. I don't know, no one's ever done that before."

"I know. It put you in danger."

"I mean-we're fine now." Matteo frowns, not knowing whether his father's voice is just serious or has gotten darker.

"You go to classes for a while, stay out of the city."

"Yes dad." Matteo says, running a hand through his hair as he watches himself in the camera. He's getting impatient and he's tired.

"Who did you talk to about this outside the family?"

"Uh..." He wants to say no one, but the fact that he spoke to Valentina about it makes it difficult to lie. He only lied once in his life, then never again. Maybe he avoids telling the truth sometimes, but he never lies.

"Don't talk about these things with people who aren't in the family, people who you can't trust. Be smart, son."

"Yes, I will." Matteo replies. Then he checks the date. Shit, it's January 6th. "Happy birthday, by the way."

His father smiles. *"Thank you. What's Marco doing?"*

"Sleeping, probably."

"Okay. Take care. We'll be in touch."

"Bye."

Matteo shuts his laptop and places it on the other side of the bed as he gets under the covers. For a second, he worries about having talked to Valentina about the incident because she's friends with Raisa who loves to gossip.

He decides to blindly trust that she won't discuss anything with anyone, then tries to go to sleep.

***

Waking up at 9am on a Monday is not something Matteo likes to do, so when the alarm goes off that morning, he curses everything that has led to him to this moment. The coffee machine in the kitchen is broken so he keeps cursing as he uses the last pack of instant coffee he finds in a cupboard.

Matteo drinks it down in three gulps. It sucks. He also doesn't know where the lecture is taking place or what it's about - he just remembers seeing a notification about a class on Monday at 10.

He figures it out on the way and arrives five minutes before it's supposed to start, happy to find Isabella waving at him from the back row.

"Can you help me with my schedule? I applied to all the courses, but I can't tell when and where they're supposed to be." He asks, placing his laptop on the small fold-out table. Isabella looks at him annoyed before she opens his laptop and signs into his university account.

"See this little tab at the top that says 'schedule'? You click on it. How did you even survive university up until now?"

Matteo shrugs. "I mostly only ever went to exams or when Vinnie told me to."

"You're a disgrace." She jokes before she waves at someone else.

Valentina takes her coat off before sitting down on the other side of Isabella and greeting them both.

"I miscalculated how long it would take to stop and get coffee." She says and places her cup on the table, smiling.

"How can you be in such a good mood in the morning?" Matteo asks her, unable to look away from how her eyes seem to shine.

"It's either this or I'm in a bad mood. And nobody wants that." She smiles as she ties her hair up in a ponytail.

The professor enters the room and it suddenly gets quiet. 'International Economics' pops up on the giant screen.

He has the same law course as Vinnie and Isabella at 12pm, so finding him as soon as possible makes the most sense for Matteo, who doesn't even know where the buildings are. He kind of zones out during the break between lectures, just following Isabella's lead while the girls talk non-stop.

How can someone always find something to talk about, he thinks as he watches Valentina and Isabella a few steps ahead of him.

"Yo!"

Vinnie pats him on the back as soon as they stop in front of a smaller building. Matteo's mood picks up then, because Vinnie always has a good energy and makes things more fun.

"I was wondering whether you'd show up since I forgot to text you yesterday." He smirks and they start walking towards the entrance.

They find four seats in the middle just as Raisa spots them on her way into the lecture hall and joins them.

It fucks up Matteo's mood a little. He can always tell when someone's into him, and Raisa isn't even hiding it anymore. It's obvious she likes him and it's less exciting to know that she'll do whatever he asks of her. Matteo knows that money is a big part of it, but sometimes he just likes to have sex when he feels like it with whomever he feels like.

Time seems to stop as the lecture drags on for 90 minutes, but soon enough it's almost 2pm and someone suggests going to lunch at a restaurant nearby.

The restaurant isn't that crowded, and they get their orders soon enough, but the lunch takes longer than expected because some people decide it would be a good idea to get drinks. It's one of those times when Matteo wishes he hadn't taken the car because he feels like he's the only sober one.

Valentina orders a bottle of prosecco to share with Isabella, with the excuse of celebrating the first day of university in 2020. Raisa excitedly joins them and suggests splitting it between the three of them.

They have to head to the last lecture of the day which Matteo shares with Vinnie, so around thirty minutes before the course is supposed to start he suggests they get going. Vinnie asks for the bill and Matteo doesn't even bother asking the girls for their share, because five minutes later the guys have all split the bill between them and left the cash on the table, with an extra tip.

"I'm definitely tipsy after three glasses." Valentina laughs with Isabella while they put their coats on. As they leave, Matteo sees her drop two hundred-dollar bills into the glass already filled with money.

It's the first time since he can remember that he's seen a woman add money to the bill and pay her part. Nobody else seems to notice, but it's enough to make Matteo respect her as a person, not just as Isabella's friend.

***

Utica, New York, United States 2020 – January 9ᵗʰ, 2020

He calls Vinnie on Thursday afternoon after he wakes up.

"Where are you?!" Vinnie shouts into the receiver to cover up the noise on his end.

"In bed. Where else?"

"I thought you'd be on campus."

"Do I even have classes today? *Fuck*, I forgot to check the schedule. What are you doing?"

"Eating."

"I want to go to New York."

"Today?"

"Yes, maybe leave in an hour?"

Vinnie hesitates, which means he's got other plans.

"I think I'm going to come tomorrow."

"How?" Matteo knows for a fact that Vinnie doesn't have a car in the States.

"I'll figure it out."

"Alright."

He hangs up and then gets out of bed to go pack a bag before he embarks on the four-hour drive to New York. His schedule says he's supposed to be in a seminar right now, so he sends a voice message to Isabella as he's on the way to the car.

"Do you happen to also have Business Psychology? Because I'm on my way to New York and I'm pretty sure my dad is tracking my progress. Thaaanks."

Isabella replies five minutes later.

Isabella sends him a Russian number, and he adds her contact as he drives before texting Valentina.

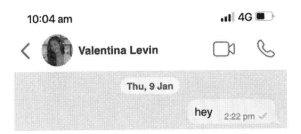

The reply comes an hour later when he's way past Albany, headed south.

Matteo looks at the road ahead waiting for her to type something else.

She doesn't. Okay, so he has to get straight to the point because she obviously knows that he didn't just hit her up so they'd hook up, like most girls usually do. It seems like Isabella and Aurora (his sister) are the only girls close to his age that he can text without sex being implied.

> u got business psychology?   3:36 pm ✓✓

He looks at the road ahead. Texting and driving are a lot of pressure when he drives 100km an hour. He decides to call her directly and speak through the car's speakers.

She picks up on the third ring. His ego tells him that she waited a little before answering to seem busy because she might want to impress him, but he knows she didn't.

"Hello."

"Hi. Uh, are you taking Business Psychology this year?"

"If you mean Organizational Psychology, then sure."

"Same thing."

"I was just at the seminar." She pauses. "Why?"

"I'm also supposed to be taking it, but I'm on my way to New York." There's a short pause where neither of them says anything because Matteo focuses on switching lanes, then he continues. "Anyway, could you send me your notes or something?"

"I can send them to you by email."

"Photos on WhatsApp are fine."

"I am taking them on my laptop, so I'll send them to you by email. If I take photos of the screen, they'll all be blurry."

She's right.

"Alright."

"Just text me your address and I'll send them to you."

"It's matteolorenzogiudice@giudicesrl.com"

"Yeah, no way I will remember that. Text me so I can just copy-paste it."

Matteo smiles at her demanding tone. "Alright. I'm driving now though."

"It's fine, I'm not going to wait around for it." She says, and Matteo can hear the smirk on her face.

"Okay."

"Well."

"Thank you."

"Okay. Byee."

"Bye." He says and the line goes dead.

He texts her his email address at the next stoplight half an hour later, and he gets the notification from valentinalevin@gmail.com just as he gets onto the George Washington Bridge to enter Manhattan.

The apartment looks just like he left it before 2019 ended, thanks to the maid coming over every week to maintain it.

He gets comfortable on the couch and rolls himself a joint, then texts Valentina to thank her.

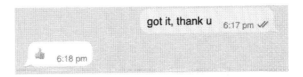

Matteo looks at the emoji for a second, before he opens the email she sent. It's a pdf of her notes taken in class, from which he understands right about nothing.

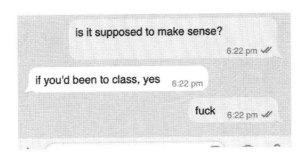

This would've been the part where she offers to explain the notes to him as an excuse to spend time with him, like all the girls who have helped him with schoolwork in the past.

Valentina leaves him on read. Well, not really read, because his read receipts are off, but she stops replying.

He's gotten through university until now exactly because he knew the right people who would help him out or he knew exactly which girl would do most of the work for him just as an excuse for them to say to their friends they hung out.

Sometimes he thinks it's just the money, but that can't be it – everyone he met at school and now university comes from rich families. Some of them are old money, others are new money families, but all of them have millions of dollars to their name.

Matteo knows what people (especially women) think of his family and how there's a certain allure to it because no one really knows exactly what they do, so there's a mystery that goes hand in hand with it being perceived as dangerous and illegal. Not that it isn't. In reality it's far worse, and Matteo knows he hasn't even seen a quarter of it.

It would take a strong woman to put up with everything that comes with joining a crime family. Matteo has never met one that could live up to the role - only girls who thought they could.

He was with Allison because she was the only person in the world who Matteo even considered worth the effort to pursue, but that's all over now (even though they still hook up sometimes).

He learned a long time ago that when feelings disappear, the only thing that keeps him from leaving her is the fear of change.

***

Manhattan, New York, United States 2020 – January 16th, 2020

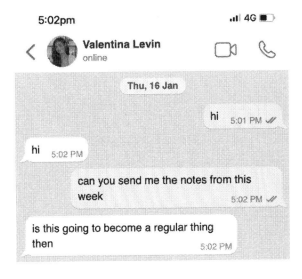

He smiles.

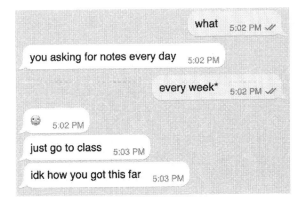

She emails him the notes two minutes later anyway.

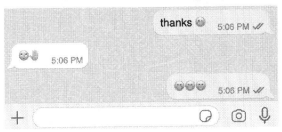

If he didn't know better, he'd think she's flirting.

***

Hamilton University, New York, United States 2020 – January 23rd, 2020

It's the first time he ever bothers going to the Organizational Psychology seminar this semester (in his defence, he's only missed two so far).

He immediately spots Valentina sitting in the corner of the last row, head buried in a book with a cover that looks like it's being read for fun, not for class.

There's an empty seat next to her and he's aware of the two girls sitting a few rows away are watching him as he walks up to where Valentina's sitting.

She doesn't look up at him until he sits down next to her. Her eyes widen and she slams the book shut, like she's reading something she shouldn't be.

His eyes fall on the title. "So, you're reading porn."

Her cheeks flush a little as she guiltily smiles and shrugs.

Then, in a split of a second, she composes herself and nods her chin at him. "Looks like you decided to show up to class after all."

"I had some free time."

His comment makes her roll her eyes, like she can see right through his nonsense. Which is exactly why he knows she's not flirting with him or trying to play hard to get; it's just the way she is. He shouldn't be enjoying it as much as he is.

"Yeah? From doing what?"

She obviously knows that he's bullshitting because he was just too lazy to come. The drive from his apartment to campus is about twenty minutes long, but he just couldn't be bothered on most days. He knows he'll pass exams somehow - he always does.

Someone sits down next to him, but his eyes are still on Valentina's face.

"Enjoying life." He replies, liking the way the look on her face changes from curiosity to distaste.

Before she can comment on it (it was obvious she had something ready on the tip of her tongue), the professor enters the room, and the voices die down.

She smells good and Matteo is surprised to find himself so aware of her close presence. He feels like he should say something to fill the silence (which never happens) but she looks immersed in whatever the professor has to say. Like she forgot Matteo was even sitting next to her (which also never happens).

"Discuss amongst yourselves. Then pick the most influential one."

He leans forward, elbows on the table as if it would help him catch up on the last thirty minutes of the seminar. Still confused, he lowers his head in Valentina's direction.

"Discuss what?"

She side-eyes him.

"Intrinsic and extrinsic motivational factors."

Matteo nods, barely even processing her answer. "Sounds…boring."

"Why are you even at university then? If you don't like it."

It's not accusatory, it's just curious. And he's thought about it before, so the answer comes quick. "I like the social life that comes with being a student. I don't need a degree." He pauses. "You?"

She shrugs. "I don't know. It's what I'm supposed to be doing."

"Says who?"

"My parents. They both got an education, which helped them make a better life for themselves.

"You're here because of them then."

"…no."

"You don't need a degree to be set for life." He nods his head towards the room. "Neither do most people here."

"Maybe some people just want get an education."

"Is that why you chose Business Psychology? To get educated?"

She's trying to hide it, but she's slightly surprised that he remembered.

"What do you want to do after it?"

She shrugs again.

"I'm probably going to work at my father's business. And I actually like psychology. It makes humans predictable."

His eyes fall on the way she's mindlessly playing with her bracelet. Looks like a nervous tick.

"What are we supposed to discuss then?" He changes the subject.

She happily obliges and turns to her laptop. "Intrinsic and extrinsic motivational factors."

"Money. Power."

"Glory." She adds and smiles at herself like she made a joke or something.

"Respect."

"We're talking in a 'working in an office' context, but sure."

She starts typing something and Matteo leans in to read off the screen.

Competition. Fun. Recognition.

"Passion." Matteo adds.

Valentina types it in then leans towards the screen and squints a little. "Which one do you think is the most influential factor when it comes to success? I say competition."

"Power."

Her eyebrows raise, and Matteo swears she looks amusingly intrigued.

"Is everyone finished?" The professor interrupts and doesn't really wait for people to answer before he moves on. "Look at what each of you put down as the most influential factor when it comes to success in the workplace."

Matteo's eyes fly over to the words Valentina typed under the second question.

V: Competition; M: Power

"The answers each one of you wrote down says a lot about how you approach success in the workplace, and in life."

Matteo considers it for a second.

Power.

His father is the most powerful man he can think of, and Matteo has always admired him for that. The way he just controls a room, how all bodies seem to turn towards him even though no one dares to fully face him, or the way he talks and people *always* listen. A person people look up to and willingly follow. A person who others would kill for - just like Paulo did with that guy in the bait shop.

"Why competition?" He asks Valentina.

Her first instinct is to shrug before she finally looks like she's processing his question.

"I think it's because I have a brother."

"That's a superficial answer."

Matteo enjoys the way she pulls her head back and how her mouth parts.

He thinks that maybe coming to class every once in a while wouldn't be such a bad idea.

Chapter 14

Matteo

Manhattan, New York, United States 2020 – February 9th, 2020

The Barone siblings come over to his apartment the week before Valentine's Day weekend, together with Marco and Isabella. While Pia and Isabella are out getting dinner in the city on Saturday night, the boys choose to stay in and have a FIFA tournament.

It always reminds Matteo of the days when they were younger and living in Palermo. He would go over to the Barone house just to stay for hours and play on their PlayStation. They stopped when they moved to New York for school.

Matteo notices it because it's the first time in two years that they decided to stay in instead of going to the club.

They order pizza and smoke joints, and it's not until they hear Isabella and Pia's voice coming from the hallway that they realize a couple of hours have gone by.

"This makes me feel nostalgic." Isabella smiles and comes inside the living room with her shoes in one hand, a bottle of wine in the other. "The boys playing videogames."

The couch is in an L shape, big enough to fit all six of them, so Pia and Isabella take the shorter part of the L so the boys can sit by themselves focusing on the TV.

"Why isn't Aurora here?" Matteo asks as he's about to start another game. "She already lives in the city."

"She said she had a date this weekend."

The boys turn their heads to look at her at the same time.

"With?!" Marco incredulously asks.

Pia shrugs. "She didn't tell me."

Eddie's mouth falls open. "And you didn't *ask*?!"

"I did, but she wouldn't say."

"She's hiding something." Vinnie observes and turns his attention back on the game.

Matteo agrees and looks at Isabella, who doesn't seem fazed by the information. "What do you know?"

Isabella looks at him surprised. "Me? Why would I know anything?"

"Because you always know everything."

She puts her phone down and looks Matteo in the eyes. "I don't know anything, I promise."

"Fine." He knows when she's lying, and right now she isn't.

"What do you know?" She asks him then.

"Nothing, obviously."

"No, like, have you noticed her being unusual?"

"I tried to take her phone at Christmas, and she got very defensive." Marco says.

Matteo nods. "Yes, and she's got this weird smile on her face and I know she's texting someone."

"Ask her then." Pia suggests, like it should be obvious.

"Like you would ever tell us about who you're hooking up with." Vinnie interjects. He's always been protective of his twin sister, more so than Matteo is with Aurora. He thinks it might be a twin thing.

"I would! But you never ask." Pia throws her hands up in defense.

"Alright, who have you slept with?"

"Eddie!" Pia exclaims, crossing her arms and looking at Matteo for a second.

It's hard for Matteo to think of her as Vinnie's twin. Even though she's about to turn 21 in April, he thinks of her like he thinks of Aurora: a younger sibling who needs to be protected. The fact that she usually keeps to herself and sometimes acts childish just enhances this image of her in his mind.

Sure, she's tall and slim and has a pretty face, but she's Vinnie's sister. The girl who was there almost as often as Isabella, who saw him throw up all over himself when they first discovered alcohol in eighth grade, the girl who cried on his shoulder five days after her dog was run over in front of their house.

"Do you have a boyfriend?" Vinnie asks then.

Pia shakes her head, relaxing, and looks at Matteo again.

"Do you have a crush though?" Isabella asks, turning to look at her.

"What? No!" She says, eyes going back down to her phone.

Isabella grins. "You do."

Eddie screams at the TV when Matteo scores a goal, which takes the attention away from the conversation.

"What do you want to do for our birthday?" Pia asks Vinnie after they've cleared two bottles of wine and are now watching some random show on Comedy Central.

Vinnie takes a hit from the bong Eddie brought and thinks about it for a second. "Uhh, whatever you want to do I guess."

Matteo smiles. Of course Vinnie is too lazy to even think about that because his favourite part is having fun - just like Matteo. Vinnie likes leaving the organisation part to his sister, just like Matteo does with Isabella. It's been working like this ever since they had their first party without parents present.

"I want to go to Ibiza." Pia says without even having to think about it.

"Oooh yeees, I vote yes!" Isabella exclaims and turns to look at the boys with an excited look on her face. "Let's go to Ibiza."

And as per usual, the boys agree with everything the girls want, because they always make it fun. All they have to do is show up.

Isabella and Pia start writing up the invite list even though it's more than two months away. Matteo likes seeing them excited.

"Should I put Allison and Sofia on here?" Pia asks in a half-accusatory half-disgusted tone as she looks between Vinnie and Matteo.

"Why do you always put them together?" Vinnie asks.

"Because they're *besties*, aren't they?" Pia replies in a sweet voice that's meant to be annoying Vinnie even more.

"Maybe they can call the police on us this time too." Isabella jokes and Pia laughs. It's that mean girl laugh that Matteo hates.

"I don't care what you do about Allison, it's your party and she's not my girlfriend anymore." Matteo tells her. He'll find someone to go home with anyway (if he wants to).

"If you invite Sofia, I'm sure she won't call the police anymore. She said she's sorry." Vinnie says.

"Are you kidding me?" Isabella spits. "If she comes, then Allison comes. And how many more times do they have to fuck you over until you move on?" she asks, looking at Vinnie.

Pia agrees by nodding and pointing toward Isabella.

"My birthday is before yours, why are we even discussing it now?" Marco groans, already annoyed at how shrill Isabella's voice gets when she's angry.

"It's our birthday, not just yours." Vinnie reminds her. "If I want to invite Sofia, I'll invite her."

Isabella gets even angrier now and stands up, taking a hold of her glass. "I'm going to sleep, goodnight."

"Aw, come on Izzy!" Vinnie yells after her but she flips him off as she stumbles back into the hallway, in search of the room she shares with Pia.

Matteo watches the door closing behind her and thinks it's unusual for her to get so upset over Sofia and Allison attending. She usually just makes snarky comments, but never gets mad.

"We stopped playing or what?" Eddie nudges him.

His head snaps back to the TV. "You wish."

***

Manhattan, New York, United States 2020 – February 15th, 2020

Manhattan, New York, United States 2020 – February 15th, 2020

He spends Valentine's Day in the club with his friends because they're having a special 'single's only' event that was suggested by Isabella a few days ago, and since Aurora didn't want to have her birthday there, they hosted 'Valentine's Dead'.

The group got dressed up and absolutely everyone was in the mood to party, which meant bottles being brought over by bottle service girls with sparklers in them, and several rounds of colourful shots done by everyone. The club was packed, Aleksi was there with his usual deliveries, so it was a successful night at the club.

Now that it's way past midnight and Matteo is on the way home in a taxi, he remembers that it's the 15th. Aurora just turned 18 and celebrated somewhere else in New York (she's attending the same boarding school in the city).

"Hello? Happy birthday!" He says, still pumped from the cocaine.

"Thank youuu" Aurora says on the other line, slurring her words a little.

Matteo frowns. "Where are you?"

"With a friend."

"Who?"

She sighs into the phone. *"You don't know him."*

"Him? Is he your secret boyfriend?"

At this, Raisa turns her head from the other side of the taxi where she was staring out the window. Matteo looks at her for a moment before returning his attention on the phone call and the buildings passing them by. The streets are still covered in snow and it's cold outside.

"Don't start, Matteo. Marco has already asked me like ten times and now I think dad is onto something. Just let me enjoy becoming an adult."

"You're not an adult." Matteo snorts. "Take care of yourself, okay?"

"I always do." She says. *"Have a good night."* She says it in a tone that means she knows Matteo's with a girl headed back from the club.

"I will. You too. But I want you at the club next month."

Although drinking if you're not 21 is illegal in the US, Matteo prefers to lower the age of people allowed entry in the club to 18. No police has ever showed up at the club, and although it might be his father's doing, Matteo has never complained.

"Promise." Aurora says, and he can hear her genuine smile in her voice.

He hangs up and looks at Raisa. She's on her phone, fingers shaking a little from the coke as she texts someone.

"Hey." He says and she looks up at him, smiling as he leans in to kiss her.

Raisa kisses more aggressive than Matteo would like, but she's crazy in bed because she says yes to everything. Plus, her nipples are pierced, which is something Matteo has never experienced before. He also knows that she's beginning to fall for the idea of him, which won't end well for her if she makes it into something more.

Raisa straddles him without any regard for the driver and starts kissing down the left side of his neck. He likes that she doesn't give a fuck when it comes to voyeurism, so he slips his hand under her black dress to find that she's not wearing any underwear.

He knows she's got daddy issues because her emotionally distant father died nearly a year ago – she talks a lot when she's drunk or high. Matteo just lets her, then fucks her real good until she can't breathe. He's not sure whether she likes it so much because he usually does all the work or if she also likes having someone listening to her problems.

He never asks her out on purpose, which is one of the things he's started doing so the girls he hooks up with don't make it into something more. He used to have an only-one-night-stands rule right after he broke up with Allison, which worked for a few months until it got boring and he had to concentrate on getting it up because he was fucking random girls or prostitutes.

Raisa kisses him as soon as they're inside the elevator, one hand going down between his legs to rub him over his pants.

She moans into his ear when they're out of the elevator and he unzips her dress before they even reach his apartment. One minute later she's naked, straddling him on the couch in the living room, looking over his shoulder at the view of the city behind him. He sucks on her pierced nipple, focusing on getting it up with all the cocaine and alcohol in his system. Without him even asking her, she gets on her knees in front of the couch and smiles up at him.

The reason he prefers having a few 'fuck-buddies' as he likes to call them, is because they already know each other's body so it's more pleasurable than fucking a new person every time. Trust is also an important part for him, ever since one of his one-night stands stole two of his watches and posted about it on her social media.

He had to come to terms with the fact that anyone who would google his name could see how much money his family has. Sort of. The statistics on the internet didn't even showcase a quarter of the wealth he knew his father had acquired over the years, but it $342 million showing up if you googled his net worth was still enough for girls to throw themselves at him.

He goes to sleep an hour later, after having had sex for forty minutes and taking a shower afterwards.

He wishes she'd be gone by the time he wakes up.

***

Manhattan, New York, United States 2020 – February 15th, 2020

Two weeks later, Aurora finally agrees to come out and celebrate that she was eighteen with her 'family' - as Matteo had put it.

"Shut up, you sound like dad." She had told him, which was kind of a slap in the face. But she came to RedLight anyway, wearing a white sundress and sunglasses.

They have their usual corner in the VIP area and there are more people at the table than usual, some of whom he doesn't really recognize (probably friends of friends). He spots Valentina talking to Isabella and Raisa, and for some reason he feels pulled to go over.

"Hi."

"Hello." She smiles.

He's not sure why he even came over, but they've become friends ever since he started attending the Organizational Psychology seminars (occasionally) and would choose to sit next to her (always).

He's gotten so used to seeing her in jeans and a sweater that her wearing a dress tonight makes him want to check her out.

"Anything interesting happened in class yesterday?" He asks after knocking their glasses together.

Valentina takes a sip before answering. "Depends on what you mean by interesting. If you're asking whether Birkin's zipper was down again today, then no. But if you're asking whether I took notes, then, as usual, yes, I did. I sent them to you already."

"I know, but I don't really understand them. They're not even entire sentences. And some abbreviations don't even make sense."

Valentina takes another sip from her straw. "I mean, I take my notes so *I* can understand them."

"Yes, but *I* can't understand them." Matteo says, mimicking her gesture and placing a hand on his chest.

She smiles. "Which ones?"

"All of them."

Valentina rolls her eyes. "And what exactly do you want me to do? Do you want me to solve your problem?"

He blinks at her. "No."

Raisa starts talking to him then and he loses his train of thought, leaving the conversation be for the moment so he can focus on her. It gets too much too quick though, because she's already asking what they're doing afterwards and he just wants to enjoy right now.

He's not sure why, but he turns to Valentina and asks if she wants to do a line in the office.

He likes being around her. It's different. Maybe because she doesn't care to impress him, doesn't care whether he pays attention to her, and doesn't shy away from speaking her mind.

Valentina downs her drink and grabs a bottle of water, then motions towards the door in the back. "Lead the way then."

Her heels echo in the empty hallway as Matteo tries to get the door open with shaky fingers. It's the fourth time he's doing this tonight, twice with the boys and then once with Isabella and Raisa before Valentina arrived.

She sits down on one of the chairs facing him. It's the first time they're completely alone. Just the two of them with no one else around.

He wonders whether he should say something, since he's the one who suggested they do this.

Matteo pushes the plate with the credit card and bill towards her and she takes it. He watches as she starts racking up two lines with a knowing smile on her face.

"What?" He asks, feeling too hot all of a sudden. She's too sober, and he's too coked up and aware of it.

She looks up at him, hands still working on splitting up to even lines.

"Are you nervous?"

"About what?"

She shrugs. "You look a little on edge."

She doesn't wait for him to come up with a reply, because she points to the plate. The lines are larger than usual – they look just like the ones he and Vinnie do when it's just the two of them.

"Too much?" She asks, looking up at him.

Matteo looks at her lips for a split second without even realizing it, then takes the plate from her to do the honours.

He smirks at her when he catches her eye. "Never."

***

The club closes a little while after 4am and Matteo refuses to stay behind because he's way too active and half of the people there are already on the way to his apartment. He grabs a taxi with Vinnie and their brothers, and by the time they reach their building there are people waiting in the lobby.

The elevator goes up three times taking ten people each and the door to his apartment stays open for twenty minutes until everyone arrives.

When he finally sits down on the couch, his legs feel numb. There are about forty people in his apartment, some of whom he still can't recognize.

He watches Valentina enter the living room with Isaac. He's one of the regular NYU rich kids at the club. Matteo knows that he used to be on the same football team as Vinnie a few years ago and that he can get quite violent when he's drunk, but that's about it.

"Who are those two?" He asks Vinnie at some point, when he sees the same two guys he saw at his table at the club and couldn't recognize.

"I don't know. Maybe they know Aurora?"

"Who left an hour ago?"

Vinnie looks at him in a strange way. "Are you okay? Are you getting paranoid?"

"I'm just going to ask them who they are."

"Matteo-"

But Matteo is already headed towards them, elbowing people out of his way. One of them spots him and they both bolt towards the hallway.

He yells at them to turn around, but he can barely hear himself over the music. By the time he reaches the hallway, the door is wide open, and they're gone.

"Fuck." Vinnie's probably right. He's getting paranoid because his brain is coming down from the dopamine he's consumed in the past few hours.

***

The crowd in his apartment goes down to half of what it initially was around 6am. Most of the people that left are chatting on the balcony waiting for the sun to rise.

Matteo has always hated sunrises. The idea that a whole new day is starting when the one he was living through hasn't even finished always fucks with his cocaine-riddled brain.

Isabella is alone on the couch, which is unlike her, so Matteo goes over and sits down next to her.

He throws an arm around her shoulders. "I didn't see you at all tonight."

"Yeah." She dully answers.

"Are you alright?"

Yeah." She smiles. "I'm just tired and I want to go back to the hotel, but I'm waiting on Valentina to finish whatever she's doing with Isaac."

"How does she know Isaac?" He asks, turning to look towards the balcony where Valentina and Isaac sit amongst the people sharing a joint. It's cold and cloudy and there's no part of Matteo that would enjoy being out there right now.

"She told me he was a year above her in middle school in Moscow. Funny how small the world is huh." She slurs and rambles at the same time.

Okay, so Isabella is more drunk than anything else. It's fine.

"Finally." Isabella sighs and gets up from the couch.

"Uhh." Valentina says with a guilty look on her face. "I think I want to stay a little longer."

"It's fine, I'll just call myself an Uber." Isabella waves it off and takes her phone out of her purse. "So, you decided you're interested?"

P. Mazilu

Matteo looks up at Valentina, who just shrugs in response. "Maybe? I haven't figured it out yet." She has this guilty look on her face, like she's doing something she knows she shouldn't be doing.

Isabella grabs her arm. "Okay, I'm going to be direct. You need new dick. I know you're on your self-discovery journey and whatever, but it's okay to be horny and it's okay to hook up with that hot guy you've had a crush on since middle school. If I were you, I would do it."

He's known Isabella since he was in diapers, so he knows she actually wouldn't do it. She's not a one-night stand type of girl, although she's had a couple of more-night stands with guys whose names are unknown.

Valentina crosses her arms over her chest. "Oh, would you really?"

Her tone is more accusatory rather than joking. Isabella flips her off before she announces her departure.

"Don't do anything I wouldn't do!" She yells as she hurries away, happy to be on the way to her bed.

Everyone comes back inside after sunrise, including a horny Raisa who places her hand on Matteo's arm while he's pouring himself another drink in the kitchen. She tells him to meet her in his bedroom in five minutes before simply leaving him there staring at the drink he just poured.

Valentina and Isaac are talking on one of the couches, away from the rest of the people who are trying to decide on a song to play on the speakers.

Matteo doesn't bother to say goodnight to either of them before he turns around and heads towards his bedroom, not knowing what to expect.

He finds Raisa on her stomach, scrolling through her phone. The little excitement he felt on his way here disappears. He nearly expected her to be dressed in something overtly sexy or already playing with herself (even though that has never happened).

"Hey." She basically purrs at him and turns on her back, spreading her legs to make space for him.

Matteo looks at her for a moment, wishing he were already hard and so he could make the whole process quicker. But he settles for crawling on top of her and kissing down her neck.

He already knows where to put his mouth to make her weak; the place where her neck meets her shoulder. Everything is easier when you know the person's weak spots. Maybe that's why he always went back to Allison in the first place.

***

Finding Valentina in his kitchen, wrapped in a blanket as she tries to make coffee in a pot takes him by surprise after he wakes up.

Before he can ask her what she's doing here or where she even slept, Isaac comes into the kitchen with a towel around his waist like he owns the fucking place.

That's what she's doing here.

As Isaac starts talking about some irrelevant football shit he couldn't care less about, Matteo gets a strong sense of apathy towards the guy standing in front of him.

Chapter 15

Valentina

Matteo drops down on the chair next to me, looking exhausted. I know it's him because no one else would just sit down all up in my space like this. He's wearing a black hoodie with the hood pulled over his forehead.

"You're *not* wearing sunglasses right now."

He sighs and takes them off. His pupils look that way they get after a night of partying.

"Where did you even go out on a Wednesday evening?"

I notice his hair is curlier than usual, the tips of it bending out over the edge of his hood.

His eyes fall on the phone in my hands. "No book today?"

I didn't bring my book today because he went through it last time [31], despite my protests.

I try to keep my face straight as I answer. "No."

He grins. "You're embarrassed of what you read?"

My mouth parts. I'm not ashamed – not *really*. I'm just uncomfortable when people read it aloud to me. What I read is like a window into my soul and there are parts of it that I'm not comfortable sharing.

"No." I huff.

He grins even wider, eyes moving to the door before his face does.

Professor Birkin enters and the first thing I see is that his pants are unzipped.

---

[31] and made jokes about the spicier scenes he saw when he flipped through it

Matteo notices too because he looks back at me and motions over to the front of the room. I nod and watch as he catches Birkin's attention by waving at him. He points to his own crotch, then back at Birkin.

I don't even watch the man's reaction because my eyes are still on Matteo's hands. He's got two rings on his left one.

Once the class quiets down and Birkin starts talking, Matteo crosses his arms over the desk and goes to sleep.

***

Hamilton University, United States 2020 – February 13th, 2020

I bring my book to the seminar next week, as a sign of protest.

Not sure against what.

He doesn't show.

***

Manhattan, New York, United States – February 15th, 2020

The club is already packed when I get there - a little before midnight because Adrik took too long for once and not me (when I asked him who he was getting ready for, he told me to mind my own business).

The two girls at the entrance don't ask to see my ID this time – I guess Vinnie must've talked to them like he said he would. They wrap the VIP bracelet around our wrists and shoots us fake smiles as they tell us to have fun.

I find Isabella and Raisa at the usual table, and Adrik disappears by the time we start talking about boys.

"Isaac's here." Raisa informs me and nods over to the table adjacent to ours.

Isabella steps closer, looking intrigued. "You know Isaac?"

"We went to the same middle school in Moscow. He was a year older than me, and I used to have a crush on him." I quickly summarise.

The whole conversation seems irrelevant to me. He's replied to some of my stories on Instagram ever since we saw each other on New Year's and even tried to ask me out on a date a few weeks ago, to which I said I had to study.

"I like him. He's nice. He used to play football with Vinnie in high school."

"Ugh, he's a football player?" I ask.

"Yes, but not the typical asshole you'd expect him to be. He's more...soft."

"And hot." Raisa adds, still looking in his direction. I check him out as he's leaning over the table to talk to one of his friends. He *does* look good. He's got the baby face and the muscles, which is a deadly combination because it's the right amount of both.

He's wearing black jeans and a white t-shirt that shows off his biceps. If he had tattoos, I would probably be going over for me right about now.

"Yes, he's hot." I agree.

"You don't seem convinced." Isabella smirks and I look away when I catch Isaac looking in my direction.

"Well, I just...when we text it's like I'm texting him because it's what I think I should be doing. Not because I *want* to." They both look confused, so I clarify. "Basically, I want to feel like I want to be doing those things."

They still look lost, but I don't know how to better explain it to them.

"Want how?"

"I don't know. Like, when was the last time you *really* wanted someone? The last time you felt desire for someone? Not in a 'I want to fuck you' way but in a 'I can't get enough of y-'"

"I feel that every day." Raisa interrupts me and I can't possibly believe that's true. Although Matteo is a nice guy to be around, I can't imagine he's *that* interesting.

"I don't think I've ever really felt that I *desired* someone. Attracted, sure, turned on, sure. But desire? I don't know. What does it even mean?" Isabella asks, understanding exactly what I mean.

"He's coming over." Raisa whispers and I look at Isaac, who hasn't moved from where he's still leaning over the table saying something to his friend.

Then I realize she's talking about Matteo, who materializes right in front of me.

"Hi." He says to me, and I can tell Raisa doesn't like it.

"Hello."

He raises his glass and I instinctively bring mine up to push them together, looking him in the eyes as I do so.

His hair is shorter, and he looks better than I remember. No rings, but the tattoo peeking out from behind his half-unbuttoned shirt is new to me.

"Anything interesting happened in class yesterday?"

Okay, so he wants me to help him with the course again and doesn't know how to ask me directly.

"Depends on what you mean by interesting. If you're asking whether Birkin's zipper was down again today, then no. But if you're asking whether I took notes, then, as usual, yes, I did. I sent them to you already."

"I know, but I don't really understand them. They're not even entire sentences. And some abbreviations don't even make sense."

"I mean, I take my notes so *I* can understand them."

"Yes, but *I* can't understand them." he says, mimicking me.

I smile because I think it's funny. "Which ones?"

"All of them."

Now I have to roll my eyes. "And what exactly do you want me to do? Do you want me to solve your problem?"

Matteo looks surprised. "No."

There's a short pause in which I just look at him, waiting for him to answer, but then Raisa tells him that she's having fun at the party and that the club night is a success. I decide it's best to leave her to do her thing and return to the conversation about Isaac with just Isabella. She feels that's my intention, so she lowers her voice.

"I think you should go for it, with Isaac."

"I don't know, it seems like so much work. How do I know it's worth it?"

"You're not marrying him, Valentina. It's just something fun you could do. Just see what the vibe is, feel him out. He's cute, and he even has an accent."

"Yes, to you. But to me, he's just a Russian speaking bad English."

She squints at me. "Good thing you both know Russian then."

"Do you want to go see the office?" Matteo interrupts us out of a sudden, and I don't even have to think about it before I down my drink and grab a bottle of water.

"Lead the way then." I say, seeing Raisa getting mad out of the corner of my eye.

Matteo takes forever to open the door but when he finally does, I go to sit down on the chair across from him.

He looks nervous, like he's overstimulated and doesn't know what to do with himself. Might have something to do with Raisa being all over him, but I'm not sure.

He pushes the plate with the credit card and bill towards me.

I notice a tattoo under his white shirt. It's new, otherwise I would've noticed it before. There's just something about tattoos on a man that makes me instantly classify them as handsome.

"What?" He asks, and I feel my neck heating up, like I've been caught doing something I shouldn't have.

"Are you nervous?" I ask, pretending like I didn't just find him attractive for a split second.

"About what?"

"You look a little on edge."

I point to the plate, changing the subject.

"Too much?" I ask, looking up at him.

"Never."

I smile at him, do the line, then watch as he does his.

"You've got cocaine in your hair." I point out and move to brush it out of the soft curls on his head. I feel the cocaine in my throat as I touch his hair and smile.

"Why are you smiling like that?" He asks, and I pull my hand back.

"I felt it down my neck."

He smiles back.

***

We end up at Matteo's apartment after the club closes at 4am, and I wouldn't have come if Isabella and Raisa hadn't insisted. I talked to Isaac in the club, but it wasn't enough to convince me he's worth the effort. I've been saying that I want a 'friend with benefits' ever since I broke up with Jamie, and yet I haven't had sex with anyone else since then.

At first it was about body image issues and my own confidence, but now I feel confident and still don't want to make the first step with Isaac.

"Who says you have to make the first step?" Isabella asks me when I tell her exactly what I'm thinking as we stand outside on the balcony, looking at the city skyline.

I love looking out into the city at night and seeing all the high-rise buildings I would see in movies as a child. Back then they seemed to be from a different world, compared to the communist style building blocks in my old neighbourhood in Moscow.

"Well, he certainly isn't."

"Maybe he didn't notice you came to the after party."

"He saw me."

And of course, as if he heard us, Isaac appears in my line of vision holding something between his fingers. When he's close enough, I can see it's a small pink pill.

"Share?" he simply asks, and Isabella and I exchange looks.

"What is it?"

"Ecstasy."

I look at the pill and the skull imprinted on it before I look it up on my phone. After checking out it's legit, Isabella and I decide to each take one quarter and have Isaac take the rest. Then Isabella pretends being called over by someone and makes herself scarce.

"That was very subtle." Isaac laughs, switching to Russian. "Where do you study?"

Ah, the classic pick-up line.

"Hamilton University near Utica."

"You're not from the city?" He asks, looking disappointed. And maybe a little cute.

"I'm from Russia."

He laughs at that, even though I didn't really mean for it to be funny, but I smile at his energy.

Okay, maybe Isabella was right. He's nice to look at and easy to be around.

"And what do you study?"

"Business Psychology."

He raises his eyebrows. "Psychology? Can you tell what I'm thinking?"

I tilt my head and look into his eyes. His pupils are already dilated, and I wonder if mine are too, but there's no way it only took five minutes for the pill to take effect.

"I think you're asking yourself if you look high."

He looks pleasantly shocked. "I was literally thinking that I swear."

"I know, I believe you." I say, feeling a small rush of warmth go through my body.

This is going to be fun.

An hour and a half later, Isaac and I are joined at the hip chatting about literally anything that comes to our minds. I know my pupils are dilated to the point where my eyes are nearly black and that I'm talking way too much, but I'm having more fun with him than I thought I would. And he *is* funny.

I see Isabella plopped down on a couch, so I excuse myself to go over and see if she's okay.

"Are you okay?" I ask, getting a déjà vu as I sit down. I look at the city behind her for a moment. The sun hasn't come out yet and I love how a lot of lights are still turned on throughout the city that never sleeps.

"I'm just super drunk." She whines, leaning her head on my shoulder. "I want to go back to the hotel."

"I have the room key."

"Do you want to come with?"

I look outside where Isaac is waiting for me on a loveseat. "In thirty minutes?"

She smiles, but there's sadness in her eyes. "Okay."

"What happened?" I ask, knowing better than to just stand up and leave.

"I just don't understand why he can't see it."

"Who? See what?"

She points to the place across the room at the bar where Matteo and Vinnie are talking.

"Matteo?" I ask.

She looks disgusted. "Ew, no."

"Vinnie?"

She nods.

"What? Can't see what?"

She shrugs. "That they all just want his money and attention. They don't care about him, and he just cares about all the wrong people."

I watch her looking at him as she talks, and everything makes sense. At some point I suspected that she might be in love with Matteo, because she always talked about how better off everyone was without Allison and Sofia, with a hint of jealousy in her voice.

But it had been Vinnie all along.

"Does he know you like him?"

She looks up at me. "Of course not." She lowers her voice. "And he never will, okay?"

I frown. "I think that's a bad idea."

"Never telling him?"

"Yes. Maybe he feels the same."

"If we were meant to be, we would've been together by now." she says and leans back into the couch. I look out at the city below us. I can see the Hudson River and I wonder how many people get to see what I'm seeing right now.

"You seem to be getting along well with Isaac." She changes the subject.

"Yes, but-"

"Stop with the excuses, Valentina! I feel like you're trying to find excuses not to enjoy the attention of a cute guy who isn't an asshole."

"I think you should listen to your own advice."

"I've never told anyone that before, you know. It feels good saying it out loud. Do you think I'm crazy?"

I look at her in awe. "What? Why would I think you're crazy? I think falling for your best friend is the most beautiful thing in the world."

"If it's reciprocated, that is."

"You won't know if it is until you tell him."

"But the friendship-"

I stand up. "I feel like you're trying to find excuses not to enjoy the being with a guy who isn't an asshole." I say, trying to mimic her Italian accent.

"He *is* kind of an asshole though." Isabella says, smiling. "Okay, I'll wait thirty minutes."

I kiss her on the cheek before I hurry back outside, feeling excited to talk to Isaac. I know it's probably the drugs, but I haven't had so much fun talking to a guy in a long time.

Someone starts rolling joints at some point, which makes everyone outside join into one big group therapy session as the sun slowly comes up. I look at Isaac's profile while he talks to one of the guys in our group. The balcony is more crowded than I'd like, but at least the view is pretty.

For a moment, I wonder whether Matteo even likes having people over all the time and if he doesn't sometimes wish to just go to sleep, but then I focus on Isaac again. His hand is on my thigh under my dress, just resting there, and part of me wants him to put it even higher, to kiss me, to do *anything*.

I pass the joint back to Isaac then head towards the door. I need to talk to Isabella.

"Finally." Isabella stands up from where she was just talking to Matteo.

"Uhh. I think I want to stay a little longer."

"It's fine, I'll just call myself an Uber." Isabella waves it off. "You decided you're interested?"

Matteo looks up at me and I shrug. "Maybe? I haven't figured it out yet."

Isabella grabs my arm. "Okay, I'm going to be direct. You need new dick. I know you're on your self-discovery journey and whatever, but it's okay to be horny and it's okay to hook up with that hot guy you've had a crush on since middle school. If I were you, I would do it."

I cross my arms. "Oh, would you really?"

Isabella flips me off before she announces she's leaving.

"Don't do anything I wouldn't do!" she yells at me and walks away.

Twenty minutes later even more people leave so I go back inside with Isaac to sit on the couch. I keep asking myself whether I want to stay, go to his place, go home, or just see where this goes. I'm in the middle of telling him about a time I missed a flight to Spain whilst being in the airport when he suddenly kisses me.

His kisses are more aggressively than I'd like them to be, but his hands are soft and slow and he's making me feel comfortable, so I go along with it.

Reality sinks in while I straddle him on the couch. I stare out at the sun coming up over the city and realize that I'm in a random apartment with a guy I've had a crush on five years ago.

I break off the kiss to look around – everyone's gone and I'm way too horny to stop now.

"What do you want to do?" he asks, lips buried into my neck.

Honestly? Have sex.

"Are there any empty rooms?" I choose to ask instead, but he understands and look like he's up for it.

"Marco isn't here today, so yes."

He keeps me from stumbling on my heels when I stand up.

It's now or never. "Let's go."

He kisses me as soon as I say the words, with a force that surprises me but also turns me on, so I let him guide me to the bedroom he was speaking of.

My dress is the first thing he pulls over my head, getting straight to the point as soon as the door closes behind me.

He doesn't bother waiting for me to take off my shoes before he turns us around and guides me towards the bed. It almost feels rehearsed, like he's done this so many times before it's become a reflex.

It doesn't last as long as I would have liked, and fifteen minutes later he's already asleep on the other side of the bed, leaving me horny and lonely.

***

Manhattan, New York, United States – February 15th, 2020

Staying up on my phone until I think it's reasonable puts me to sleep for a few hours until the sun wakes me up at 2pm. It's too hot under the covers and my throat is uncomfortably dry.

Isaac is still asleep so I get out of bed as quiet as I can, wrapping the blanket around me. I cover a naked Isaac with another blanket before I make my way towards the kitchen.

"Coffee." I say to myself and look at the coffee machine on the counter. My father uses the same one, but I can't find capsules, so coffee in a pot it is. I've never done coffee in a pot in my entire life, nor have I seen anyone but my grandmother do it.

Holding up the blanket around my body while also making coffee turns out to be harder than I'd hoped. The fact that I've only slept two hours and didn't take my makeup off makes me even more uncomfortable. I hate waking up anywhere else other than my bed, and today I am once again reminded why.

I hear someone walking down the hall in my direction and I panic because I can't recognize the steps. Matteo appears from around the corner, and before I can even explain myself (he stops in his tracks when he sees me), Isaac also makes an appearance. With a towel around his waist. Great.

We all say hello to each other, and I turn around to focus on the coffee, letting the two of them fill the silence.

"I need to go; I have an appointment today." Isaac says, looking at me. "I'll text you." He winks and walks back towards the bedrooms.

Matteo and I both watch Isaac walk away, and I pretend not to notice when he turns to look at me.

"What?" I finally ask, feeling as if he's trying to ask something without asking it.

"How was it?"

"Excuse me?"

"Isaac, I mean."

I cross my arms over my chest, gripping into my blanket. "It was okay."

He smiles. "I never thought he had it in him."

"What do you mean?"

Matteo shrugs. "I didn't think he'd be the type to sleep around."

I scoff. "I don't sleep around either."

"I didn't say you were. I was just saying that he's softer than most guys, and I didn't think he'd actually make a move."

Well, if I'm completely honest with myself, that explains the average sex - the type of sex I had with Jamie towards the end of the relationship. Sex just for the sake of having sex. For the sake of the guy having an orgasm before he can go to sleep. Boring. But still it felt good to feel someone inside me after a long time of doing it myself.

But he was very sure of himself…in hindsight, it might've been the drugs. Or maybe Matteo doesn't know what he's talking about.

"Well, you seem to know him better than I do." I say, turning around to check on the coffee.

"Did you do drugs?"

"Don't I always?" I ask, not really joking.

It isn't something I am proud of, but every time I'm in the city I end up doing bad things and feeling guilty about them the next day. But then it all goes away, and I crave yet another dopamine rush because nothing else does it for me anymore. I feel like I've watched all the movies and shows there are to watch, and I haven't read since I left Italy last summer.

I realize I zoned out when Matteo walks over to the window and opens it to let some fresh air in.

"So?" he asks, leaning against the counter.

I look at him confused. "So what?"

"Did you do drugs?" he repeats.

"Haven't I already answered that question?"

"I meant with him."

"Yes."

Matteo raises his eyebrows and looks at the boiling coffee. "Hm." He pauses.

"Everybody does drugs in the city." I tell him, which is also something I've come to realize ever since I started coming to the city on weekends.

"In theory, yes, but I think 'drugs are everywhere' would be more accurate." My eyes go to the tattoo on his leg "I just always thought Isaac was judgmental about this stuff because he plays football."

"Looks like you're the judgmental one, hm?"

I turn off the stove and push the pot away from the heated circle.

"Like you didn't judge him at first for being a football player."

I try to keep a straight face. "No, I didn't."

"Yes, you did." He mocks me.

We hear a door close and footsteps echoing from down the hall, so we just look at each other until Isaac appears.

"My Uber's going to be here any minute. Thanks man." He says when he comes into the kitchen, fully dressed in his clothes from last night. He goes over to shake Matteo's hand and kisses my temple.

Just then, Raisa enters the kitchen in Matteo's shirt and nothing else, smiling from ear to ear. Her smile falters when she spots Matteo and I on the other side of the kitchen, facing each other.

"Good morning." She snaps in my direction, even though her eyes are trained on him.

I take a step back and fight the urge to roll my eyes.

Isaac says goodbye to her as well and the three of us look at each other as the front door closes shut. Raisa looks at me in a knowing way, her eyes are urging me to tell her what happened.

"Valentinaaa." She theatrically says and places a hand on her hip. "Tell me *everything*."

I shrug. "It was okay."

"He lasted ten minutes huh?"

I turn around and look for some coffee mugs, trying to think of a polite answer. I don't want to tell them it was average and only mildly satisfying because it had nothing to do with Isaac; there were two of us in that bed last night, and I could've made it more fun if I really wanted to, but I guess I just wasn't feeling motivated enough. I also know that she has a big mouth and would go around telling people.

Matteo is also here, and I still haven't figured out whether I trust him yet. I know he's overheard some of my conversations with Isabella [32] and has never once said anything about it [33]. I take out three coffee mugs and place them on the island counter, facing Raisa again.

"No, it wasn't that. It was nothing out of the ordinary, that's all. It was… nice."

"Hm." Raisa trails off, looking at Matteo. "Do you have any spare clothes? My dress is…stained."

"First door on the right is my closet." Matteo tells her.

"I'm going to go take a shower. You want to join me?"

I look down at the coffee empty mugs, feeling embarrassed for some reason. Maybe for her, maybe for being here and feeling extra, maybe for Matteo as well.

"No, I showered when I woke up." Matteo bluntly replies.

I don't look at Raisa's face as she says 'okay' and leaves.

The interaction hangs in the air until I finally decide to break the silence.

"You could be nicer to her, you know."

"Why would I be nicer than my usual self?"

I can't give him an answer (because on a foundational level, I do agree with him), so I settle for pouring the coffee into the mugs.

"You have to pour a little cold water over it, so the grounds go down." Matteo says and I understand maybe half of what he just said.

---

[32] or maybe he wasn't even listening

[33] mostly he probably just doesn't care - which works out great for everyone

"What?"

"The coffee, when you make it in a pot. If you don't want coffee grounds in the mug, you must pour cold water over it while it's still hot."

I notice that my blanket begins to slip so I set the pot down and grab it with both hands. My phone buzzes on the table and I check to see that Isaac just texted me he got home.

"Isaac texted me."

I guess he's a part of it now. And who else is there to talk to about this anyway?

"Already?"

"Yes."

"He must live close by."

I chew on my lip as I overanalyse Isaac texting me so soon. "Do you think it's a good or a bad sign?"

Matteo takes one of the filled coffee mugs and goes to sit down on a highchair by the island counter. "A sign for what?"

I watch him take out a pack of cigarettes and an ashtray from one of the drawers.

"I don't know? A sign that's like a preview of how my relationship with him is going to develop."

He shakes his head as he lights his cigarette. "Women always think men think too much."

I raise my eyebrows. "How so?"

"You had sex and now you expect something between you to change."

"Something *does* change though."

"No, it doesn't."

"We've seen each other naked, and orgasm. Well, in his case." I ironically add, getting a sudden urge to defend my opinion and playing defence. "It's like a barrier to intimacy."

"For you," he tilts the hand holding the cigarette towards me, "but for us," he points back to him, "it's just a way to release an urge."

"I'm not saying we're something more because we had sex, I'm asking you if you think *he* thinks we're something more. I don't want him to get clingy because he'll do something to turn me off, but if he gets too distant, I'll eventually regret it when I get bored."

It sounds selfish to say it out loud, but it's how I feel and I'm not sure Matteo understands anyway.

"I think you're overthinking it. Real bad." He concludes and takes the first sip of his coffee, already halfway through his cigarette.

"Can I have a cigarette?" I ask.

He holds the pack out to me.

I walk closer until I'm standing at the table next to him, one hand holding my mug and the other holding the blanket. He places the cigarette between my lips and lights it up.

"Thanks."

The coffee is a 5 out of 10 but it's the only coffee we have in this apartment, and I can't be bothered to wait for Uber Eats right now.

"I know I overthink, but I do it less often now. I used to do it with my ex-boyfriend when I was younger."

"You should just see where it goes. Go with the flow."

Going with the flow is what all of my almost-friends-with-benefits said to me when I tried to at least make a connection with them before we had sex, which always lead to nowhere. I feel sorry for Raisa. She probably heard the line from him too, but under different circumstances.

"Well, that's what I'm trying to do, but he texted me right after he got home. I don't want to have to talk to him." I whine, and I realize I'm being childish.

It's one of those situations where you wake up after having made plans while drunk, terrified of having to follow through the next morning.

"Then don't." He says, as if it's the most obvious thing in the world. "You don't have to do anything you don't want to, Valentina. You always have a choice."

"I don't want to be mean."

He laughs at that.

"What?"

"Saying no doesn't make you mean. It just saves you both the time and effort."

Matteo and I smoke another cigarette in comfortable silence; me standing up and looking out the window at the city, and him on his phone. The coffee tastes like something died in it, but I choose to pull through because I need to sip on something during my morning cigarette.

Raisa eventually joins us, fully dressed in some of Matteo's clothes, saying she put her dress in his laundry basket.

I feel like it's time for me to leave. "I'm going to go."

"Do you have milk and sugar?" Raisa asks.

"The coffee sucks by the way." I warn her before I go back to my room to get dressed.

On the way to the hotel, I realize that even though the coffee was one of the worst I've ever drank, Matteo never complained.

Chapter 16

Valentina

Moscow, Russia– March 2020

Our dad tells us about the international lockdown two days before it's announced, so he gets Adrik, Raisa, Aleksi, and I on a plane back to Moscow before the entire world starts panicking.

Another couple of weeks later, our university announces that it would be switching to remote teaching.

And along with it went my freedom.

***

Moscow, Russia – May 24th, 2020

Four days before the Business Psychology exam and 2 months after the entire world went into lockdown, Matteo calls me.

"Hello?" I answer, happy to get a break from forcing myself to study.

The last couple of months at home have been bittersweet. On one hand, I had so much time to get back to what I used to love doing when I was younger. On the other hand, it's the first time since I was fourteen that the entire family has been forced to cohabit for more than a month at a time. I'm still being treated as a child, even though I was basically pushed out of their nest six years ago. They want me to behave like an adult yet they only treat me as a child.

"Come to Italy and let's take the exam together."

I stop writing. "Excuse me?"

"The exam, on Monday. It's at two."

My first exam is on May 4th, and it's for the class Matteo and I have in common.

"Why would I ever even consider doing that?"

"I can't pass this. I haven't even downloaded the app yet."

"It's an online exam. You can cheat. It's practically open book."

"I wouldn't even know where to look in the book, Valentina!"

"How is that my problem?" I provoke him, simply because I'm bored, and his desperation amuses me.

"I'll be very happy and forever grateful if I pass this exam."

"You know that's not a good enough reason for me to fly to Italy during lockdown." I stand up from my desk and start walking around the room.

"Okay, let me try again. The flight is only four hours and I'll send the best private jet I can find to pick you up at nine on Thursday."

"Try again."

"You know the weather in Moscow is shit and lockdown sucks, and it's twenty-four degrees here and my room has a sea view."

I look out my window. The sky is grey and I can't even see the sun, and everything is muddy and wet.

"Did you actually google the weather in Moscow?"

"Yes, because I knew you wouldn't agree if you didn't get something out of it."

"I haven't agreed yet."

I hear him sighing at the other end. *"Don't make me beg. Leave me my dignity."*

"Fine. I'll send you the address of the airport where you can pick me up."

"Okay."

"Okay."

Chapter 17

Matteo

Palermo, Sicily, Italy – May 28ᵗʰ, 2020

When they were forced to move back home to Italy because of a global pandemic, Matteo didn't think about the fact that he would be spending more time with his father, which meant that he could see first-hand how much work Matteo was putting into his studies.

His father kept asking about exam dates and upcoming projects, and it all came down to Organizational Psychology, which was the only course where he didn't have someone who could help him pass.

Well, he knew he had Valentina. And he realized that begging her to come would be his last resort.

During the early hours of Thursday, May 28th, a private jet departed from their landing strip outside Palermo and set off towards Moscow, where it would pick up Valentina at 8am. By the time Matteo wakes up at 12:30pm, Valentina has already texted him that she'll be landing in 30 minutes.

He gets into the shower quickly and lets his siblings know that Valentina's coming over to take the exam. Their parents have been out since yesterday and Matteo has no idea when they'll return. At least there's a little peace and quiet in the house, save for the chef and the maid during the day, who barely ever make themselves known anyway.

A black SUV pulls up in the driveway in front of the house and Matteo watches Valentina climb out, carrying two bags. She says something to the driver before walking up the pathway leading to the main door.

Soon enough, the doorbell rings throughout the house.

"We have to write an essay?" Matteo groans twenty minutes into the exam after copying all multiple-choice answers from Valentina. He decided to take the desk because Valentina insisted on sitting on the couch by the window with the sea view.

"It's not that complicated." Valentina reasons, leaning back into the cushions. "Just write what you think creates the most efficient work environment. You're the one who runs a club, you should know this."

Matteo thinks about the people who work at the club.

"So...money then." He concludes.

She scrunches her nose.

"What? Is there something else that can make people want to work?"

She crosses her arms over her chest and leans back into the cushions. "Yes."

"What?"

"Purpose."

"Purpose." He repeats.

"What else?"

"Money."

"Is that why so many people are unhappy with their jobs? Someone who works because they like what they do delivers better results." She argues. "If money were the answer, there wouldn't be any unhappy workers."

"We're talking about work efficiency. Not life satisfaction."

"Someone who doesn't like the work performs worse than someone who does."

"That means they aren't getting paid enough. People will do anything for the right amount of money."

She decides to give up on the conversation and focuses back on her screen.

Matteo argues his point of view in writing, and the word count is reached fifteen minutes later.

"There, it's done." He says, turning back to look at her.

Valentina nods but doesn't look away from her screen, still typing.

Matteo looks out at the Tyrrhenian Sea shining in the sun behind her and thinks about how he's never had a girl in his bedroom just sitting on her laptop. It feels strange but comfortable at the same time.

Maybe it's weird because it's not weird.

"Okay, I'm done too." She says as she looks him in the eye and smiles.

Matteo clicks on the button to turn the exam in and shuts his laptop, happy to be done with exams for the semester.

"How did you even get through the rest of your exams?" Valentina asks, following him with her eyes as he stands up from the desk and goes over to open the balcony doors.

"I paid off a professor to pass one, Vinnie helped me with two, and Raisa another one."

"Did you fly her in too?" She sarcastically asks, making fun of him going to such lengths just to pass his exams.

"I called her."

She looks at him, annoyed. "And you didn't think to suggest that when you called me?"

Valentina does this sometimes – pretends to be displeased with something he did because it's fun for her.

He grins at her. "You didn't either."

She follows him outside without saying a word and sits down on one of the chairs against the wall. There's a round table in between two chairs, so Matteo sits down across from her and takes out a cigarette.

He holds out his pack to Valentina, but she waves him off and stands again. "No, thanks."

"You quit smoking?" He asks, but she already walks back inside.

She's holding a Marlboro Gold pack when she emerges on the balcony again. "No, I brought my own. You smoke truck driver cigarettes."

Matteo lets out a surprised laugh. "What?"

"The Marlboro Red ones? They're the strongest. They're what, a ten?"

Matteo shrugs and lights up his cigarette before offering her the lighter. He watches her face as she looks down at the cigarette between her lips.

They smoke their cigarettes in silence while watching the sea, even though Valentina seems to be in her own world.

"If I had this view every day, I would never have any worries, ever. Just listening to the waves, feeling the sun." She says after a while, exhaling the last bit of smoke. He watches her put the cigarette out in the already filled ashtray

"Ha. You think that, but it's not true." Matteo answers, also putting his cigarette out.

Valentina turns her head to him, surprised. "Why wouldn't it be true?"

She bends her right leg up on the chair and hugs it by the knee.

Matteo suddenly gets the urge to roll and smoke a joint, so he tells her he'll be right back and stands up to go inside. He finds his rolling stash in its usual spot in his nightstand and brings it outside.

"Yes, good idea." Valentina smiles.

Matteo rolls a joint as she struggles to take off her hoodie and tie her hair up.

"It's like thirty degrees here. Back home it's raining." She pouts and watches his fingers skilfully rolling the paper into a joint.

Matteo looks up into her eyes as he licks the paper. "What were we talking about before?"

"You said you're sad even though you basically wake up in an ocean view room every day."

Matteo cocks his head and lights the joint. "I didn't say that. I just meant that people who live here also have problems and worries. Everybody does. When you're used to the same view since you're born, it can get...boring. Not extraordinary."

He takes three long drags before blowing them out and passes the joint to her. She takes it and turns back towards the sea, closing her eyes at the sun.

Her face shines in the sun and Matteo feels like he can't look away for some reason. He feels like he's seen this exact image before, even though he knows he hasn't.

"Are you bored?" She asks, letting out smoke towards the sea.

Matteo shrugs, turning to the water.

"I don't know. Sometimes, maybe."

"If being bored is your biggest problem, it means I made life too easy for you, Matteo."

That's what his father always used to tell him every time he would see Matteo in a bad mood. He'd ask him what's wrong, and Matteo would tell him he's bored. His father never seemed to understand that being bored was bordering burnout and depression. Matteo's almost certain his father doesn't have any feelings. Always looks detached from everything and everyone, and there's nothing that moves him, nothing that can break him.

"If being bored is the problem, then you have it easy."

Matteo looks at Valentina, almost shocked. "What?"

She shrugs and takes another drag before passing the joint. "That's what my dad says to me every time I complain."

"So...you understand." Is all he says and leans back into the chair, looking out at the sea.

"Being bored? Yes. I think it's one of the worst things to be in life. And what's even more absurd, I actually feel guilty about it."

"Why?"

"Because rich kids shouldn't complain about anything, right? We can have anything we want."

Matteo smiles at the way she says 'rich kids', like the two of them aren't exactly that. But he gets it. When you have all the money you could ever imagine, even more than you could ever imagine spending, things that once seemed extraordinary become ordinary.

"When you have everything you could possibly want, nothing is exciting anymore. Eventually, there's nothing to want anymore." Valentina adds and takes the joint Matteo is holding out. "It's sad."

"That's why you think this view would make you happy, because you don't have it every day." Matteo concludes, proving the point that started the discussion in the first place. The conversation turned deeper than Matteo expected.

Valentina rolls her eyes. She doesn't admit when he's right and she's wrong during class, and she won't admit it now either.

They sit in silence once again, listening to the sea create small waves crashing against the cliffs below.

"Do you think it's possible to keep life exciting?" He asks her out of nowhere.

"Yes."

"How?"

Valentina opens her mouth to answer but Matteo's phone starts ringing. It's Isabella Facetiming him.

"Hi."

"Are you done with your exam?" She asks in Italian. Matteo turns the camera to show Valentina. She waves. *"Valentinaaa! Are you in Sicily? This is perfect! Let's talk about Vinnie and Pia's birthday because for some reason she thinks I should be helping her with it."*

"Don't be mean." Matteo tells her in Italian, then switches to English. "Didn't she say she wanted to do something in Ibiza?"

"Yes, but everything is closed because of the new laws. She was crying when she called."

Matteo snorts and looks at Valentina, who is too focused on the sea to even listen to their conversation.

"I think I have an idea." Matteo says after thinking about it for a minute. "I know some guys on the island, I can arrange a yacht."

"Yacht party?! She'll love that. I'll tell Vinnie too."

At this, Valentina turns her head to look at the phone.

"I'll call them now." Matteo says and Isabella ends the call.

Valentina passes the joint and watches Matteo look up someone in his contacts before holding the phone up to his ear. He knows Marcus from the last time he was in Ibiza.

Marcus knows his father because he's been helped by their company before (Matteo doesn't know the details), and has sworn his loyalty to their family, telling them he'll help them anytime when they're on the island (with anything they could possibly need – and that includes illegal shit)

"Ciao Matteo!" He answers in Italian.

"Hi, I need a favour."

"Anything."

"My friends' birthday is tomorrow, and I can't find anywhere to celebrate it. I need a yacht with a staff and a DJ."

Valentina looks at him with a look that makes Matteo feel weird, but then he realizes they're both high. After all, he has access to the best weed in Italy.

Marcus tells him to wait on the line while he makes a call, so Matteo looks down at his slides, listening to the song that plays while he's on hold. His eyes travel to Valentina's ankles, and he raises his eyebrows when he spots a small tattoo.

"Okay, it's done." Marcus says and Matteo can hear the pride in his voice. *"There's a yacht waiting for you in Port Eivissa* tomorrow *at eight pm. I'll be waiting with a bus at the airport tomorrow, just let me know what time."*

Matteo smiles and passes the joint. "Perfect. Thanks, Marcus."

The line goes dead and Matteo places the phone down.

"What? Is it done already?" Valentina asks, surprised.

"Yes."

Matteo texts their Italian group chat about the details. All of the Barone kids, his own siblings, as well as Isabella and Ariana are in the group.

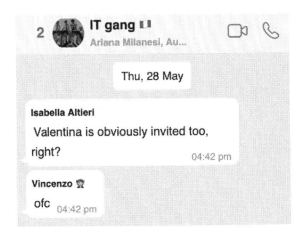

"You're coming too, right?" Matteo asks when he reads the message.

Valentina shrugs. "When is it?"

"Tomorrow."

"Matteeeoooo." Aurora sings from inside.

"Out here." He answers her in English.

"We're going to Ibiza- oh, hello." Aurora says, stopping in her tracks when she sees Valentina. She looks at Matteo for a second, then back at her, smiling. "You're coming too?"

Valentina looks down at her shirt. "I only have this outfit with me. I planned on going back today."

"I have an entire closet full of clothes, you can borrow mine." She offers, waving it off. Matteo frowns at her. Since when is Aurora nice to anyone?

Valentina is looking at him questioningly, silently asking him if it's okay.

"You can stay here until you want to leave, we have enough guest rooms." He answers.

"Great, then I want to have a shower, like, now." She says, standing up. "Show me to my room?"

Aurora takes the joint from her and sits down in her place, crossing one leg over the other. "I'll be here."

Matteo leads Valentina to one of the guest rooms down the hall, the only one that has a bathroom and a closet.

"Thanks. Do you have towels?" Valentina asks as she looks around the room before going over to the bathroom. "Never mind, I see there are towels here. Thanks."

She looks genuinely happy to be staying over, and it's nice to have someone stay over for a reason other than to fuck him. On the other hand, why doesn't she want to? He's never had a girl stay over without sex being implied and it throws him off a little. He's also never met a girl his age who wasn't attracted to him.

Matteo returns on his balcony, where Aurora is currently sitting with an extinguished joint between her fingers. He sits down in his seat and takes it from her fingers, making a point of lighting it up.

"Since when are you two friends?" Aurora asks, unnecessarily wiggling her eyebrows.

"Since- I don't know." It occurs to Matteo just now that he first became aware of her last summer. "Last year? She's Isabella's friend."

"Why is she here?"

"I already told you, she helped me take an online exam. I flew her in from Moscow."

"Hm."

"How do *you* even know her?"

Aurora looks like she panics for a second, but she quickly composes herself. "I've seen her around. I like her."

"You don't like anyone."

She ignores him and goes on to talk about why she's even on his balcony. "I just graduated from high school on a random Thursday, no ceremony, nothing. I think I might just die if I don't have some human interaction with someone who isn't my family." She dramatically changes the subject.

"We're going on a trip to Ibiza tomorrow, I don't think you should be whining about it." Matteo finds himself saying, feeling not like himself but like his father.

"You sound exactly like dad." Aurora jokes and rolls her eyes. "Have you even seen him today?"

Matteo shakes his head.

"Can I get some clothes?"

The two of them look towards the door, where Valentina's standing with a towel around her body and wet hair.

Aurora stands up and waves her hands excitedly. "Of course. I'm going to make you look like you were born to live here."

Valentina throws Matteo a confused look, but all he can do is smile and shrug, having no idea what Aurora even means.

Aurora comes back eventually, long after Matteo finishes the joint.

"You haven't moved?" She asks, dropping down on the chair.

Matteo doesn't even know how much time has passed since he's been sitting in the chair he usually sits in, looking out to the sea.

He can't even remember the last time he just sat here, simply staring out where the water meets the sky. He's been trying to figure out what makes Valentina so sure she would never be unhappy with this view that he hadn't even realized he hasn't gotten bored by just sitting there.

"What else am I supposed to do?"

"We should go out tonight. It's nearly six."

"We're on a national lockdown, Aurora." Matteo reminds her.

"Yes, but I'm going to lose my *mind* if I have to stay in this house for one more day! Dad comes and goes whenever he wants, why can't we?"

Because dad *has the police on payroll,* Matteo thinks, but doesn't say.

"Pia also wants to. Come on, let's convince Vinnie and Isabella and let's all go out! We can show Valentina around, we can't just keep her inside until tomorrow."

"What about me?" Valentina asks, stepping outside. She's wearing a short white satin dress Matteo has seen Aurora wear around the house before.

"I was just telling my brother that we have to go out tonight, we can't just keep you inside instead of showing you beautiful Palermo."

"I wouldn't mind." Valentina says and sits down on the bench by the stone railing, facing the two of them. "But isn't Italy on lockdown because you have the highest death rate in the world or something?"

"Exactly, so the streets are going to be empty, even better!" Aurora concludes.

"What about the police?"

Matteo looks at Valentina and nods, agreeing with her question. Aurora waves it off. "Eh, no worries. We'll deal with them if it gets to it. I'll text the group chat."

Aurora leaves after that, and Matteo lights up a cigarette.

"Do you know each other?" He asks Valentina, who's typing away on her phone. She looks younger than usual in the white dress and semi-wet hair.

"Who? Me and your sister? Not really. I just know she's your sister."

"Hm."

"Why?"

"No reason."

Valentina doesn't ask any further questions, so Matteo also focuses on his phone.

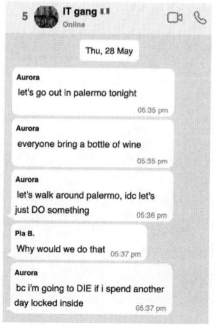

Matteo thinks about his father for a moment. If he'd hear them complain about being locked in a giant mansion by the sea with a pool and everything they could possibly want, he'd laugh at them and tell them to come back down to earth.

But Valentina's right, when you have everything, nothing feels exciting anymore. Living in lockdown during a pandemic in a nine-bedroom house can become depressing, especially if you know, deep down, that you should be more grateful about where you are and what you have. Matteo never realized he'd been bored and burnt out until Valentina came to Italy. Every day has been the same, but he's gotten used to it. Just went through each day without feeling anything other than just *meh*.

Being home months at a time hasn't happened since before he went to boarding school. He never appreciated the sea before either.

"Don't your parents mind you being in Italy during an international pandemic?"

Valentina looks up from her phone. "I just texted them. They're not excited about it, but they'll deal. My dad travels for work anyway."

"He owns a business, right?"

"Right." Valentina answers, with a hint of hesitation in her voice.

Matteo doesn't mention it, but he remembers her telling Isabella about how her parents are trying to keep someone dying a secret. He also remembers his first instinct saying *mafioso*, but then she explained that her father is a businessman and that they were just being secretive about it.

Sometimes Matteo forgets that although his reality *does* exist, there are very few people in the world who are in it as deep as he is. Born into it, stumbling upon the truth when young, doing jobs that get more serious and dangerous each time, using drugs to make money to buy other drugs, and so on.

Also, he tried googling her name to find her dad, but all he got was a link to her Instagram and Facebook. She didn't post as much as the other girls Matteo followed, and she definitely looks better in real life than in photos.

"What are you thinking about?"

Her question anchors him back into reality. He's never been asked that directly. He also can't really answer the question truthfully.

"How things aren't always what they seem."

She lights up a cigarette and turns around to watch the sea, smiling up at the sun. Matteo looks back at his phone screen.

Pia asks if it's okay to meet up in front of their house in twenty. Matteo sends a thumbs up emoji before deciding to go change out of his tank and shorts into something more appropriate for going out. He finds a pressed white linen shirt and clean jean shorts in his closet.

Good enough.

"Let's go get the wine first." Aurora speaks as soon as he appears in the downstairs foyer.

They go down to their wine cellar, stocked to the brim with wines produced by their own company, some of the bottles being ever older than Matteo.

"Il Giudice 2010?" Valentina reads off a bottle she picks out. Matteo walks over and takes the bottle to read the label.

"Yes, it's the batch from 2010. It's good wine, I think. I prefer spirits."

"Yes, but *Giudice*? Wait, are all these Giudice?"

"It's our family winery."

Matteo doesn't tell her that you can find this type of wine in every supermarket selling alcohol in Sicily, if not all of Italy.

"Do you sell it?" She asks anyway.

"Some of it." Matteo answers and picks out a random bottle. "Let's go."

Chapter 18

Matteo

They take Matteo's convertible, with Vinnie sitting in the passenger's seat holding a bag containing two bottles of wine. Pia, Aurora, and Valentina are sitting in the back, already sharing the bottle from 2010. Marco and Eddie chose to stay home and play FIFA, and Isabella is waiting for them in front of the restaurant in the city.

The drive takes fifteen minutes because there's not even one car in sight, and the city feels different when it's deserted. The sun is setting behind them and the silence is eerie as Matteo parallel parks in front of their closed restaurant.

"It's weird, right? The silence." Aurora says in English, hopping out of the car without even opening the door, then grabs a bottle from Vinnie's bag.

"Shouldn't we at least be wearing masks?" Valentina asks, looking around.

"Don't be a loser." Pia laughs and shakes her head, taking the bottle from Aurora's hand. "There's no one around. Salute!" She raises the bottle and takes a long sip from it.

"Yes, that's the spirit!" Aurora cheers her on and goes to throw an arm around her shoulders.

Matteo and Vinnie look at each other. It's obvious, to Matteo at least, that the two of them are trying, for some reason, to show off in front of Valentina. They would never be this excited about drinking wine in the streets of Palermo. The boys have done it numerous times before, but Pia and Aurora were never with them. Is this what they think Russians do for fun?

Isabella shows up five minutes later with a smile on her face. She hugs Valentina first, and soon enough they just settle on aimlessly walking around the city drinking the wine. Matteo and Vinnie trail behind Aurora and Pia, who in turn are following Valentina and Isabella a few steps behind. They share a joint as they walk, completely unbothered about the thought of someone looking out the window and seeing them.

Half an hour later, when the sun has completely set and the moon is slowly starting to show, they find themselves in front of the Port, with two out of five bottles already empty.

"Let's just sail to Ibiza now." Pia points to a boat in the marina, slurring the last part of her sentence.

They all sit down on the benches facing the boats, sharing two opened bottles between the six of them.

"I can't believe you live here." Valentina says to no one in particular as she looks around.

"You've never been to Italy?" Pia asks with the same condescending tone she talked to Valentina earlier. But Valentina doesn't even seem to care, nor notice.

Instead, she smiles.

"I have, and every time I come here, I feel like I belong."

"Too bad you were born in Russia then."

Matteo and Isabella exchange looks. Okay, so Pia *is* being meaner than usual.

"Shit, police!" Aurora says and stands up when she sees two Carabinieri walking towards them. They don't even notice their group until they're running away, following a laughing and screaming Aurora.

The two men yell something as they chase them up the street.

"Do we even know where we're going?" Valentina yells from behind him, and before he even thinks about it, he turns left and then right, running down on two small streets.

He doesn't stop until he knows where he's running to, finally coming to a halt in Pretoria Square, sweating and out of breath. When he turns around, he sees everyone else is in the same state, except Aurora and Valentina, who have smiles on their faces.

"What is this?" Valentina asks after everyone's had a moment to breathe and the bottles are doing the rounds again.

"Piazza Pretoria." Isabella answers and points towards the fountain in the middle of the plaza surrounded by old buildings. "And that's the fountain."

The Pretoria Fountain looks even more beautiful at night, when the streetlights around it shine on the statues and reflect in the water.

Valentina walks up to the black fence surrounding the stairs leading up to the first level of fountains. "Can't we go see the top fountain?"

Isabella tries the gate, which is usually opened during the day. "It's locked."

Valentina takes a gulp from the bottle, closing her eyes and scrunching up her face as she does so, before handing it to Aurora.

"Help me up." Valentina says. "The fence isn't even that high."

Everyone looks at each other, hesitating. Save for Isabella who doesn't even question it before giving Valentina a boost over the fence.

Everyone except Pia ends up jumping the fence. Aurora goes first, followed by Marco and Eddie, then Vinnie, and finally, a sighing Matteo.

They follow Valentina up to the second level of the fountain.

"Have you talked to Sofia about Ibiza tomorrow?" Pia asks Vinnie from where she's now leaning against the closed iron gate.

"I tried calling her for the past three weeks, but it goes straight to voicemail. I think she's ignoring me."

Isabella huffs and takes the bottle from him.

"I had a dream about this two days ago." Valentina says and kneels on the concrete. She places the palm flat on the water, as if she were testing its temperature.

Isabella looks away from Vinnie, trying to fake excitement. "About being in Palermo?"

"No, about swimming in a fountain. Also, I'm drunk."

She takes off her sneakers and steps into the fountain.

"Dio mio!" Aurora screams in an excited tone, walking up closer to her.

Valentina laughs and takes the bottle from her, before walking backwards and finally sitting down in the water.

Aurora joins her without saying anything else.

"You're not allowed in the fountain." Matteo points out.

He's getting paranoid about the Carabinieri returning and arresting them for being outside their homes, not to mention hopping over the fence and basically violating a historical monument.

"Like you ever give a shit about the rules!" Aurora laughs at him in English, and he flips her off.

"Oh, come on Matteo. No one's around to judge you." Valentina mocks, standing up and walking in his direction with a mischievous grin on her face.

"Don't you even think about it." He says, stepping back.

"You live here and you *never* got into this fountain?"

"Why would I want to get into the fountain?"

"You asked me how it's possible to keep life exciting." She cocks her head. "The first step is doing something new every day." She smirks, knowing she just won the argument that had started this morning.

Matteo knows she's right, and what's fair is fair. He toes off his sneakers, then his shirt, then throws his wallet on the ground before getting into the fountain.

"I can't believe my eyes!" Isabella exclaims and tells the three of them to get closer to each other so she can take a photo. Vinnie also laughs as he takes photos, and Matteo finds himself laughing along. Maybe it's the wine, maybe it's that he's seen this fountain a hundred times before but never once thought about swimming in it until today.

"It's kind of nice." Aurora says as she swims over to Valentina to take the bottle.

Matteo leans back against his palms and looks up at the sky. Everything seems to stop for a few moments, and it's just him, the sky, and the water. He smiles, feeling a wave of unfamiliar happiness wash over him.

"Merda!" Pia's voice loudly echoes through the square, and Matteo's surroundings suddenly turn into red and blue flashes. He watches the police car pull up in front of Pia, and two different men get out.

They order the five of them to come down this instant, threatening them with prison time and high fines for breaking lockdown in the first place.

Matteo sighs and stands up from the fountain, already forgetting those few seconds of complete peace and serenity as he looked up at the stars while drunk on wine.

"What's the problem?" He asks them in Italian after grabbing his wallet and walking down the steps barefoot. He stops on the other side of the fence from the police and Pia.

"The problem is you're trespassing and you're breaking a nationwide lockdown. May I see all of your IDs? Also, can the blonde come out of the fountain before we call for backup and take you all to jail?"

Matteo takes out his driver's license and a 100 Euro bill before handing them over to the guy who just talked. He motions to Aurora to get out of the fountain.

"If you think this will work you're mistaken, Mr…" the officer trails off as he reads his name, voice trembling at the end. "Oh. Mr. Giudice?"

"Yes, and that 'blonde' is my sister, Aurora." Matteo adds, pointing to Aurora, before placing both of his hands in his pockets and relaxing.

The other policeman double checks his ID as well, looking at him then at the photo about five times before handing the ID back to him. The 100 Euro bill didn't make it back, of course.

"Have a good night." The first to talk smiles at him, before bowing his head and going back to the car.

By the time they leave the Square everyone is out of the fountain and over the fence anyway, mood ruined. Vinnie hands his jacket over to Valentina, who obviously didn't think that getting herself wet while wearing a white dress would be a bad idea.

"Let's just go back to the car, I'm bored." Pia groans after not having said anything for ten minutes while the rest of them finished the bottles.

"I drank, I can't drive." Matteo says.

She rolls her eyes and looks away, crossing her arms over her chest. "Then let's order a taxi."

"Why are you in such a bad mood today?" He snaps at her.

Her cheeks turn pink, and she looks at him with an angry look on her face without saying anything.

"There's a taxi station a few streets away."

"What did you tell the police to make them go away?" Isabella asks him once the two of them and Valentina naturally end up a few steps behind the rest of the group.

"I gave them a hundred and showed them my ID."

"They recognized the name, obviously." Pia says, not turning around.

"Do they know their names?" Valentina asks her and Matteo knows she's asking a question she already knows the answer to. What he doesn't know though, is *why*.

"Vaguely." He answers for Pia.

"Why?"

Aurora interrupts their conversation by calling over a free taxi van coming down the street in their direction.

They all pile inside and Vinnie hands the driver two hundred Euros, apologizing for them dripping over the seats. They drop Isabella off first before they set off East towards Aspra. Pia is sitting between Vinnie and Matteo while Aurora and Valentina each lean against a window, contently smiling as they look out of them.

"Did you have fun on your first ever day in Palermo?" Aurora asks, turning her head to look at Valentina.

"Yes, I did. I'm sure it's even more fun when the city isn't locked down." She makes eye contact with Matteo as she says it, and neither of them break it until Aurora sits up straight. The car stops in the middle of the road, across from the gate leading to the Barone residence, a hundred meters away from their own home.

"See you tomorrow, the plane leaves at six thirty!" Matteo yells after them.

Five minutes later they're already walking down the long driveway leading up to the house.

"I love the smell." Valentina sighs and looks up at the trees as she walks.

"What smell?"

It literally smells like nothing.

"The smell of the sea…it smells like summer. I want to live here."

"Why would you want to live here?" Matteo laughs, not intending to sound judgy. They stop in front of the door and the girls wait for him to unlock it.

"Why wouldn't I want to live here? The air is…different. I feel like everything is different. I even like the people here more than I do back home."

"You've only met us, though."

Valentina looks up at him with a smile as she struggles to take off her sneakers by the door.

"I've been vacationing in Capo d'Orlando for over ten years. There's a clear difference in the personalities of people who grow up in sunny places and those who grow up in places where it's mostly bad weather. I notice the difference between the people in Russia and people in Italy. Especially the boys."

Matteo rolls his eyes. "Italian boys being a thing is just a stereotype though. I can name a few who would be worse than your Russian boys."

"Yes, but you know what I mean."

"I do."

Aurora is just standing there, looking between the two of them as they talk. She grabs her stuff and slips into her house slippers.

"You can have the matching pair, Valentina." She says and points to the matching white slippers. "I'm going to bed, see you tomorrow."

She hugs them both and kisses Matteo on the cheek before hurrying up the stairs. They walk upstairs in silence.

"Do you have pajamas?" Matteo asks her when they stop in front of his door, since it's the first one right by the stairs.

"Yes, Aurora gave me some."

"Alright."

He places a hand on the doorknob and looks at her one more time.

"Goodnight."

"Goodnight."

He takes a quick shower with his playlist on shuffle before he changes into his sleeping briefs. Just as he's about to go out on his balcony to smoke his end of the day cigarette (he's too lazy to roll), there's a knock at the door.

Valentina is standing there in his sister's cotton pyjamas holding up a cigarette and a lighter.

"I wanted to smoke my goodnight cigarette, but I realized I don't have a balcony and I didn't want to smoke out the window." She explains.

Matteo steps aside and she waltzes in, asking if she can take the half-filled water bottle from the desk.

"Just take a new one out of the fridge." He answers and points to the minifridge in the corner.

She joins him outside and sits down where she first sat down this morning. The only light on his balcony is the one above them, and he can see her lips are dark red from the wine she's been drinking.

They smoke in silence for a couple of minutes while looking out into the darkness. Matteo thinks about everything that happened today, and how different it felt from the past two months, which have gone by on autopilot.

The Italian rap song that was just playing inside changes to PPP by Beach House.

"I love this song." She smiles and closes her eyes.

Matteo listens to it for a while. The song feels like getting home after a long day at the beach, feeling content. He used to feel like that when he was younger and everything around him seemed easy.

"Why did you play stupid today?" He asks out of a sudden.

Valentina turns to look at him, surprised but still relaxed. "When did I play stupid?"

"When Pia was trying to belittle you and you didn't play into it."

"Ah." She waves it off, the bracelets on her wrist making that sound they always do. "Whatever that was about, it's not about me. I don't even know her, so that's her problem to deal with."

"What about when you asked if the police knew our names?"

"Sometimes my instinct tells me when it's better to be underestimated."

Matteo puts out his cigarette and watches the small orange spark fade into darkness. "Do you ever do that with me?"

She tilts her head and blows out smoke, her tongue poking out between her teeth as she smiles. "What do you think?"

There's a spark in her eye that he noticed the first time he saw her back in Taormina but hasn't seen again until now. He smiles and looks back down at the ashtray, feeling a bit dizzy from the wine, the cigarettes, and the joint he smoked with Vinnie earlier.

"I think you're way smarter than you let on."

She playfully squints at him and puts out the cigarette without breaking eye contact. "Which tells me the same thing about you."

Valentina smiles at him once more before standing up and grabbing the bottle. "I had fun today, thank you."

He nods and looks at her bare legs for a split second before looking back at her face. She looks tired now, but her eyes still look the same as they always do.

"Goodnight."

She waves as she leaves the balcony without looking back at him.

"Goodniiight." She sings.

The door to his room closes a few seconds later.

Matteo chain-smokes two more cigarettes as he looks out into the darkness, listening to the waves and the song playing in the background, thinking about nothing. He goes to bed ten minutes later, his mind blank.

When he closes his eyes, all he sees and feels is that endless moment when he was in the fountain, the water up to his neck as he looked up at the sky.

He falls asleep without anything playing in the background for the first time in months.

Chapter 19

Valentina

Palermo, Sicily, Italy – May 29ᵗʰ, 2020

I wake up in an unfamiliar room with a dry mouth, feeling completely disoriented. It takes me a few seconds to realize that the cream-colored ceiling and the matching drapes don't belong to my bedroom in Russia.

Fragments of my dream come back to me as soon as I completely wake up. I try to shake them off, bury them somewhere deep in my brain where I'll never find them again. It's a new day, but the view I have of the trees doesn't look like rainy Russia.

Then I remember that I'm in Sicily, sleeping in a guest room at Matteo's house. I sit up and groan, rubbing my eyes and running my hands through my hair. I can still taste the wine from last night.

My mom wasn't too happy about me being in Italy during a world-wide crisis, but getting out of the house after two months feels good. My dad didn't even read the messages I sent in the group yesterday.

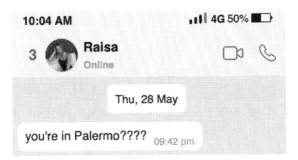

"Shiiiit." I say under my breath as I read the message she sent last night. While I was on the balcony. Smoking with her crush. I didn't even think of telling her about it. How does she even know?

I check Instagram as I get out of bed and pull the curtains to the side so I can open the window. The sun blinds me from the left but I love it, and for a moment I forget about Raisa.

Today

you're leaving me on read????

09:41 am

I groan and set the phone down. I need to brush my teeth and wash my face first before I can deal with unnecessary drama.

There's a voice message from Raisa waiting in my notifications bar while I change into a pair of black shorts and a white shirt. I play her voice memo, finally, as I try to put my hair up in a ponytail. No one warned me it would be 27 degrees in Italy, yet here we are.

"I saw on Isabella's story that you're in Palermo, she posted you and Matteo in the fountain...anyway, how come you're there? I would've loved to come with. When are you coming back? Are you back already? Miss you!"

I resist the urge to roll my eyes at myself in the mirror. She's never said 'miss you' to me once in her life.

Coffee.

And a cigarette.

I mentally prepare myself to send a voice message to Raisa explaining everything (I don't know why I feel like I owe her an explanation – I don't, I haven't done anything wrong), as well as ask Matteo for coffee.

The worst thing about being at someone's house is feeling like a toddler who needs to ask every time they want something. I'm also not sure what my boundaries with Matteo are now, because we've gotten along better than expected. My expectations were the usual chit chats I had with him every time we saw each other, nothing out of the ordinary.

But it felt...comfortable. It was *weird* - because I expected it to be and it wasn't. I genuinely enjoyed myself in what feels like forever since we were forced to stay inside, and he even got two new tattoos. I haven't gotten a new tattoo in ages.

"Soooo Matteo and I take the same Business Psychology course and he asked me to help him during the exam." I open the door. "Yes...so he flew me out and I helped him pass, and then I stayed over because it's Vinnie's birthday today."

I let go of the button and think about what else to say. I don't know if Vinnie or Pia want to invite her, but there's no point in lying. I press the corner of the screen again.

"It's a yacht party in Ibiza today at eight or nine, I don't know for sure. They invited me because I was here, and I said yes. I don't even have my own clothes, I had to borrow Aurora's. Oh, and they showed me around Palermo yesterday, which is why we were in that fountain." I chuckle and knock on Matteo's door before ending the voice message.

I wait a few minutes then knock again. I hear some groaning from inside, so I take it as him being awake. I also need coffee more than I need him to like me right now.

"Matteo?" I ask, looking over to his bed. I can only see a mop of brown hair between the pillows and blankets. He mumbles something in Italian under his breath.

"Yes? What."

He turns his head, and I can see his eyes are still closed.

"I want some coffee, but I don't really know my way around here."

"There's a cook downstairs, ask him."

"But I'm-okay, I'm not embarrassed but I feel bad-"

He makes a dramatic show of huffing and puffing and turning his back to me.

I stare at the tattoo on the back of his shoulder.

Not a morning person then.

"Make it the new thing you try today then." He sarcastically says and I just stare at his back for a second before I flip him off with both hands. I hear him say something in Italian, so I just turn around and close the door behind me.

I see that Raisa has already replied to my voice message as I walk down the stairs. It doesn't take me long to find the kitchen and thankfully, it's empty. There's a coffee machine on one of the counters with the pods next to it.

"Eaasy." I tell myself, forgetting about my phone.

The coffee is done two minutes later, and I press the ice button on the fridge to make it instantly drinkable. I go back upstairs, happy that I am surrounded by 0 people.

I need a cigarette.

Shit, but I don't want to smoke out the window in someone else's house like a lunatic.

Matteo will just have to deal.

I knock on the door again, but don't wait for a response this time before I slowly tip toe in. He's still sleeping, so I try to go over to the balcony without making a sound. My slippers don't cooperate, but I manage to open the doors and walk outside with just one hand and without waking him up.

It takes me a minute to take in the view. Every time I come to Italy for the summer after having spent time either in Moscow or New York, I feel like I'm a different person. Or maybe more myself. It's the weather, for sure. I don't even like the weather in those cities 80% of the time.

"I can only wear 20% of my wardrobe during the weather I get 80% of the time." I say to myself, then start looking for my lighter. I realize it's already on the table from yesterday.

"Math in the morning? My head hurts."

I look to my right, horrified. Matteo is standing in the door with the blanket under his armpits, hair dishevelled and unimpressed about my presence. He looks well rested and almost like a baby. What changed?

The bags under his eyes are gone.

He's got the most resting bitch face I've ever seen, lol

"Is that coffee?" He asks, sitting down across from me at the table.

"Yes, but it's-" I watch him take the coffee to his lips and take two large gulps "-mine."

He takes a cigarette from my pack and lights it up, then leans back facing the water. I get a flashback from last night in the fountain, when I was looking at his face from this angle.

I remember looking at him the moment he relaxed for like, five seconds. The way he looked up at the sky, how his eyes reflected the light of the moon and sparkled for a second.

I also remember the moment he realized the police were there and came back down to reality. He looked like the saddest boy in the happiest place on Earth, and my heart broke for him, for whatever reason.

As I watch him shamelessly drink my coffee and smoke my cigarettes without a care in the world, I tell myself that I cannot feel sorry for this man. Nor can I allow myself to even consider him cute.

I feel like it's my mother talking, but after last night, he's come dangerously close to me considering him an interesting man. Boy. Whatever. I can't even entertain the idea of him being subjectively good looking. I don't even think about it – my instinct just *knows* I shouldn't.

My train of thought takes me to Raisa, who I still haven't replied to. I don't even remember what we were talking about.

Right, Vinnie's birthday. I feel weird about inviting a friend of mine to Vinnie's private birthday party in Ibiza.

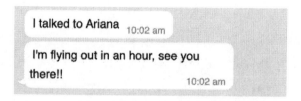

"¡Se deve autoinvitarsi, dille almeno di portare Aleksi!"

For a moment I think Matteo's talking to me, but then I see him holding the phone up to his mouth to send voice memos. All I understood was 'auto-invite' and Aleksi, which tells me everything I need to know.

"Who are you talking to?" I ask.

"Vinnie. Your friend is coming too."

I squint at him. "'My friend' is your friend too."

Matteo pretends not to hear me as he lights another cigarette.

"And don't act like it's such a drag that she's coming. You know exactly why you want Alex there."

He rolls his eyes. "Did I say anything? You're the one getting defensive."

I don't bother telling him I heard it in his tone, the way he told Vinnie that Raisa invited herself in Italian, thinking I can't understand him. I know Spanish, or at least I understand it from all the telenovelas I used to watch and the course I took in high school. And Spanish kind of sounds like Italian. I know I'm right.

"Did you even understand me?" He asks after a while of both of us typing on our phones.

"Pretty much, yes."

"What did I say?" He asks, not believing me.

"That Raisa should bring Alex if she invites herself, like it's the least she could do."

He looks impressed and annoyed at the same time, which tells me that I'm right. "Don't you think it's a bit much to invite herself to Vinnie's birthday?"

"Do Vinnie and Pia mind?"

"Vinnie said it's okay."

"Then what's the problem?"

"Do I need to say it out loud?"

I sit up straight. "Yes, do it."

"She's obviously coming here because I'm here."

I mean- he's not wrong.

"Maybe the world doesn't revolve around you." I say.

"I get a feeling that hers does."

I get the same feeling too. But I'm not going to let him know that. He needs to treat Raisa more like a human and less like a...I don't know.

"Helloooo??" Isabella's voice rings out from Matteo's room.

Matteo mumbles something in Italian up to the sky, just as Isabella appears on the balcony. She has a smile on her face and a bag in her hand.

"Buongiorno!" she tells us, then steps directly in front of me, blocking my sun.

"Why are you here?" Matteo asks. "Who let you in?"

Isabella ignores him and looks at me. "I had the best idea of what we could do today."

"What?" I ask at the same time as Matteo asks "Isn't Ibiza enough?"

"Will you shush?!"

Matteo shrugs before leaning back and lighting up another one of my cigarettes.

"Valentina, come on. We must be there at one."

"The plane leaves at six." Matteo interjects once again.

I turn to look at him. "I thought you said six thirty yesterday."

"Yes, but if I tell Isabella six thirty, she will be there at seven."

Isabella waves him off. "I'll be there on time, leave me alone."

"What do you want to do then?" I ask, changing the subject.

"There's this Romanian woman in Palermo that my mother used to go to, and she's still taking appointments "under the table", as long as the clients keep their mouths shut."

"You're going to that fortune teller?" Matteo asks, almost laughing.

"Hey. My mother went when she was my age for the first time, and Pandora has been mostly right."

"Her name's Pandora? You can't be serious."

"I didn't ask you to come, now did I? I asked Valentina. She'll do us both."

They both look at me expectantly. Isabella with hope in her eyes, probably happy she has someone to go with; Matteo with an incredulous look, as if he's asking me whether I believe in the whole thing.

"I'll come with, obviously." I smile at her. "We'll see if she's right in a few months, won't we?"

"Do you believe that bullshit too?" Matteo asks, sounding disappointed.

"I believe the world is full of things we can't explain, and yet they make sense." I tell him, not knowing where it really came from. I just spoke it out loud. They look at each other.

"Did you smoke without me?" He asks me.

I decide to ignore him. I stand up and tell Isabella that I will get dressed quickly before we can go.

***

We take Isabella's white convertible Mini Cooper to Palermo. Driving parallel to the sea lifts my mood and I'm also happy that I get some alone time with Isabella, because I've noticed something has changed since the last time I saw her. Maybe that's why she's going to look for answers.

"How have you been?" I ask her as I watch the trees pass us by.

"Since yesterday? Good."

"You know what I mean."

She sighs. "Yeah. I don't know. My parents are getting divorced and all I can talk to Vinnie about is how Sofia has been ghosting him for the past two months."

"I completely forgot Sofia even existed."

"Yeah, me too. Until he brings her up."

"I think he needs closure."

"I don't care anymore. I feel like it's time for a fresh start."

As I look out to the sea, at the horizon that fades into the sun, I think she's right. I feel like my life has for some reason entered a new phase as well. It's like I can feel a change is coming, and there's a weird feeling in my stomach that I can't place.

"Do you believe in spirits?" She asks me then, just as we enter the empty streets of Palermo.

"I believe we are all connected, spiritually. But I can't say I believe in spirits. I don't *not* believe in them either."

An Italian song comes on the radio, and she screams, turning the volume up. We dance along to it until it comes to an end, and then Valentina pulls the car over into a parking spot.

"We're here."

We're standing in front of a small cream building with a giant door in the middle, blocked by an iron grid. Isabella rings the doorbell three times before the intercom buzzes. The iron grid moves to the right and folds against the wall.

Isabella turns to me and smiles. "It's already mysterious, I love it."

The gate opens into a cold, dark hallway with stone walls and one door at the end. A pipe coming from somewhere above the ceiling is dripping on the concrete. The sound echoes against the walls, making me feel uneasy. Isabella knocks on the door and steps back, crossing her arms over her chest.

"Chi è?" a voice behind the door asks.

Isabella answers something in Italian then waits for an answer. We look at each other but nothing happens.

"Maybe we should-"

The door creaks open.

"Come in, come in." the voice from earlier switches to English.

A woman in her early to late fifties is standing there, welcoming Isabella in. She's dressed in a white floral floor-length dress and golden jewellery. Her face is framed by a bandana made of golden amulets that shake lightly every time she moves her head.

"And who are you?" She asks when she sees me. Her accent sounds just like my mother's.

"Shouldn't you already know that?" I try to make a joke, closing the door behind me. Pandora doesn't find it funny. She turns around and leads us down the hallway.

The room is small, very intimate, and I feel slightly uncomfortable being here. For some reason, the moment she looked at me I felt naked. Pandora goes over to the bookshelf by the barricaded window.

"Sit down." She says without looking at us.

Isabella and I sit down on the two chairs by the table. When Pandora turns around, she's holding a deck of cards and a few candles in one hand, and a crystal pendulum in the other.

"Not both of you!" She exclaims, nearly laughing. "Just one. The other one goes outside."

"Why can't she stay with me?" Isabella asks.

"If I'm doing a reading I can't have two different spiritual energies in my field."

"Well, whatever that means." I say and stand up instantly. "I'll just wait out in the hall."

"No, you wait in the library. First door to the right."

I follow her instructions and end up in a very sunny room with a view of the street. I stare out at the deserted road for a few seconds before I take my phone out.

Raisa lets me know that she'll be landing in 5 hours so I text a thumbs up emoji then lock my phone, checking the clock again. It's already been fifteen minutes. How long are fortune readings even supposed to last? What does Isabella have to know that's taking so long? What is she telling her? I feel uneasy again, unlike I felt yesterday. Today feels different.

The fact that he seems stressed for no reason makes me instantly calm down because I can see that I'm doing the same. I'm in the apartment of a Romanian witch, waiting to get my future laid out in front of me.

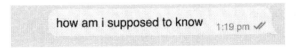

As if on cue, I hear Isabella calling my name. We meet by the door. She looks very happy and pleased with what she heard. It relaxes me enough to trust the process.

"Your turn."

I take my seat in front of Pandora, who is busy shuffling the cards and looking at an unlit candle.

"Light the candle for me please." She says. Her thick accent reminds me of my mother once again.

I do as she says, using the lighter in my pocket. The candle burns slowly, small at first, before it suddenly pops. It lengthens itself out, then remains straight and warm.

Pandora nods at the candle then places the cards on the table. She makes a semicircle with the deck before leaning back in her chair.

"Take out three cards and place them in front of me. Those will be your past, present, and future."

"I thought this was more like a Q&A" I say, fidgeting in my seat. I'm still nervous for some reason.

She doesn't answer me. She just looks down at the cards, expecting me to pick. I let out a deep breath and go by instinct, picking without thinking. I place them faced down before her and she turns them around.

The first one is of a defeated man on the ground with swords in his back. The second one has three women dancing with cups in their hands, and the third one is turned upside down, so it looks upright to me. There are two naked people on there that resemble Adam and Eve, with an angel in the sky above them.

VI The Lovers

"I see betrayal in your past."

I try to think of a time where I felt betrayed. Nothing comes to mind, so I relax. It's obviously untrue.

"Someone kept something from you, maybe a family member. And you felt betrayed."

My mind instantly goes to that night I overheard my parents talking about the people that died. 'People' as in, more than one person. How they said they told their families that they got lost at sea.

Pandora looks at my face and nods, knowing she's spot on.

"Your present is the three of Cups."

"This one looks more promising." I say, still trying to make jokes to cover my nervousness.

"You're having fun. Right now, you're surrounded by people you love, your soul tribe."

I think of Isabella waiting for me in the same spot I waited for her. Raisa has been my stable friend throughout my life, but recently I've been feeling like we've drifted apart. We've both changed since last year. Something is different.

Isabella has also been by my side for five years now, and I feel we're more like sisters rather than friends. It's just easier with her, more natural.

"The card represents celebrations, dancing. Sex, sometimes. In love, it represents a third party, family or friends, another person. A ménage à trois, a love triangle."

I look at her amused but she looks dead serious.

"What about my future?" I ask, getting optimistic.

"Your future is the Lovers. Reversed."

"Why does it matter if it's reversed?"

"The card represents romance, opposites attracting. The duality and balance of physicality, fire, and emotions, water."

"Does that mean I'm going to fall in love?"

She continues, as if not having heard my question. "If it's reversed, it means this love brings unreliability with it. Separation, conflict."

Then I wouldn't even be in love? I'm done with all of the toxic things that come with a dramatic relationship. It's just not attractive anymore.

"You doubt the cards." Pandora observes.

"No, it's not that-"

"Pull three more."

I do as I'm told, without bothering to ask why. At this point I've realized that she just goes on doing her thing and asking her questions is useless.

I pull three more cards and she cleans up the rest, placing them in order, faced up. "Huh." She says, looking at the card on the top of the deck.

There's a naked woman on it, in what looks like a mirror.

XXI The World

I see Pandora look at it for a second, her eyes big, as if she'd just realized something.

"What is it?" I ask.

"I see childlike optimism, rebellion. Playfulness, charisma. Someone powerful…" her look turns more serious (I didn't think it was even possible) as she stares at the cards in front of her.

"What?"

"No, that cannot be."

"What?!"

She looks at the flame. "Forta invincibila." she almost whispers. I don't know if it's Italian or Romanian, but I can tell it means invincible force. She snaps out of her trance and looks back at the cards.

She looks at the third card, touching it lightly with her fingers. "The Moon."

"I like the moon." I say, trying to fill the silence. I don't like this at all.

"It's reversed."

"Is that bad again?" I sigh.

"No. When it's reversed it means joy, enlightenment."

"Is this how my lover is going to be?" I ask her.

She doesn't answer, which lights a spark of anger within me.

"I have no idea what's going on. You have to tell me."

"I am telling you what the cards mean. You must understand them yourself."

"But you're a fortune teller. Doesn't that mean *you* have to tell *me* things?" I ask, finding her more annoying than anything else at this point.

"You're a very smart girl. That's why I told you the meaning of the cards, not my own interpretation. It's up to you to interpret them. Then we'll discuss next time."

Next time? Is she serious? She must know I'm not from around here.

"Why did it last longer with Isabella? Is it because I'm not Italian?" I ask.

"You are not from Italy." She says and starts gathering the cards. Is she agreeing with me? Correcting me? What is she doing?

"No."

Her lips turn into an almost unrecognizable smile. Then she stands up and goes to put the cards back in their place.

"If you ever come back to Palermo, visit me again."

I stand up as well, glad that it's finally over. I learned nothing. I watch her back as she fumbles with something on the bookshelf.

"I don't come to Palermo often."

"If you do, visit me."

"I vacation with my family in Capo d'Orlando here every summer." I say, hand already on the doorknob.

Pandora turns her head to look me in the eye. She has the same look she had as she looked at the World card.

"Since when?"

"Since I was little."

Recognition flashes across her face. "Listen to your dreams." Is all she says after that, then turns back to her bookshelf. I take it as my cue to leave.

The sun is right above us as we drive out of Palermo and up the coastline back to the Giudice house.

"What did she tell you?" Isabella asks and turns her eyes away from the road to look at me.

"Literally nothing." I say. "Did she tell you anything?"

"Yes. She told me that I held back in my past. That I took on too much and refused to accept help. That I've been hiding something from myself for so long that I've become numb. Which is obviously true, because- you know." She says, referring to her crush on Vinnie. "My present is a fresh start and something big is coming. She told me fate is turning the wheel in my favour."

"That sounds good. What about your future?"

"She said that I'm going to have to juggle multiple priorities and career options. That I'll be victorious in the end."

"Well, your sounds better than mine."

"So you're saying she didn't tell you *anything*?"

"I swear! She only let me pick the cards and then told me what they meant. But she didn't say anything about...nothing like what she told you."

She raises a hand, still looking at the road. "Wait. She let you pick out the cards? She didn't shuffle them herself? That's weird."

"Why?"

"She didn't do the same thing to me."

"I think it's because I'm not Italian."

"You're joking right?! That's definitely not the reason. She's a witch of gypsy origins, she is not one to discriminate. What else did she tell you?"

"That I'm supposed to understand them myself."

"Huh. That's weird."

"That's what I thought. At least she told me to listen to my dreams." I say, sarcasm dripping on my words.

"Do you at least remember any cards?"

"The Lovers."

"That's a good sign! Was it the future?"

"Yes."

"Ooooh. Do you think it's Isaac?"

No.

The fact that I thought of no one when I saw the card meant Isaac was definitely not someone I would see myself with long term. The fact that my mind whispered 'Matteo' for a second when she said power has been buried in the back of my mind. Along with my dreams she told me to listen to.

"No." I answer. "Plus, it's summer. I want to enjoy myself, have fun. I think we should hang out when I'm in Sicily with my family. Is Capo d'Orlando far away?"

"Are you kidding? It's not even that far! A two-hour drive, tops." she excitedly says. "We'll definitely hang out. Maybe I can come over to your house, since I live in the city and I love the beach."

"We can just tan all day and read books." I say, also getting excited about having something to do, and someone to do it with.

"Oh, it's definitely a plan."

Neither of us says anything about how the situation in Italy could turn from bad to worse. We've seen our futures today, and even though I'm too petty to admit it, they both look promising.

Chapter 20

Valentina

Palermo, Sicily – May 29th, 2020

Matteo is in the kitchen when we get home, eating a sandwich and scrolling through his phone.

"We're back." Isabella announces and doesn't bother to take her shoes off as she waltzes over into the kitchen. She tells him everything Pandora told her, leaving the Vinnie part out.

"What did she tell you?" Matteo asks me.

"That there's a very unstable relationship in my future." I half-joke, going over to the coffee machine.

He watches me put the pod in and press the button. "Do you believe that she's right?"

"I think that if I believe she's right, she will be."

"The plane leaves at six thirty, so we'll have to be there fifteen minutes earlier. We leave at five fifty." Matteo says, changing the subject.

"What do we have to be there fifteen minutes early for?" Isabella argues.

I leave them to their childish bickering so I can go upstairs and have a cigarette with my coffee, then go take a quick bath. It's already half past three and two hours to take a bath and get dressed is cutting it really close.

I knock on Aurora's door, asking her if she'd let me raid her closet so I can have something to wear in Ibiza. She agrees, and I choose a black dress with a low cut in the front held together by a small bow.

"No, you can't wear your sneakers with this dress. Here." she says as soon as she sees my intention to leave. She holds out a pair of black Valentino platform sandals.

"I don't really like heels."

Aurora looks outraged. "Yes you do. You just don't know it yet."

I can't say no to her. Her childlike personality reminds me of Adrik's, and I feel like she's dear to me for some reason.

"Do you know my brother?" I ask her as I take the sandals from her.

Her face changes. I see it change from amusement to horror. She knows him.

"What? Who?"

I could swear I've seen them talk at least once before in my life.

"Adrik Levin? You go to the same school. He just graduated."

"Yes, I- I've seen him around."

She's acting weird.

Maybe she's the secret girlfriend

The thought seems ridiculous as soon as I think about it.

"You remind me of him." I tell her and smile.

She smiles back, but it doesn't reach her eyes.

I spend an hour in the bath before I force myself out of it. The more I think about Aurora and Adrik, the more it makes sense. Adrik's pictures were from Capo d'Orlando, which is a couple of hours away from Aurora. The girl in the pictures was also blonde, dressed fashionably like Aurora. I should've asked her if she has a boyfriend. Adrik would lose his mind if he found out.

By the time I get around to doing my makeup, my mind is already made up. I'm 99% sure they're dating, and it seems such a surreal thing to me that I don't know what I should even do with the information.

The clock on my phone shows 5:30pm by the time I'm done with everything. I tie some of my hair back with a bow clip, then throw all my belongings in the YSL bag Aurora gave me yesterday.

There's a knock on my door and I yell 'come in', because I'm on my fourth try of making my winged eyeliner be identical on both sides.

Matteo appears in the mirror, standing by the door. I see his eyes checking me out for a split of a second before we make eye contact in the mirror.

"Are you ready?"

"Five minutes."

He groans, throwing his hands up in defeat, and turns towards the door to my room. "Why can no woman in this house ever be ready on time?!" He yells into the hallway.

I hear Aurora's voice ringing out in the hallway, coming from her room. "Go smoke a joint or something to relax, Matteo!"

I laugh but then I catch Matteo's look in the mirror, so I stop.

"We're going to be there on time, why are you so stressed?"

Matteo turns around and leaves, so I focus on my eyeliner.

Ten minutes later I'm downstairs, putting on a black jacket that Aurora gave me. Matteo is standing by the door, holding a bottle of wine and checking his wristwatch every ten seconds. He's wearing a pair of loose jeans and a black t-shirt, looking more stressed than usual. It's like he's a different person than he was yesterday. Somehow, I've been feeling like a different person too.

Something happened.

"Are you okay?" I ask him.

He stops looking at his watch to turn his head up at me. He looks surprised that I asked that question.

"Yes, why?"

"You're acting weird."

"I don't like being late." He lies, running a hand through his hair.

"That's a lie."

"Aurora? Che diavolo are you doing?!" He yells up the stairs.

Aurora appears on the stairs, smiling at her phone as she slowly descends. "Chill, Matteo."

"Don't tell me to chill. You're being rude, everyone is waiting for you outside."

Aurora isn't even listening to him, but she's completely dressed and ready to go. Matteo takes the phone out of her hand and holds it above her head where she can't reach.

"Give it back, Matteo!"

"What, you're talking to the secret boyfriend again?"

Aurora's face flushes and she looks at me with a scared expression on her face. That's when I know for sure that my theory is right. Somehow, out of all the possible universes and realities, my brother managed to land Aurora Giudice. Maybe I judged them both too quickly. Him being too...Adrik for Aurora, and Aurora being too high maintenance for Adrik.

It's none of my business.

But I feel like I need to talk to someone about it. Matteo obviously knows *something*, but Aurora's scared of him finding out. Why?

"I'll scream." She warns him, but Matteo doesn't give a fuck as he opens the door and points towards the driveway. There's a black van parked by the fountain, with a guy waiting to open the door for us.

"Go and I'll give you your phone in the car."

Aurora spits something at him in Italian then crosses her arms, marching outside.

Matteo and I exchange looks, and I'm not sure what to even think. His sister is dating my brother, and for some reason they feel the need to keep it secret. That's why I can't let it go. *Why the need to keep it a secret?*

Marco and the Barone kids are already inside, with Vinnie and Pia being in extra good moods because it's their birthday. Aurora gets her phone back and doesn't say anything for the rest of the way to the airport. I don't either.

***

The flight leaves two minutes earlier than scheduled, which Isabella doesn't let him forget until we land in Ibiza. The whole vibe instantly changes, and the air is thick with anticipation.

There's a bus waiting for us so we get inside, but it doesn't leave the airstrip. Four more planes land in a span of thirty minutes, and soon enough more people join us on the bus. Raisa and Aleksi, together with Isaac and one of his friends, coming from Russia. Ariana and two guys I've never seen before coming from Milano, and the last plane apparently comes from New York. At last, Allison and three more people I've seen at the parties in the city climb onboard.

"No Sofia?" Vinnie asks, looking disappointed.

Isabella and I exchange looks, having chosen to sit together. Raisa sits down across from me in the seat next to Matteo. Her face changed as soon as she saw Allison, and she apparently decided to change her seat and leave Aleksi sitting by himself in front of us.

"Thank God we're here." She smiles, and I can see Matteo throwing me an annoyed look over her shoulder.

When Raisa turns to greet him, I put my hand into a fist and show it to him, as if telling him to be nice. He rolls his eyes and looks at her face, trying to pay attention to what she's saying. He's a grown man, and no one is forcing him to do anything he doesn't want to.

"How old is Matteo?" I ask Isabella. The bus has just left the airstrip and is on the way to the port.

"Twenty."

"When does he turn twenty-one?"

"In July. Why?"

I shrug. "I was just wondering."

She eyes me curiously but doesn't comment on it.

I want to tell her about my theory, about how my brother might (100%) be dating Matteo's little sister. I also want to tell her about what the fortune teller said, and how she was very cryptic at the end. I want to tell her about the dream I had last night that I can barely remember anymore after a day of trying to forget it. I succeeded, except for the part where I was holding a gun to Matteo's chest and he grabbed my hand, before passionately kissing me with force.

We're on our way to a private yacht to celebrate Vinnie and Pia's birthdays, not a joint therapy session. It'll have to wait. Who knows, maybe by then it wouldn't matter anymore. Maybe I'll even completely forget the way his lips felt on mine. Definitely.

Chapter 21

Matteo

Palermo, Sicily – May 29ᵗʰ, 2020

2pm

His father calls him as he's smoking a joint on his balcony, staring out at the sea with nothing on his mind. He remembers waking up two times before actually getting out of bed.

First time, it was Valentina saying his name that brought him back to reality. He was still semi-unconscious when he told her something he cannot remember now.

The second time, it was a pair of flip flops slapping against the ground that had stirred him awake. He couldn't fall asleep after that, so he got out of bed.

Isabella's idea of the girls going to see a psychic put him in a better mood. Their childlike excitement made him happy inside, like he was surrounded by people he could trust. That's why he allowed himself to make the occasional snarky remark. He decided that the two of them could hold their own against him.

The moment his father calls though, his good mood shatters. It's on their own private App, which means it's going to be a discussion that is not meant for anyone else's ears.

He places the joint in one of the cigarette-holders of the ashtray and swipes his finger across the screen.

"Hello?"

"I just got off the phone with the chief of police." He says, sounding tense.

A feeling settles in Matteo's stomach and doesn't leave.

"And?"

"I tell you to stay at home while the world is on lockdown, and you're going out swimming in a monumental fountain, drunk?"

He isn't yelling, but his voice is loud and stern. Matteo doesn't know what to say, so he says nothing.

"Say something, Matteo!"

"What do you want me to say? You're telling me to stay locked up in my room while people are dying outside, but you yourself don't do as you preach."

His father huffs on the other end, and Matteo hears him slam his fist on the desk in his office.

"Listen to me, Matteo Lorenzo Giudice. My father's name, my name, are your own name as well. Lorenzo Giudice did not build an empire and then die in vain protecting it for you to be swimming around in fountains with Russian whores."

The feeling in Matteo's stomach expands to his chest, his legs, turning into anger. His heart is beating faster now, and the waves below seem to be more aggressive.

"Nothing happened, they let us go. Why are you making a big deal out of nothing?"

"They let you go because they read your second and third name, not your first."

"What's your point?" Matteo asks, getting impatient. He knows what's coming, but he wants it done already. He knows he's about to be reminded of not doing enough.

"You haven't earned your place in the company that benefits from the privileges you abuse."

Matteo is way too high to register the gravity of his words. He's still angry about the 'Russian whore' comment. Like he hasn't noticed how his father turns his phone upside down sometimes when they're having dinner, or how he would smile then compose himself after catching himself falter?

But Matteo expected him to have affairs, it's not like they were uncommon, especially in their society. There was the Paulo Barone scandal, when he cheated on Vinnie's mom. Then there were Isabella's parents, who are now getting divorced after years of her father having numerous affairs.

Matteo has never heard his parents arguing about anything other than how absent his father was. No one ever implied there might be a mistress. If his mother noticed, she never said anything.

But Matteo noticed. Yet it wasn't a card he was ready to use against his father.

Sometimes it's better to be underestimated.

It's Valentina's voice that says this, so he coughs and comes back to the conversation.

"And what do you want me to do? Earn my place in the company? Is that what you're saying?"

His father would never call him just to scold him. He knows that time is the most priceless resource there is. Everyone has the same amount of it per day. Those with infinite amounts of money can buy it from those who can't afford to do the same.

"If you want to be respected by the police, you're going to have to do a lot more than collect shipments and drink at the club."

What he's trying to say is; if Matteo wanted to be more respected by his father and have his independence, he would have to get his hands dirty.

He'd hoped that driving around with a body in the trunk would be enough.

"Do you want me to kill someone? Is that it?"

"I never said that."

The feeling retreats to his stomach, and Matteo suddenly understands. His father thinks it's time for him to do the initiation ritual.

"You want me to do the initiation ritual."

"I want you to do whatever you want to do."

Matteo has always known, deep down, that this day would come. He just didn't expect it to be today. Their father explained the rules to him and Marco about five years ago, when they discovered the drug den in their garden.

He knew that all men born into the Giudice family didn't have to swear loyalty to a family they belonged to by blood. It was a given; loyalty was implied. That's how they were raised, that no matter what, family comes before everything else.

He doesn't want to do it because he doesn't want everything that comes with it: responsibility, guns, raids, corruption, blood, *death*. It's not because he thinks he can't handle it – if there's anyone who would be able to keep the family business going for generations, it's Matteo.

Marco is too soft sometimes. He prefers reading and playing video games. He's also too close to Eddie to not talk about what goes on in their family.

Aurora is out of the question. Not because she's a woman, but because she would be too overwhelmed by everything and is not a born leader.

Vinnie and Eddie would be second to Matteo, maybe. Paulo raised them to be athletic, they were both captains and excelled in their fields: Eddie on the ice rink, Vinnie on the football field. But they're too hot-headed, too physical, and less practical.

Matteo is a balance of both. His father knows it, and Matteo knows it too. He's smart but can also be barbaric if need be. He would never back down from a fight.

He knew it the moment he was dismissed from being a captain on their football team in middle school. He started out when he was little, when his father urged him to take up any sport, and like most Italian boys who were still raving about having won the world cup in 2006, he chose football.

A few years later at just thirteen years old, he was already playing at university level. A scout came from Torino, asking if he would be interested to play for the Juventus junior team. Matteo said yes, the scout said he'll be visiting him the next day, and Matteo excitedly told his father that same evening. But the scout never came.

His father consoled him, then urged him to take up another sport. When Matteo found out it had been his father's doing, he took up boxing. It was a good way to get out all the anger he had buried inside himself, directed towards his father.

Four years later, after having defeated everyone there was to defeat in any championship his coach could find, he quit. His father has never urged him to pick up a sport since then.

Matteo proved what needed to be proven to get him off his back. All that's left now is graduating from university. And apparently, being initiated into the Family.

"Matteo?"

He comes back to reality. His soul knows what the only choice is. He's always known his destiny, maybe even before he was born.

"I will do it." He hears a sharp intake of breath on the other end. His father is surprised. "But not this weekend. I'm going to Ibiza today."

"I will talk to you on Sunday. Have your guests leave by then."

Matteo feels angry again. His father hasn't said anything about Ibiza, because he knows. He knows everything, sees everything, always. And the only way to stop that from becoming his entire life is by *becoming* his father.

There's a bittersweet taste on his tongue, and as if his father could hear his thoughts, he speaks again.

"And before you ask yourself how I know you're going to Ibiza, think about who you called to help you. And ask yourself, who did he ask for the yacht, and the bus, and to keep police away? Those people that helped Marcus? Ask yourself who they work for. In our world, Matteo, you're merely an Associate."

An Associate - the lowest of the low.

In the organization's hierarchy, there were five levels of authority. There is his father, who is the head of everything and everyone. The king. His right-hand man, his Consigliere, was the only one with the authority to speak on his behalf. The second level is the underboss, who leads the Caporegimes, the captains. The fourth level under the captains are the soldiers, who usually carry out the day-to-day to-do list of the organization.

The lowest level are the associates, who are helpers because they asked for help or are getting paid for some type of work. That's what Matteo is. Running his club and collecting shipments is all he really does, and he's fine with it.

"I'll see you on Sunday at noon. Get some rest before we see each other."

In other words, don't do too many drugs because this is important.

The line goes dead.

Matteo stares out at the sea, wishing to forget the conversation that just took place. The sun is dimmer now, and there are clouds in the sky, announcing possible rain.

They carry a message.

There's no going back now.

***

Friday, 3:40pm

Isabella and Valentina have been gone for over three hours now, and Matteo has been driving himself insane thinking about the initiation ritual. He just wants a distraction, and this weekend is perfect for that. He wants to get the airport, get to Ibiza, get on that yacht, and get wasted. So wasted he parties through the whole day into Sunday, where he'll sleep for a few hours before his father will wake him up.

It feels as if Sunday is the day his old life ends and a new one starts.

He texts Isabella, tries calling her even, but she doesn't answer. He thinks about it for a minute, then texts Valentina as well.

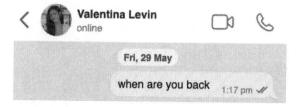

His mind drifts off, wondering what a psychic might tell him if he ever went to one, just out of curiosity.

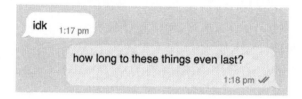

There's a knock on the door in his room. It's so faint he barely hears it.

"Come in!" He yells into the room. He sees Marco enter, still wearing his pyjama bottoms.

The phone buzzes in his hand, getting his attention.

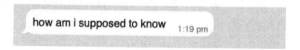

By the time the girls are back it's past four and Matteo has to make himself a coffee to stay awake. It's hot and he just ate two portions of Carbonara made by Romeo. As soon as the girls' voices echo down the hall, Romeo says goodbye for the day and leaves.

He argues with Isabella for a few minutes, then asks Valentina about her future. She looks uncomfortable as she makes a joke about the answer.

Two hours later, after having taken a shower and smoked the remains of the joint, Matteo is ready and impatient.

He checks on Aurora first, who is only half dressed and texting on her phone. There's a smile on her face, which makes Matteo angry for some reason.

"Can you please get dressed so we can leave? You can be on your phone later."

"I already did my makeup; I just have to get dressed."

"A van is already picking up the Barone family. Be downstairs in ten."

She waves him off and annoys him even more, because she knows it pisses him off when she pretends not to care.

He goes to find Valentina next, hoping she's ready by now. He knocks on the door and opens it after she yells 'come in'. She's in the bathroom, already dressed and bent over the counter, face close to the mirror. She's wearing a black dress and matching heels, and Matteo's eyes dart over the back of her legs for a second. When he looks up, she's already looking at him with a look that tells him she saw him checking her out.

"Are you ready?"

"Five minutes."

Matteo throws his arms up, groaning. She's not ready either.

"Why can no woman in this house ever be ready on time?" He asks, voice loud and directed at the hallway so Aurora can hear him too.

"Take a chill pill, Matteo!" Comes her response.

Valentina laughs at that, her lips turning into a thin line when she sees that Matteo doesn't find it funny.

"We're going to be there on time, why are you so stressed?"

Her eyes are warm in the mirror, looking back at him with genuine kindness. She doesn't annoy him like Aurora does, because she's not doing it to spite him.

He turns around and leaves. Maybe if he's already by the door, everyone will just magically move faster. He just can't wait to get to the open bar on the yacht and drink his body weight in Vodka Red Bulls. Get the Initiation out of his mind.

Matteo goes down to the wine cellar and grabs a bottle, which he opens in the kitchen. He pours himself a glass. He hears a pair of heels upstairs heading for the staircase, so he downs the glass and goes to find a reusable cork in the drawers.

By the time Valentina's downstairs, he's already at the door, checking his watch for the tenth time.

"Are you okay?"

His heart starts beating faster. He feels exposed, like she knows the reason he's acting weird. Adrenaline rushes through his body.

She noticed.

Out of all the people who have been around him today, she's the one who noticed. Isabella, Marco, Romeo, Aurora, all of whom have known him since he was a child, didn't think he was acting strange. Valentina did.

"Yes, why?" He asks, composing himself after a few seconds of surprise.

"You're acting weird."

"I don't like being late." He says and runs a hand through his hair. There's a lot of nervous energy building up in his body.

She frowns, pursing her lips. "That's a lie."

"Aurora? Che diavolo are you doing?!" Matteo yells up the stairs, tearing his eyes away from Valentina.

Aurora appears on the stairs, still on her phone. "Chill, Matteo."

"Don't tell me to chill. You're being rude, everyone is waiting for you outside."

She doesn't even look like she cares what he's saying, so Matteo takes the phone out of her hand and holds it above her head.

"Give it back, Matteo!" She says, grabbing the air under the phone.

Matteo smirks, feeling a strange enjoyment in tormenting his sister a little bit more. She always does it to him first, and there's a part of Matteo that loves vengeance.

"What, you're talking to the secret boyfriend again?" He asks, knowing very well she'll be horrified.

Aurora's face flushes and she looks at Valentina for a moment, then back at Matteo.

"I'll scream." She threatens. He stops himself from laughing and goes over to the door, having had enough.

He opens it with such force it nearly slams into the wall. "Go and I'll give you your phone in the car."

"You're just like that!" Aurora says before she walks away.

She knows that comparing him to their father is one of the worst things she could say to him. If she hadn't used it so often, it might have had an effect on him now.

Matteo and Valentina look at each other before she grabs her bag and steps out first.

The ride to the airport is silent, and he knows they must wait for a few more people from the Ibiza group chat to land before they can depart.

He expects to see Allison climb on board with a few of Pia's friends from New York, and he also sees it coming when Raisa sits down in the empty seat next to him.

It's Vinnie's fault, really. He's the one who chose to sit in the row in front of him, hoping that Sofia might show up with Allison.

"Have you seen Sofia?" Vinnie asks Allison, who sits down next to him.

She shrugs, eyeing Matteo and Raisa.

Maybe having Raisa here would solve the Allison problem, Matteo thinks. Maybe she'll finally leave him alone willingly, decide to not be there for him anymore. Maybe then Matteo would be able to completely move on.

"I haven't talked to her since we went back home. From what I heard from her mother, she got really sick at the beginning."

"Is she okay now?" Vinnie asks, clearly worried.

"Honestly? I don't know. Her phone is off, and she hasn't been online since March."

"Haven't you talked to her mother?"

"No, I haven't. There's been a lockdown in New York too, I didn't think about her that much." Allison says in an accusatory tone. She's accusing Vinnie of accusing her of being a bad friend, maybe.

"Don't you think it's weird? What if something happened to her?"

"Like she died because she got sick?" Allison asks, and then looks back at Matteo.

He can tell by the look in her eyes that she is in fact worried about her friend. The feeling comes back in his stomach and doesn't leave until they land in Ibiza.

The yacht Marcus had arranged for them is way better than expected. It waits for them in Port Eivissa, with three different lounging areas that open right over the water. It has four different levels, five bedrooms, seven bathrooms, and enough space to host the twenty people that would be onboard, including the staff. Some of the guests are Pia's friends, some of them are Vinnie's friends, and Matteo knows them all (by face, not by name).

By the time he's up the steps and into the open bar area looking out into the sea, he's ready to drink. Aleksi is by his side with a reassuring smile, telling him without words that he has what Matteo wants.

I love this guy.

Matteo sees Ariana Milanesi looking at him with a smile on her face as she talks to Pia and Raisa, probably about her semester abroad in Amsterdam. Raisa is looking at him too, and so is Pia. Okay, they were talking about him then. Aleksi is pouring him a drink, and Matteo feels like he can trust him despite being Raisa's brother.

"Let's get drunk." He tells Aleksi, who smirks.

After all, these are the last thirty-six hours of his life where he can get away with being a careless teenager. Everything that comes after Sunday is a big unknown.

Chapter 22

Matteo

Saturday 1:30am

Matteo's next three hours are filled with Vodka Red Bulls, lines of cocaine done in the bathroom, and trying to escape both Raisa and Allison at the same time. Vinnie is nowhere to be seen, still upset about Sofia (maybe), and Isabella and Valentina have been talking on one of the lounge chairs since they've arrived.

Eventually, after they sing happy birthday at midnight and cut the cake, Raisa finds him alone smoking a cigarette on the deck. She leans against the railing and smiles up at him, her eyes filled with lust.

He feels like he needs to say something to fill the silence. He can't seem to remember what they ever had to talk about. Luckily, she takes over.

"I haven't seen you all night."

Matteo nods, feigning interest. "I've been around."

Over her shoulder, he can see Allison approaching them, and has no idea whether he should be relieved or panicking.

"I've been looking all over for you!" She tells him, bluntly ignoring Raisa. It speaks for Allison's superiority complex, which is one of the reasons Matteo broke up with her.

"What do you want?"

Both women seem surprised by his rude tone. His pulse is racing and he's looking for a way out. He can't handle this right now, not in this state.

They're sailing along a shoreline, which means they're next to Spain. Matteo knows they're on their way to Barcelona. The boat trip should last about 9 hours, and it should be arriving around 6am. From there, they would be taken to the airport and back to their countries at 9.

"Who wants to play a drinking game?" Isabella shouts from the lower deck.

A few shouts of approval come from all around the yacht, and fifteen minutes later everyone is down on the lower deck.

Matteo notices that Aurora is gone, as well as most of the people who came a long way and didn't do any drugs. They pull up some chairs in a circle and sit down, a table full of cups, bottles and ashtrays between them.

There's, Matteo, with Vinnie and Aleksi to his right. Pia and the guy she's been hooking up with are next to Aleksi, followed by Isaac, who's friends with the guy. Next to Isaac and right across from Matteo sits Valentina, legs crossed as she talks to Isabella.

How can they still find something to talk about?

He can spend hours just being in the same room with Vinnie without acknowledging each other.

Next to Isabella are Marco and Eddie, laughing at something only they could understand. Finally, next to Eddie are Ariana, Allison, and Raisa, with Raisa conveniently sitting next to him.

"There's this game called Picolo, it's an App on my phone. I put the names in, and it tells us what to do. I'll read and you just have to do as I say." Isabella explains.

Matteo is too drunk to understand any rules for any game, so being told what to do and when to drink is convenient.

They play the game for a few rounds, and people are entertained. The game gives them challenges such as 'the last one to stand up has to down their drink' or 'those who don't have blonde hair take a shot', but it gets boring pretty fast. Soon enough, people are asking for more interesting challenges.

Isabella buys the extension.

"Okay, there are different levels. The fourth one is a dirty one, so I'll leave that out." She half-jokes. Nobody complains, so she starts a different level of the game.

These are more daring, and it gets everyone's attention.

"Isabella." She reads her name out loud. "Who do you think gets more hammered at parties? Vinnie or Matteo?"

Everyone laughs as Isabella looks between the two of them. Obviously, she picks Matteo. He must drink two times. He can't argue though; he feels drunk and high at the same time, and he's convinced Vinnie is more sober than he is.

Matteo is sweating a little after dancing for a few hours, but he's feeling good now. The moon is high up in the clear sky and the cold breeze seems to sober him up.

"Vinnie, give out a drink for as many guys there are in the group."

There are six guys and six girls, so Vinnie tells the girls to drink.

Matteo looks around the room. As Isabella keeps reading the next challenges, he entertains himself in his head by pairing up everyone. He starts with Valentina and Isaac. Then Pia with her friend, Jared? Jason? Anyway. He doesn't even think about him and Raisa as he jumps to Isabella. Isabella with who? Maybe Vinnie? No way. He loses his track of thought by the time he tries pairing Raisa with anyone. He also realizes that there are seven boys, not six.

"Matteo?"

Everyone is looking at him, leaning back in his chair.

"You have to kiss the youngest player here."

Matteo coughs and thinks it's going to be Aurora, but then remembers she's not here.

"Who's younger than me?" he asks.

"When are you born?" Raisa asks, even though they both know she's in a year below him in school.

"July." He answers. "1999."

"You're a Cancer?" She asks, faking surprise.

Valentina chimes in. "You don't act like one."

All the girls Matteo has met who knew his birth date have told him the same thing. That he's not like a Cancer at all. When he asked them what that even means, they would explain: 'a romantic man', 'easily jealous and protective', 'sensitive'. And the worst one? 'Affectionate'. They always blamed him for not being affectionate enough.

"So, who's younger than him?" Isabella asks, eyes looking back down to her screen. She's getting impatient. So is Matteo.

"I'm younger." Raisa concludes. "I'm in June 2000."

"Anyone else?" Isabella asks.

"I'm July 22nd." Valentina answers.

Suddenly, the air around Matteo feels strained, like there's not enough oxygen for everyone. Their eyes meet and Valentina chews on her bottom lip, eyes wide as she looks through him again.

What is she thinking about when she's not here?

"We're close enough." Raisa nervously chuckles and before Matteo can ask what she means, his face is grabbed by a pair of sweaty hands. His eyes tear away from Valentina as his lips touch Raisa's. The kiss doesn't last long, but he pulls away too late anyway.

His eyes look for her again, book she's looking down at her drink now.

"I'm in April 2001, so you should've kissed me you idiot!" Marco yells from his seat, and everybody laughs, easing the tension.

"Alright, this one's good." Isabella says, getting everyone to quiet down. "We must go clockwise, saying one thing we have never done. Those who have done it have to drink. Matteo starts."

Matteo's confused for a second.

"It's Never Have I Ever." Ariana explains, seeing his face.

"I know that game, okay." He says, sitting up straight in his chair. "Never have I ever..."

His eyes trail off from the ground as he thinks of something he's never done. His mind is suddenly blank. He's always done everything he's ever wanted to do. Playing this game with these people will get them all drunk.

Matteo smirks. That's the point.

"Never have I ever had to make coffee for myself in someone else's house." He says, eyes flickering to Valentina.

She looks at him and scrunches her nose in disapproval, but her eyes are playful. She's the only one who drinks, flipping him off in the process.

"My turn." Raisa says, a little bit too eager. "Never have I ever been arrested."

The feeling in Matteo's stomach returns. It had disappeared the moment he did the first line with Aleksi in the bathroom.

Marco, Vinnie, Eddie, Isaac, and himself drink.

"When have you been arrested?" Valentina asks Isaac.

"I got into a fight when I was in Moscow." Is all Isaac says. Valentina doesn't press any further, as expected. Matteo can't help but think that Raisa would've wanted to know more. After all, she's the one who started the whole conversation.

"What happened?" Raisa asks, leaning over Matteo to get closer to Isaac.

Matteo can't help but smile. He's always right about people.

"Never have I ever had sex with someone in this game." Allison says, taking the attention away from Raisa.

Matteo, Raisa, Valentina, Isaac, Pia and her friend all drink. Matteo sees Eddie and Marco reaching for the cups but stopping. They fidget in their seats, looking around.

"I guess I'm not the only one then." Allison spits, getting his attention.

Raisa turns to look at her, and Matteo can't see the face she's making.

"Never have I ever had a dream about someone here." Ariana says, trying to ease the tension between the girls.

Valentina and Matteo make eye contact, and Matteo playfully squints at her. She averts her eyes and looks back at her lap. It's the first sign of insecurity she's ever shown in front of him. He leans forward, watching her still looking down. Her hands are playing with the glass, but she doesn't drink from it.

Who's acting weird now?

As if she had heard him, she looks up at him, eyes strange.

Allison, Raisa, and Vinnie drink, then it's Marco's turn.

"Never have I ever had sex in the sea."

Some people laugh, and everybody drinks.

"You've never done it?" Isabella asks Valentina, shocked. Valentina's drink is still resting in her lap, her fingers playing with the rim of the glass.

"No. Is it even enjoyable with all the water?"

Her back is straight again, and she doesn't look insecure anymore. Maybe Matteo's mind imagined it.

"The water lessens the feeling, yes." Matteo answers her.

She doesn't look at him to acknowledge his answer. She doesn't have to because Isabella is quick to take her turn.

"Never have I ever jumped in a fountain." Isabella shouts, laughing.

Matteo meets Valentina's eyes again, and she's changed. A small smile plays on her lips and her eyes are alive, daring, as if she knows he had noticed her moment of weakness.

He takes the cup up to his lips, and she does too, before looking away. He lets out a breath he didn't know he was holding and looks at Raisa. She has placed a hand on his leg, pursing her lips, asking for a kiss.

Matteo feels bad embarrassing her in front of everyone by not kissing her, but he also knows he won't kiss her out of pity. He hates everything about this.

"Never have I ever felt infinite." Valentina's voice comes from his right.

Matteo turns his head, and he's back in the fountain, leaning back against his palms, looking up at the sky.

He takes the cup up to his lips, and she does too, eyes meeting once again. This time, neither of them break eye contact.

The feeling in his stomach seems to have spread through his entire body, amplified by the dopamine in his brain. It doesn't feel *bad* anymore, like something's about to happen.

It feels like adrenaline. It feels like cocaine should feel.

He doesn't see who drinks, he also doesn't see if anyone noticed their...whatever it was.

"Never have I ever gotten a tattoo." Isaac says.

Matteo and his brother, as well as Vinnie, Eddie, and Valentina, drink.

He remembers the tattoo he saw on Valentina's ankle, as well as the one on her back. Matteo had never asked about them, but he suddenly feels the urge to know what they mean. He's sure they each must have a meaning.

"Never have I ever been in love." Pia's hookup says.

Allison, Raisa, and Isabella drink. Matteo debates for a second but doesn't end up drinking. Whatever that was with Allison, it wasn't love. It was something else. Comfort? Lust? Chemistry? He doesn't know.

Allison stands up from her seat and throws her drink in his direction. Everybody startles when Matteo catches the glass with his hand, saving his own head from being hit by a glass.

She doesn't say anything else as she marches up the stairs towards the bedrooms.

"What a drama queen." Isabella says, and Raisa agrees.

"Never have I ever cheated on someone." Pia says.

"Allison should've drunk." Vinnie adds and those who know their history laugh. She would always accuse Matteo of cheating on her, but in the end, it was her who cheated on him.

No one drinks, so it's Aleksi's turn.

"Never have I ever stolen money from my parents."

Everyone drinks. Everyone but Matteo and Valentina. Isabella notices this.

"Wait, you two never stolen money from your parents' wallets? Not even a coin!?"

They both shake their heads.

Matteo would never even think about stealing from his father. He would notice, and if he didn't, Matteo wouldn't be able to stand the guilt. It's just not something he would do. Stealing is not something he wants to be a part of. His mind goes to the dark place of initiation rituals and gang wars, so he downs his drink.

"For some reason, I just can't steal from my dad." Valentina says, and the world seems to stop for a moment.

Then he feels the drink he had just downed in his stomach not agreeing with his decision, so he stands up.

"Let's do a line." He says to everyone.

"It's my turn still." Vinnie objects, but he's already taking his baggie out, ready to lay out some lines for everyone.

"Go ahead, then." Matteo urges him, not sitting down. "Someone turn the music up!"

"Never have I ever wanted to do something I might regret while drunk." Vinnie says, reaching for a plate.

Matteo looks at Valentina for a second, before turning to Isabella. He catches her looking at Vinnie with a face full of regret, and the feeling returns to what it was.

It's not a bad feeling, it's not nerves. What is it?

It's just...*knowing*.

Instinct.

Vinnie racks up a plate full of white lines, enough for everyone to have seconds. It gets passed around, and Isabella continues the game, but people slowly start losing interest.

Matteo's not sure when it happens, but at some point, he reaches his peak. He passes that threshold, where the alcohol and drugs don't affect him anymore. He could drink his body weight in alcohol right now, and he would still feel sober. Everything is...great.

The last thing he remembers feeling real is watching the sun come up on the horizon as they sailed closer and closer to Barcelona.

***

Sunday, 9:30am

The first thing he sees when he wakes up are the open balcony doors. There's a breeze coming through from outside, making the curtains dance. His mind is cloudy, and then he slowly realizes it's Sunday, and that he's not on a yacht anymore.

That can't be.

He's sweating and feels completely empty inside for some reason, but he's not hungry. He looks out the window to the sea, and it all comes back.

It's as if a gate has been opened, and all the memories from what seems like a dream come crashing down on him.

Matteo remembers watching the sun come up over the horizon with Vinnie and Isabella, the last ones standing. Raisa had tried to stay awake but denied when he had offered her a line. Eventually, after seeing that Matteo wasn't going to invite her to bed, she went to sleep with Ariana. The rest of them also eventually went to sleep, saying they had to be up in time for the plane at 9.

He turned around and saw Valentina looking at the city they were slowly approaching. His impulse was to go over to her, so he did.

As if she heard him coming, she turned around. Matteo remembers her right cheek glowing in the sun. How her brown eyes reflected the sunshine as they followed him moving closer.

"What are you doing?" He asked, placing his hands on the railing. He looked out at the tall buildings of Barcelona in the distance, feeling small.

"Thinking." Valentina answered.

"About?"

"About the 'how to make life exciting' theory."

They looked at each other. Her pupils were huge, and she was rambling but smiling, eyes wide.

"Did you come to any conclusions?" He asked.

"Yes. It's basically doing something you have never done before every day. It's the game we just played. How could life be boring then?"

The light in her eyes showed hope, faith. They showed the child within her that he only ever saw in Aurora anymore.

"Maybe you're right."

They stood there in silence, and Matteo remembers feeling comfortable with her without having to talk.

The ship docked and eventually the engine stopped too.

"Never have I ever jumped overboard fully clothed." She said out of nowhere.

Matteo remembers the cold water against his skin after he jumped overboard, laughing as he did so. Valentina looked at him incredulously after he got back on the deck, dripping wet but proud of himself. He doesn't remember when Vinnie and Isabella disappeared.

"Never have I ever done a line on the highest deck of a yacht." Matteo said, and something in Valentina's eyes changed.

It wasn't hope, nor excitement, not even hesitation. The way her lashes fluttered softly as she breathed his words in, nostrils flaring, told him it was something else. His drunk mind thought, *desire.*

They talked nonsense as they watched the sun come up on the loungers of the top deck. When it was nearly time to go to the airport, Valentina insisted on getting something to eat – the only person Matteo has ever met who was hungry after doing coke. He indulged her and they made their escape before everyone started coming out of their rooms.

They took off running on a side street by the port, laughing because they were the first one to get off the boat.

They had stopped by a street vendor who was illegally operating despite the restrictions, where they got a change of clothes [34]. They changed in an alley, and he remembers her smiling, hair pulled back by a handkerchief, wearing a linen shirt too big for her.

When Raisa asked her if she was coming back to Moscow, Matteo remembers feeling sad. But then Valentina explained that all her stuff was back in Palermo, so she would be leaving on Sunday.

That was the moment Matteo had decided not to go to sleep.

When they boarded the jet with the Barone kids, Isabella, and his siblings, the two of them were the only ones who didn't fall asleep within the first five minutes.

"I don't need sleep." Matteo explained after they'd been looking at each other across the aisle without saying anything, just chewing their gums and grinning.

I feel like I'm dreaming anyway, he thought but didn't say out loud.

"Me neither." She had answered, so they both stood up and went over to the bathroom to do another round of lines.

They talked about everything; about Valentina growing up in a post-soviet looking Moscow apartment building before her father's business took off and about Matteo spending his days at the restaurant when he was a kid. He leaves the murder part out, but it was still nice to reminisce with someone about those days.

He remembers the sun setting over the sea as they sat on his balcony, chain-smoking joints and listing things they'd never done. She had started it when they had first sat down with cups of coffee and a joint.

"It seems easy, but I've been trying to think of ten things I've never done before. It's hard."

They spent hours listing things they have never done, things they've done, things they wished they would have done. They talked about their tattoos, and Matteo regrets that he can't remember everything she had told him. He remembers the moon on her ankle, which meant following her intuition, always.

---

[34] because Matteo was dripping wet and Valentina was getting tired of walking around in heels and a dress.

When it got dark and they had finished what was left, Matteo told her that his father wanted to have guests over tomorrow and they would need the room. He remembers her face falling a little but agreeing to leave before sunrise.

He arranged the plane for her with shaky fingers, then informed her the car would be waiting at four in the morning. There was not enough time to fly her to Moscow and also bring his father back to Palermo.

Valentina changed the subject by talking about them being the same zodiac sign, and they agreed that they didn't consider themselves cancers. They talked about astrology, the stars, the moon, and the sun. They talked until Matteo remembers her standing up and saying goodnight.

He looks at his room. Her laptop, which had been resting on the window seat for the past few days, is gone.

He walks outside with a cigarette between his lips and sits down in his usual spot, facing the sea. Her seat is empty, but her lighter is on the table.

He smokes as he stares out the sea, feeling like he has just shifted realities, yet everything looks the same. The four days he spent with her don't feel real. The last twenty-four hours seem like a parallel universe, something his mind just made up. Something he dreamt of.

Reality comes crashing down on him from all sides, and his brain is struggling to hang on to any trace of dopamine left in his body, to the memories of her.

It all seems fuzzy now.

Being with her felt like a fever dream.

Chapter 23

Valentina

Somewhere on the Balearic Sea, Spain – spring/summer 2020

Saturday 01:15am

The first thing Isabella and I did as soon as we saw the open bar was get two gin and tonics. We sat down on two of the lounge chairs on the lower deck. They were facing the sea we're leaving behind, so we watched the sun setting over the horizon.

We didn't realize how long we had been talking until they announced the cake.

By the time we're at our fourth G&Ts, it's already dark.

"Have you noticed that all the girls here besides the two of us are drooling over Matteo?" She asks, a mean streak in her voice.

"I have, actually."

Gossiping with Isabella is different from doing it with Raisa. With Isabella it feels as if we're discussing something; with Raisa it feels more like talking behind someone's back.

"I bet you fifty right now that as soon as Ariana comes back to Hamilton, she'll be all over him."

"Who? Vinnie or Matteo?"

"Matteo, of course. Why would you say Vinnie?"

"I don't know. I just thought she'd flirted with him before. Wasn't that why Sofia called the police at New Year's?" I ask her, remembering our conversations about their NYE party.

"Yeah, you're right. But I think she's changed her mind the since last time you saw her. Vinnie isn't even interested anyway; he's still crying about Sofia missing his birthday."

"Has she ever missed one before?"

"Not since they were fifteen, no."

"Well, six years with someone is a lot. I think he just needs time to get over her. Her not being here might be the best for everyone."

I look up at the stars that have appeared since we first sat down. I take a deep breath and the salty air tickles my nose.

"I'm tipsy." I let her know, smiling.

She throws me a smirk, but her face falls and becomes serious, looking at something to her right. I turn my head to see Allison approaching us, sporting a very fake smile.

"Have you seen Matteo?" She asks Isabella.

"No, I haven't." Isabella replies with her resting bitch face. Something about the way she's looking at Allison makes me laugh. I bite my lip when Allison throws me a piercing look.

"What's so funny to *you*?" Her tone is aggressive as the completely turns to face me.

"Her face." I explain, not even lying.

Allison looks me up and down before holding her head up and leaving.

"She's mean." I say, unable to hold my laughter in anymore.

"She's frustrated, is what she is."

I look on the upper deck, where Pia and a guy I've never seen before are making out against the railing.

"Do you think Pia is also frustrated?"

"What? Why would she be?"

I shrug. "I don't know. I feel like every time we interact there's a...vibe. Like apathy, towards me."

Isabella frowns for a second, thinking about it. Her features relax as realization crosses her face.

"I know which interactions you mean, from yesterday. But yeah, makes sense."

"What does she have against me?" I ask.

When Matteo had commented on it, I told him that whatever it is, it has nothing to do with me. But when I noticed her throwing me ugly looks from across the plane earlier, I got the feeling that it is in fact personal.

"Well, she has a crush on Matteo."

I'm surprised by her response. I don't even know where to begin; I want to know why Isabella thinks Pia has a crush and what it has to do with me.

"What does it have to do with me?" I decide on asking.

"He's attracted to you. That's why she's in a bad mood every time you're around. She's usually okay."

"What?"

I swallow as I think about my dream. Up until last night I didn't even think of Matteo as someone I'd be subjectively attracted to. I feel as if the thought of seeing him as a guy I'd be attracted to had been pushed back deep into my subconscious the moment he looked at me with superiority a year ago. I'd asked him to hold the plate up for me and he gave me a look that rubbed me the wrong way.

It seems that for the past twenty-four hours, those deep parts of my subconscious are unwillingly pouring into my reality.

"He's attracted to you." Isabella repeats, like it should be obvious.

"He's not."

"Why wouldn't he be? It's no secret that you have those good Russian genes."

I smile. "Okay, but still."

"Honestly? I don't think he knows it either." She says looking towards the second deck, probably searching for him.

"Then why do you say that?"

My mind needs to talk it out so I can put the idea of Attractive Matteo to rest. Not to rest. To death. He's good looking, sure. But so are most of the guys I know.

The only difference is that there's something about Matteo that sets him apart from everyone else in my head. That's why I never even went there in the first place.

There's something alluring about him, a magnetic energy. Everything he does is for his own pleasure, yet there's a certain darkness to him that seems to follow him everywhere he goes. His eyes are warm, genuine, but he always looks like they're hiding something behind them. He's holding something back, there's something he doesn't allow the world to know. Something that scares him, which makes me want to *know*.

"The way he looks at you? I feel like he's always looking at you."

"He's not."

She shrugs. "Maybe not *always*. But often. I saw it earlier when you went to get our drinks. All those girls were talking to him, trying to get his attention. You just walked past, got our drinks, came back. He followed you with his eyes the whole time, and those girls saw it. We can feel when the guy we like doesn't like us back."

There's a sadness in her voice, so focus on her instead of my own inner freak-out session.

"You don't know if Vinnie likes you back though." I try, sipping on my drink.

"If he did, we would've been together by now."

"You like him, and you haven't said anything. Maybe he's doing the same."

"Yes, because I don't want to ruin our friendship."

"Have you ever thought he might think the same?"

She shakes her head like it's a foreign concept to her; a concept she's not willing to consider as being possible.

I give up on trying to be sensitive. "Then get over him."

"What?"

"Get over him. Move on. If you're so sure it's completely impossible, move on. You keep telling me I need to have sex with random guys, but you haven't gone out with *one* guy since I've known you." I bluntly tell her, then finish my drink in one go.

I know she's not a virgin, but she never talks about *any* guys, ever. Ever since she told me about Vinnie, she sometimes talks about him. Other than that, no one.

"I'm just not interested in them. No one's...I don't know. No one interests me."

"Besides him."

"Besides him." She agrees.

"Why haven't you given up then?"

She looks confused, but I don't ask again.

"I don't know."

"Yes you do. And I know it's not because you're delusional."

She sighs, her shoulders slouching. "Sometimes I feel like there's a look in his eyes."

"What look?"

"Like...like he wants it too."

I lick my lips. "Next time just kiss him."

"It's not that simple."

"But what if it is? What if it is that simple? Are you going to wait until you're both eighty and single to kiss, only to realize that you could've done in sooner?"

"No, he- I've grown up with Vinnie and Matteo by my side. I've seen their whole lives – they like making the first step. If they want something they get it. They're not-they don't get shy; they don't get nervous."

"Everybody does. You just have to pay attention."

"I know what you're saying, but I *know* them, sometimes even better than they know themselves. That's how I can tell you Matteo is attracted to you, without him realizing it maybe, and why I know Vinnie isn't in love with me."

"Okay, let's say he's not in love. But he does love you, and I'm sure he's thought about it too."

She doesn't seem convinced.

"Let me put it this way. Is your relationship to Vinnie different to the one with Matteo?"

"Of course it is, I have a major crush on Vinnie. Matteo is just...Matteo."

"That's not what I meant – do they behave differently with you? Do they treat you differently?"

She shrugs. "I don't know, I've never paid attention to how he treats me."

I frown at her. "Maybe you should. I will too. Then we can say for sure if you need to move on or not."

She smiles, agreeing. Then she downs her drink and stands up.

"Who wants to play a drinking gaaaame?" She screams from the top of her lungs out into the sky.

I laugh, completely forgetting about the whole Matteo thing for a moment.

When fragments of my dream start coming back into my conscious mind, I am glad Isabella had the idea. A drinking game is exactly what I need.

***

Everyone joins us on the lower deck around a table we took from inside. Aurora and all of the people (besides Isaac's friend who is also Pia's hook-up) I don't know have gone to sleep.

I watch Pia and the guy kissing as they sit next to each other, and for a second I wish I were her. I miss...I don't know. Liking someone. The act of kissing. I feel like I've been deprived of everything since we were put into lockdown. Not that I was too active before.

I look over at Isaac next to them, engrossed in his phone. He tried making conversation throughout the night, but I mostly spent it talking to Isabella in our own little bubble. I don't know if he's just not interested anymore or if he feels that *I'm* not really interested anymore, but he stopped trying to make an effort. In a weird way, I'm glad. The only reason I miss it is because I liked flirting and feeling wanted.

My eyes catch Matteo's stare, and I wonder if he knows Pia likes him. He must know, he's smart and self-centred.

I smile to myself.

Isabella proceeds to explain the rules of the game, and we play it for a while until people get bored and stop paying attention. I tell Isabella to buy the expansion of the game because the other levels look interesting and it only costs $5.

"Isabella, who do you think gets more hammered at parties? Vinnie or Matteo?"

Everyone laughs as Isabella looks between the two of them. I look over at Matteo, who seems to be having an inner conflict. He's probably trying to convince himself he's not as drunk and high as he actually is.

"Vinnie, give out a drink for as many guys there are in the group."

Even though there are seven boys, he tells us six girls to drink. We happily obey, cheering at the fact that we're women. I find it funny how Allison and Raisa clearly don't like each other yet they sit together pretending to be friends.

"Matteo has to kiss the youngest player here." Isabella reads, her head snapping up in my direction.

A feeling settles in my stomach that I've never felt it before.

Yes I have. It was today in the car; I remember it vividly. I know I'm younger than Raisa, and the thought of kissing Matteo amplifies the feeling every time I think about it.

"Matteo? You must kiss the youngest player here."

Matteo coughs. "Who's younger than me?" He asks.

"When are you born?" Raisa asks, pretending not to know she's younger.

"July seventh. 1999."

"You're a Cancer?"

I smirk. "You don't act like one."

"So, who's younger than him?" Isabella asks.

"I'm younger." Raisa concludes. "I'm in June 2000."

"Anyone else?" Isabella asks, and subtly looks in my direction.

My throat feels dry as I speak up. "I'm July 22nd."

I chew on my bottom lip as I zone out for a moment. I suddenly have trouble breathing and all I can think about is I don't want it to happen.

Not like this, a voice in my head whispers.

I realize that I'm chewing on my lip to the point that it starts to hurt.

"We're close enough."

I look up just in time to see Raisa kissing him. His eyes are open and it's clear he's uncomfortable. The sight of him kissing another girl triggers something in me that I can't describe. I know he sleeps around, I've heard stories, gossip, even details of his sexual drive and preferences from Raisa. But I've never seen him kiss anyone.

It doesn't bother me. On the contrary, it makes my drunk mind wonder what would've happened if it had been me.

How would it feel?

I feel like I already know

"I'm in April 2001, so you should've kissed me you idiot!" Marco yells from his seat, and everybody laughs.

I feel a weight lifted off my shoulders, like the air is breathable again.

"Alright, this one's good. We must go clockwise, saying one thing we have never done. Those who have done it have to drink. Matteo starts."

"It's Never Have I Ever." Ariana explains when Matteo doesn't start.

He sits up in his chair, and I find myself following the way his muscles flex as he does so.

"I know that game, okay. Never have I ever...never have I ever had to make coffee for myself in someone else's house."

I immediately look at him and scrunch my nose to feign disapproval, but I must give it to him- he played fair. I flip him off as I take a large sip of my drink.

"My turn. Never have I ever been arrested." Raisa says, and I nearly face-palm myself.

Marco, Vinnie, Eddie, Matteo, and Isaac drink.

Seeing Isaac drink makes me forget how embarrassed I am for Raisa. "When have you been arrested?" I ask.

"I got into a fight when I was in Moscow."

"What happened?" Raisa asks, leaning over Matteo. She touches his thigh as she does so and he smiles. I look away.

It's Allison's turn. "Never have I ever had sex with someone in this game."

Isaac and I drink, as well as Matteo, Raisa, Pia and her friend. Marco and Eddie look at each other subtly, then around the group. My instinct says they're being shady, but I can't tell why.

"I guess I'm not the only one then."

I look at Allison, whose words come out with hatred, pointed at Matteo. Raisa turns to stare at her and make a disgusted face. But Allison is looking at me, like I'm the one responsible for it.

"Never have I ever had a dream about someone here." Ariana says, trying to ease the tension.

My eyes involuntarily trail to Matteo.

I remember him being close, his breath on my neck as he closed the distance between us. In my flashbacks I forget the gun I was holding to his chest. Remembering it somehow makes me feel at ease because I'm reminded of what it was – just a dream. I've dreamt of boys I know before. I've dreamt of having sex with Vinnie when I was younger. Now I can't remember anything other than it was in a room painted red.

Listen to your dreams. Pandora's voice echoes in my head as if she's right next to me, saying those words.

This was just another dream I had because I haven't spent that much time in one place with a guy in months. With anyone really, since the pandemic has become a thing. It's normal. There is no premonition or message in the dream. Maybe just one: I'm horny and desperate. And right now, drunk.

Something in my reality catches my attention and I realize it's Matteo squinting at me. His eyes tell me he's mocking my concentration as I look straight through him. A rush of panic goes through me.

I avert my eyes, wondering if he can read my exact thoughts. He looks at me like he knows exactly what I'm thinking about. I am very aware of him still watching me as I fumble with the rim of my glass.

Maybe this is what Isabella meant when she said he's always looking at me. But I'm also always looking at him – it's just our *thing*. It's not because we're attracted to each other, but because we can communicate without words.

We've done it in university before, we've done it at parties before – mostly when someone said something stupid or something that we thought was so unfunny it was funny. But it was never for any other reason than satirical amusement. Neither of us have mentioned it – we don't have to.

I'm drunk.

I feel angry at myself for letting him think I'm shying away from one of his confrontations. Just because I had a random dream, and a Romanian witch told me to listen to my dreams? I need to remember who I am.

"Never have I ever had sex in the sea."

Everyone drinks expect for me.

"You've never done it?" Isabella asks me, genuinely shocked.

"No. Is it even enjoyable with all the water?"

"The water lessens the feeling, yes." Matteo answers.

"Never have I ever jumped in a fountain." Isabella shouts, laughing.

Memories of that night come back. My heart fills with joy as I remember being in that fountain with Aurora and Matteo. We make eye contact again, and this time I smile at him. His eyes smile back but I break the eye contact as we both take a sip.

I see Raisa looking at our interaction before turning her head to Matteo and pursing her lips, asking for a kiss.

I feel mortified for her, I don't know why. Maybe it's because I know how Matteo feels about her and how it looks to everyone here. I feel bad about judging her, but then I see the way Matteo looks at her, and he looks as horrified as me.

"Never have I ever felt infinite." I say without even thinking.

Matteo turns his head, and I know he's back in that fountain looking at the stars. I saw the moment he felt infinite, how happy it made him even if only for a few seconds. I also know he considers it a moment of weakness, and I want him to know I know.

I look him in the eye as we both raise our glasses to our mouths. He's already looking at me, but this time I don't break eye contact.

The feeling starts pulsing through my whole body and I suddenly realize why the dream had such a huge impact on me. It's because of how I remember feeling. It was adrenaline, mixed with fear and something else.

Craving. Wanting. I remember wanting him so much, wanting him to kiss me, to touch me, to do *anything*.

"Never have I ever gotten a tattoo." Isaac says, pulling me back to reality.

I drink but don't see who does because I'm too focused on staring at the floor.

"Never have I ever been in love." Pia's hook-up says.

I don't drink, and I don't even have to think about it. I see some people drinking, and then suddenly, Allison stands up.

I see her glass flying in Matteo's direction, drink spilling all over his shirt. My heart stops, thinking it's going to hit him in the head and knock him out, but he catches it so fast it scares me.

There was a certain precision, a certain skill to how aware he was, even in his drunken state. He saw the incoming danger and his body reacted before my mind could even understand.

How?

I watch Allison march away in the direction of the stairs, still shocked by the sudden act of violence from her.

"What a drama queen." Isabella comments, shaking her head.

"Never have I ever cheated on someone." Pia chimes in.

"Allison should've drunk."

A few people laugh but no one drinks, so it's Aleksi's turn.

"Never have I ever stolen money from my parents."

Everyone drinks. Everyone but Matteo and me.

"Wait, you two never stolen money from your parents' wallets? Not even a *coin*?!"

We shake our heads.

"For some reason, I just can't steal from my dad." I say.

My relationship with my dad is a loving one. Sort of. I know he loves me; I know he cares for me, and I know he's a very loving husband and father. He's just not the emotional, affectionate type. He raised us to be respectful, always tell the truth, and most importantly, to always be fair.

The reason I wouldn't steal from him is not because he would scream or ground me or whatever – I've never seen him get upset in his life. Raise his voice? Maybe. But never for no reason.

No, his disappointment and disapproval would be more damaging to my mental health, and no money is worth that feeling I get when I know I've let him down. I'd rather ask him for it directly. He rarely says no anyway.

"Let's do a line." Matteo suddenly says to the group and stands up.

I think it's a great idea, but I stay silent.

"It's my turn, still." Vinnie objects while taking out the drugs.

"Go ahead, then. Someone turn the music up!"

"Never have I ever wanted to do something I might regret while drunk." Vinnie says and reaches for a plate.

Everyone drinks; not because they're paying attention, but because they want to do lines and Allison killed the mood.

Once the second line is down my throat, my dream has been pushed out of my mind and I don't care anymore.

I smile and ask Isabella whether she'd like to get refills.

"As if you don't already know the answer." She answers and gets up from the chair, linking her arm through mine.

***

Saturday 5:25am

I'm watching the buildings of Barcelona moving closer and closer while the sun slowly warms by back. I look at the tall buildings in front of me, suddenly feeling insignificant and at the same time the most powerful being on earth. Like everything is possible in this moment.

I think about my time in Sicily and how it's coming to an end, and I wonder if I'll feel different once I'm back in Moscow. Is there a way to make life exciting while I'm locked up in my room and people are dying outside? How can I not think about how the world seems to be going to shit and at the same looks as if it might be getting better?

I think about the game, and how I mostly drank, but there were some things said that I have never done. Didn't I tell Matteo that life can't be boring if you do something new every day?

I've never been arrested - nor am I planning to. I've never cheated on someone, I've never stolen money from my parents. These aren't things I want to do anyway. But I've never had sex in the sea, and I've never been in love. These are things I *want* to do.

I get the impulse to make a list about things I've never done and start doing them. Then I remember what I had said I'd never done.

Had I ever felt infinite? Did I even drink? I can't remember. I only know Matteo has.

I turn around to look for him, but he's already walking towards me with a childish grin on his face. I get a weird sense of déjà vu, like I've seen this before, like I've known him all my life.

"What are you doing?"

My heart starts beating faster and I'm not sure if it's because of all the cocaine I did with Isabella or if it's something else.

"Thinking." I answer.

"About?"

"About the how to make life exciting theory."

We look at each other, my eyes looking for the meaning in his. His pupils are so big his eyes are nearly black, but there's that light in his eye that's always there.

"Did you come to any conclusions?"

"Yes. It's basically doing something you have never done before, every day. It's the game we just played. How could life be boring then?"

He smiles down at me.

"Maybe you're right."

We stand watching the city in comfortable silence for a while. As the yacht pulls into the port and the engine stops, I look at the water below. I suddenly feel the urge to jump.

The sun is warm on my back and for some reason I feel hotter than I should. "Never have I ever jumped overboard fully clothed." I say.

He just stares at me, confused for a second. He understands. Then, without saying anything else, he takes a few steps back and run towards the railing. He uses his hands to jump over it, and I watch him fall from the first upper deck into the water.

He comes back dripping wet with his hair pushed back out of his face. He's grinning from ear to ear, looking very proud of himself. His face is boyish and he looks three years younger now, out of breath but happy.

"Never have I ever done a line on the highest deck of a yacht."

The moment he says it I feel a switch turn on in my brain.

The feeling returns in my stomach and there's something else to it; it feels earthy, whole, *incredible*, because he said exactly what I *wanted* him to say without realising I wanted it.

I take a deep breath and my vision gets blurry. The feeling spreads through my body, takes over me, and then time stops.

***

Saturday 8:45am, Barcelona

He's telling me about how he tried escaping Raisa and Allison when Isabella suggested the drinking game.

He talks fast when he's on drugs.

I can still follow him though, and he appears to be able to keep up with how much I can talk, not minding it one bit and not looking bored. He looks like he's actually listening, only interrupting when he has something even better to add.

"I want to eat something because even though I'm not hungry, I can feel my stomach growling and I don't want to pass out."

He's leaning back on his palms like he did back in the fountain, legs stretched and open, face pointed to the sky.

"Where from?"

"I don't know? The first thing we can find."

He doesn't put up much of a fight, but he lets me know he's not hungry.

Saturday 9:20am, airport

"You're coming back to Moscow, right?" Raisa asks once everyone is on the runway. There are four different jets with four different destinations parked in front of us, ready to go any time.

I see Matteo looking at me, shirt unbuttoned and hair curling at the sides as it dries under the sun. I feel the sadness in his eyes, reflecting mine right back to me.

"I still have all my stuff in Palermo." I realize and can't help but smile. "I need to pick it up, I'll be back tomorrow."

She makes a face as if to say 'do whatever you want', then heads off towards the rest of the group going to Russia.

As I watch Matteo's back in front of me on the stairs, I decide I don't want to sleep until I'm on a plane back to Russia.

Saturday 10:35, somewhere above Spain

Everyone falls asleep as soon as we board the jet, so I'm left watching a downloaded episode of the Kardashians on Netflix. The gum I'm chewing to death is stale and I can't focus on anything.

I look in Matteo's direction. He's on his phone but he's looking at me.

I instantly understand that he's in the same situation as me. We smile at each other and for a second I feel stupid, but I don't care. I'm not scared of him judging me at all – I have nothing to prove to him, I don't care what he thinks of me. That small amount of power he had over me during the drinking game shook me to my core. It can't happen again.

"I don't need sleep."

Once again, he reads my mind.

"Me neither."

Chapter 24

Valentina

Saturday 1:23pm, Palermo

A black van with tinted windows is waiting for us when we land, and we drive Isabella home first.

"We'll talk." She tells me, then closes the van door with a bit too much force. She doesn't acknowledge anyone else.

"What's up her ass?" Eddie laughs from his seat in the third row next to a sleeping Marco.

"She just hasn't slept." I say, feeling the need to protect her even though I know that can't be it.

Saturday 2:02pm, Matteo's kitchen

"Coffee?" Matteo asks.

I watch Aurora disappear up the stairs, leaving the two of us alone in the cold hallway.

"Sure."

I lean against the island counter as I watch him start the process of making coffee.

"Aren't you hungry?" I ask, realizing he probably hasn't eaten since we had cake at midnight.

Matteo presses the button on the machine after having place the pod in. "Obviously not."

We're wearing matching white XL linen shirts from the street vendor we found by the port. He knew Matteo because he greeted him by name, then offered us a change of clothes when he saw Matteo wet.

I find myself staring at his tattoos. My eyes trail down to his leg, where the two scales of justice are inked into his skin.

Giudice

"What does your name mean?" I ask. "Does it mean justice?"

Matteo looks up at this. "Judge. But it can also mean justice. Why?"

I point to the tattoo on his leg.

"The scales of justice." I say, remembering reading something about it. "Your brother has the same one."

"We got them together when I turned sixteen."

Saturday 3:12pm, Matteo's house

"I still can't get over this view. I'll miss this." I say, not really knowing if I meant just the view or something else.

"It's not like you don't go on vacation. Don't you go to Capo d'Orlando every summer?"

This surprises me, so I stop rolling the joint to look at his face.

He's leaning back against the wall of his house, but his head is turned to watch me at work. I find it harder and harder to look him in the eye. Maybe because there's always this *look* in them that makes me feel as naked as Pandora's did.

Like I can't hide anything because he's really listening and paying attention. I know he notices things normal people don't. I don't know why though.

"I do. How did you know?"

"Vinnie told me."

I don't ask why because it's irrelevant.

"I don't know if we will this year though, I hope so. I don't remember the last time I was excited about coming to Italy for the summer."

"What changed?"

The air feels thicker. Something in me that tells me we both know the answer.

I take the diplomatic approach. Not lying, just avoiding the truth. "I think being in lockdown for two months gave me a new perspective on life."

Hey, if politicians can do it, so can I.

"How so?"

I shrug. "I don't really know. Maybe I know myself better now. Also, I don't know if we will come here this year because of the pandemic. I hope we do."

"Are your parents stressed or what?"

"My mom, a little. My dad doesn't really care. I don't think he does. He's not in Moscow right now. Where are yours?"

I don't even know who Matteo's parents are. Are they even together? The house seems so big, bigger than mine, and yet I haven't seen anyone but the three of them. There's food on the table and everything is extremely clean, yet no one's here.

"My father is on a business trip, and my mother is at our vacation home in Taormina."

"Is it the house from last summer?"

"When you wore the red dress?"

My heartrate picks up. I didn't expect him to remember.

"Yes." I breathe. I need to focus on the joint.

Maybe doing drugs with him was a bad idea. My will to push back any attraction towards Matteo is nothing against the extra dopamine in my brain.

"Yes." He answers.

I forgot what I even asked.

Saturday 4:18pm, Matteo's balcony

"I think I know why I like this view." I say as we smoke the second joint. He rolled it this time, complaining that I took too long with the first one.

We turn to look at each other at the same time.

"How so?"

"I grew up in a two-bedroom apartment in Moscow. In one of those post-soviet era buildings, you know? It still has bullet holes in it, I see them every time I pass it."

His eyes grow wide, and he looks like a kid again.

"For real?"

I nod. "It's not that impressive, really. Life in Moscow seems more...grey."

"How is it here then?"

"Golden."

He nods and looks back at the sea. "I never thought I took it for granted until you came."

That makes me feel warm inside. I pass him the joint.

"Did you grow up here?" I ask him, referring to the house.

"No, in Palermo. Do you remember where we picked up Isabella?"

I squint. "Sort of."

"I used to live in the townhouse across from it."

"Wasn't there a restaurant? Where you parked."

He smiles at the fact that I remember. "Yes. That's our restaurant. But the building has three levels, and our house was there."

"Really?" I ask, excited. "That's so cool, that you have a restaurant."

"Yeah, I used to hang out there after school every day. Free food and I could do what I want."

"What did you do?"

He shrugs. "I don't know. I read, I drew, I played with toys or in the kitchen. With Vinnie. Did my homework...sometimes." He grins and looks down then back up at me.

"You look like a child." I tell him then. I can't help myself.

My phone buzzes on the table and I see it's 4:20.

"Four-twenty." He says, reading my mind once again, and passes me the joint.

Raisa texts me to ask whether I'm awake and I send her a thumbs up.

She calls me then, and I realize she's probably already in Russia. Time seems to have no meaning, and I feel like two seconds have passed since I was on the yacht.

"Who is it?" Matteo asks when he sees me roll my eyes.

"Raisa."

He groans then, and I get the instinct to tell him off, but I remember that I had just rolled my eyes at her.

I can't concentrate on what she's saying because Matteo is making faces when I silently threaten to turn the camera if he doesn't behave.

Raisa eventually gets annoyed and says she's going back to sleep.

"How do you know her?" He asks me after he's made sure she hung up.

"We grew up together, and our fathers grew up together. Her dad he...he died."

He nods, letting me know he knew that already. Raisa probably told him herself. I wonder how much she knows about him. Not from other people, but from his own mouth.

"They used to be business partners."

He's still nodding, but I can see his thoughts are somewhere else now.

"So, you're like Vinnie and I." He concludes after a while.

I light the burnt-out joint between my fingers.

"I don't think that's the best way to describe it. She feels more like...a cousin rather than a sister. I'd say Isabella is more like my Vinnie."

A look crosses his face when I mention their names. I don't open the subject.

Saturday 6:56pm, Matteo's balcony

The sun is setting over the sea as we do the second line since we landed. The wind blows some of it away but neither of us says anything.

"Nature wants some too." I say and he laughs at that, like it's the funniest thing he's ever heard.

"If you think about it, if drugs come from nature, they theoretically can't be that bad." He tells me.

"Coke doesn't come from nature. Coca leaves, maybe."

"I meant weed. Or mushrooms."

"I've never tried those."

"Never?" He asks, surprised.

"Do you think I'm some kind of drug connoisseur or something?" I joke before taking the cold coffee to my lips.

"No, but you're still awake and no one's ever stayed up with me this long. I assumed you know your way around parties and afters like I do."

"You don't go to sleep after parties?"

"Sometimes no. Depends on what I'm doing."

There's a sexual connotation to his words and I wonder if that's what he meant. His eyes tell me nothing.

"I've never stayed up this long, but I don't feel tired."

"That's the new thing you can do today then. Not sleep for a whole day." He says and grins at me. I don't tell him I've already officially done that.

"Yeah, never have I ever been awake for a whole day."

He raises the bottle of wine we've been sharing between us throughout the day and goes to take a sip.

"It's empty. Let's get another one."

Saturday 7:11pm, Matteo's kitchen

He goes into the wine cellar, and I wait for him in the kitchen, making us another round of coffee. I hear laughter coming from the garden, so I go over to the windows in the foyer. I see Aurora laughing as she lays on the grass with her phone to her ear.

I wonder if she's talking to Adrik.

I see someone cutting the roses a bit further away. When he turns his head, I squint.

Romeo?

He's our housekeeper/ house manager when we're in Italy and even when we're not, and he's been at our house for over five years now. I must be imagining things. They're wearing the same type of jacket, that's all.

"Got it."

"You have a nice garden." I say when I see Matteo emerging in the hallway from the door that leads to the cellar.

"Yes, our housekeepers do a good job."

"You have a gardener?"

"Not really. One of our house managers Romeo tends to them."

It is him! Should I say hi? The feeling in my stomach tells me *no way*.

I follow him up the stairs, but not without checking twice whether it's actually Romeo or not. At this point I don't even know what's real and what isn't.

Saturday 9:18pm, Matteo's balcony

"It seems easy, but I've been trying to think of ten things I've never done before. It's hard."

We're still outside and it's colder now. I'm wearing one of his jackets as we smoke cigarettes.

"Let's find ten together." He suggests, putting his cigarette out in the ashtray.

"That neither of us has done? That's going to be even harder."

"No, like you five and me five."

"Okay. I've never...had sex in the sea."

Matteo rolls his eyes. "That doesn't count. It has to be original."

He doesn't comment on the sex thing like I would expect a guy to, and my inner child feels safe with him now.

"Fine. Never have I ever skydived."

"Okay, that's a good one."

"Have you?"

"I have. I know a guy in Taormina."

"You know everyone on this island, don't you?"

He shrugs, and his eyes turn dark. "More like they know my father." He mutters.

"What?"

He coughs. "They know my father, not me."

I cock my head. "You don't seem so happy about it."

"Why would I be? I haven't done anything to deserve their respect or earn any favours."

"Most of the people I know brag about their fathers." I say before I can think.

Most people also don't think of respect and favours as currency.

My dad does.

"Yeah, well." He pauses. "Most fathers aren't like mine."

He doesn't say it in a superior tone, he says it like he wishes things were different.

"What does your tattoo mean?" I ask, getting the hint to change the subject.

He tells me that the scales on his calf mean justice, balance. I tell him I have the word 'balance' tattooed on my lower back. When he asks me to show it to him, I tell him I can't. I feel myself blushing, so I look down for a new cigarette.

"Okay, what about the other ones?" I ask, taking the attention off me.

He explains them to me quickly, like he doesn't want to get into them right now, so I don't ask further. The discussion about his father seems to have really bothered him.

"You tell me yours now. The one on your ankle?" He asks. "And on your back?"

I'm surprised he noticed.

"This is the moon." I say and hold out so he can see the tattoo. It's a small half-moon tattoo. "I got it to remind myself to always follow my intuition." I don't elaborate because his mood has shifted, but I still smile and try to look for any sign that I should leave.

He forgets to ask about the one on my back again, so I don't say anything. Something has changed.

I try to ease the mood by going back to our list, and we make a game out of it: the first one to get to ten wins.

We give up half an hour later because we have too much to say and can't concentrate. We're also avoiding the fact that not coming up with things left to do with your life is sad. Bittersweet, in a fucked-up way.

Sunday 00:01am, Matteo's balcony

We snorted the last line an hour ago, but at this point I don't feel like it has any effect on us anymore. I'm completely awake, feel great, and Matteo is back to being in a great mood.

"My father is hosting this thing tomorrow, and there are a lot of guests coming." He starts, playing with my lighter.

"Okay."

I get that feeling in my stomach again, but it's accompanied by dread. I know what this means: I need to leave.

He coughs, and it's the first time I see him looking uncomfortable in my presence. "We need the room, that's why. You are welcome- I mean, you could've stayed longer if things were different."

"I'll leave before the sun comes up."

"You'll take our jet, of course. I'm going to text the pilot now."

His fingers shake as he types out the text. A few minutes later he looks up from his phone.

"Okay, the jet is arranged. But it leaves at four thirty the latest – it has to fly to get my father and bring him back here before noon."

A wave of sadness washes over me, taking me by surprise. I try to hide behind my smile. He's too out of it to even notice anymore.

Sunday 01:11am, Matteo's balcony

"What are you thinking about?" I ask him when I notice that the silence is unusual.

"My birthday."

"What about it?"

He turns his head, and I can see the bags under his eyes in the dim light of the balcony. He looks tired, but content.

"I was thinking about what to do. I'm turning twenty-one. I can legally drink in the US."

"It's not like that has stopped you before."

"Yeah." He pauses. "Why did you say I'm not like a cancer?"

"Because you don't strike me as one."

"You don't strike me as one either."

"What do you know about astrology?" I ask him. It comes out more condescending rather than surprised. I didn't mean to.

"I've had other girls tell me that I'm not like a cancer man, whatever that means."

"No, I mean in general. Those things you read online tend to be sexist."

He raises an eyebrow. "Okay. Tell me then."

"I found this astrology book in a shop one day and I read about my sign, that's why I can tell you facts." I say and he laughs.

"Go ahead then. Tell me how they're supposed to be."

"Sympathetic. Gentle, kind."

"I'm not nice?"

"I didn't say that. I think you're nice, but you're not nice."

"Thanks." He sarcastically says, but I know he understands exactly what I mean. He's not nice, he's fair.

Balanced.

"We prize security above else." I add. "And I feel like that's not true for me. The feeling of knowing how my life will be like for the next fifty years is terrifying."

"Why? Do you already know how it's going to look like?"

"No, but I'm already out of things to do."

"That's a very pessimistic way to look at the future."

He's right.

"What else?" He asks, lighting another cigarette.

"I know we are ruled by the moon." I say, and we both look up at the moon.

"Does this have something to do with the tattoo?"

"Yes, it has a lot of meanings. And I find new ones sometimes."

We sit in silence for a while and I try to think of more things I read in that book.

"I know I read cancers have a difficult time trusting and have psychic abilities due to the moon."

He doesn't laugh like he did with Isabella.

"Also, we care what people think of us. Which I can't relate to."

"I don't believe that." He says.

"I don't care if you do." I retort and smiles, nodding, accepting that I won this round.

Sunday 01:56am, Matteo's balcony

I look at him as I say goodnight for the last time. A wave of nostalgia that I can't explain crashes into me, bringing every cell of my body to life. Every moment since I've stepped on this island has given me a weird feeling of melancholy mixed with…freedom.

It's like I knew I was going to love it here, but already regretted it ending.

When I'm back in my room, I spend what seems like hours staring at the ceiling, waiting for the moment I need to get up and go to the airport.

Sunday 04:49am, somewhere up in the clouds

Time doesn't feel real as I see the sun come up for a second time over the horizon, this time in the air, not in the water. It's different now, the feeling is replaced with dread and emptiness. A full day has passed since I've seen the sun come up the first time, but this time I'm alone on a plane back home.

Even the jet feels different now, like I've jumped timelines.

I close my eyes and eventually fall asleep in the eerie silence wearing heavy on my soul.

My life has been feeling like lucid dream, and everything before seems insignificant, like it happened in another dimension. A switch has been turned, and I can't find it so I can turn it back off.

What makes it painful is that I'm experiencing an emotion I've never felt before, and I can't make it go away if I can't logically understand it.

It was a day where time stood still. It didn't exist. And yet somehow, it's been forever etched into my soul.

Chapter 25

Matteo

Palermo, Sicily – June 1ˢᵗ 2020

The initiation ritual doesn't take place on Sunday, as Matteo had expected. His father came home in the evening, not at noon like he had said. He was in a good mood, despite their last phone call (he probably had more important things to worry about than his son's behaviour) and didn't even talk to Matteo until the next morning on Monday. He had been in his office with Romeo since he had arrived.

On Monday, he comes into Matteo's room. He never does that. He usually calls him to his office or talks to him when they bump into each other on their estate. But he never comes into his room. He's also the only person in the house who doesn't knock. He knows the house belongs to him, along with everybody in it.

"Hello." He says and goes to sit on one of the chairs by the table. Matteo is watching reruns of The Office in the background while scrolling on his phone. He's been doing that ever since he woke up on Sunday.

Everything seems grey now. The sun has been hiding behind the clouds since yesterday, and it's cold.

"Hi." A feeling of worry settles in his stomach as he locks his phone.

"How are you?"

Matteo shrugs. "Alright. What's up?"

His father looks at him and Matteo hates this. He does this sometimes; he'll just stare into his soul, as if he were reading his thoughts, trying to see what the best approach would be.

"It will happen this Sunday."

Matteo is confused. Then he remembers. Now he feels afraid, and he knows his father can see it, maybe even smell it on him. He hates himself right now.

"Okay."

"Don't be afraid."

"I'm not *afraid*."

Matteo sits up straight.

"It's okay to be scared. I was scared when my father swore me in."

This is the first time he's ever admitted weakness to Matteo. He wonders if he'll see more of it once they start working together. Seeing his father admit he can feel anything (or at least used to in the past) makes him appear more human.

Matteo has never heard him say 'I love you' to anyone, ever. He sees him kiss his mom on the temple sometimes, but they seem more like friends rather than partners. He knows they don't sleep in the same room, but they both travel a lot. The only times the whole family is together is during birthdays and other celebrations.

The first two months of remote university and work were unusual; everyone in their family was home. They would eat dinner together more than once a week (which was the only time all five of them were in the same room, ever), which is something they stopped doing when Matteo left for boarding school.

"Do you have any questions?"

"Where's mom?" He finds himself asking.

His father's expression changes.

"You know she's in Taormina."

"Why isn't she here?"

His father's face is expressionless, as always.

"Why are you only asking now?"

Matteo shrugs. "I'm spending a lot more time in the house than I did in the past twenty years."

His father thinks about it.

What is there to think about?

"Do you even love her?" Matteo asks out of a sudden.

"Of course I do." His father answers automatically. It sounds rehearsed.

"Okay."

"Why are you asking me this?"

"Just curious. Why do you care?" He daringly asks.

Sometimes he likes to see how far he can take it until his father's face shows any kind of emotion. Anger, rage, confusion, even disappointment - anything. Disappointment is the worst one, but at least it's something.

It shows he cares enough to feel.

"Because you've never brought it up before."

The *Feeling* comes back. He looked it up online yesterday after the whole talk with Valentina about intuition and whatever. He literally googled the unknown feeling in his gut and after rabbit hole of threads and forums, he found something.

Someone wrote that if you think about something and you get a feeling in your stomach, it's your intuition speaking. If you feel it in your chest, then it's your own mind playing tricks on you.

"Is that all there is?" Matteo asks this only to be cryptic and play with his father a little bit longer, see if he can get a reaction out of him. He wants to see if his father feels guilty, because then it confirms he's having affairs.

But it's not guilt that takes over his face. It's something else.

It's fear.

Then, anger.

"I would suggest you mind your own business until you earn the right to pry into mine."

Matteo is quick to react. "Is mom a business then?"

His father's muscles tense under his shirt and Matteo knows he won this round.

"I'm going on a business trip to St. Petersburg this week, I will see you on Sunday."

Matteo nods and watches his father leave without as much as a goodbye. He turns the volume back up as soon as the door shuts.

***

Palermo, Sicily – June 7th 2020

The suit is tight on his arms when he puts it on. He hasn't worn it since Christmas, when he looked at himself in the mirror and saw his father.

Now, as he looks at himself again; hair gelled back, tie around his neck, he sees his father again. Which unsettles him because it's the one thing he had always tried to avoid. The one thing he knows for sure about his life is that he doesn't want to turn out like his father.

"Look at you." Aurora says from the mirror in the hallway. "Where are you going looking so radiant?"

"Fuck off."

Their father appears in the doorway from the kitchen, holding the newspaper he was reading and a cup of coffee.

"Language." He says, like they've never heard him curse before. "We leave in ten."

"Where are you going?" Aurora asks.

"Church." His father answers for the both of them.

Aurora makes a displeased face. "Why didn't you invite me?"

"Do you want to come?" Matteo provokes her, smelling her game from a mile away.

She scrunches her nose. "Of course not."

They watch her sling a bag over her shoulder and grab the umbrella from its holder. "I'm off."

"Where?" They both ask at the same time.

Aurora smiles sweetly. "Church."

No one says anything as they watch the door close behind her.

***

It's been raining since Wednesday, and everyone he sees on the street seems to be in a sombre mood. Italians need sun to thrive.

It's a little past twelve when they arrive at the restaurant. It's clearly been renovated during the pandemic; the inside is wider now and there are more tables. The lamps are gone, having been replaced with chandeliers that hang from the ceilings.

The whole atmosphere has changed. It doesn't say 'family-friendly' anymore. It says 'black tie business dinners', or that type of restaurant that you just know has expensive food that comes on miniature plates.

"Looks nice." Matteo observes as they walk through the empty restaurant towards the back door. It opens into well-lit hallway with five doors: two on the left, two on the right, and one at the end.

The two on the right are offices, the two on the left lead up to their old home and down to the wine cellar, and the one at the end is a storage room.

To his surprise, they go through the door that leads to the wine cellar.

Once they're in the cellar, his father opens another door, hidden behind the last barrel in the back. Matteo never even knew it existed.

They go down another set of stairs and arrive in front of a door.

Behind it is a large, cold room, filled with candles and people. Men.

There must be around twenty people here, most of them his father's age, sitting in a circle of chairs. It reminds Matteo of the game they played at Vinnie's birthday.

Then, sitting on one of the chairs, he finds his grandmother Angelina. His father's mother. She's sitting there knitting like she sometimes does, listening to something Paulo Barone is telling her.

Matteo recognizes Romeo, as well as Isabella's father, Franco Altieri. He remembers never being sure whether Isabella's father had any involvement in this.

Now he knows.

He wonders who out of Franco and Paulo might be the Consiglieri. He knows the consiglieri is the one in charge after the boss, even though the underboss is second in command according to the hierarchy. The consiglieri is the right-hand man, the advisor; the only one who can influence his father.

He imagines it must be Isabella's dad. He's a lawyer specializing in criminal law, or something like that, if Matteo remembers correctly.

Paulo is way too physical, too good at practical things (like his sons are), to be a consiglieri. Matteo has seen him carry out tasks, talking to people, closing deals, but he rarely ever sees Franco. Franco, who seems too soft and too intelligent to be the underboss.

It all makes sense now.

The voices echo off the walls but they go quiet the moment they're aware that their leader is here. (With his degenerate son, who is to be sworn into the organization.)

Matteo knows he must take the oath of Omertà; the code of silence their father had told them about years ago. Only then will he officially be a part of *Cosa Nostra.*

He looked it up this week. He has to swear loyalty to the organization; swear that he won't talk to any authorities, the government, or any outsider about *anything* starting today. They're supposed to be merely people who owe them favours. Those who don't owe them favours are irrelevant, and those who don't qualify as irrelevant are enemies.

Matteo will basically have to swear to ignore any illegal activities he sees. He's also read that he must kill someone, but he's sure that can't be true. It's only a thing you read in books or see in the movies. Plus, he doesn't really trust Google.

"Buongiorno." His father says, then proceeds to greet everyone.

All of the men who were sitting before are standing now. Everyone wants to shake his hand, greet him personally, show their respects. Everyone that is, except for his consiglieri, underboss, and his mother.

Once everyone but Matteo and his father are sitting, Grandma Angie stands up and places her knitting utensils on the chair.

"Now that my son and grandson are *finally* here, let's start."

***

First, his grandmother presents him to the rest of the men. The first people he's formally introduced to are Franco and Paulo, consiglieri and underboss, whom he already knows.

Then his grandmother introduces Romeo (who he also knows), Vincenzo, Pablo, and Gianluca, the caporegimes – the captains. The ones who did all the dirty work, people who have killed other people.

Romeo has always been around, and he's a good man. Matteo has grown closer to him than to his own father. He can't even imagine Romeo holding a gun, let alone kill someone. But Matteo knows he's always carrying a gun and has been serving his father since before Matteo was even born.

"Gianluca and Pablo work in New York, so you will be under them while you're there." Grandma Angie explains, before moving on. Her Italian is posh, old-fashioned. She can speak fast sometimes, but rarely with her grandchildren. Sometimes she has a hard time understanding when they speak amongst themselves, but Matteo knows she always *understands* what is being said.

The next people he meets are soldiers; some from Romeo's team, some from Vincenzo's. Matteo doesn't bother to learning their names, but he recognizes one of them. He's the only one that looks closest to Matteo's age. His name is Luca, and Matteo remembers him from his early days growing up in the restaurant. He was always *there*.

He's the son of the guy who got shot.

"Luca is Romeo's nephew. He is the newest member of our organization; he joined two years ago."

Matteo is surprised. He never bothered to ask himself whether Romeo had any family. As far as he was used to, *they* were Romeo's family. He also didn't know the person who got shot was Romeo's brother.

"The rest are in New York."

His grandmother turns to the rest of the group. Matteo realizes there's no empty chair for him to sit on except for his grandmother's.

"Matteo will be sworn into the organization, and I will initiate the ritual. He will be serving under Romeo as a soldier, to be trained by Luca."

Matteo and Luca exchange glances. What could Luca even teach him? How to fight? Matteo already knows how to fight.

"If anyone has anything to object, you may speak now."

The room is dead silent.

Now is Matteo's chance to say something. Choose his path, pick one of the two versions of himself, and play that role until death.

Two futures lay ahead of him: one where he lives off his father's money, works as an 'associate' in the club. He'll settle for a woman who can handle him when he gets bored of her and goes off with someone else. They'll have children and he'll rarely see them, but he'll swallow his guilt by throwing money at them and ensuring they have a pleasurable life.

The second future is one where he takes the oath and enters the world of organized crime; his own family – just on the dark side of the coin. That's all he can know for sure; the only thing he can see ahead of him. Everything that comes after is a big black unknown.

It feels like the beginning of the end again.

His mouth stays shut, but his heart is screaming.

"Alright. Before you swear your loyalty to Cosa Nostra and become a Man of Honor, you need to hear the commandments by which we operate."

"Like in the Bible?" Matteo asks in disbelief.

Another round of whispers, this time talking about how he can't keep his mouth shut like he should.

His grandmother doesn't seem phased; she just continues.

"One. No one can present himself directly to another of our friends. There must be a third person to do it."

Matteo has no idea what that means, but he just swallows and lets her continue uninterrupted.

"Two, never look at the wives of friends."

Don't get caught screwing someone's wife, classy.

"Three, never be seen with cops."

Obviously.

"Four, you're always on call."

He wants to object to this but his grandmother sees him opening his mouth and throws him a warning look.

"Five, appointments must always be respected."

Matteo rolls his eyes.

"Six, wives must be treated with respect."

Her eyes glow as she recites the rule, like she came up with it herself.

"Seven, when you're asked for any information, the answer must always be the truth. Eight, money cannot be appropriated if it belongs to others or to other families."

Basically don't get caught stealing.

He can't possibly believe that there's no corruption within the organization itself.

"Nine; there are certain types of people who cannot be a part of Cosa Nostra. Anyone who has a close relative in the police that wasn't planted by us, anyone with a two-timing relative in the family, anyone who behaves badly and doesn't hold moral values."

Matteo wants to laugh.

Moral values? Behaving badly? What would you call hiding a body or extortion for example?

"Ten." His grandmother's voice echoes against the stone walls, trying to get his attention. "Our approach is defensive. We don't act, we *re*act. We have enough wealth to last a lifetime of generations, and our duty at the end of the day is to protect it and add to it in a *legal* way."

She looks at Matteo now, because she apparently feels like he's the only one in this room who needs an explanation. "If anyone tries to take what is rightfully ours, we have the right to defend ourselves."

Seems fair.

She's talking like it's an everyday occurrence, like it's a normal life to be leading. It only dawns on him now that it *is* an everyday occurrence for every single person in this room. And at some point, it will be normal for him too.

Grandma Angie turns to look him in the eye. "Matteo Lorenzo Giudice, are you here to swear to follow Omertà and pledge your loyalty and allegiance to the Giudice organization, with St. Michael as your witness and protector?"

A small wave of whispers settles among the people in the room. What happened?

"Be quiet." His father's voice echoes, and everybody shuts up.

"Yes." Matteo answers after he realizes that everybody's looking at him, waiting for him to answer.

Grandma Angie goes over to her seat and takes a picture out of her purse. Her vanilla smell seems to follow her wherever she goes.

She's holding a picture of the archangel Michael, a catholic Saint. Matteo knows it's her favourite Saint out of all of them; the one she's been praying to every night since she was four.

That's how she was raised by her mother – her father died fighting the Russians in Stalingrad. She married Lorenzo Giudice in 1966 and had their first son, Lorenzo (Matteo's father), in 1975. Matteo doesn't know what really happened – all he knows is that his grandfather died during a war in 1999 (he looked it up – it had something to do with a Yugoslavian war) and his father took over.

"Do you swear on your life by Archangel St. Michael, champion of justice, healer of the sick, guardian of the people, that you will respect Omertà with death as punishment for breaking it?"

Matteo laughs inside his head.

The fear of death means nothing to him at this point. He has no opinion whether this is good or bad, whether these people are good or evil. He knows it just needs to happen.

"Yes."

She comes over to Matteo, and his nostrils are filled with her scent as she takes his right hand. She is holding a small needle, which she uses to prick the skin of his index finger.

Blood comes out, and she places the photo under it so it would drop onto it. After a few droplets fall, his father stands up and comes over. He has a lighter in his hand - he had asked for one earlier and Matteo gave him the one Valentina had left behind.

"As head of Cosa Nostra and grandson of our founder Lorenzo Giudice, I welcome you, Matteo Lorenzo Giudice, to Cosa Nostra."

He hands Matteo the lighter and the picture. Matteo sets fire to it, then watches it burn.

The saint has his hands up in prayer and is looking at something above him. His face is engulfed by the flames, and then slowly, but surely, his body is too.

Matteo sees himself in the angel or whatever he is and lets the picture burn in his hand. At some point it the fire starts burning his fingertips, but he doesn't care.

A few seconds later it turns into ashes and falls onto the floor. People are whispering again, and he asks his grandmother if he has done something wrong.

"No, no, it's fine." His father assures him, which seems to calm down the people who had something to comment.

"Why are people whispering then?" Matteo asks, knowing very damn well everyone can hear him.

"The picture was supposed to be passed around quickly while you take the oath with a hand on your heart."

"Why didn't you say anything?"

"Because it's fine either way."

His grandma chimes in. "The only ceremony that allows holding the picture while it burns is when someone takes over as head of the family. Your father did that twenty years ago, exactly on this day."

Matteo frowns. If his grandfather died in 1999, why did his father only become boss in 2000?

He doesn't ask, and the initiation comes to an end. People stand up from their chairs and come over to shake his hand and congratulate him. His father announces lunch and drinks on the house upstairs; everybody cheers.

Afterwards, Matteo watches the people around him talk to his father, laugh at his jokes, asking him when there's time on his schedule for a quick 'business meeting'. His father is diplomatic and seems to know everyone's names, who their families are, their past, and their futures.

Everyone in this room right now, everyone on this island, respects him. It's a respect that's accompanied by decades of work, mixed with authority and fear.

His phone buzzes at some point during their lunch – it's the first time Matteo has ever eaten at the same table as his father in the restaurant.

He checks the notification from his Italian bank.

You have received €200,000.00 from L. Giudice

He clicks on the notification and looks at what his father wrote as a reference.

Well done

He has always said he was never going to be like his father. Yet somehow, in a fucked-up way, he wants to be *exactly* like him.

NEVER HAVE I EVER
done something like this

Chapter 26

Matteo

Palermo, Sicily – June 26th 2020

It's grandma Angie's birthday today, so Lorenzo made an exception and gathered the whole family at her house for dinner. The 'family' meaning the extended family that includes the Barone and Altieri families as well.

Grandma Angie lives in the townhouse next to their old house in Palermo. It's a four-bedroom building, wall-to-wall with their old house, which she and her husband bought when they got married.

The building looks almost historical from the outside, as well as on the inside with its giant paintings and crystal chandeliers. She used to host Easter and Christmas dinners there until last year, and it's the biggest townhouse Matteo has ever been in. It has four floors, the ground floor being the restaurant.

She has been sleeping in the same bedroom for over fifty years, almost half of them without her husband by her side. As soon as Matteo and Vinnie were born a couple of months apart, his father's childhood bedroom became theirs when they would visit her.

Vinnie's grandparents had died before he was born, shot dead on the street, so grandma Angie raised the Barone kids like they were her own grandchildren.

Isabella and Pia would sleep over in their uncle's old room, whereas Marco and Eddie would sleep in a room that was once their grandfather's study.

After they grew up and moved away, two of the rooms were turned into guest rooms and the study was converted back into an office. Matteo never knew who used it, but he knows now that his grandma most likely does.

She *knows*.

She knows everything. Since the beginning of time.

They are sitting down at a long table in the dining room, with Matteo's father sitting at the head of it. Their grandma usually sits at the other end, but right now she's too busy in the kitchen to sit down.

The dining room is the largest room in the house – she always tells the story of how she insisted on buying this home *exactly* because of the large dining room. She loved to cook and wanted to have a large family to host dinners for. Her 'husband, soulmate, partner in crime' indulged her.

Matteo wonders how she fell in love with him. Did she know he was in Cosa Nostra before they got together?

He looks out the floor-to-ceiling windows and can see right into Vinnie's old apartment. Someone else lives there now, with the Altieri's being the only ones who have not yet moved out of the city.

The birthday lunch has three courses that are accompanied by wine from the Giudice collection. The wines are as old as their grandmother (almost), and they sometimes sell on auctions for over $40k.

"Matteo, you're awfully quiet today." Grandma Angie says when she finds him on the balcony sipping on his wine glass.

"I told you happy birthday already."

"You did, but that's not the point."

"What's the point then?"

"How are you adjusting to your new position?"

Matteo almost rolls his eyes.

The 'new position' is nothing to write home about – he's doing the same thing he's done since he was forced into lockdown: nothing. Absolutely fuck-all.

The initiation ritual was the most interesting thing to happen to him this month, followed by his grandmother's birthday.

"I don't have anything to do. I figured it was more for show." Matteo says, a part of himself happy that that's what it's like.

He half-expected to be called up and asked to kill someone this month. Every time his father called him, his heart would stop. But it was never anything serious. Just driving around and picking up a few more shipment than he's used to. Other than that, nothing new. Matteo realizes now that he had made it bigger and darker in his head.

"What did you expect?" Her voice is careful, but a small smile is playing on her lips.

"I don't know, I thought I'd have to kill someone."

"Oh."

Why isn't she denying it?

"Is it true then?" He presses.

She doesn't answer, which annoys him.

"Why are you avoiding the answer? Are you ashamed of what you're doing? If I have to take responsibility for everything *I* do in my life, you should too."

"Yes." She finally answers.

"Yes what?"

"You'll have to kill someone."

A chill runs through Matteo's entire body. His mouth goes dry even though he just drank from his glass.

It is true then.

"What if I don't want to?"

"You will want to, eventually."

Her tone shakes him to his core. She said it like it's the most natural thing in the world.

"I don't want to kill anyone. Are you going to force me to and then kill me if I don't?"

She's laughing now, but Matteo isn't having it. How can she laugh right now?

"Is this your infinite generational legacy then? Killing people?"

His grandmother raises her arm at him and he flinches, even though they both know she won't hit him this time.

"Watch your mouth." She threatens. She's shorter than everyone in their family, but the most respected. Her word is the only one that can go above his father's.

After the tension eases, she proceeds to explain what she meant. "We will never hurt you, Matteo. I can guarantee you that our duty is to protect you. However, you will have to kill someone eventually. Nobody can stop that from happening. We won't point you at someone and tell you to go kill him."

"Then why would I ever kill someone?"

His grandmother finds this amusing. "If someone pulled a gun at you with the intention to kill you, what would you do?"

"Shoot him."

Matteo answers automatically, without even thinking. He looks at his grandmother, ashamed of his instinct. But she smiles at him and places a hand on his arm.

"Exactly. Once that happens and you keep it to yourself, that's when you'll be officially considered a member. Because you proved you kept your oath."

"Can't I just…not sleep with someone's wife? Not steal?" He knows it's a stupid question, so he changes directions. "What if I never *have* to kill someone?"

Her eyes are overcome by darkness.

"Then count yourself lucky."

"Have you ever killed someone?"

She chuckles, nervously. "If I die tomorrow, I can say that I have no regrets I take with me to the grave."

Matteo watches her look out onto the street below as she takes a sip.

"Do you know what Omertà actually means?" She asks. You swore to it, but do you know what it means?"

"Yes, it means I can never say anything to the police if it ever comes to it, to save my own ass. Basically, I swore not to be a snitch."

His grandma scrunches her nose at the word.

"I don't like that word."

"Sorry. But I know what the oath means." She doesn't seem convinced. "I know what Omertà means, Nonna."

Her eyes soften at the nickname. It's what they would call her when they were younger.

"You know what it means, okay. But do you *understand*? You swore to lead your entire life, up until death, by the Omertà. That means, everything that happens in your life from now on will be settled between us. Our own rules, our own justice system. The government and any other outsiders cannot be involved, cannot know. You can't go back, and you can't back out."

The Feeling comes and settles deep into the pit of his stomach.

Matteo feels like it never left since the beginning of June.

"You took the blood oath and were sworn in like a boss would. You must honour that."

"Yeah...that's what I mean." Matteo tries to appear stronger than he is. He didn't think it through in depth. He thought it would just please his father. Nothing has really changed, so it must've been for show.

"Does that mean I can just go up to anyone and kill them and everyone has to be quiet?" Matteo spits. The way his grandmother is talking makes her seem like she's not a grandmother anymore.

She's a woman in her seventies who has been the 'silent head' of the family for over twenty years now; ever since her husband got shot.

Matteo had never met his grandfather; he died a few months before he was born.

"You swore your loyalty to Cosa Nostra, and there are a few basic rules to follow. Everything else is dictated by the laws of nature, good and evil. We have values and morals, we're not animals."

Matteo sees his opportunity. "There is no good and evil." He says it in a mocking tone, mimicking his father's words.

His grandmother's eyes change. "What did you say?"

"There's no good and evil. People make it so." Matteo repeats.

His cheek starts stinging and he realizes that he's just been slapped. His grandmother's shaking now, looking enraged.

"Never say that to me again! You understand? That is how the devil thinks."

Matteo wants to tell her that it was her own son who had said that to him, but he keeps his mouth shut.

"Don't make me force you to come to church every Sunday."

Matteo grins. It's funny; her thinking she can force him to do something. But she likes to be respected and even feared sometimes (*don't we all?*), so he pretends to be terrified and she goes back to being 'Nonna'.

"I'm proud of you." She tells him before they go back inside.

It leaves a bittersweet taste in Matteo's mouth; he's happy to hear it from her, but what she's proud for, he has no idea.

He joins the rest of his family at the table.

"What are you doing for your birthday?" Isabella asks.

"Sorry?"

"Your birthday? In two weeks? I need to know what your plans are."

"Why, you busy next month?" He asks, only to pester her a little. Once he gets the desired reaction, he answers her properly. "I haven't thought about it. Everything is still closed, isn't it?"

"They're going to open some venues late July." Vinnie chimes in, having listened to the conversation.

Matteo isn't really invested in talking about his birthday right now. Why does everything always happen around his birthday?

First, he had to discover the drug den in their back garden right before he turned sixteen. Now he swore his loyalty to Cosa Nostra, which was now, sort of, also *his* thing. His birthday is the last thing on his mind.

"I liked the boat party. I think I'm going to do that. Start in Palermo, end up in Taormina. And I want to be the captain."

"You want to steer the boat?" Vinnie asks, incredulously.

"Yes, but not a *yacht*. We can take one of the motorboats on our dock."

"Those are motor *yachts,* Matteo." Isabella says. "And you need a license to drive those."

His first instinct is to tell her he could get one of those if he wanted to, without much hassle. But he bites his tongue. It would be a stupid idea.

But I could if I wanted to.

The ease with which the thought occurs to him, and the adrenaline it sends through his body, nearly scares him.

He could, in theory, do whatever he wanted to. No one would give a fuck, would they?

The idea that everything in the world is possible, no matter how right or wrong, makes everything feel infinite. In a dirty, evil, perverted sort of way.

***

Palermo, Sicily – July 7th 2020

He wakes up before noon on Saturday. It's not until he stretches, the sun warm on his face, that he realizes it's his 21st birthday today.

Isabella had planned something after he asked for her help – he wanted to have fun again, and the lockdown restrictions had been loosened at the beginning of the month.

She asked him who he wanted to invite, and when he really thought about it, only nine people came to mind. Obviously, it would be the Barone kids and Isabella, and his own siblings. He also thought about Valentina because he kind of missed her vibe and he knew she was in Capo d'Orlando at the moment. He also wished he could invite Aleksi without Raisa being involved, but he had texted him a few days ago and he was in Russia. His mother was sick and he couldn't come.

The final invite list ended up being eight people and himself. Isabella went along with the idea of taking one of the boats from Palermo to Taormina. She asked everyone to get tested before attending, then hired a captain and one waiter.

It would take around seven hours to get from their dock in Palermo to their dock in Taormina, and Matteo took care of arranging the alcohol.

"What about coca?" Vinnie had asked him a few days earlier when he had given him a list of things he needed for the party.

"I don't feel like it." he said. "There won't be that many people."

He doesn't feel like it today either, he thinks, as he sits up in bed. He can hear people downstairs already, even though it's not even 12.

There's always a feeling of detachment on his birthday. People treat him like he's special; pretend they're friends and post pictures they might've took together at some point, even though they haven't talked in years. Relatives call, and then he must make small talk and tell them about his life before pretending to care about theirs – if he doesn't, his grandmother will hear about it.

The shower takes longer than usual, and Matteo doesn't get out until the glass is foggy and his skin starts prickling. He leaves his phone on the nightstand, avoiding the notifications that are piling up, and goes downstairs.

There are a lot more people in the kitchen than usual, sprawled out across the open space that opens up into the living room. Aurora and Pia are talking on the couch, already dressed for a party. Next to them, Marco and Eddie are playing FIFA.

In the kitchen, Isabella and Ariana are drinking coffee. He forgot that Ariana confirmed her attendance last minute.

"Where's Vinnie?" Matteo asks when he doesn't see him.

"Out for a smoke." Isabella answers. "Happy birthday!"

Everybody stops talking to come over and congratulate him for turning 21. By the time he hugs Ariana, Vinnie and Valentina emerge from outside, smiling at each other.

"Happy birthday you little weasel." Vinnie laughs as he goes over to hug him.

Matteo responds to the hug, happy to see his best friend, then looks at Valentina over Vinnie's shoulder. She's smiling at them as she holds what looks like an Aperol Spritz in her hand.

Vinnie lets go of him to make way for Valentina. She's wearing a dark leather skirt with a white long-sleeved blouse and Air Force 1s. His eyes drift to the drink in her hand.

"I see you've already started." Matteo jokes, motioning to her drink.

"It's your birthday, isn't it?" She responds with the same energy, before she hugs him. "Happy birthday."

She smells sweet, like flowers and something else, and her hair is soft in his palm.

"Thanks." He says when they pull away.

"Is that what you're wearing?" Isabella asks when she sees him come back into the kitchen.

He throws his arms up and looks down at himself. "What's wrong with my fit?"

He's wearing a pair of jean shorts and a white band t-shirt.

"Everybody's dressed for a party." Ariana lifts her leg slightly to show her heels.

"So? When I have fun I like being comfortable, I don't care about looking good." He answers, maybe a bit snarkier than intended. He hasn't had his morning coffee and cigarette yet, it's not his fault he's cranky.

He can feel the girls' eyes boring holes into the back of his head as he goes to press the button on the coffee machine. The coffee is done soon enough, and he goes upstairs to his room to drink it by himself.

As he smokes a cigarette with his coffee, he thinks about changing his clothes. It would make him look like he cares about how other people see him, so he decides against it. What else is he supposed to wear anyway? A *suit*?? Why do people care so much about how they look and not at all about truly having fun?

"We're leaving at three, Matteo!" Isabella yells up at him from somewhere in the garden below.

He acknowledges her by yelling something back, then goes back inside to pack an overnight bag. Right before he leaves his room, he remembers to go take some cash and the weed bag with him. He might've said no to cocaine, but there's no way he won't smoke a joint with his friends on his birthday.

***

"Has anybody seen my cigarettes?" Valentina asks at some point during the evening. They're far out into the sea right now, heading at medium speed towards Taormina.

Matteo is sitting on the upper deck playing poker with his boys when she comes over and interrupts them.

"What do you smoke?" Vinnie asks.

"Marlboro Gold."

They look down at the table where their cigarette packs are sprawled out. She's clearly eyeing the Marlboro Gold pack next to Matteo's stuff.

Matteo points to it. "That's mine."

She props her hand on her hip. "Since when?"

"Since I got it yesterday."

"You smoke the Red ones."

"They don't sell them at the corner store anymore."

He's not lying. He's been smoking Gold for a few weeks now.

She extends her hand, pretending to not have heard him. "I'll have my pack now."

"When did you lose it?" He asks, pretending to not hear her.

"An hour ago."

"I've been at this table for- well, okay, for less than an hour. But this *is* mine."

She looks annoyed now, probably thinking that he's lying because of the way he's grinning.

"Are you serious? This is mine."

"No it's not."

"Does it matter? I have an extra one, you can have it Valle." Isabella chimes in from across the deck.

She's sitting with Ariana and Pia on a velvet U-shaped couch. The sun has already set but it's still light outside, and the mood has been comfortable and chilled from the beginning.

"We're bored." Ariana adds, pouting. "Let's play a game."

Matteo and Valentina look at each other, and she rolls her eyes, choosing to go with Isabella's solution.

"We're already playing a game." Vinnie argues, motioning towards the money and cards on the table.

The look that Isabella throws towards Vinnie is enough to make him sigh and officially end their game. Matteo groans and protests, making it more difficult for everyone to enjoy themselves. It's his birthday though; he has the right to have a little fun by creating drama.

He's only been drinking beer and has smoked the occasional joint, which made him feel hazy.

"It's my birthday, we should play something I want to play."

He plops down on the couch, in the empty spot where the left side of the U-shaped couch meets the middle.

Isabella doesn't seem pleased with him doing everything in his power to be annoying, but there's nothing better to do anyway.

"What do you want to play then?" Valentina asks. Her voice is louder than usual, with a hint of irritation in her voice. She's sitting next to him on the edge of the middle part, holding a drink.

Matteo can't do anything but shrug. "How about the game we played last time?"

Isabella grabs her phone from her lap. "Which one? Picolo? Alright. Does everyone agree?"

Isabella doesn't wait for everyone to agree before typing their names in and starting the game. The first few tasks are boring, and Matteo can't help but complain.

"Maybe you should play the game of buying your own cigarettes and shutting up." Valentina says after another one of his complaints.

"Maybe you should remember when you finish your-"

"Can we not?" Isabella interjects. "There's a dare for you Matteo. You must down your drink or kiss the player to your right."

Matteo looks at Eddie without even thinking.

"That's your left." Valentina says. She lifts her head up and looks down at him, no expression on her face. Then she leans over, closer to him, resting her elbows on her knees. Her eyes are searching his – she wonders whether he'll actually do it or not.

Matteo has never given it too much thought – yes, sometimes he finds himself checking her out or looking at her, but that's because she's objectively good looking. Not even that - she's beautiful. But he respects her in a way that automatically doesn't allow him to go further than that.

She leans in closer, and he does too, their eyes saying everything their mouths aren't.

Are you going to pull away before I do?

They're so close now he can feel her breath on his lips. She smiles then; a lopsided smirk that dares him to take the final step. He's the man, after all.

330

"Well?" She asks, and he can hear the grin in her voice without having to look away from her eyes. "Are you asking yourself how to lie about the cigarettes right now?"

"Oh, I can't take this anymore!"

Before Matteo understands what's happening, his head is being pushed forwards. Then, a pair of soft lips on his.

She tastes like the Sangria she's been drinking ever since they got on board. Sweet, warm, like summer. His eyes close and his mouth opens out of instinct. Her tongue on already against his lips, searching for his.

A small sigh comes out of her mouth then, but it's covered by the song playing on the speakers. He doesn't miss the sound she makes though, and it immediately sends blood to his groin.

Matteo doesn't realize he's been pushing back against the hand until he loses his balance.

"Was that so hard?" Isabella is standing up next to them, looking pleased. She's laughing, and Valentina is rolling her eyes, feigning being ashamed.

He brushes it off and tries to make a joke of it.

The game continues as usual, but Matteo can't focus anymore.

He wants more.

He wants to know what makes her make that sound so he can hear it over and over again.

"Are you even paying attention?!"

Isabella is on his back again, looking at him expectantly.

"What?"

"Are you incapable of doing a simple task?" Isabella groans, skipping over whatever challenge it was that involved him.

Matteo spares a look in Valentina's direction.

She's not looking at him but she's proudly smiling to herself.

They've been playing this game for months now; a silent game where the only rule is winning. They never talk about it but they both kept score.

And right now, she's *definitely* winning.

Chapter 27

Valentina

Moscow, Russia - June 23rd, 2020

The weeks after I came back from Sicily went by in a haze. I spent them mostly watching movies and eating snacks, which led me wondering whether I was bordering on being depressed. Every day seemed to be exactly like the one before and sharing the same space with my family for days on end turned very toxic very quick.

By the middle of June, Russia came back to pre-lockdown levels, which also meant that my social life had a dramatic increase. Not only did I have Raisa calling me almost daily to go out and do something 'fun', as well as Isaac asking me when I was free 'to hang', but I also had my parents drag Adrik and I to business meetings and formal lunches.

My mother had commented that I had gained a little weight at some point during one of those lunches, which triggered my memories of being an insecure teenager with an undiagnosed eating disorder.

Every time I come back to my hometown and spend some time with my parents, I come to the realization that the experience is bittersweet. I saw a post that said 'your parents' house has everything you need but peace', which rang deep into my bones.

Then I end up feeling ungrateful and end up hating myself a little bit more.

It's Adrik's birthday today, which brings us to our uncle Boris' house on the outskirts of Moscow. I've always thought it's more of a palace rather than a home, because it is way too enormous for a single man like my uncle to live in alone.

We used to spend Christmas at his house when I was younger and we were still living in our apartment in the city.

I never knew how 'formal' that Christmas experience was until we started spending it at our own home, just the four of us.

I'm wearing a white and red polka dot dress my mother asked me to wear (apparently my uncle Boris bought it for me as a gift last Christmas).

The driveway is immense, always filled with cars parked around the fountain in the middle. A large stone staircase with koi ponds on either side leads up to the wooden door that always creeks. The main entry of the house is held up by tall marble columns that sport the Russian flag, which has always looked very conservative and outdated to me.

I'm wearing heels, so I walk slower than usual, trailing behind my family as we go up the steps in silence.

Two valets greet us in the foyer and take our coats before they show us the way to the dining room, even though we've been here before.

The table is long enough to sit twenty people, but there aren't even that many here. I can see Aleksi and his mother talking in hushed tones on one side, and my uncle sitting on across from them. He's sipping his whiskey and scrolling on his phone, mumbling something to himself as he does so. There are a few men and women I don't know and who I bet Adrik doesn't know either, yet they're here for some reason.

I instantly notice that Raisa isn't here. I didn't think to ask her because I just assumed she would show up like she always has.

The first course is served, and after two glasses of wine, the function becomes more fun.

I actually enjoy talking to my mother about the books we've been reading, after all the men at the table excused themselves to 'go talk in private'.

"Are you having fun?" I ask Adrik after noticing that he's spent most of his time on his phone. I bet he's talking to Aurora.

He looks up at me and throws me an annoyed smile. "What do you think?"

"Be nice." Our mother hisses. "Boris invited us here."

"But it's *my* birthday." Adrik notes. Mom shoots him a warning look, which causes him to roll his eyes and return to his phone.

Half an hour later, the men return into the room and only dad and Boris sit down. The rest say their goodbyes and leave.

"Raisa isn't here." My mother observes, making conversation with Valerya. Valerya is Raisa and Adrik's mother, a tall woman with green eyes and black hair. She looks exactly like I would imagine Raisa looking in thirty years. She's always been very quiet and elegant, keeping to herself and choosing to follow her late husband's lead. I've always thought of her as the epitome of elegance and calmness.

My ears perk up at the sound of her name. "Where is she?" I ask, genuinely interested.

"She's in Mallorca."

My eyes widen. "With whom?"

"With a guy she met."

"When?!"

When did she even have time to meet someone new? I feel like I've been inside for the past few years (even though it's only been a couple of months), and she's already out there travelling with a guy?

"A few months ago, while she was at dinner."

A few months ago was lockdown, so the guy must be rich enough to make her leave the house.

"Who is he?"

"Some guy from South Korea, who's doing an Erasmus semester in Moscow. His parents have a few mobile communications companies in Asia." Her mother explains, eyes sparkling.

I don't know why it bothers me, but the fact that Raisa didn't tell me makes me wonder why.

"Do you have anyone, Valentina?"

I knew the question would come at some point during the evening. It always comes up at any family event.

"No, I don't." I cough. "There's no one who interests me right now."

My uncle throws me a look and so does Adrik.

"What?"

"What do you mean, no one interests you? What does that even mean?"

"It means I want someone I like, someone…exactly how I like it."

"Do you really think you should have such high standards and expectations?"

I make a face. "And why the hell not?"

"Valentina." my mother gasps, not expecting my outburst.

"There aren't many people to choose from, and the older you get the harder it will be to find someone."

I roll my eyes. "There are *literally* billions of people on the planet."

"Not in our tax bracket and social class."

His face doesn't move.

"So? Who says I can't date or marry someone who doesn't have as much money as I do?"

"You won't."

"But what if I will?"

"Where would you meet someone like that? At your private school? At your vacation home in *Italy*?" He spits the last word like Italy is a place he'd never go to. I'm not sure if he ever has, actually. He's always been very vocal and open when it came to his strong opinions about the rest of Europe, especially Italians.

"I'm just saying. If I fall in love with someone who doesn't have as much money as I do, then I'm not going to care about what anyone has to say."

He chuckles in a very patronizing way that makes my blood boil.

"First, *you* don't have any money. Second, get back to me when that happens."

An awkward silence settles in the room as I shift in my seat, avoiding the stares from my parents. It's been a long time since I've gotten into a 'debate' with my uncle. Usually, he'll say something racist or sexist, but he's never commented on anything related to me before.

My father stands up and raises his glass. "Let's toast to those who couldn't be with us today." Everyone follows him, including my uncle who mumbles as he stands up. "To Volkov and Raisa."

Valerya places a hand on her chest and thanks him.

"Biggest lie ever told." My uncle mumbles as he takes a long sip from his glass.

"What?" Aleksi asks, the first words he's spoken in the past two hours.

"He's drunk." My father interjects, but Aleksi and I both heard him right.

"What do you think? That he got in an accident last year? At night, on an empty road? Where the cameras happened to not be working?" my uncle laughs.

Aleksi and I exchange looks. I get a bad feeling in my stomach and I'm not sure whether it's showing on my face, but Aleksi continues anyway.

"What else could have happened? That's what we were told."

"Someone killed him." My uncle says without even blinking.

"Oh my God." Valerya cries.

"I think that's enough." My dad says and walks over to Boris, reaching for his glass.

Why doesn't he look as shocked and worried as everyone else in the room?

"What does he mean?!" Aleksi asks, voice getting louder. He's nearly screaming now, even though I've never seen him as anything but calm.

Boris and I make eye contact from across the table, where my dad is holding him back.

"Open your eyes, Valentina."

I frown. "What?" Okay, he's way past drunk now.

"You've played stupid for a long time now." He adds, but then my dad manhandles him out of the room, saying something I can't hear.

I look at my mom, who looks worried. Not about what Boris said, but for my dad.

"What was that about?" I ask her.

She composes herself and shoots me an innocent look. "Oh, nothing. Come on sit down, finish your drink, and let's go home."

***

Moscow, Russia - June 26th 2020

"I think I might be going insane."

The rustling in the background lets me know that Isabella is turning around on the other side of her bed for the hundredth time. The video call has been going on for over two hours now, and neither of us has said anything for the past half hour.

I'm sitting cross-legged on my bed, doodling in a blank notebook that I bought ages ago just because it looked nice but never used.

"Why?"

"I'm bored out of my mind."

"How could you be bored? You're next to a beach."

"Ugh, but it's not like that, really. Everyone lives outside of town and the boys have their own thing going on anyway. Who am I supposed to go out with? Pia? We're not even allowed to go out, there's police going up and down the street."

"Why don't you just join the boys?"

"They're either playing video games or going out having sex with girls from Tinder."

This catches my attention for some reason. "What?"

I look at the screen now. Only half of her face squished against a pillow is showing, but she still looks good.

"Yes. They talk to girls on Tinder and then go out somewhere and they have sex."

"How? Where?" It's the most interesting thing I've heard in weeks. "Why didn't you tell me before?"

"I didn't think you'd enjoy the tea."

"I always do!" I whine. "I've read like, four books in the past few weeks. I need real life entertainment, not just my imagination."

I don't tell her that I had another dream about Matteo after Adrik's birthday fiasco. I haven't even told her about the first one, and it feels weird to keep things from her.

He was pressing me up against a wall, and his hands were in my hair, keeping my head back. I don't remember what I told him, but I remember him kissing me. I remember how good the kiss felt and how he kissed exactly the way I liked it.

"Well, Vinnie has been seeing this one girl he met for the first time a month ago, and Matteo has had two? Or maybe it was three dates? He only had sex with one of them though, he's weird."

"How is he weird?"

"I don't know. I think there's something weighing him down."

"Like what?"

I can see her shrug. *"Maybe something with his dad, I guess? He was acting weird today at his grandmother's birthday."*

"My birthday is on the 22nd." I tell her, wanting to change the subject.

"We should do something in Italy."

"I could come and spend time at our vacation house in Capo."

Her face lights up. *"Yeeees and we could spend a week there just existing."*

I instantly feel happier, but then it fades out when I think about having to ask my parents for permission.

"I'll ask my parents. Getting them to agree is the hard part."

"Let me know, and then I'll see how I'll get to you. It's also Matteo's birthday next week, so we can go to Palermo then!"

"When is his birthday?"

I remember knowing this at some point.

"The seventh."

There's a long pause in which both of us think of completely unrelated things.

"So...you'll talk to your parents and let me know?"

"Yeah. Sure."

"I'm going to go shower and get into bed." She says and we say goodnight before she hangs up. I watch the screen for a moment, my mind already in the future. I check the time.

10:55pm

My mom's voice is coming from down the hall, and she sounds happy, so I take it as my cue to go and ask her about Sicily.

I open my door to find her at the top of the stairs, talking to someone on the phone.

'Can I talk to you?' I mouth.

She shushes me with her hand, then giggles into the phone. Okay, she's drunk. Who is she even talking to?

"I'll talk to you tomorrow. Yeah, goodnight." She says and takes the phone away from her ear. "Is everything okay?"

She's back to being worried mom now.

"Yeah, I wanted to ask you about my birthday."

"Come talk to me." She says and starts walking towards the master bedroom.

My parent's room is at the other end of the hallway, and it opens into my dad's office, which also has a separate door for 'the public'. When I was younger, I would sometimes see people sitting in the armchairs by the door, waiting to go in and talk to him.

I watch her walk over into the ensuite bathroom, stopping by her sink to take off her makeup. She looks happy and a little too smiley from the drinks but seeing her like this makes me warm inside.

"What did you want to talk about?"

"I want to do something for my birthday."

Our eyes meet in the mirror. "What do you want to do?"

"I want to go to Sicily and stay at our house in July. Like a birthday month. And before you say no, I'm going to go insane if I must stay inside for one more day. I will just go and detox and read and lay in the sun and talk to no one." I ramble, not wanting to give her a window to say no.

"You know there's a global pandemic happening, right?"

I sigh. "Yes."

"And you know I can't possibly believe that you're going to Sicily and won't see a single person there."

"Who would I even see?"

"Isn't your friend Isabella from Palermo?"

Oh, right. I forgot I told her about my friends. Well, not *all* of them; I left some of them out (Matteo, mainly).

Amusement sneaks on her face when she sees I have nothing to say for myself.

"Please, as a birthday gift."

"I'm not even sure you can travel."

"I know I can. Dad does too."

"But your father-"

"Has more important things, yeah yeah. Pleeease? I won't ask for anything ever again."

She scoffs at that.

The moment I hear her sigh though, relief washes over me. She caved.

"Fine. But you're only going if you won't leave the house." She sternly says then starts taking off her clothes.

I go to hug and kiss her, thanking her for letting me go. I don't tell her that she's also partly the reason I want to leave for a while and get some peace of mind.

"When do you plan on leaving?" She asks me as I'm on my way out.

"I was thinking in a week on Friday. Or wait, no. The 2nd. I think that's a Wednesday."

"Fine. But you also have to ask for your dad's permission."

I nod and blow her a kiss before happily going back to my room.

"Why are you so happy about?" Adrik startles me.

He's leaning against the wall with his phone in his hand.

"I'm going to Italy next week."

His eyebrows shoot up. "Why?"

"For my birthday. I need the beach and the sea. Aren't you bored here?"

Adrik just shrugs.

"Do you want to come with?"

He makes a face. "Why would I want to come with?"

"I don't know. Just thought I'd ask."

"I'm fine here." Is all he says before he pushes himself off the wall and walks to his room.

A few seconds later I'm already on the beach in my head. Only a few more days, then I'll be on sitting on an *actual* beach in Italy with a drink in my hand.

Chapter 28

Valentina

Capo d'Orlando, Italy - July 2nd 2020

I landed in Italy last night, at the same landing strip we used last summer to go to Taormina. My mood shifted as soon as I stepped foot on Italian ground. It was like I wasn't Valentina Levin anymore; I was just someone going to their favourite place.

It didn't feel like home, but it was definitely the only place where I could just *be*.

Isabella came over this morning and settled into the first guestroom across the hall from my room, excitedly listing all the things we could do: reading on the beach, ordering in and eating our faces off, finding underground clubs or raves etc. When I asked her what she wanted to do today, she just said 'beach'.

Now here we are, sitting on the lounge chairs on the beach in front of the house, reading our books and enjoying the sun. We're on a mission to get tan before Matteo's birthday, so we're pretending like we're not melting under its rays.

"Should I ask around about raves?" She asks out of a sudden.

"I mean, are there any here?"

I feel like I need a party where I can just go have fun, let loose and maybe kiss a cute guy or three. At this point, I've forgotten what fun even is, not to mention that even the thought of being around people again gives me a weird feeling. Like I'm uncomfortable. I've gotten used to being by myself in my own energy, without anyone disturbing it.

Even being with Isabella is different; I feel like she's changed since the last time I saw her. She's gotten skinnier, and she's obviously avoiding talking about Vinnie. Maybe it's just in my head.

"Ugh, wait." She says.

I hear some rustling coming from her phone, then a familiar voice saying 'che fai'.

"I'm on the beach." She says in English.

"Con chi stai?"

"Valentina." She answers and turns the camera towards me. I wave at Matteo then look back at my book.

"Hi. Listen, I need your help with my birthday party."

Isabella chuckles. "Meaning what?"

"Meaning, I just can't focus on it right now, but I wanna do something, and you always have the best ideas."

"You love kissing my ass."

"I will literally do it if you want me to. Just help me."

"Fine. Who do you want to invite? Just send me a list."

"And I want a yacht."

I see Isabella rolling her eyes under her sunglasses. "A small one. Mattco, you cannot drive a boat."

This makes me laugh. "Do you actually want to drive a boat?"

"Can you help me or not? Please?" He whines on the other end, completely ignoring my question.

"Fiiiine. I guess we can-"

"We can go from Palermo to Taormina and spend the night at our house." Matteo interrupts her, and I can hear the excitement in his voice.

"You give me the invite list, first of all. And second of all, everyone needs to be tested before coming. I'm not fucking around with my health."

"You're on a beach with another person, from a different country."

"And you want to organize a *party*."

There's a sigh on the other end. *"I'll take care of sending tests before the party."*

"Good. Send me the list."

"Thank you, you're the best! Mwah!" He says, making a kissy noise.

"Byeee." She turns to look at me over her sunglasses after ending the call. "You're coming."

"Am I even invited?"

She scoffs like I've just insulted her.

"I mean, I don't want to intrude on a small-"

"Since when do you care?!"

"I don't know-"

She raises her hand to stop me from explaining myself further.

"It's Matteo. He'll invite you."

An hour or so later, she gets a text.

"See?"

She pushes her phone in my face. It's a screenshot of a list of names, and I spot mine in the middle.

"I told you he'd invite you."

My brain tells me that he invited me just because I was there when he talked to Isabella, but I just smile. I wanted a party, and now I have one.

Palermo, Sicily - July 7th 2020

I woke up at seven in the morning so we could arrive at Matteo's house in Palermo before he woke up. Isabella had arranged a private driver to take us from my house to his, but that didn't help my mood. The fact that I didn't even get the chance to have a coffee and smoke a cigarette before we left made me irritable and cranky.

We arrive in front of his house a little past eleven, and I'm glad I know the place because I know exactly where to find the coffee machine.

The Barone kids and Ariana are already in the kitchen. We greet each other and I ask whether anyone would like some coffee. Isabella and Ariana nod, and then Vinnie comes over and asks me if I want a drink.

"After I have my coffee and cigarette." I mumble, feeling bad that my mood doesn't match his.

"Do you like Aperol?"

"Sure." I say and manage to give him a smile.

I take my cup once it's ready and go outside to the terrace overlooking the sea. Vinnie joins me a few minutes later, right as I'm about to light my cigarette.

He's holding two Aperols and watches me alternate between the cigarette and the coffee.

"You're in a bad mood." He observes, a small smirk playing on his lips.

"Not for long."

We make small talk while we take sips of our drinks, and he tells me how he started going out despite the restrictions a few weeks ago. He leaves out the part about the girl from Tinder and asks me if I've heard from Sofia instead.

I make a confused face. "I'm not even friends with her, so no."

"Nobody's heard from her in weeks, maybe even months. Her mother told me she went to visit some relatives up north, but I'm not sure whether that's true. And she hasn't been answering me either for the past couple of weeks."

I can see he's stressed about it, worried even, but it's normal to care.

"Has she done this before? When you were broken up or had a fight?"

Vinnie shakes his head. "No, never. And her mother loves me, I used to talk to her when Sofia wouldn't talk to me."

We hear raised voices from inside, and I know Matteo must've come downstairs. I feel my heart beating through my entire chest for some reason, and I wonder whether it's just the coffee kicking in.

"I think Matteo's up." Vinnie says, changing the subject.

We put our cigarettes out and I follow him to the door.

"Happy birthday you little weasel." Vinnie laughs and walks in front of me to hug Matteo.

Our eyes meet over Vinnie's shoulder as they hug. He's wearing shorts that show off his leg tattoos and a white shirt. *Objectively*, he looks good.

"I see you've already started." He jokes and points to my drink.

I'm happy to see him. "It's your birthday, isn't it?"

I hug him too and wish him happy birthday. He smells really good, like he just got out of the shower. The tips of his hair are still wet, and I notice a tattoo under his ear that I hadn't seen before.

"Thanks."

We pull away and I step back before I even think about how close we are.

"Is that what you're wearing?" Isabella asks him.

Matteo looks down at himself. "What's wrong with my fit?"

"Everybody's dressed for a party." Ariana says.

"So? When I have fun I like being comfortable, I don't care about looking good."

He goes over to the coffee machine and that's when everyone switches the subject. At some point he goes upstairs, only to emerge with a smile on his face, saying he's ready to go. I double check that I haven't left my cigarettes outside before I follow the group out the door.

We set off towards Taormina around four. The boat is a nice cream-colored motor yacht with two decks and warm lights.

Isabella and I settle on a couple of lounge chairs, and I toe off my sneakers so I can tan my feet.

Ariana brings over a jug of Sangria and sits down on the empty chair next to us. She looks out onto the front deck, where the boys are getting undressed.

Isabella and I exchange looks, then turn our head back to the boys.

I imagine she must be watching him, since she's put her sunglasses on to be less obvious.

My eyes trail over to Matteo, who's already in his blue trunks, laughing at something Marco has just said. The tattoo on his chest glistens in the sun, and he runs his fingers over it.

Our eyes meet across the deck and I panic for a second, like I've been caught doing something I shouldn't have.

He smirks at me and I turn my head, only to see Ariana waving at him. I realize then that I wasn't the one he was looking at.

The boat stops at some point, and I spend the next hour trying to avoid looking over at the guys. They're jumping in the water, screaming and laughing amongst themselves.

Their voices echo through the air, and I get a sense of contentment watching them. I'm happy for them, or maybe I'm happy just for being here. I don't remember the last time feeling this content.

Maybe the last time I was in Italy.

***

It's already dark outside, and the mood has shifted since we've smoked a few joints and the lights on the upper deck have been turned on. We're supposed to be in Taormina in less than two hours, and I can't find my other pack of cigarettes.

My semi-drunk self needs to chain-smoke while talking to the girls on the couch. A laughter catches my attention and I look over to where the guys are sat around a table.

Of course.

"Has anybody seen my cigarettes?" I ask, walking over to their table. They've been playing poker for nearly an hour, and I've been looking everywhere for the past fifteen minutes.

I immediately spot the pack of Golds on the table.

"What do you smoke?" Vinnie asks me.

"Marlboro Gold."

"That's mine." Matteo immediately says and points to the pack.

"Since when?"

"Since I got it yesterday."

"You smoke the Red ones."

"They don't sell them at the corner store anymore."

I roll my eyes and extend my hand. "I'll have my pack now."

"When did you lose it?" He asks, pretending not to have heard me.

"An hour ago."

"I've been at this table for- well, okay, for less than an hour. But this *is* mine."

He grins at me like he usually does when he's trying to be smarter than me, which instantly annoys me.

"Are you serious? It's mine."

Matteo shakes his head, remaining calm. "No, it's not."

Isabella speaks up from her spot on the couch. "Does it matter? I have an extra one, you can have it, Valle."

"We're bored, let's play a game." Ariana whines. For some reason, she's annoyed me today as well.

Matteo and I make eye contact. I can't help but roll my eyes once more before walking over to Isabella.

"We're already playing a game." Vinnie says. When he sees Isabella won't budge, he sighs. "Fine. Let's play something."

"It's my birthday, we should play something *I* want to play."

The boys walk over to us and Matteo sits down to my left.

"What do you want to play then?" I ask, having had enough of his attitude.

Of course, he shrugs. "How about the game we played last time?"

After a few challenges in a row, Matteo complains. "Why is it so boring?"

Two more dares after, he groans again.

I don't hold back this time. "Maybe you should play the game of buying your own cigarettes and shutting up."

"Maybe you should remember when you finish your-"

"Can we not?" Isabella says, then looks down at her phone. "There's a dare for you Matteo. You have to down your drink or kiss the player to your right."

It takes me one second to realize that I am on his right because he's on my left. He dumbly looks at Eddie.

"That's your left." I tell him, almost laughing.

I lean in closer, still not over the fact that all he's been doing since he got here is complain.

There's no way he'll do it. Or maybe he will? Him saying no would be a little embarrassing for me.

He leans in closer as well, which makes me follow his lead, not wanting to seem insecure.

Pull away.

My mind goes back to the cigarettes and I smile without thinking. The fact that we're closer than we've ever been before doesn't faze me.

We've been this close before

"Well? Are you asking yourself how to lie about the cigarettes right now?"

Isabella throws her hands up in a desperate manner. "Oh, I can't take this anymore."

I know what she's about to do before she actually does it.

Our lips meet halfway, and I get an instant déjà vu. Suddenly, I want to continue the kiss, and I feel that switch going off in my head, turning to a setting I didn't even know existed.

Isabella pulls her hand away and Matteo slips backwards making her laugh. "Was that so hard?"

"More than it looked." Matteo jokes.

Isabella continues. "Matteo, who is more likely to end up drunk in a ditch? Vinnie or Eddie?"

Matteo doesn't seem to hear her. He looks like he's somewhere else, thinking about something that has nothing to do with Isabella's question.

She steps closer to him when he doesn't respond. "Matteo? Are you even paying attention?!"

"What?"

"Are you incapable of just doing a simple task?" She groans, tapping on the screen to skip the question.

I see him looking at me and I understand now that he was probably thinking about the kiss. It doesn't even count as an actual kiss; it's like we're in fifth grade, playing truth or dare for pecks.

I spend the rest of the game looking anywhere else but at his actual face. I catch him turning looking at me a few times, but I convince myself that it's just in my head. After all, the reason I am so caught up in the kiss is because I haven't come into contact with a guy who wasn't family in months.

The kiss wasn't even that good, anyway.

Taormina, Sicily – July 8th 2020

We arrive at Matteo's house a little before midnight. Their dock is small and dimly lit, made from a stone that looks ancient.

The boat is slowly reversing as we emerge down the stairs, waiting to disembark. I'm way past tipsy now, and I'm not sure whether I'm more drunk or stoned.

"Let's continue this in my room!" Vinnie suggests and everyone cheers.

On my way to the lower deck, I realize I forgot my phone charger, so turn around to go back upstairs. I let Matteo and Marco slip past me before I quickly climb the last steps.

It's not on the table nor by the bar, but I find it squished between some cushions on the couch.

I realize how eerie the place is as I slowly walk down the stairs, trying not to trip. Even though it's dark and I can barely see because there's a strange fog hanging low in the air. And the *silence*. The silence is the worst part.

I see Matteo waiting by the stairs on the lower deck, but he appears to look right through me as I come down.

The lights on the yacht have been shut off and everyone but the two of us has already offboarded.

I can hear the others chatting as they walk up the steps leading through the trees and up to the house.

"Did you find what you were looking for?" He asks me as I walk down the last couple of steps. His voice is tense, and for some reason it rubs me the wrong way.

"No. I was looking for *your* pack." I sarcastically say, just to provoke him.

"I don't know what you want to hear from me." Matteo sighs, his Italian accent getting heavier, like it always does when he's trying to dramatically articulate himself. He looks stressed, like he needs a break from life.

I immediately soften. "I was just joking."

It's the first time we've ever had to put a disclaimer to our little unspoken 'let's see how far you can take it' game (or whatever it is that we're doing).

He huffs, looking annoyed that I felt the need to explain myself.

It makes him look like he can't keep up.

We stand there at the bottom of the stairs, looking at each other, neither of us saying anything.

I look down at his lips just in time to see his tongue move across them. An earthy feeling settles into the pit of my stomach, and I realise that I am *incredibly* attracted to him right now.

I don't know who gives in first, but our mouths collide before our bodies even touch. His lips taste more like Tequila now and his mouth is warm. One of his hands comes up to the back of my neck, hot against my skin.

Matteo pulls me closer to him, and our bodies are touching all over for the first time. His smell is everywhere, filling up my senses and turning me on. Our tongues seem to be working in sync, like we already know what to do.

Everything else around me fades to black as I focus on how kissing him feels. He's the best kisser out of everyone I've ever kissed, because it's like he already knows *exactly* how I want to be kissed. He kisses with just the right balance between rough and slow, deep and gentle.

I sigh into his mouth again, pushing my lower body up against his by instinct. He bends down a little and I throw one of my arms over his shoulders when his hands come down to grip into my hips.

He walks me backwards until my back hits the wall. The collision puts pressure on his body against mine, making me tremble at the friction.

We keep kissing for I don't know how long, Matteo's cold hand pressing against my neck right under my earlobe to keep me in place.

A scream of laughter comes from somewhere above us, and it's enough to break the bubble we have stepped in.

He's still holding my head back slightly, our heavy breaths mingled together as we come back to reality. I look at his face, realizing that I have never seen it so close to mine, not even during the dare a few hours ago.

His eyes are different, almost completely black now from what I can tell in the moonlight. I want him to kiss me again, but the moment has passed.

Matteo lets go of me and steps back, leaving all the parts of me he touched cold.

"We should uh-" he says, voice hoarse, which lets me know that it was as intense for him as it was for me.

I follow him off the boat and onto the dock. He stops to check his pockets, making sure he hasn't forgotten anything, and I feel like the energy in the air is suffocating me.

There's a heat coming off his body as he silently walks in front of me, and I wonder if he can hear my heart pulsing in my throat.

I wonder what he's thinking when he's silent.

I can usually tell what people are thinking and feeling by their body language and their expressions. We learned this last semester in Business Psychology, and it has been my favourite course so far. But it's different with Matteo.

He stops for a moment and looks over my shoulder, as if to double check whether the boat is still there. I want to joke that it won't float away, but something has changed between us, so I bite my tongue.

He goes up the steps and we only stop when we reach the stairs leading up to the second floor. I remember seeing these steps a year ago, liking how they spiralled up along the column like a snake.

Where do I sleep?

I don't ask out loud, but I'm suddenly aware that Isabella never made any remarks about our sleeping arrangement.

"Where does Isabella sleep?" I ask instead. My voice comes out croaky, like I've been eating sand and am in desperate need of water.

He starts walking up the steps. "In a guest room. That's where she usually sleeps when she comes here."

We arrive on the second floor and the balcony door separating the hallway from the outside is already open. There are loud voices and music coming from a room, and Matteo stops in front of the door, placing his hand on the knob.

I look at his hand, then back up at him. "Well? Open it."

My words die in my throat, and I can't even figure out why. I can't even think because I get the sudden urge to kiss him again.

He's the one to take the first step this time, and it's not as soft as it was before. He grabs the back of my neck and tilts his head to make my mouth more accessible.

The way he kisses me, like he *wants* it, makes me weak. It ignites something in me I forgot even existed.

My hands grab his face to bring him closer, if it's even possible. I sigh into his mouth and his fingers tighten their grip into my hair.

We pull away for a second, our chests still pressed together. The air around me us feels heavy and I can tell we're both confused and surprised at the same time.

It's like months of pent-up tension I wasn't even aware of have just been released.

I look into his eyes, and I can tell he wants this as much as I do. I bite my lip when I feel his hands slipping down to my waist.

I'm the one to lean in first this time, and the way he smirks before we kiss tells me everything I need to know.

Same.

"Where's Valentina?" Isabella's voice comes from behind the door.

I pull away. "Go." I tell him and he opens the door, not having to be told twice.

I haven't been in the room before, but it looks like it must be a guest room. Everyone turns to stare at us.

"Speaking of the devil." Isabella grins, then she looks at my face. She squints her eyes at me before looking at Matteo.

My eyes focus on something else in the room, lips still burning. He isn't saying anything right now, and I ask myself whether it's because he's repeating the kiss over and over in his head, like I unwillingly am.

I know what I said about wanting to kiss a cute guy, but this is not what I meant.

I hate this. I hate that it was so good and so short that it left me wanting more. And what I hate most of all, is that out of all the people in the world, it had to be *him*.

Chapter 29

Matteo

Taormina, Sicily – July 8th 2020

Matteo doesn't know what came over him when he first kissed her. All he knows is that the moment he saw her coming down the stairs, and the way her eyes sparkled when she made the cigarette comment did something to him.

He's never thought about kissing her until the moment Isabella pushed their heads together and their lips touched. The sound she made in that moment rang through his entire body and made him want to do it again.

Now, as they enter the room where the rest of their friends are sitting and drinking, it's all he can think about.

"Speaking of the devil." Isabella says and looks between the two of them.

Matteo wonders if she can tell what they did.

Valentina sits down next to her and takes the drink out of her hand. She seems to be in her own world somewhere inside her head, so Matteo tears his eyes away from her and goes to sit next to Vinnie.

If he glances in her direction more often now, he doesn't notice. Suddenly it's like he's very aware that she's in the room, sitting on the couch across from him.

"Your birthday is also in July, isn't it?" Isabella asks her as she refills their glasses.

Valentina nods, eyes flickering to Matteo for a split of a second. He only catches it because he was looking at her first.

"The 22nd." She answers.

"Are you going to be in Italy for it?"

"Yeah, probably. I've already talked to my mother about it."

"And we're all alone in that big house." Isabella whines. "We should all do something."

Valentina hesitates and looks around the room. Everyone is watching and listening to their conversation now, and she looks intimidated.

"Maybe she doesn't want to invite us." Pia says with a mean hint in her voice.

As usual, Valentina doesn't react. She just smiles at her then looks somewhere else, which only seems to annoy Pia even more.

"It's not that, I have fun with you guys. I'm just not sure about the 'being outside if it's illegal' thing." She rambles.

Vinnie motions to the room. "I mean, we're all here now."

"Yeah, but my parents aren't that-"

"Oh God, who even cares what their parents think?!" Pia groans in Italian, rolling her eyes.

Valentina looks confused. "What did you say?"

Pia plasters a fake smile on her face. "Just that I love your outfit." Then she adds 'you fool' in Italian.

"Are you okay? Why are you being so rude?" Matteo snaps back in Italian.

Pia looks embarrassed now, just like she did when they were in Palermo and Matteo called her out.

Isabella shoots Matteo a curious look, probably surprised that he cares enough to get involved.

"I'm bored, I'm going to go to sleep." Pia decides then. She downs her drink and slams the empty glass on the table.

"She loves drama." Vinnie says once the door shuts behind her.

"Maybe we should go too." Valentina suggests. "We have a train in the morning."

Vinnie looks sad. "To go where?"

"Back to my house in Capo."

"Yes, we're going to have a few weeks just to sit in the sun and do nothing." Isabella smirks, downing her drink as well.

"Why don't you stay for a few more days, and then we can all go back together?"

"Because I want to be surrounded by female energy, gossip, and drinks, not you smelly idiots with your awful jokes." Isabella smiles, then turns to Valentina. "Let's go."

Valentina agrees and stands up, placing her drink on the table. "Goodnight."

Matteo watches the two of them leave the room.

With Ariana being the only girl left, she quickly grabs everyone's attention. Her sights are obviously set on either Vinnie or Matteo and they're all way past tipsy.

Eddie and Marco are in their own world, talking on the couch in the corner and laughing at something only the two of them would find funny.

At some point, Vinnie brings up Sofia again, which makes Matteo groan and roll his eyes. Vinnie is sitting one of the chairs at the table now, and Ariana has taken his place on the bed next to Matteo.

"I think something happened to her."

"Like what?" Ariana asks, leaning into Matteo. "Something *bad*?"

"Or maybe she's just ignoring you." Matteo suggests.

"I'm going to go over to her house next week."

"That's a bad idea man."

"Why? She can't just ignore me forever."

"Maybe she just wants it to be over." Ariana butts in. "And yes, going over to her house is a bad idea. She might get a restraining order."

"Are you serious? I haven't done anything to her! If anything, she did something to us at that New Year's party." Vinnie argues.

"Exactly. Just take the win and move on. There's plenty of other girls." Matteo says, eyes drifting to Ariana to prove a point.

Vinnie rolls his eyes at the insinuation. "I can't leave things unfinished like this."

"Maybe she's your karma for what you've done to other girls." Ariana grins.

Matteo points at her. "She has a point."

Ariana winks at him then, and that's when Matteo knows he could sleep with her tonight if he wanted to.

"Whatever, I'm going to sleep." Vinnie mumbles, turning his head to Eddie and Marco, who are still talking. "You two, go chat shit in Marco's room."

"What about me?" Ariana pouts, looking at Matteo.

"You can sleep in my room tonight. Or with Pia."

"Okay." She doesn't clarify where she wants to sleep, but Matteo intuitively knows what's about to happen.

Marco and Eddie are the first ones to leave the room, and Matteo follows Ariana, closing the door behind them.

His own room feels cold, so he goes over to the air conditioner to turn it on and make it warmer. Ariana is sitting on the couch, typing on her phone.

"You cold?" Matteo asks as he sits down across from her so he can roll a joint.

"Not really."

The conversation feels a little forced, like it's a very bad scripted foreplay before what they both know is most probably going to happen happens.

She watches him roll the joint, the occasional nails typing on the screen and the AC being the only sounds filling the silence. Her lips curl into a smile when his tongue darts over the paper so he can roll it shut.

He nods over to the JBL speaker in the corner on the windowsill. "Put some music on?"

"Sure."

She plays some Italian rap everybody knows while Matteo lights up and pulls the ashtray in the middle of the table.

He passes her the joint after a few long drags.

"Did you enjoy your birthday?" She asks when she passes it back.

He nods. "Yeah, you?"

"Mhm. I always have fun when I'm on a boat." She lets out smoke through her nose and pauses for a second before speaking again. "I didn't know you were that close with Valentina."

Matteo finds it weird that she brings her up. "She's more Isabella's friend, but we get along. I like her."

Ariana smiles, but Matteo can tell it's forced. He wonders what Ariana could possibly have against Valentina. Pia also has no real reason, which means that they probably feel threatened that they're not the only good-looking girls.

"Does she bother you?" He asks.

Ariana shakes her head. "Oh, no. I was just wondering. She's alright."

Matteo nods, not really buying it.

"How come you didn't invite Raisa?"

Matteo makes a face then. "What? Why would I invite her?"

She rolls her eyes. "Because you sleep with her?"

"So? I don't have to invite every girl I fuck to my birthday."

The way he says it doesn't seem to faze her. "She was at Vinnie's birthday though."

"That was Vinnie's choice."

"She has a boyfriend now."

Matteo raises his eyebrows. He can see through her act, but it's late and the weed is making him horny. "Good for her."

"I think she liked you."

"Good for me I guess." He smirks, running a hand through his hair as he takes a few more drags.

"Bad for her." Ariana chuckles, tucking a strand of blonde hair behind her ear.

"Why is that?"

"Because you're a fuckboy."

He's not offended in the slightest. He knows he has this reputation, and the truth is, he has had sex with more than a handful of women, but he has never given them false hopes or told lies to get them into bed. They're the ones that choose to do it, *willingly*, and then get bitter because they catch feelings he doesn't return.

"Why are you here then?" He daringly retorts.

She doesn't seem to shy away from it, and smirks instead. "For fun, why else?"

He puts the joint out in the ashtray and stands up. Ariana watches him walk over to the bed and take off his shirt before sitting down at the edge of it.

She nods to herself before following his lead, taking off her dress on the way to the bed. Their eyes meet as she straddles him and places her hands behind his neck.

Her lips are soft, and she tastes like weed and alcohol. She kisses with way less tongue than Matteo would like, but she's hot and kind of nonchalant in an attractive way.

The sex ends up being better than average as she lets him do most of the work, but when he falls asleep that night, he feels satisfied with the way his birthday turned out.

***

Taormina, Sicily – July 18th 2020

Vinnie, Pia, and Eddie ended up leaving five days after his birthday to go to their home in Capo d'Orlando with their parents, which left Matteo and Marco alone in Taormina for a few days.

They got bored three days in and decided to go back to Palermo, but their father called Matteo just as they were about to leave, instructing him to stay in Taormina because he was on his way.

As usual, he didn't give any details as to why Matteo had to stay behind and Marco was free to leave, but Matteo suspected it had something to do with the Organization.

For the first couple of days his father just had meetings in his office without paying attention to him. This annoyed him even more, because he was just supposed to wait around with no explanation whatsoever.

He tried passing the time by playing video games and occasionally texting Ariana, but at some point, he got bored of that too. Ever since they had sex on his birthday, she's been texting him and sending memes, which, okay, *does* entertain him a little.

She doesn't care about how it looks that she's the one texting first. She also doesn't seem to mind that she's the one initiating a conversation 90% of the time, which Matteo finds refreshing.

Sitting in his room playing FIFA online with Vinnie, Matteo decides he's had enough.

"I'm gonna take a break." He says into the headset.

Vinnie agrees on the other end and Matteo shuts the TV off before he stands up. His father has been in the office with Romeo all day today, and now it's nearly seven. He's going to ask why his father insisted he stayed here, since he hasn't said much in the past few days.

The office is at the end of the hall, the wooden double doors closed, as usual. He hears hushed voices talking behind them, so he hesitates to knock. He knows his father doesn't like to be disturbed, but that doesn't mean Matteo has to waste his time doing nothing.

"This is serious." His father's voice comes from the other end of the door.

Matteo's hand is already raised, ready to knock.

"Are we sure?" Romeo asks.

"All the signs point to it."

Paulo Barone is also here then, not in Capo with his family like Matteo had assumed.

"I've gone through the security footage of the last two years, and there is no sign of a rat." Romeo says then.

The blood in Matteo's veins goes cold.

"We're going to ask our informants to keep an eye out. For now, no one else knows about Siracusa but the three of us. Let's keep it that way."

Matteo hears a chair scraping against the floor, so he quickly knocks.

"Yes, Matteo?"

He opens the door and walks in. "Why did you ask me to stay in Taormina? I've been bored for the past few days."

His father is sitting at the desk with a cigar in his hand. Paulo is in the corner by the drinks table, and Romeo was just about to leave.

"We'll talk about it tomorrow. Right now you need to drive Romeo to the landing strip."

"You asked me to stay behind so I can be your driver?" Matteo groans. "You have other people for that, I'm sure."

"Don't be a smartass and do as I say."

Matteo rolls his eyes and waits for Romeo to leave the room first before following him out.

***

His father calls him into the office the next day before noon. He's alone, standing in one of the corners by a giant painting of Enzo Giudice.

"It's time for your training." Is all he says.

"What training?"

"You'll see."

"I thought Luca was supposed to train me."

"He's going to show you the ropes when you're in New York, yes. But right now, you'll do it with us."

Before Matteo can ask who 'us' is, his father pushes on the right edge of the painting, and the wall in the corner moves. Matteo is speechless.

"What is this?"

His father doesn't answer as he steps through the door. Matteo follows him and watches as the door closes behind him, leaving them in complete darkness.

A few seconds later, a light turns on to reveal a spiral staircase descending into darkness. He follows his father down a few flights of stairs, nearly getting dizzy at how fast they're going.

When they stop in front of a black door, Matteo's pretty sure they're one or two levels underground now.

"There's three people who know about this room. You're the fourth."

His father pushes the door open, and Matteo's breath dies in his throat. It's a fucking armoury. The three walls in front of him are filled to the brim with guns: everything from pistols to handguns to proper machine guns.

Paulo is looking at a gun hoisted up on the wall, turning around when he hears the door open.

"What is this?" Matteo asks again.

"This is our Scogliera armoury." Paulo answers, hoisting a bag that was on the table in the middle over his shoulder.

"Is it even legal to have these guns?"

No one answers, so Matteo takes it as a very blunt 'no'.

"Why are you showing me this? Are you going to train me to shoot?"

His father nods and hands him a pistol from the wall. "Take this and follow us."

Matteo doesn't even know what to say as they leave the room once again, the door closing behind them with a thud.

Somehow, they end up in the garage, then out in their back gardens. They silently walk through the iron gates separating the back garden from the woods on the cliff, and after a few more minutes, they're in an open field that can't be seen from anywhere inside the house.

There's a short stone wall in front of them with bottles and cans on top of it, and Matteo immediately recognizes it as a shooting range. They stop a good fifty meters away from the wall.

Matteo's palms are sweating around the gun when Paulo drops the black bag on the ground. When he opens it, Matteo can see a bunch of smaller guns inside, alongside two machine guns.

"So by training you meant shooting training."

His father nods, then points to the bottles on the wall. "Try to take one out."

Matteo points the gun towards them, but nothing happens when he presses the trigger.

"You have to take the safety off." Paulo explains, and before he can step closer to show him how, Matteo pulls on the small silver switch at the end of the gun, making it click.

Paulo and his father exchange looks with raised eyebrows.

"Alright, now point it to the-"

He pulls the trigger, and the gun barely makes a sound. The bullet misses the bottle he was aiming at.

"It's not loud at all." Matteo notices, looking at the gun with a scorpion engraving in the leather handle.

"It's a silent gun." Paulo explains, before he comes closer and teaches him how to properly hold it, one hand over the other. "Now look right above the barrel. Don't rush."

After two more tries, Matteo finally hits a bottle. On the next try, he knocks over a can.

"Good." His father speaks for the first time since he's started shooting. "You're better at this than expected."

"Why are you teaching me how to shoot? Does this have anything to do with your conversation yesterday?"

"What conversation?"

Matteo drops the hand holding the gun to his side. "I overheard you talking about a mole."

"We don't have moles, Matteo. We have *rats*."

The way he says it is cold, like there's no worse thing in the world than being a rat.

"What does that even mean?"

His father and Paulo exchange looks. "It means someone is leaking information to our enemies."

Matteo wants to roll his eyes but doesn't. He knows better than that. "What enemies?"

"Other families. Families that have wronged us in the past."

He's being avoidant. "Wronged us how?"

"Killed our men, for example."

"Who was killed? Last thing I remember, *we* were the ones that had to hide a body about a month ago."

"It doesn't matter who was killed."

"When did it happen?"

"It also doesn't matter."

"How can you even be sure? This is-"

"We have informants."

"But Romeo said there's nothing unusual on the cameras."

"We don't have video proof, but-"

"Then how can you even know for sure?"

"They know about some of our drop off zones and times, and our secret storage spaces that only the closest people in our family know of. It's information that couldn't have come from anywhere but inside this family."

"What happens to rats?"

Paulo takes clicks the safety of his gun and points to one of the bottles lined up on the stone fence before taking it out. Matteo watches in awe then turns back to his father.

"Who is it?"

"We don't know for sure."

"I don't want to kill anyone, especially if you're not sure!"

His father's face is stern. "You took an oath."

Matteo's heart starts beating faster. "That wasn't in the oath! You told me I wouldn't have to shoot people!"

"I didn't tell you that."

Matteo takes a step back. "Fine, grandma told me then. It doesn't matter because I don't want to kill anyone."

His father doesn't answer as he takes the machine gun and holds it out for Matteo to take.

"Try this one now."

Matteo exchanges the pistol for the machine gun, which is heavier and harder to handle. There's a lens at the end of the barrel, so he squints an eye as he points it to a bottle. He takes it out on the first try.

"Good, now take twenty steps back and try again."

He does as asked, taking two more bottles off the wall. "This one's easier."

"And deadlier. But you're a natural." Paulo adds, a proud look on his face. His father nods along, and it's the first time in ages that Matteo has seen him so obviously proud.

"What's in Siracusa?" He asks when they're done an hour later, on their way back to the house.

"We planted a fake story to weed out the rat, and Romeo is over there right now to set it up. If it all goes well, we'll have our rat by the end of August."

***

Taormina, Sicily – July 20th 2020

His father leaves the next day, saying that he has some business to take care of in New York with Paulo, but not without telling him to be in Taormina at the beginning of August.

Matteo finds himself alone in the house when he wakes up, so he gets some coffee from the kitchen and goes to sit on the upper terrace overlooking the sea.

His mind takes him back to what Valentina said about never being sad if she were to live at sea. He isn't sad, but he's bored, so he texts Vinnie, Ariana, and Isabella, asking each of them what they're doing.

Vinnie's reply comes first.

Matteo rolls his eyes and doesn't even bother replying. He's over the whole thing already.

His phone vibrates again just as he lights his second cigarette.

Isabella's texts come in then, so Matteo switches to that conversation.

She sends a photo of herself holding a half-empty glass in her hand, sunglasses on her nose. Valentina is sitting on the lounger behind her, reading a book. Images of the kiss against the wall come into his brain, then of the one on the boat.

He'd be surprised if Valentina invited Ariana, and even though he doesn't want to admit it, he'd also be a bit...disappointed.

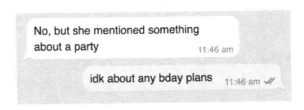

He goes back to the conversation with Isabella.

Before Matteo can go back to the conversation with Ariana, Isabella is facetiming him. He absentmindedly runs a hand through is hair before answering.

"Yes?"

"She said yes!" Isabella says, moving the camera so it shows Valentina.

She lifts her head up from the book she's reading and looks at the screen. Her eyebrows rise and she smiles. *"Hi."*

"So, you're doing something for your birthday then?"

"Hello to you too." She sarcastically answers. *"But yeah, I was thinking about a pool party here."*

"Who did you think about inviting?"

"You're invited Matteo, if that's what you mean."

Matteo rolls his eyes. "I meant in general. I know *I'm* invited." He grins.

"I guess I kind of have to invite everyone who heard me talking about it." She says to Isabella.

"You don't have to invite anyone you don't want." Matteo says.

Isabella scoffs off camera. *"You wouldn't understand."* Her face comes back on the screen. *"Anyway, what are you up to?"*

"I'm *insanely* bored. Can I come a day early?"

"You mean tomorrow?"

"I mean right now."

Isabella turns her head to look at Valentina, and Matteo can't tell what she's doing, but Isabella rolls her eyes. *"Yes, you can come over. Everyone will be coming tomorrow night anyway I guess."*

Matteo smiles. "Great, I'll take a car and drive down there."

"Can't wait." Comes Valentina's sarcastic voice from off-camera before he hangs up.

Matteo's mood has shifted now, and he's happier than he's been in days just at the thought of getting out of here and going over to Capo d'Orlando.

He goes upstairs to pack a bag with some clothes and swimming trunks. Isabella sends him the location and he checks Waze to see how long he'll be, then texts Isabella his ETA.

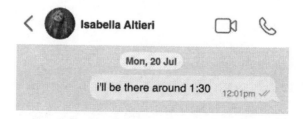

He finds the keys to the Mercedes in the hallway, then checks the conversation with Ariana.

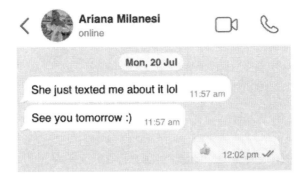

Matteo gets into the car and presses the button to start the engine.

Chapter 30

Matteo

He beats the GPS by fifteen minutes, but the gate is closed when he arrives, so he calls Isabella. The gate opens a couple of minutes later and he drives the car all the way up to the front of the house.

A feeling of peace and happiness settles in his stomach as soon as he gets out of the car with sunglasses on his nose and the bag in his hand.

The girls greet him by the door. Isabella is in her bathing suit and Valentina's wearing an orange sundress. She looks tanner now than the last time Matteo saw her, and she's not wearing any makeup.

She looks *good*.

"Well, here goes our girl time." Isabella groans but goes to hug him anyway.

"Where can I drop off my stuff?" He asks Valentina after they also hug. She smells like the perfume she always wears mixed with the sea.

"You can stay in Adrik's room, since he didn't want to come."

Matteo looks towards the stairs. "Thanks, but I don't know where that is."

"Up the stairs and to the left, then down the hall and the first door on the left."

When he returns downstairs, the girls are nowhere to be seen, so he goes into the kitchen first, where he finds a glass filled with Aperol Spritz. He grins as he grabs it and heads outside to check if they're by the pool.

He hears laughter coming from the beach, so he follows the narrow path paved with stones, where he finds the two of them. They're lying on two lounge chairs under an umbrella, with a table between them. There's another identical setup right next to them, so he goes over and takes a seat, setting his drink down on the table.

"So…what do you do for fun?" He asks after a few minutes of silence.

Valentina lets the book fall on her thighs, and Matteo notices she's taken off the dress, leaving her in a yellow bikini. He can see some small tattoos he didn't know she had on her waist, her ribcage, and behind her ear. He remembers talking about their tattoos back in Palermo a month ago.

"We just exist." She answers, pushing the sunglasses on top of her head. Her voice is monotone, like she's annoyed, but there's that twinkle in her eye that lets him know she's playing.

They get into the water fifteen minutes later, because Matteo can't sit still for too long. The girls bring their glasses into the water, giggling about the two guys playing catch with a ball in the water a hundred meters away.

The whole beach, as far as Matteo can see, is divided by stone fences, each house on the coast having its own private area.

"Who are they?" Matteo asks, swimming over to stand next to Isabella so he can drink out of her glass. She groans in protest, but he presses a kiss to her temple and drapes an arm around her shoulders.

"They're our neighbours." Valentina answers. "I think they moved in this summer; I haven't seen them before last week." She turns her head to look in their direction again. "How old do you think they are?"

"Old enough." Isabella wiggles her eyebrows.

"Do you know them?" Valentina asks him before she takes the glass up to her lips to take a sip.

Matteo rolls his eyes. "Yes, because all Italians know each other."

Valentina flips him off and takes another sip.

"Don't drink all my alcohol, you should've brought your own!" Isabella protests when Matteo goes in for another drink, slapping his hand.

He turns to Valentina then, whose eyes widen as she takes a step back. She raises her arm to put some distance between them. "Don't you even *dare*."

Matteo grins. "You know I have to now."

Valentina squeals when he makes a sudden movement, giving Matteo the perfect opportunity to grab her glass. She watches him down the entire glass and splashes him right in the face.

"You have to go inside and get us all drinks now." She concludes, swimming over to Isabella for refuge.

"Yeah, I'm not going to do that."

She shoots him an annoyed look, which only makes him smirk.

"I'll go. I have to go to the bathroom anyway." Isabella says, turning around to face the beach.

"Just pee here." Matteo tells her.

"I'm not a degenerate like you." Comes the answer, and they both watch her swim to the shore with two glasses in hand. Isabella grabs Matteo's glass as well and makes a point of downing it before walking up to the path, disappearing behind the tall living fences that shield the house.

Then it's just the two of them. Matteo is suddenly aware of the fact that it's the first time they've been alone since they kissed. He looks at her, only to see that her eyes are trained on his bicep tattoo. When she looks up, she knows she's been caught checking him out.

"So..." She starts, absentmindedly weaving her arms through the water. "How have you been?"

"Are you trying to make small talk with me?"

"What if I'm genuinely interested?"

"Are you?"

Her jaw clenches but her eyes remain playful. "Did anything interesting happen on your birthday after we went to sleep?"

Matteo thinks of telling her about Ariana but decides against it. "We drank, then went to bed." It's not lying, *per se*. But for some reason he doesn't think it's relevant to bring up sleeping with Ariana right now. "It was a fun night."

The sentence changes something in her brain, and he sees the exact moment her mind goes back to them kissing that night.

She swallows. "Yeah."

He takes a step towards her, and she brings a hand up to her mouth out of reflex. She's biting her nail to hide a smirk as she glances up at him, her stare following him as he comes even closer. She's looking at him with an expression that says they shouldn't be this close, like she's contemplating whether she should do something that hasn't even happened yet.

Her hand drops from her mouth when Matteo touches her waist underwater, bringing their chests together.

"What?" He asks, looking down at her. He sees the right side of her mouth twisting up into a smile.

She shakes her head, smile spreading as she tries to stay indifferent to their closeness. "Nothing." Her nails scrape across his belly underwater, and she bites her bottom lip in a daring way.

It ignites something in Matteo's core which makes his blood flow directly to his crotch. "Stop."

"Or what?" Her mouth opens, grin widening because she knows she's in control right now.

He kisses her without a second thought, hands moving directly to her ass.

She exhales into his mouth, making that *sound* as she grabs his face to deepen the kiss. Matteo presses their bodies together before lifting her up, her legs wrapping themselves around his waist underwater.

The way she kisses is incredible; it's deep and dirty, like she's enjoying it, and it's *exactly* what Matteo likes. It's turning him on so much it's almost ridiculous, and his brain goes to her saying she's never had sex in the sea.

The thought excites him even more, so he tangles one of his hands in the back of her hair, gently pulling at the roots. She moans, and unlike before, it's an outright moan that points to pleasure.

"Fuck, don't do that." She says into his mouth.

He smiles. "Why?"

"It turns me on."

Her blunt answer makes the insides of his brain collapse, but she continues kissing him and grinding herself against him. Matteo could swear his knees just went weak, so he tries to compose himself.

She suddenly pulls her face away and untangles her legs from his waist. "Shit."

Matteo turns his head to where she's looking, and they see Isabella appearing from behind the bushes, focused on carrying three glasses at once.

He lets go of her and takes a few steps back, nearly tripping over himself.

"I've got refiiiills!" Isabella yells. "Come get them while they're cold!"

Valentina starts walking towards her without sparing another look in his direction. He stays put and tries to think of literally anything else but her, so the effect she had on him wouldn't be visible once he gets out of the water.

When he finally sits down on his sunbed, the two of them are talking about going and chilling by the pool. He watches Valentina sipping on her drink, purposely avoiding his eyes. When she finally looks in his direction, their eyes meet.

She looks flushed from what has just happened and also a little guilty, which makes Matteo raise his brows and daringly smirk at her.

They spend the next half hour by the pool in silence, Matteo and Isabella on their phones and Valentina reading.

"I'm out again." Isabella whines from where she's laying on her stomach on a towel next to Valentina. They said they wanted to get that afternoon tan, but Matteo remained on the sunbed, hiding from the sun.

"Me too." Valentina agrees.

"It's your turn to make drinks."

Matteo realizes they're both looking at him. "Wha-me? Why me?"

"Because we were *incredibly* generous and took you in." Comes Valentina's answer. Matteo cocks his head in response.

"I want Mojitos now; I'm bored of Aperol." Isabella says then.

Matteo raises his hands in defense. "In case you forgot, I'm new here. I don't even know where the drinks are."

Isabella turns to Valentina then, who groans and stands up from her towel. Matteo smiles and stands up, gesturing towards the house. "Lead the way."

He watches her ass as she walks ahead of him into the house, stopping next to the fridge and pointing at it.

"This is the fridge."

He looks down at her. "Thank you."

Her lips look soft, and her cheeks are pink, obvious against her sun kissed face. Her eyes are lighter than he remembers, almost like dark honey, and Matteo takes a moment to just admire her beauty.

She coughs as she takes a step back, almost hitting the wall behind her. "What?" she asks and pushes the damp hair out of her face. "Why are you looking at me like that?"

He shrugs, unable to hold back a smile. "You look beautiful."

Valentina rolls her eyes then. He places his left hand on the wall beside her head, her eyes following the motion before she looks back at his face.

"Why are you rolling your eyes?"

"Does that line usually work on girls?"

It's his turn to roll his eyes. "Why would I need a 'line'? You already kissed me."

Valentina crosses her arms. "To get me to have sex with you? I guess." Matteo laughs at that, which annoys her even more. "What's so funny?"

"You think that's what I'm trying to do here? Get you to have sex with me?"

"What else then?"

"What if I just like kissing you?" he mocks her accent.

Her eyes flicker to his lips for a split of a second before coming back to his face.

"You're full of shit Matteo." She says, but her smirk gives her away.

"Like you aren't."

Her eyes widen as she tries to feign innocence. "I'm not the one who initiated this." She gestures between their chests.

His eyes stop on her cleavage, at how incredible way her breasts look being pushed up by her crossed arms. "Are you saying I forced you?"

She looks annoyed now because she definitely caught him looking. "I'm saying you started it."

"And you were happy to continue."

She cocks her head. "Oh really?"

"Mhm. And I also think you actually enjoy it."

"How could you tell?"

He slips his hand between her legs, catching her off guard and making her gasp in that really sexy way that turns him on.

"You're wet." He concludes.

She doesn't push his hand away from its place. "Oh please. We just got out of the pool, this doesn't prove anything."

"Why don't you mind me touching you then?"

She seems distracted because she answers back with a 'hm?'.

"You haven't pushed my hand away." He says, slipping his hand inside her bikini. "And you're *definitely* wet."

"I read this book." She starts, stuttering when his middle finger enters her. "That said that...fuck."

Their faces are closer now than they were when they first started talking. "That said what?"

"That the body reacts to sexual cues even though the mind isn't turned on. It's like a reflex."

Matteo licks his lips and tries to slip another finger in, which makes her grip into his arm to steady herself.

"We're- Isabella could walk in."

"So?"

Valentina makes a face. "I don't want- "

"Then let's be quick."

"You don't honestly think you can make me cum just like this." She bluntly states.

"Who said I wanted to make you cum?"

Her nostrils flare, signalling annoyance. "You wanna know what I think?"

"Do I?"

"I think you're *really* overrated, and I also think that most of the things said about you are just exaggerations."

"What things?"

He starts moving his fingers in lazy up-and-down motions, only to see what it would do to her.

"I don't know, about how the sex is incredible, and you know exactly what-ah, what you're doing. Because-" She stutters when he pushes his fingers further in "-because I don't think you do."

He sarcastically pouts. "Don't I?"

She shakes her head. "I think you get girls in bed with your cheesy lines and make them fall for you to the point where they can't tell average sex and good sex apart anymore."

"You seem to have thought about this a lot, hm?"

She shrugs. "Just an opinion."

Her legs unwillingly shake when he curls his fingers towards himself and keeps rubbing them in a constant rhythm. Her eyes flutter as she bites down her lip.

"I've never heard any complaints." He cockily continues as he picks up the pace, rubbing his fingertips against the same spot over and over again.

"Fuck." She breathes, her grip tightening against his arm.

"What's that?" He asks, stopping his movements.

"You can't just..." She lets out a frustrated moan.

"You like it then?"

"Don't make me say it."

"Oh, but I *want* you to say it."

"You're a fucking- "

"Valle? Matteo? Helloooo?" Matteo pulls his hand out instantly. "Where's my Mojito?"

Valentina ducks out from under his arm and rearranges her bikini just as Isabella enters the kitchen with a smile.

"I couldn't find the ice." Matteo coughs and goes over to the fridge.

"It's probably in the freezer." Isabella says and walks over to the other side of the counter. Matteo turns his back to her, hoping his she doesn't notice him trying to hide a boner.

Valentina is leaning against the counter, looking out of breath and a little shocked.

"Are you okay?" Isabella asks her while Matteo looks through the cupboards for alcohol and soda.

"Yeah."

"You look out of breath."

Matteo smirks to himself as he places the empty glasses on the island counter, trying to think of things that would make his hard-on go away faster. Looking at Valentina doesn't help.

"Yeah, I think I'm getting…I don't know. It's hot outside and I've had too many Aperols without any water." Valentina rambles, purposely avoiding Matteo's glare.

"I guess you're not used to Italian heat combined with drinks."

"Yes Valentina, it's from the *Italian* drinks, those are the strongest!" Matteo sarcastically adds as he pours the rum in the ice-filled glasses.

Valentina looks at him and he smirks as he takes his fingers up to his mouth, licking them clean. Her eyes widen and she turns her head to Isabella, cheeks turning pink once again.

"What, you mean the Aperols we just drank?" Isabella asks, oblivious.

"Yeah, those overrated Aperols." Matteo grins.

Valentina flips him off, which satisfies him even more. "They're overrated because they're good."

"Just make those mojitos already." Isabella groans, motioning to the half-filled glasses.

Matteo obeys and pours the soda, adds some mint, then pushes a glass towards Valentina while Isabella grabs hers. "Salute!" She says, lifting her drink.

"Salute!" Matteo repeats, eyes locking with Valentina over the counter as he takes the drink to his lips.

The girls leave to go back to their towels, and Matteo remains by the counter, checking his phone. Ariana texted him something about the party tomorrow, but he can't seem to focus on it.

He looks in their direction again. Valentina's on a towel, laying on her stomach next to Isabella, chatting and laughing. The sun is bright up in the sky which makes the pool water look like glitter. He feels thirteen again, where even the wind got him popping a hard-on. He's hornier than he remembers feeling in months, maybe even years. Maybe it's from the three Aperol Spritzes they drank while on the beach.

It's like ever since they kissed, the dynamic between them has shifted. She's much more comfortable calling him out and commenting on the dumb shit he says or does, and he's not holding back from saying exactly what he thinks. In a weird way, they're more comfortable with each other now, and there's a tension in the air that makes him unsure whether it's only in his head.

He's only known her for a year now, but looking at his best friend sitting there with her, laughing under the same sun they've always known, awakens a feeling in him. He feels like they've been doing this since the beginning of time, like he belongs exactly here with Valentina and Isabella and no one else.

Matteo realizes he feels at peace, like he did in that fountain that night.

Chapter 31

Valentina

Capo d'Orlando, Sicily – July 21st, 2020

Isabella and I spend the rest of the day by the pool until the sun starts to set on the horizon and it gets too cold to chill in a bathing suit.

"I want to order pizza."

I look up from my book to where Matteo is sitting by the edge of the pool, his legs in the water.

"Yes, *please.*" Isabella groans. "I'm so hungry I could die. Where are you ordering from?"

"I know a place."

Matteo and I make eye contact for a moment before his eyes drift back to the screen. A few seconds later he starts talking to someone in Italian, so I zone out and try to focus back on my book.

The pizzas arrive twenty minutes later, and we sit down at one of the tables on the terrace.

"What time are people arriving tomorrow?" He asks me with his mouth half full.

"I don't know, I guess around seven or eight. Might be sooner."

We eat our pizzas in peace after that, deciding to watch a movie before going to bed. We're all tired from sitting in the sound all day, and tomorrow's going to be a busy day.

As I get into bed with Isabella that night, my skin feels like it's glowing.

"It was okay, right?" She asks me in the darkness after we've done our going-to-bed routines. We would set a speaker in the bathroom as we took turns showering and doing our skincare, before getting into bed. There are guest rooms she could sleep in, but she preferred feeling 'at a sleepover vacation'. I agreed.

"Was what okay?"

"Matteo being here."

My throat goes dry as flashbacks fill my brain. "Yes, it was alright. He's…fun."

"I'm happy you two are getting along."

I turn on my side to look at her. "Really? Why?"

"Because it's the first time one of my close friends actually liked him and didn't end up sleeping with him."

A feeling settles in my stomach, and I'm not sure whether it's guilt or sorrow.

"I used to get along with Allison before they began dating. And I also liked Ariana before she stopped being the person I knew."

I don't want to lie and tell her that I'd never sleep with him. "He's okay."

"Happy birthday!" she says out of a sudden, before showing me the screen of her phone. "You're twenty now!"

Capo d'Orlando, Sicily – July 22nd 2020

I wake up after Isabella the next morning, judging by the fact that she's not in my room. She's talking in Italian to someone downstairs, and I remember that Matteo is also here.

My morning routine goes on for longer than usual because I'm procrastinating on going downstairs.

Finally, I emerge in the kitchen after I got bored upstairs.

"I drank your coffee." Is what Matteo says when he sees me.

"Great, thanks." I sarcastically answer. I walk over to press the button on the machine.

"Happy birthdaaay." Isabella sings, coming in from the garden. "I made us birthday Mimosas."

The love I feel for her in this moment is the only confirmation I need for my 'should I ever even consider sleeping with Matteo or not' dilemma. I would never do anything to ever hurt or lose Isabella, so the decision not to do it is fine for me.

She looks at me making myself coffee and scoffs at Matteo. "I told you not to drink her coffee."

He shrugs and checks his phone. "Vinnie is landing in two hours. Asked if we wanted to pick them up at the airport."

"Sure."

He looks at me, eyes softening. "Happy birthday, Valentina."

Ninety minutes later I was still getting ready for the airport, and Isabella was already calling both of us downstairs.

"How come I'm the first one to be ready?" She yells from the bottom of the stairs.

"Un fottuto minuto!" Comes Matteo's voice from down the hall.

I'm not sure what he said, but I'm pretty sure he threw a swear word in there.

I set down the perfume and look at myself in the mirror one last time before I leave my room.

"Can you see what's taking him so long?" Isabella asks me when I'm about to take the first step down the stairs. "The driver is already outside."

"Sure."

I walk over to Adrik's room, which is wide open.

"What are you doing?" I ask when I step inside. Matteo is at the wall containing some of Adrik's photos. He's looking at a photo, and he seems to be ready to leave.

"This photo." He says, pointing to the wall. "It looks familiar."

I know it's a photo of Adrik and Aurora before I even see it.

"Why?"

"I feel like I've seen it before."

He turns his head to look at me. I watch his eyes go down to my body, then back up to meet mine.

The air in the room feels thick all of a sudden.

He smells good, which only makes things harder.

"You look good." He observes.

"I know." The words fly out of my mouth before I actually think about it. He smirks at that, eyes falling to my lips. I can tell that he knows exactly what he's doing, on purpose.

"What."

His right hand comes up to the back of my head, where he softly pulls at my hair, making my head tilt upwards.

My lips inch out towards his out of reflex, and he closes the gap so they can touch. He doesn't kiss me though.

Judging by the way his eyes sparkle and the way I can feel his lips bend up into a smile against mine, I realize he's taking the piss.

"Isabella's waiting." Is all he says against my lips before he lets go of my hair and takes a step back.

"Are you serious?" I ask, not moving from my spot.

He grins. "I never am." Then he walks out the door.

He just played with me, what the fuck.

I'm not sure whether I'm annoyed or horny, or both, but I compose myself before going downstairs.

The ride to the airport is silent and for some reason, I can't breathe.

I'm looking out at the scenery passing by so quickly I don't get to fully process it.

My legs are crossed so we can have enough space, meanwhile Matteo's sitting across from me, legs stretched out so mine are between his. Our knees bump against each other every time the car goes over a pothole, and every single time I feel it, the area he touches catch on fire.

Nobody seems to notice that the air is thick or that my throat is so dry it hurts.

He's already looking at me when my eyes wonder over to him.

His eyes move down to my crotch, then back at me.

I raise my brows and shake my head, silently and sarcastically asking him whether I can help him with something.

Matteo grins and nods. I roll my eyes and move my head so I can look back out the window, hoping that the airport is less than five minutes away.

"Okay, what's going on?" Isabella asks, and suddenly I'm back in the car, aware of where I am.

"What do you mean?"

Matteo looks at me. "I think she doesn't like the silence."

"Exactly! You're both holding Mimosas and no one's drinking or saying anything. Valentina, it's your *birthday*."

I raise my glass and they both bump theirs against it, saying 'salute' at the same time.

Thankfully, the landing strip is right around the corner and the Barone siblings are already there waiting. They're all dressed up for a party, and I instantly feel at ease.

Today is my birthday; it's supposed to be fun. And easy. And filled with memories.

I don't look at Matteo at all during the ride back to the house.

***

The rest of the people I invited show up around 8pm, and I'm already dressed. I'm wearing a black sundress with sneakers, because I'm not about to wear heels for no reason whatsoever.

The pool party is in full swing about an hour later, and I feel like I'm the only sober one. Isabella is already on her third Gin and Tonic, while I'm still trying to finish my first. She's talking about Vinnie as I look around the garden, feeling like I want to do *something*.

It's like every time I had some time to think, my mind would go to how we kissed, and it would make me want it *more*.

He's talking to Ariana by the pool now, and she has her hand on his arm. She's been laughing since she arrived, and Matteo is not *that* funny.

"Are you even listening to me?"

"Sorry, I'm not."

"Are you checking out Isaac?"

I look to where she's pointing, realizing that Isaac and Vinnie are sharing a joint right behind where Matteo and Ariana are.

"Uh, maybe."

"Is something wrong? Do you not feel comfortable?"

I shake my head. "No, it's not that."

"You've barely drunk anything. Usually, you're already four drinks in and have had a line or something."

"I'm fine. I just feel like…I don't know. Like I want to do *something*. My energy is all over the place."

"Do something? Like what?"

"I don't know."

"Or maybe do someone?"

She wiggles her eyebrows, and I know she's referring to Isaac.

"With Isaac? I don't know."

"You've already done it and it was fine. Plus, he wouldn't have come all the way from Russia for no reason."

"I don't know if I like him or not."

"You said the sex was great. And he's an easy choice if you feel horny."

"Hmm, maybe. I don't know. I guess I want something new."

"What about Matteo?"

I panic inside for a second. "What?"

"Matteo? I mean, isn't he also a potential, *you know*?"

My face contorts in confusion mixed with pretend disgust caused by the thought of it.

I'm overthinking again.

"I mean – wouldn't you mind?"

No idea why I asked that.

"Why would I mind?"

"You said that I'm your only close friend that has never slept with him."

"Yes, but then I thought about it this morning. You're my girl best friend and he's my boy best friend, and you would be the first girl he hooks up with that I actually like." She smirks.

Something weird happens in my body when I think of Matteo and me having sex. She looks like she's excited by the idea. Which makes me feel even guiltier about what has already happened and cannot be taken back.

My face turns to look in his direction. "He looks like he's interested in Ariana though."

"Oh, yeah, they had sex."

"When?"

"On his birthday, after everyone fell asleep."

He told me that everyone went to sleep that night, why would he lie to me? Or avoid the truth?

"They've been talking a lot actually; I think it might turn into something serious."

"Really? I can't imagine him like *that*."

She rolls her eyes. "Serious as in, they have sex, and he also enjoys her presence as a friend. Texting when it's not a booty call-" She pauses to look at me when I laugh at the word. "That's how they say it, isn't it?"

"You don't like Ariana then?" I ask her.

"Meh. She's okay at parties. Otherwise, I don't really care for her. I think she can be fake sometimes."

"Fake how?"

"I just don't trust her. She's too friendly."

I throw her a look. "Too friendly?"

"It feels forced sometimes. She's not usually friendly and fun, only when there's guys around."

"Oh, so she's a guys' girl."

She smirks. "Exactly. She reminds me too much of Allison, and I don't like that."

We both look in her direction again, but this time Matteo is looking at us.

"Shit, I think he's onto us." Isabella giggles as she waves him over.

He says something to Ariana before walking over.

"What are you gossiping about now?"

Isabella motions towards where Ariana is now texting on her phone.

"What about her?"

"What's the deal?"

He shrugs, throwing a look in my direction. "I don't know? She's…nice."

"Alright."

"Why do you even care?"

"Because I can't go through Allison 2.0."

"It's not like-"

"Yes, it's exactly like that. You had sex first before even getting to really know her and she's easy to talk to, and now she's all you know."

Matteo's eyes flicker to me just as Vinnie calls him over.

I down my drink to process the entire conversation with Isabella from start to finish.

"Another one?" She asks.

"Actually, let's do some shots."

It's a big house, but the music is still thumping through the walls when I arrive upstairs an hour later. I left Isabella to go and grab a jacket because it's getting cold. I'm way past tipsy now, and I kind of wish I had something to sober me up.

Matteo is just leaving Adrik's room, followed by Ariana.

"What's up?" He asks as soon as he sees me, sparing a glance in her direction.

"I'm going for a smoke." Ariana tells him before walking towards the stairs, not even acknowledging my existence.

My head softly starts moving to the beat as we look at each other, neither of us saying anything.

I realize that we're alone for the first time since the party started.

He's the first one to break the silence. "Do you want a line?"

"Do you have?"

"Yes, Vinnie brought it."

"Sure."

We walk into Adrik's room, and I shut the door behind me while he walks over to the table. I notice that Adrik's red LED lights on the ceiling are turned on.

I take a seat on the edge of the bed, watching him as he takes a plate out of the drawer and places it on the desk. I feel the impulse to ask what he was doing with Ariana since the lights are on, but I cough and try to focus on what he's doing.

Matteo turns his head to look at me. "Are you having fun?"

His question pulls me back to reality. "Yeah, I am."

"You don't look like it."

I scoff at him. "I am."

"Okay." I can tell he doesn't believe me, but he's done with the conversation.

He comes over to sit on the bed, holding out the plate in front of my face. I take the rolled-up bill he's holding.

There are two highway-sized lines there, so I look at him incredulously.

"What?"

"I've never seen lines like these."

Matteo motions to the plate, so I do the line in one swift motion. He looks surprised for a second, then takes his turn. Once he's done, he settles the plate on the desk and sits back down next to me.

The room is so silent that I can hear the music from outside through the open window.

"I need a drink." I say, then order my legs to help me stand up.

"It's on the desk."

Right. I brough my glass upstairs.

"I came up to get a jacket." I remind myself.

"I'll wait here."

After taking a jacket out of my dressing room, I go back to my brother's room.

Matteo is still on the bed, but looks up from his phone when he hears me come in. He checks me out again, then pockets his phone and stands up.

Neither of us says anything, and I'm currently thinking about him and Ariana having sex, wondering why he didn't mention it to me when I asked.

"When I asked about your birthday, you didn't tell me about Ariana."

"You asked me if we did anything interesting."

I roll my eyes at his answer, even though he sounds genuine. "You don't find that interesting enough?"

"I didn't lie to you."

"I wasn't accusing you of lying. I was just wondering why you didn't mention it to me.

"Because I thought it wouldn't be interesting to you."

"Alright." I decide to take his word for it. "Let's go."

He nods and hides the plate in the drawer of Adrik's desk. I wait for him by the door as I shut off the lights, which leaves the room dark red. I turn around to leave once he's close enough.

His hand suddenly grips into my wrist, turning me around.

"Does it bother you?" he asks.

"Does what bother me?"

"Me fucking her."

I can't contain my laugh. "Why would it bother me?"

"I don't know."

"*Should* it bother me?"

"No."

"Okay then."

His hand quickly moves from my wrist up to the left side of my face, pulling me in towards him. My instincts take over without thinking about it, and I kiss him back.

His body presses against mine, blocking me against the doorframe.

Matteo's other hand moves between my legs, his cold fingers making my inner thighs tremble.

"Let's not." I breathe out against his lips, right hand coming to the back of his neck. My body isn't cooperating because it wants to feel *more*.

He whines. "Why not?"

"Because it's weird."

I kiss back, still gripping into his shoulders.

"Why is it weird?" It's dark but I can see his features, and he looks a little sad and disappointed.

I shrug. "There are people here, you're Isabella's best friend, and we shouldn't be touching like this in the first place."

"You don't like it?"

One of his fingers slips into my underwear, catching me off-guard and making me moan in surprise. I look up at him.

"Of course I enjoy it."

"Then what's the problem?"

"I just told you."

Someone calls my name from downstairs, which sets off alarm bells in my mind. Apparently, in his too, because his hand pulls back immediately.

Vinnie is at the top of the stairs when Matteo and I walk over to him. He looks at me first, then at Matteo, then back at me. "We're about to light another one, and Isabella told me to come find you."

"Yeah, I'm coming."

Matteo mumbles something under his breath that sounds a lot like 'not yet'. I pretend not to hear him as I follow Vinnie down the stairs.

Matteo pats me on the shoulder before bringing the finger that was inside me to his mouth, licking it.

I flip him off and hurry down the stairs, hoping Vinnie didn't notice anything suspicious.

Capo d'Orlando, Sicily – July 23rd, 2020

Everyone sang happy birthday to me at midnight, even though it's more symbolic rather than factually accurate, making me uncomfortable but happy.

We did some shots after, then Isaac tried to flirt with me for what seemed like forever before Isabella finally saved me and brought me out by the pool half an hour later.

Matteo and Vinnie are in their own world, talking on the other side of the pool.

"What do you think they're talking about?"

We've been people watching for the past twenty minutes since we sat down.

"I don't know, what do boys even talk about all day?"

"No clue. And I have a brother at home."

"They seem to have a very interesting discussion. Matteo looks serious, like he's scared even."

"How can you even tell?"

"I know him."

He turns his head, as if he could feel we were talking about him. We make eye contact before he turns back to Vinnie.

"Something's off with him." Isabella notices.

"You think?"

"He's hiding something. I think it's about Ariana."

The two of them start walking in our direction, and he looks over at Ariana, smirking. I avert my eyes.

I know I'm supposed to be leaving tomorrow (my mother asked me to be home after my birthday – that was the deal), and the thought makes me sad.

The night becomes in a blur, and after a few more shots everything goes blank.

Isabella wakes me up the next day, telling me that my driver is downstairs, waiting to take Isaac and I to the airport.

Capo d'Orlando, Sicily – July 23rd, 2020

Four hours in and I still can't sleep during my flight back. Isaac fell asleep as soon as we took off, but I'm just staring into darkness.

When the sun comes up on the horizon over the clouds, time and space stop feeling real. I don't know how long I actually look out the window, but the next thing I feel is the plane wheels coming in contact with the ground.

As I step outside and down the stairs into a very rainy and cold Moscow, I suddenly get overwhelmed. Someone laughs behind me, and I turn around to see Isaac talking to the pilot.

I still feel out of place when we climb into the van and greet our family driver. I get the urge to cry, but I'm not sad. It's the lack of sleep and the thought of the upcoming jetlag.

Or maybe it's not.

Maybe I've gotten so used to being around him for three days non-stop, that it's weird not feeling his energy anymore.

It's weird but it's not. I just don't know how to describe it.

Not sad.

Just…empty.

Somehow.

Chapter 32

Valentina

Moscow, Russia – August 25th, 2020

A month has passed since I was in Italy for my birthday, and time seems to be infinite. I miss that energy so much that I've started listening to ABBA and watching foreign movies taking place during the summer.

Our courses start again in October, but I have no idea whether they'll be online or in person. Sometimes I find myself hoping they would happen in person, because I feel like I need to be in my own space, doing my own thing.

Spending time at home with my parents is nice, because I don't have to focus on surviving. But it gets tiring after the third time my mother tells me to pick up my clothes or not eat food in the bed. I need to be on my own again, and I also miss my friends.

"Are you listening to ABBA?" My mother asks, stepping inside my room with a shocked/excited look on her face.

Oh, and she also comes in whenever she feels like it.

"Yes, I like their songs."

She used to play it all the time when we were growing up, in the car or at parties I got to witness as a child.

"Are you in love?"

The question makes me laugh somehow. "What? Who would I be in love with?" It's unexpected.

She smiles and nods. "I see."

I groan. "You see what exactly?!"

"Nothing."

The Hotel Frederick, with the West Virginia Building in the background. *Author photo*

1907

Retail

J.W. Valentine was out as a partner at one Huntington department store, and Eugene Anderson of Portsmouth was in, creating the Anderson-Newcomb Co., capitalized at $125,000.

The business had started back in 1894 as Valentine's dry goods store on 9th Street, and W.H. Newcomb had joined the business a year later; together, Newcomb and Valentine had moved to a larger three-story brick building on 3rd Avenue in 1902.

But now Valentine was bowing out, and Anderson was taking his place... and the store would continue to grow.

In 1913, the partners built a three-story annex, then added three more floors to the main structure in 1920. The company outlasted competitors like Deardorff-Sisler and Morrison's. It was an innovator: the city's first store with a switchboard and the first

"Can I help you with something?" I sarcastically asks, making her roll her eyes and smile.

"You need to pack; we're going to Italy for your father's 45th birthday."

"Since when?"

The information brings a weird feeling with it. I don't know whether it's happiness or anxiety.

"Since he decided yesterday. A friend of his is playing in the opera and he wants to see it."

"Dad doesn't even like opera."

"But his friend does."

"Who's the friend?"

"A family friend. You don't know him."

"Who else is coming?"

"The immediate family."

"So, Boris is coming too?"

"Yes. And Romeo."

"Alright."

I like Romeo, and I don't like Boris, so I guess it evens out.

"Pack lightly. We won't stay longer than three nights."

"Yeah yeah."

I text Isabella about me going to Italy before my mom even leaves the room.

***

Capo d'Orlando, Sicily – August 27th, 2020

My father's 45th birthday is a bigger deal than I expected it to be. Both of the guest rooms are filled (by Boris and Romeo), and there are people downstairs who are waiting for the pre-drinks to finish.

It's mostly people from Russia; some I recognize from former events, and then Aleksi, Raisa, and their mother.

"Raisa has a boyfriend now." My mother tells me when it's just the two of us outside with Adrik, waiting for the last town car to arrive. "He's from New York."

Why is she telling me this like I should care?

"I thought he was from South Korea." I answer, catching Adrik silently laughing.

"They broke up. This one studies Law."

"Alright? Why are you even telling me this? Please don't go all Boris on me."

"I'm just saying, she's happy with her choices."

"And I'm not?"

"What choices?" Adrik laughs, but I agree with him.

"Exactly."

The car pulls up in the driveway as dad's car leaves, but the conversation stays with me a long time after that.

The opera is in a nearby town, so the ride is longer than I'd like but we get there eventually.

There are a lot of people there, and we cut the line because Boris talks to someone at the entrance, who leads us all the way up to our seats on the first floor. They're box seats, which are basically balconies overlooking the entire atheneum.

I've never been in such a giant theatre, opera, or whatever it's called.

I get the seat between Adrik and Romeo, thankfully not next to my mom. She looked like she wanted to continue the conversation when we entered the balcony.

I don't focus on the show, not really, but the music is okay, and I can kind of understand what story they're telling in Italian.

Romeo stands up to clap along as the soprano is about to finish the last song, looking as happy as I've ever seen him. I stand as well and he leans over to me then. "Let's go before everyone starts to leave."

"Alright."

He coughs up blood, all over my face and chest.

Before I can even process what's happening, I see a bullet enter the left side of his temple in a split of a second.

My mother is the first one to start screaming, followed by Valerya and Raisa. Within seconds, everyone around us is screaming and panicking as Romeo falls into me. My arms feel numb when I try to hold him up. I can see that I'm holding him, but I don't feel like I'm holding him.

I look around to where the bullet came from, still not moving from my spot. I'm paralyzed by fear and the possibility of the next shot taking me out. There's a reflective flicker of light coming from the technical room right above the stage.

The light goes out then and Romeo drops to the floor, head turning weirdly against the edge of his seat. Blood is gushing out of his temple now, and I can see parts of his brain on the floor and on my shoes.

My mother yells at me as she grabs my arm, but her voice feels like it's coming from somewhere far away.

There's a ringing sound in my ears – I get them sometimes, randomly, but it's never been this loud.

As I stare down at my hands, the reality of what has just happened slowly enters my consciousness. The blood tastes exactly like I expected it to. My hands shake, and I realize it's my mother violently pulling at my arm.

"We need to leave *now*, Valentina, for fuck's sake!"

I look down at Romeo, whose eyes are open as he blankly looks at my ankles. There's no trace of life in them.

In the midst of people running and screaming and pushing each other to flee towards the exit, my father is talking at Boris.

I look down at Romeo again as my mother physically forces me to follow her.

What did you do Romeo?

It's only when I'm in the car with my family that I start to have thoughts again.

The first thing I notice is that it's a bulletproof van now, unlike the one we had arrived in.

The second thing I notice is that my father, Boris, and I are the only ones who have not once panicked since Romeo got killed right in front of us.

Chapter 33

Matteo

Capo d'Orlando, Sicily – July 22nd

As soon as Vinnie and the rest of Valentina's guests arrive, the atmosphere around Matteo changes. He's not as relaxed anymore, and he feels like he has to take care of five things at once before he can actually enjoy himself.

First, there's Ariana, who has been texting him more than usual since he woke up this morning. Then there's Vinnie, who keeps asking him if he's okay and if he's having fun, which forces Matteo to smile and assure him that he's okay.

The third reason is the photo he saw in Valentina's brother's room, which he now knows he's seen before. In Aurora's room, above her desk.

Valentina is also somewhere in the mix because he's fully aware of her presence now. He knows where she is at all times without even having to look, his consciousness unwillingly shifting to wherever she is.

Ariana is telling him something about her life in the past two days, but all Matteo can focus on now is that Isabella and Valentina are talking about him.

"I'll be right back." He says to Ariana before walking over to the two of them.

"What are you gossiping about now?"

Isabella motions towards where he just came from in response.

Matteo doesn't look back to where Ariana is surely watching him. "What about her?"

"What's the deal?"

Matteo shrugs, unwillingly looking at Valentina. She's already looking at him, watching to see how he reacts.

"I don't know? She's...nice."

"Alright."

"Why do you even care?"

"Because I can't go through Allison 2.0."

"It's not like-"

"Yes, it's exactly like that. You had sex first before even getting to really know her and she's easy to talk to, and now she's all you know."

Matteo instantly knows that Valentina realizes omitted telling her about Ariana. Her face doesn't betray her though, not even as Vinnie calls him over.

Ariana tells him to come upstairs at some point, and he's way too high and horny to turn her down. It lasts less than last time on his birthday, and this time they get dressed afterwards. She stayed the night a few weeks ago, but the vibe is different now.

Matteo knows that there's cocaine in the desk drawer but he's not in the mood to go through it with Ariana right now.

"I'm ready." She says eventually, after fixing her hair in the mirror for the third time.

He follows her out of the room.

He sees Valentina before she sees him as she's coming up the stairs.

"What's up?"

His eyes go to Ariana, and he feels like he's just been caught doing something he shouldn't have done.

"I'm going for a smoke." Ariana huffs at him and walks past her to the stairs, obviously ignoring her.

They're alone for the first time since her birthday party started.

"Do you want a line?" He blurts out.

"Do you have?"

"Yes, Vinnie brought it."

"Sure."

They walk into Adrik's room, and she sits down on the bed while Matteo takes care of the rest. The air in the room feels uncomfortable, and she doesn't look like she's having fun. She doesn't even look like she's here right now.

"Are you having fun?"

"Yeah, I am."

"You don't look like it."

She scoffs at him. "I am."

"Okay."

He doesn't believe her, but lets it go as he walks over to sit on the bed next to her.

Valentina looks at the plate, then back at him.

Matteo smiles. "What?"

"I've never seen lines like these."

He motions to the plate, surprised to see her do it all. He's surprised because he's never seen a girl do that, like *that*.

Her lips move. "I need a drink."

Matteo's head turns to right. "It's on the desk."

"I came up to get a jacket."

"I'll wait here."

He checks his phone while she's gone, seeing that Vinnie and Ariana had texted him.

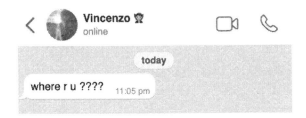

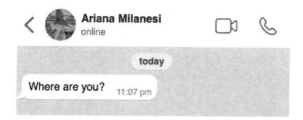

Ariana Milanesi
online

today

Where are you?   11:07 pm

He tries to figure out how long he's been alone with Valentina when she comes back wearing a jacket, her face flushed from the coke.

He stands up from the bed, making a list of things he can't leave in the room in his head.

"When I asked about your birthday, you didn't tell me about Ariana."

The sentence throws him off.

"You asked me if we did anything interesting."

"You don't find that interesting enough?"

"I didn't lie to you." He says, and technically, it *is* the truth.

"I wasn't accusing you of lying. I was just wondering why you didn't mention it to me.

"Because I thought it wouldn't be interesting to you." He also means this.

"Alright. Let's go."

Matteo can't tell whether she actually believes him or not, although he kind of hopes she does.

As she shuts off the lights, he thinks about the possibility of it bothering her. A lot of girls get attached quickly and start expecting…something.

He grabs her wrist when she's about to leave. "Does it bother you?"

"Does what bother me?"

"Me fucking her."

She genuinely laughs. "Why would it bother me?"

"I don't know."

"*Should* it bother me?"

"No."

"Okay then."

He's not sure why, maybe because she smells incredible and her lips are right *there,* but he doesn't want whatever this is to come to an end yet.

He pulls her towards him by holding her face, and she kisses him back without a second thought.

Their bodies are pressed together and he brings his hand between her legs, smiling when he feels them buckle.

"Let's not." She says against his lips, but her hands come up to the back of his neck nonetheless.

"Why not?"

"Because it's weird." She answers before kissing him again.

He feels disappointed. "Why is it weird?"

"There are people here, you're Isabella's best friend, and we shouldn't be touching like this in the first place."

"You don't like it?"

One of his fingers slips into her underwear, making her moan in that special way that Matteo likes.

"Of course I enjoy it."

"Then what's the problem?"

"I just told you."

Vinnie calls her name from outside the room, and Matteo panics. He didn't really care whether Isabella found out, but he never thought about telling Vinnie.

He's at the top of the stairs when they walk over to him. He looks at Matteo first, then at Valentina, then back at him. "We're about to light another one, and Isabella told me to come find you."

His voice is weird, like he already *knows* what just happened.

"Yeah, I'm coming." She says.

"Not yet." He mumbles, knowing that it'll fluster her, which is fun to watch. Valentina pretends not to hear him as she follows Vinnie down the stairs.

Matteo doesn't give up on it though, patting her shoulder so she would pay attention to him. He makes sure she sees him lick the finger that was just inside her, and she flips him off in return.

Mission accomplished.

***

Capo d'Orlando, Sicily – July 23ʳᵈ

He spends his time by the pool after they all sing happy birthday to Valentina, talking with Vinnie and Marco about Marco's recent luck with girls.

"It's like they're all attracted to me now for some reason."

"Because you're legal."

"I'm twenty."

Matteo sometimes forgets that his little brother isn't sixteen anymore.

"Or maybe it's because they've been inside for so long." Matteo jokes.

"If they want someone to stay inside with, I'm good with that. Which one would I even pick though?"

"Which one do you enjoy talking to?" Vinnie asks him.

"Petra."

"Then her."

"Why would you even suggest moving in together?" Matteo interjects, still not over the idea of Marco moving in with a random girl.

Marco tuns to leave. "I'm not going into discussions about relationships with you Matteo, I know how that ends."

"And why is that?"

"You always tell me not to get attached."

"So?"

"I'm going away." He smirks, waving over Eddie.

"Have you ever had a girl you just liked talking to?"

Matteo looks at Vinnie, trying to figure out why he asked that. "Like you enjoy her presence, without any expectations or not being there just to fuck her?" He elaborates.

Matteo thinks about it. "Not really."

"Not really, or no?"

"Not really."

Matteo can't lie and tell him that the description matches no one ever. He thinks about that time after Vinnie's birthday, when he stayed up until the next evening with Valentina.

Just because they enjoyed being around each other. When he didn't have to check his phone or thinks of ways to entertain himself to avoid awkwardness.

She was *interesting* and she talked about things he's never talked about with anyone else before. He could be himself around her, and sex wasn't even on his mind that night, nor on that day when he ended up in bed with Ariana.

But she's also insanely attractive. Not only hot, but beautiful too. And smart.

Sure, he'd like to have sex with her, it would probably be enjoyable. And if it never happened, fine.

"Are you even listening?"

"Not really."

"Are you high?"

"Aren't you?"

Vinnie laughs at that.

Matteo still doesn't know how to bring up Valentina. They always talk about what's going on in each other's lives, especially when it comes to girls.

"Is something going on with Valentina?"

"What do you mean?"

His eyes unwillingly travel to where he knows she's talking to Isabella on the across the pool.

"You're being weird."

It's the second time today that someone uses the word to describe him. He turns his head to look at Vinnie. "How am I being weird? What does that even *mean*?"

"You came out of that room together and you were gone a long time."

"I was with Ariana."

"Doing what?"

"Sex."

"And what were you doing with Valentina?"

"Lines." He looks in her direction again. He remembers wanting to lift her dress up and put her face against the wall. But for some reason, he couldn't bring himself to act on any of his thoughts. "She's attractive, I don't know."

"She is."

The way Vinnie says it is genuine, with no intent behind it, but the thought still bothers him for a split second before he pushes it out of his mind.

"I don't know if it's a good idea."

This makes Matteo pay attention. "Why?"

"She's Isabella's friend, and Isabella cares about her. And she's the only one you haven't hooked up with. It might get complicated."

"What? If we have sex?"

"No, even if you make out."

"Why would it be?"

"Would you want to do more then? I know you. And a good kiss is basically the gateway to being okay with having sex."

"Maybe she wouldn't be a good kisser."

"I don't think you'd think that." He pauses when surprise takes over Matteo's face. "Because you're attracted to her."

"I'm attracted to a lot of people."

"Come on man, you know what I mean. She's *exactly* your type. From her body type all the way up to her personality. She's sort of like you, but more stable."

Matteo snorts in surprise. "Stable?"

"Yeah, I don't know. Drama free, I guess. Her only drama would be you."

"I don't have drama."

"You always do though."

Vinnie knows him better than anyone, and Matteo knows he's right. He can't hide anything from him, and he also can't lie to him. The only thing he can do is avoid the subject.

"But you haven't done anything yet, so just take your horniness out on someone else."

"Like whom?"

Vinnie looks at him like it's obvious. "Ariana."

Matteo's face scrunches up out of instinct before he can even think it through.

"See? She's great." Vinnie sarcastically says as he pats him on the back.

As they return to the group dancing on the other side of the pool, he glances in Ariana's direction. She catches his eye and smiles. He smirks at her, deciding then that he'll be sleeping with her tonight, because it's the easiest choice right now.

***

He realizes that most of the people have gone home the next day after he wakes up. Ariana is still sleeping in his bed, and he finds Isabella is in the kitchen downstairs.

"Where is everyone?" She asks him when he walks over to the coffee machine.

"They all left before noon. Valentina left me the keys to lock up when we leave."

"When do you go to Palermo?"

"In a few hours."

Matteo lets her know he's driving.

"What are you going to do about Ariana?" she asks when they sit down at the table outside on the terrace. The sun is high up in the sky and it's incredibly hot.

"What do you mean?"

"She's still here, isn't she?"

"Why do I need to do something about her?"

Ariana comes outside then, completely unaware of what they were just discussing.

"I'm going to get a refill." Isabella says, throwing him obvious glances as she leaves.

Ariana takes her place. "What are you up to today?"

His brain goes completely blank, so he shrugs. He almost sees it coming when she starts talking about her flight being from Palermo. She asks him if she can stay with him until her next flight to Milan. Matteo doesn't object, so she thanks him by leaning over and kissing him.

He isn't really bothered about it, so he just goes along with it.

Chapter 34

Matteo

Palermo, Sicily – August 20th, 2020

Ariana ended up staying for almost an entire month, and to Matteo's surprise, she hasn't rubbed him the wrong way yet. It was actually unexpectedly nice, and he sort of misses her when he wakes up alone.

He wasn't really bored at all during her stay at his house, and he also hasn't thought about the dream he had on the first night Ariana stayed over. Which reminds him of the fact that he also hasn't thought about the situation with Valentina since they had left her home.

The thing is, Ariana always came up with things for them to do. She invited him out for lunch or to go shopping before he could even think about his day. It's as if she was making sure he didn't make any other plans. She would sometimes suggest going for coffee or to see a movie. Matteo went along with it, because what else was there to do?

Then, they usually went back to his place and had sex.

At some point, it became a habit. She listened to him, always agreed with him, and even did everything imaginable in bed.

He knows she's the cousin of one of their soldiers in Sicily, but she has no idea because she thinks her whole family is in Milan. At least, she doesn't seem to have a clue.

His father calls him down for lunch after he showers and gets dressed for the day. Matteo wonders whether his father is aware of Ariana or not; he had no idea he was even home until today.

A table is set up for them in the back of their garden overlooking the sea. His father is looking out towards the water, puffing on his cigar.

They eat in silence for a while, until Matteo finds it too weird not to speak. "Is this about the whistle-blower? Or the fact that I've had a girl over for a month?"

"Both, sort of."

Matteo waits for him to elaborate.

"There was a call made outside of our house yesterday evening that had a number blocker."

"A number blocker?"

"Someone made a call that came from our driveway yesterday evening, which connected to our cell phone tower-"

"What cell tower?"

"The one on the cliffs a few streets away. Everyone within an eight-mile radius who uses their phones can be tracked by us."

Matteo gets an uneasy feeling in his stomach. "Why can't you trace it?"

"We can't see the number, because the call was made by a device with a professional signal blocker."

"How do you know it's the mole?"

"Only the people on our payroll know about that cell tower. And the person who used a blocker obviously doesn't want to be traced and found."

"And there's no way to trace it?"

"There is, but it will take a few days to connect to the device's signal. We have to trace it back before it was blocked before we can trace it in real time."

"Alright, why are you telling me this?"

"Who was here yesterday?"

"I was. And I don't even know what a cell phone blocker is."

"What about your girlfriend?"

"She's not my girlfriend."

His father isn't impressed nor looks like he cares, still waiting for the answer.

"She was here too." Matteo states. "I don't think she knows what a signal blocker even is"

"Who else?"

"I don't know. Maybe Marco? Aurora? I don't know, I don't keep track of people. I thought you would've had cameras installed by now."

"The ones at the entrance by the gate didn't show anyone for the past three days. But I will think about increasing security until we find the rat."

"What does this have to do with me?"

"If we track the device and find him, it's your job to go after it and find him."

Matteo wants to ask what that means, because he's rarely sure whether his father is talking about the legal or illegal version of his words; does 'find him' mean 'take him out' or just 'report back'?

"I'll let you know when it's time."

Matteo chooses not to overthink it and focuses back on eating.

Once they're both done with their lunch they ask for coffee and pull out their cigarettes.

"Paulo asked me to talk to you."

Since when does Paulo ask to talk to me through my dad?

"What about?"

"You and Vinnie."

Matteo is surprised. "What about me and Vinnie?"

"If you can get him to stop looking for Sofia."

The uneasy feeling comes back, this time settling in his entire body, all the way through to his bones. It's a feeling of *knowing* what happened without actually knowing what happened.

"Why?"

There's no logical reason for his father to be talking about Vinnie's girlfriend, let alone use her first name like he knows her.

"Paulo thought it ended after she ratted him out at your New Year's Eve party."

The way he uses the verb 'ratted' makes Matteo feel sick.

"So? He likes her, I guess."

"Has he tried to contact her?"

"I think so."

"And did she answer?"

"Shouldn't you already know this if you have a cell tower? Vinnie is right next door."

Matteo suddenly realizes that his father can also probably see everything he's doing on his own phone.

"Don't worry, we don't track the phones of our family. Nor the Barone family. I am asking you sincerely."

"I don't think she replied, no."

"So, it's obvious she won't be coming back to him. Get him to stop trying."

"I can't tell him what to do, and I also don't want to tell him what to do."

His father looks at his face, as if to check whether Matteo means it or not. He does.

"How do you know who Sofia is? And why isn't Paulo talking to me directly like he usually does?" Matteo asks.

"I know her because Paulo told me what happened. And I told you."

"Fine."

"So, you'll talk to Vinnie?"

"No, it means fine, I believe you. But I won't try to influence my best friend just because our fathers want to control him."

"But you do understand that she won't be responding, right?"

"Why wouldn't she?"

The silence is heavy, and Matteo already knows.

"Are you sure you want to know?" His father asks then.

He thinks about it then. If it's the worst-case scenario he can think of right now, he doesn't want to know, because then it would mean lying to his best friend about it.

Matteo's stomach feels uncomfortably empty as he speaks. "Did you actually *murder* someone because they called the police?"

"We don't act, we *re*act." His father reminds him of the tenth commandment in the Oath, skirting around Matteo's question. "My duty at the end of the day is to protect you and this family."

This triggers Matteo's anger. "You pay off the fucking police, I think we're protected enough."

"In Sicily, yes. But what if it had happened somewhere else?"

"And what about the 'no women and children' honour code?"

His father pulls his head back. "Where did you hear that?"

"I know enough about how things work by now to know that it is an unspoken rule."

"Yes. We don't hurt children, under any circumstances. They are off limits. And we don't hurt innocent men and women either. But if someone deliberately wants to cause us harm, we will take measures to defend ourselves. Sofia wasn't a child, nor was she an innocent woman."

"She's my age."

"You're not a child, Matteo. You're a *man*. And I would think you'd know by now that someone who calls the police out of spite is not someone that can be trusted. She dated Vincenzo for so long and yet she's not loyal to anyone but her own impulses. It's dangerous to have someone like that around."

"That still doesn't-"

"She decided to take away your freedom, Matteo, when she called the police."

"And her plan didn't work out, so why kill her?"

"You'll understand some other day."

Matteo shakes his head. "No, I won't. And I won't tell Vinnie what to do."

"Fine."

The coffee has already gone cold, and Matteo isn't in the mood to finish his cigarette anymore.

"I'm going up to my room."

"We haven't finished breakfast."

"I'm not hungry anymore."

"Are you bothered by what I just told you?"

"You didn't *tell* me anything." Matteo says, trying to convince himself by doing so. His father never admitted to it – he just tried to reason with him.

"Alright. I'll contact you within a week."

***

Palermo, Sicily – August 25th, 2020

The next five days after the talk with his father have been filled with near heart attacks every time his phone starts ringing. Because every time he thinks that it might his father, telling him they've found the mole and sending Matteo over to kill it.

His phone starts ringing, and to his horror, it is his father calling him. He tells Matteo to meet him and Paulo by the door that leads to the garage, right at the end of the west hallway downstairs.

His heart is nearly beating out of his chest as he descends the stairs and walks through the arch separating the dining room from his father's office.

The two of them are nowhere to be seen, so he pushes the garage door open.

Seeing his godfather and his father holding sniper rifles is not what he expected to see.

"What's going on?"

"We think we found the guy." Paolo explains, still looking down at the rifle like it's something precious.

Matteo doesn't even need to ask any more questions, but his entire body gets goosebumps, like he's gone cold from the inside out.

"Where is he?"

"He's in Capo d'Orlando now."

"Who is it?"

"We still can't see the number, but we can track the device which tipped off the tower."

"Do you want me to go to Capo then?" He asks, voice hoarse, secretly hoping the answer would be negative.

"Yes."

"I don't have any army training or whatever I need to be able to handle a fucking sniper."

Paulo bursts out into a genuine laugh, even though Matteo has no idea what's so funny about the situation.

"We're showing you today, and you'll leave tomorrow."

They go back out into the garden, where Matteo had lunch with his father just a week ago. The table is gone now, and there's a brick wall in its place.

"Where are the targets?"

"You can't see them with the human eye."

They show him how to use the rifle, then show him how to shoot from different heights, how to adjust the gun, and how to look through the lens so he can have a clear shot.

By the time he goes to sleep at night, he can't think about the gun in the bag by his bed anymore. He falls on his back, exhausted from the day he had, and goes to sleep immediately.

***

Capo d'Orlando, Sicily – August 27th, 2020

He arrived in Capo yesterday and spent the entire day in an apartment his dad father gave him the keys to. He watched the monitor tracking the phone so much he sees green dots everywhere.

Paulo told him to never be closer to the guy than fifty meters, and not further than three kilometres. The guy is close by today, somewhere near Vinnie's house, on the coast.

He was also advised to follow him if he ever left the house. When Matteo asked whether he could drive by, they immediately told him no. Whoever the person was could notice a random car driving by and destroy the device.

Matteo wakes up early on that Thursday morning, and the first thing he does is look for the green dot on the map.

It's exactly where it was yesterday.

When he orders a burger for lunch right after noon, the dot is where it always was.

By the time he's hungry again the sun has start to set, so he orders takeout for dinner as well. The dot is where it-no it's not.

His heart starts beating faster as he sees the dot has moved away from him, eight kilometres East to be exact.

The drill says to put the earpiece in and find out where the location is. He calls his father as soon as he's in the car.

"He moved. I looked the address up on Google and it's a theatre. Can you see how long he's been there for?"

"One hour."

"How long do the plays usually last?"

"Two hours, maybe. Three."

"Check if there are any shows at Vittorio Alfieri."

"I'll get you in through the back."

By the time Matteo arrives, there's a guy waving at him. He follows the guy to the back entrance, and they cross the empty hallway together until they reach a staircase. The guy leaves without saying anything, nor asking what Matteo has in the duffle bag.

"Go all the up the stairs until you reach the top of the stage, cross the bridge behind the lights and go into the room at the end."

"Who was that?" Matteo asks as he runs up the stairs.

"He's the security chief for the theatre."

"Why do you trust him with this?"

"Because he's too scared to say something."

The answer runs a chill through his bones, but he's over the bridge above the stage now.

"I'm here."

"Slide the window open and close the curtains."

He locks the door and does as told before he sets up the sniper to face the crowd.

"How am I supposed to locate them?"

"Just look through the audience with the lens."

"Who am I looking for?"

"Someone familiar."

What does that even-

Valentina is there.

She's wearing a red dress that exposes her shoulders and makes her look like she was born to wear those type of dresses, in these types of places. His eyes fall on her cleavage, as always only revealing enough to leave the rest of imagination.

Why is she here?

And why is she sitting next to Romeo?

He watches through the lens of his gun how she leans over to talk to Romeo. He laughs, like they've been friends for years.

"It's him." Matteo says to no one in particular.

The orchestra starts playing louder, quicker, and the opera singer raises his voice. He belts out what is probably the last couple of minutes of the final act.

"What?" His father's voice is stern on the other end.

"It's Romeo. The mole is Romeo."

"What? No, that can't be. Romeo has been around since I was five years old."

"I'm telling you, it's him."

There's silence on the other end, but the entire theatre is filled with the rest of the performers' voices as they join the soprano for the finale.

His father won't make him kill Romeo. Not here.

"Shoot him."

His heart stops.

"No."

"Now."

Matteo looks through the lens again; the plus in the middle placed on Romeo's chest.

"What if I miss?" Matteo asks, suddenly very aware of his heart beating in his ears. He can't hear anything else.

"The man he's sitting with is one of the most dangerous people in the world. His family has killed a lot of our people over the last century. And Romeo has helped them do that."

How does he know who Romeo is sitting with?

Matteo's stomach sinks to the floor the moment the realization downs on him. His father must've known it was Romeo all along.

There's applause as the last high note finishes.

"Matteo, you won't have another chance. He knows we're looking for the rat."

Matteo takes a deep breath and looks back through the lens. Romeo is standing now, leaning towards Valentina to whisper in her ear.

He grits his teeth and closes his eyes for a second. He swore his life to his father two months ago. If he doesn't shoot Romeo, someone else will. Then he himself will be either killed or forever exiled from his family.

Things aren't meant to be like this.

He opens his eyes.

Then pulls the trigger.

THE END
Round I